Dear Reader,

Since the publication of *Hummingbird* in 1983, your
response to my books has been gratifying and overwhelming. It, more than anything else, has prompted
the decision to bring back two of my titles that have
been out of print and unavailable for some time.
Those of you who missed them the first time around
kept asking for them, kept demanding that they be
published again. Your insistence was relayed to the
publisher in New York, who listened.

So it is in response to your requests that Jove brings
back again, in this single volume, *Forsaking All
Others* and *A Promise to Cherish*.

These love stories are not new, but they have
endured. Thank you, kind readers, who have waited
so patiently for their return. My unending thanks, too,
for your lasting support, which has made all my
books bestsellers over the years.

LaVyrle Spencer

**"You will never forget the incredible beauty and
sensitivity of LaVyrle's gifted pen."**
—*Affaire de Coeur*

The Bestselling Novels of LaVyrle Spencer

THEN CAME HEAVEN
A triumphant story of faith and love . . .

"Touching." —*The Chattanooga Times*

SMALL TOWN GIRL
A country music star rediscovers her heart . . .

"Warm and folksy." —*Kirkus Reviews*

THAT CAMDEN SUMMER
A shunned divorcee finds unexpected love . . .

"A modern fairy tale." —*People*

HOME SONG
A secret threatens to tear a family apart . . .

"Tug[s] at readers' heartstrings." —*Publishers Weekly*

FAMILY BLESSINGS
A widow is torn between her family and new love . . .

"A moving tale." —*Publishers Weekly*

NOVEMBER OF THE HEART
True love blooms for two hearts from different worlds . . .

"One of Spencer's best." —*Kirkus Reviews*

BYGONES
A moving story of a family at a crossroads . . .

"A page-turner." —*New York Daily News*

FORGIVING
A beautiful story of family ties renewed . . .

"A lively story." —*New York Daily News*

BITTER SWEET
The poignant tale of high school sweethearts reunited . . .

"A journey of self-discovery and reawakening." —*Booklist*

THE ENDEARMENT
A woman's love is threatened by past secrets . . .

"A tender, sensual story." —Lisa Gregory

MORNING GLORY
Two misfit hearts find tenderness . . .

"A superb book."   *—New York Daily News*

SPRING FANCY
A bride-to-be falls in love—with another man . . .

"Incredible beauty."   *—Affaire de Coeur*

THE HELLION
Sparks fly between a lady and a hell-raiser . . .

"Superb."   *—Chicago Sun-Times*

VOWS
Two willful lovers—one special promise . . .

"Magic."   *—Affaire de Coeur*

THE GAMBLE
Take a chance on love . . .

"Grand."   *—Good Housekeeping*

A HEART SPEAKS
Two of her favorite novels—*A Promise to Cherish* and *Forsaking All Others*—together in one volume.

YEARS
Across the Western plains, only the strongest survived . . .

"Splendid."   *—Publishers Weekly*

SEPARATE BEDS
First came the baby, then marriage . . . then love.

"A superb story."   *—Los Angeles Times*

TWICE LOVED
A woman's missing husband returns— after she's remarried . . .

"Emotional."   *—Rocky Mountain News*

HUMMINGBIRD
The novel that launched LaVyrle Spencer's stunning career . . .

"Will leave you breathless."   *—Affaire de Coeur*

Titles by LaVyrle Spencer

FORSAKING ALL OTHERS
THEN CAME HEAVEN
SMALL TOWN GIRL
THAT CAMDEN SUMMER
HOME SONG
FAMILY BLESSINGS
NOVEMBER OF THE HEART
BYGONES
FORGIVING
BITTER SWEET
THE ENDEARMENT
MORNING GLORY
SPRING FANCY
THE HELLION
VOWS
THE GAMBLE
A HEART SPEAKS
YEARS
SEPARATE BEDS
TWICE LOVED
SWEET MEMORIES
HUMMINGBIRD
THE FULFILLMENT

LaVyrle Spencer

A Heart Speaks

JOVE BOOKS, NEW YORK

THE BERKLEY PUBLISHING GROUP
Published by the Penguin Group
Penguin Group (USA) Inc.
375 Hudson Street, New York, New York 10014, USA
Penguin Group (Canada), 90 Eglinton Avenue East, Suite 700, Toronto, Ontario M4P 2Y3, Canada
(a division of Pearson Penguin Canada Inc.)
Penguin Books Ltd., 80 Strand, London WC2R 0RL, England
Penguin Group Ireland, 25 St. Stephen's Green, Dublin 2, Ireland (a division of Penguin Books Ltd.)
Penguin Group (Australia), 250 Camberwell Road, Camberwell, Victoria 3124, Australia
(a division of Pearson Australia Group Pty. Ltd.)
Penguin Books India Pvt. Ltd., 11 Community Centre, Panchsheel Park, New Delhi—110 017, India
Penguin Group (NZ), Cnr. Airborne and Rosedale Roads, Albany, Auckland 1310, New Zealand
(a division of Pearson New Zealand Ltd.)
Penguin Books (South Africa) (Pty.) Ltd., 24 Sturdee Avenue, Rosebank, Johannesburg 2196,
South Africa

Penguin Books Ltd., Registered Offices: 80 Strand, London WC2R 0RL, England

This is a work of fiction. Names, characters, places, and incidents either are the product of the author's imagination or are used fictitiously, and any resemblance to actual persons, living or dead, business establishments, events, or locales is entirely coincidental. The Publisher does not have any control over and does not assume any responsibility for author or third-party websites or their content.

A HEART SPEAKS

A Jove Book / published by arrangement with the author

PRINTING HISTORY
A Heart Speaks is a one-volume edition of *Second Chance at Love's
Forsaking All Others* (October 1982) and *A Promise to Cherish* (February 1983).
Jove one-volume edition / July 1986

Copyright © 1982, 1983 by LaVyrle Spencer.
Cover design by Morris Taub.
Author photo © 1995 by John Earle.

ISBN: 0-515-14082-1

JOVE®
Jove Books are published by The Berkley Publishing Group,
a division of Penguin Group (USA) Inc.,
375 Hudson Street, New York, New York 10014.
JOVE is a registered trademark of Penguin Group (USA) Inc.
The "J" design is a trademark belonging to Penguin Group (USA) Inc.

PRINTED IN THE UNITED STATES OF AMERICA

49 48 47 46 45 44 43 42 41 40

FORSAKING
ALL OTHERS

With love to
my friend
Dorothy Garlock

CHAPTER
One

"NORTH STAR AGENCY," answered the voice on the phone.

Allison Scott crossed her ankles, rested a heel on her desk, and leaned back in her ancient, creaking swivel chair. "I need the sexiest man you've ever seen and I need him right now," she said, smiling.

"Hey, who doesn't?" came the glib reply. "Allison, is that you?"

"Yes, Mattie, it's me, and I mean it. I need the man to end all men. He's got to be handsome, honed, with hair the color of waving wheat, blue eyes—but I could get by with brown—a jaw like Dick Tracy's and a nose like the hand of a sundial, a body like—"

"Hey, hey, hey! Hold on there, girl. What are you using him for anyway, a screen test?"

"Not quite. A book cover."

"*A what!*"

"A book cover." Allison's voice became exhilarated. "I got the offer about a month ago, and I said I'd see what I thought after reading the book. It came in yesterday's mail, and I took it home last night, read it from cover to cover, and decided to give it a try. I just called New York and—oh, Mattie, this could be the break I've been waiting for. They'll be sending a contract within the week. Now all I need from you is Mister Right for the cover."

"Let me get his vital stats on paper and look through the

files and see what I can come up with. Okay, shoot."

Allison's feet hit the floor as she reached for the manuscript, flipped to the right page, and followed the words with her finger. "Blond, blue eyed, virile, handsome, about twenty-five years old, six feet, sinewy...God, Mattie, can you believe they really believe men who look like that are worth anything?" Allison slapped the manuscript closed in disgust.

Mattie's voice came back critically. "Were you hired as a book critic or cover artist?"

"All right, I deserved that. It's really none of my business what these star-struck authors put between the covers. This is a chance I've been waiting for, and if they want me to give them a picture that'll convince the readers people fall in love at first sight and live happily ever after, that's what I'll give 'em. You just send me the raw material and watch me!"

"Okay. So describe the woman."

"Ah, let's see..." Again a slender finger scanned a page. "Oh, here it is. Early twenties, ginger-colored hair, blue eyes, tall, willowy. And listen, Mattie, hair color is important, seems the readers tend to notice if it's wrong, so shoulder length and ginger, right?"

"Ginger it is. Let me see what I can dig up, and I'll get the photos over to you in tomorrow's mail."

"Okay, Mattie, I appreciate it."

"Hey, Allison?"

"Yeah?"

A brief silence hummed before Mattie asked guardedly, "Is he back yet?"

Allison Scott's back wilted. Her elbow dropped to the desk, and she rubbed her forehead as if to ease a sudden shooting pain. "No, he's not. I'm really not expecting him anymore, Mattie."

"Have you heard from him?"

"Not a word."

Allison thought she could hear Mattie sigh. "I'm sorry I asked. Forgive me, huh?"

Allison sighed herself. "Mattie, it's not your fault Jason Ederlie turned out to be a first-class bastard."

"I know it, but I shouldn't have asked."

"My skin's gotten a lot tougher since he disappeared."

"I know that, too. That's what worries me."

"What do you mean by that!"

Mattie backed off at Allison's sharp tone. "Nothing. Forget I said it, okay? The glossies will be in tomorrow's mail."

The click at the other end of the line ended any further questions Allison might have posed, but her ebullient mood was gone, snuffed away at the mention of Jason Ederlie's name. Pushing his memory aside, she swiveled abruptly, rocked to her feet, and thrust belligerent hands deep into the pockets of her khaki-colored jeans. Standing with feet spread, she stared out the ceiling-to-floor windows that overlooked downtown Minneapolis. The building was old and drafty but spacious and bright, thus well suited for a photography studio. At one time it had housed the offices of a flour-milling company that had long ago turned to carpets, subdued lighting, well-insulated walls, and piped-in music.

But as Allison stared out unseeingly, the only music she heard was that of aged water pipes overhead, the clang of the expanding metal in ancient radiators that heated the place—but never quite adequately, it seemed.

The January cold had condensed moisture on the north-facing panes. Now and then a rivulet streamed down and joined the drift of ice that had formed at the corners of the small panes. With the edge of a clenched fist Allison cleared the center of a square, but the view beyond remained foggy.

Her fist slid down the cold glass, then rapped hard against an icy frame.

"Damn you, Jason, damn you!" she exclaimed aloud. Her forehead fell to her arm and tears trickled down her cheek as she indulged in the memory of his face, his voice, his body, all those things she had learned to trust.

Abruptly her head jerked up and she tossed it defiantly, sending her hair flying back in a rusty swirl of obstinance. She dragged the back of one wrist across her nose, sniffed, dashed the errant tears from her eyes, and swallowed the lump of memory in her throat. "I'll get over you, Jason Ederlie, if it's the last thing I do!" she promised the empty studio, the sky-line, herself. Then Allison Scott turned back to the balm of work.

* * *

It was a simple book, an uncomplicated story of a man and woman who meet on vacation on Sanibel Island, look at each other while sparks fly, make their way into each other's arms within fifty pages, out of them by a hundred, right their misconceptions some fifty pages later, and regain bliss together as the book ends. Perhaps because the hero's description matched that of Jason Ederlie, Allison had found herself lost in the pages. Maybe that, too, was the reason she'd at first been reluctant to accept the contract to do the cover art, for without Jason to pose, something would be missing. But realizing what a boon it would mean to her career and her finances, she'd accepted, even though it galled Allison that women readers sopped up such Cinderellaism as if it really happened.

Allison Scott knew better. Cinderella endings were found only in paperback romances on the shelves of the grocery store.

At the end of the day, reaching for a can of spaghetti and meatballs at the PDQ Market, she felt the bluntness of that fact all too fully, for she hated the thought of walking into the emptiness awaiting her at home, now that Jason was gone.

Home. She thought about the word as she drove from downtown Minneapolis around "the lakes," as they were loosely called. There were five of them—Calhoun, Harriet, Nokomis, Lake of the Isles, and Cedar—forming the heart of the beautiful "City of the Lakes." Allison lived on the west side of Lake of the Isles, in a second-story apartment in a regal old house that had been well preserved since the turn of the century.

She could barely see the first-floor windows as she turned in the driveway and threaded her Chevy van to the detached garage at the rear, for the snow had been inordinately heavy this year, and the banks beside the drive were shoulder high. She closed the garage door and glanced at the frozen surface of the lake. Shivering, she tucked her chin deep into the collar of her warm jacket as she headed for the private stairway running up the outside of the house.

Home. She turned the key but dreaded going in, a feeling she'd been unable to overcome during the last six weeks. As she moved inside and shut the door on the subzero temperature, her eyes scanned the living room that she'd carefully decorated to bring a little bit of summer into the Minnesota winters—gleaming hardwood floors, the old kind they don't lay any more; the Scandinavian import rug she'd searched so long to find, with its clever blending of greens, yellow, and white in an unimposing oblique swirl of design; airy rattan and wicker furniture with fat cushions of a green-and-yellow print that brought to mind warm, tropical rain forests; a multitude of potted palms, scheffleras, philodendrons, and more, flourishing on windowsills, tables, and on a small white stepladder in front of four long, narrow windows; lime-and-white Roman shades of woven wood that added to the tropical air; a pair of French doors leading to the summer sun porch overlooking the lake; a hanging lamp with white wicker shade that matched the floor lamp behind her favorite renovated wicker rocker with its rolled arms and thick pillows. And everywhere an impression of light and space.

Yes, it was like a breath of summer. Oh, how she'd loved this place . . . until Jason.

But now whenever she returned it was only to remember him here, slouched in the enfolding basket chair that hung from the ceiling, in one corner, his heel resting on the floor as he made the thing go wiggly-waggly, all the while teasing her with those gorgeous grinning eyes or that sensuous pair of lips that photographed like no others she'd ever caught in her viewfinder.

Jason . . . Jason . . . he was everywhere. Leaning over his morning coffee at the glass-topped dining table with its chrome-and-wicker chairs, often as not with one leg thrown over a chair arm, foot bare, swinging in time to the music he always seemed to hear in his head, whether it was playing on the stereo or not. Jason . . . sprawled diagonally across the squeaky old bed, studying the ceiling with fingers entwined behind his neck, talking about making it big. Jason . . . digging through the clothing that had hung beside hers in the closet, searching for just the right look that'd finally catch some producer's eye. Jason . . . blow-drying his razor-cut hair in the bathroom, nothing but a towel twisted around his hips, whistling absently as she leaned against the doorway watching him . . . just watching. Jason . . . spread-eagled on the living room floor, teasing, tempting, while The Five Senses sang, "When I'm stretched on the floor after loving once more, with your skin pressing mine, and we're tired and fine. . . ."

Jason, with the face and body of Adonis. It had never ceased to amaze Allison that he should have chosen such an ordinary looking girl as herself. He was beauty personified, a spellbinding combination of muscle, grace, and facial symmetry that spoke as poignantly to the artist in Allison Scott as to the woman in her. With Jason before the camera there could be no poor shots—his face wasn't capable of being captured at an unflattering angle. So while she'd had him, business had soared. Sport coats, leather goods, candy bars, road machinery—it seemed there was no product Jason's face could not sell, or so thought Twin Cities ad agencies.

Meanwhile, the portfolio of photos grew, and they made plans for a fashion layout in *Gentlemen's Review* magazine. It had been Allison's dream. But to sell to *GR*, to even approach them, Allison needed between three and four thousand photos. So she shot him everywhere, in every light, in every pose, against every background, learning with each clicking of the shutter to love him more.

And then six weeks ago she'd returned home to find half the closet empty, the razor gone from the bathroom, a damp towel over the sink, and the entire collection of negatives gone, too, and along with them, her dreams. He had left one thing—their favorite photo of him, blown up to poster size, on the four-foot easel in the living room. Across the bottom of it he had scrawled, "Sorry, babe . . . Love, Jason."

The easel stood now at the far end of the room, in the opposite corner from the hanging basket chair. Its pegs were empty, for when Allison had finally admitted that Jason wasn't coming back, she'd taken that overblown ego symbol, with all its memories, and stuffed it behind a bunch of unsold works stacked against the bedroom wall. She could hide the photo, but it seemed she could not hide the hurt. For it was back as keen as ever, resurrected by a simple thing like a two-dollar romance for which she'd agreed to do the cover.

Only she needed Jason to do it.

She turned away, toward the small kitchen alcove where she heated the spaghetti and ate it standing up, leaning against the kitchen cabinet, for she dreaded sitting at the table alone with Jason's image shimmering again as if he were still there, opposite her, as he'd been for the better part of a year.

Damn that story! Damn that hero who had to bring Jason's memory back all fresh and vibrant! Damn Mattie and her innocent questions!

The spaghetti tasted like wallpaper paste, but it filled the hole, and that's all Allison cared about anymore. Mealtimes were to be endured now, not savored as when there'd been the two of them together.

The way the apartment was arranged there was little to distinguish where the kitchen stopped and the dining area began. They ran together, then on to become the living room. Leaning now against the cabinets with a kettle in one hand and a fork in the other, Allison studied the empty easel, wondering where he was, who he was with, if he was modeling again. As tears filled her eyes, she thought: Damn you, Jason Ederlie, if you ever come back expecting to find your gorgeous face and body still haunting me from the ,corner of the living room, you'll be sadly disappointed!

But the fork dropped into the kettle, the kettle into the sink, and her head onto her arms as despair and regret welled up in her throat.

The following day was one of those grim efforts to make a living. Working with a pre-set camera, Allison spent six hours taking elementary-school pictures of gap-toothed second-graders, measuring the distance from camera to nose with the string that dangled from the tripod. It wasn't art, but it paid the rent on the studio.

By three o'clock in the afternoon, when the school session finished, the temperature was already dropping outside. Allison pulled a fat, fuzzy bobcap low over her forehead, wound a matching scarf twice around her neck, and headed for the van and downtown.

The ice on the studio windows was thick, the floor drafty. But the promised portfolio of glossies was in the mail. A quick check with the answering service turned up nothing needing immediate attention, so Allison headed home, her spirits a little higher than they'd been yesterday when she'd faced the empty apartment.

She made a cup of hot cocoa, slammed a tape into the tapedeck, and curled up against the puffy pillows of the sofa to see what Mattie had come up with.

Inside the mustard-colored envelope was a note in Mattie's writing: "Sorry they're not all in color, but I pulled some that looked as if coloring would be right. Love, M."

The girls came first, a bevy of fifteen faces, some in color, some in black and white, all with shoulder-length hair, as requested. One by one she laid them on the end table and against the cushions of the sofa. Some of the faces were passable, but none bowled Allison over. Semi-perturbed, she started looking through the men.

A smiling face with one tooth slightly crooked, giving an appealing little-boy look. Another with a sober aspect that somehow lacked character. Next, a glamour boy whose face was handsome enough but who somehow made Allison sure he wouldn't have any hair on his chest—for the poses she had planned, that was important. Next came a rugged type who'd adapt well to a Stetson and cigar.

But when the rugged type fell face down with the others, the cup of cocoa stopped halfway to Allison's lips, her eyes became riveted, and her back came away from the pillows. For a long moment she only stared, then her hand brought the cup toward her lips, and the next thing she knew, she'd burned her tongue.

"Ouch, dammit!" Depositing the cup and saucer on the glass-topped coffee table, she rose to her feet, scattering male faces from lap to floor as she held the single, striking face at arm's length.

"Holy cow," she breathed, stricken. "Holy . . . holy . . . cow." The face seemed too perfect to be flesh, the hair too disorderly to be accidental, the eyes so warm they seemed to reflect the change beneath the light from the table lamp. The nose was straight, with gorgeous nostrils. He had long cheeks and a strong jaw. And the mouth—ah, what a mouth. She studied it as an artist, but reacted as a woman.

The upper lip was utter perfection, its outline crisp, bowed with two peaks into perfect symmetry—a rare thing, no matter what the untutored layman might think. The lower lip was fuller than the upper, and the half smile seemed to hint at amusing things on his mind. Flat ears, strong neck—but not too thick—good shoulders, one leaning at an angle into the picture. He wore what appeared to be a wrinkled dress shirt with its collar askew, not the customary satin showman's costume, nor what Allison had come to think of as the "Tom Jones Look"—open-necked shirt plunging low underneath a body-hugging, open suit jacket. Still, she smiled.

I'll bet any money there'll be hair on his chest, she thought.

Allison flipped the picture over.

Richard Lang . . . 4-11-57 . . . blond . . . blue.

She read the words again, and somehow they didn't seem enough. Richard Lang . . . 4-11-57 . . . blond . . . blue. God, was that all they had to say about a face like this? Who was he? Why hadn't she ever seen his photo in the North Star files before? He had the kind of features photographers dream of. Bone structure that created angles and hollows, beautiful for shadowing. The jaw and chin seemed to be living, the mouth made for mobility. She imagined it scowling, smiling, scolding. She wondered if it were as mobile in real life as it seemed on paper. Something said "dimples" when there actually were none, only attractive smile lines on either side of his mouth, as if smiling came easily.

Richard Lang.

Twenty-five years old, blond hair, blue eyes, face as captivating as . . . but Allison stopped herself just short of finishing, "Jason's."

Richard Lang, you're the one!

She leaned the eight-by-ten glossy against the base of a table lamp and backed off, studying it while she unbuttoned her cuffs, then the buttons up the front of her shirt. She reached for her cup, took it a reasonable distance away while blowing and sipping, and studied the face, already posing him, figuring the camera angles, the lighting, the background, which could not be too involved lest it detract from that face.

There wasn't a girl in the lot pretty enough for him. The

girl, she could see, was going to give her trouble. It had been made clear to Allison that in the photograph the hero must appear to be overcome by the heroine, yet that was going to be hard to do with a face like his! It would overshadow any other within a country mile!

Allison, you're getting carried away.

To bring Richard Lang back into perspective, Allison deposited her empty cup in the sink, clumped into the bedroom, flung off her shirt, squirmed out of her jeans, and snuggled into a blue, fleecy robe, thinking all the while that when she returned to the living room she'd find the flaw she must have overlooked.

But he leaned there against the base of the lamp, more handsome than she'd remembered, making her hand move in slow motion as she zipped up the front of her robe.

She wished the photo was in color. Maybe his skin wasn't as clear as the black and white made it appear. Maybe he had freckles, ruddiness, sallow coloring. But she somehow knew his skin would be as smooth and healthy as a lifeguard's. Still searching for flaws, she thought maybe he has a horrible temper. Catching herself, she scolded, well, what does that matter, Allison Scott! You're taking his photo, not his name. If he has the temperament of a weasel, it's no affair of yours!

Nevertheless, it was hard to sleep that night. She hadn't been this exhilarated about her work since Jason had left.

The following morning she called Mattie to request more glossies of girls, and the two agreed to meet for lunch. Over steaming bowls of chicken-and-dumpling soup at Peter's Grill, Allison found herself hungry—actually hungry!—for the first time in weeks.

When Mattie asked which male model she'd chosen, Allison produced the photo of Richard Lang and laid it on the table between them.

"Him!" Mattie pointed a stubby finger. "I knew it! I knew he was the one you'd pick. All I had to hear was blond and blue, and I had him pegged in a second. He's just the type you can do wonders with on film."

"I'm sure as hell going to try, Mattie," Allison said thoughtfully. Then, studying the photo, struck again by his perfection, she asked, "What do you know about him?"

"Not much. He doesn't seem to give a fig leaf for what he wears. The times I've seen him he's been in battered-up tennies, washed out blue jeans, and wrinkled shirts that look like no woman ever touched an iron to them. Kind of strange, since most of our clients tend to overdo it when they dress for a booking."

"Mmm . . . so I noticed. His shirt looks like it's been through the Hundred Years War, and his hair . . . lord, Mattie, would you look at that hair! It's . . . it's . . ."

"Natural," Mattie finished.

"Yeah." Allison cocked her head and eyed the photo. "Natural, just like the rest of him. I wonder what the giant flaw is going to be when I get a look at him in person."

"Probably ego, like most of the pretty boys we handle."

The thought was depressing. "Probably," Allison agreed, stuffing the picture away again. "You don't have to teach me about ego in male models. Not after Jason Ederlie."

"I'm sorry I brought him up yes—"

"No, Mattie, it's okay." Allison held up her palms. "If I can't be adult enough to accept his being gone, I shouldn't have invited him to move in in the first place without any commitments on either side. It was . . . it was an idyll, a dream. But it's over, and I'm done licking my wounds. I'm going to throw myself into my work and make a name for myself, and when it's made I'll choose the man I want to live with, he won't choose me."

"Well, when you do, honey, why don't you make him a nice, stable plumber or grocer or accountant? Somebody who smiles at more than just himself in the mirror."

"Don't worry, Mattie. I've learned my lesson. When I find him, he'll be generous, humble, and honorable, and he'll dote upon my every desire."

Mattie laughed. "Hey, wherever you find him, could you pick up two—one for me?"

They laughed together, Mattie in her size sixteen slacks and Allison with her shattered illusions. But in the end Allison wondered if such men existed.

CHAPTER

Two

THE OLD GENESIS Building had two elevators, one for passengers and one for freight. Naturally the old relics were both out of order when Allison got there, so she was totally out of breath as she unlocked the studio door after climbing six flights of stairs.

The phone was shrilling, and she tore across the room to grab it, puffing breathlessly as she answered, "Ph...photo Images."

"Hello, this is Rick Lang. I was told to call this number, that you may possibly have a booking for me over there."

"Rick...L..." Suddenly the light dawned. "Oh! *Richard* Lang! The one in the photo from North Star's files."

"Right, but I go by Rick."

Allison was caught off guard by the pleasant, unaffected voice on the other end. It was deep, masculine, and easy. If she was looking for shortcomings in the man, his voice wasn't offering any clues.

"Rick...all right. Listen, I never make decisions from photos alone. I'd like to see you before we sign any contracts, okay?"

"Sure, that's understandable."

The image of his face came back to Allison, suddenly making her feel like a damn fool for insisting. What could she possibly find wrong with a face like that?

"Please understand, I'll be relying heavily on this job to

16

bring in other similar work. If there's anything about you
that—"

"Hey, sure, I understand. Sometimes black-and-whites can
be misleading."

Of all things, Allison felt herself blushing. Blushing! Talking on the phone clear across a city where he couldn't even
see her, she was stammering and blushing while he maintained
perfect poise.

"When are you free?"

"I'm my own man. When would you like to see me?"

"How about tomorrow at one o'clock?"

"Fine."

"Can you come up to my studio?"

"Sure, if you tell me how to get there." She gave him
instructions on where to park and what to do if the creaking
old elevator was still balking, and more careful instructions on
what to do if it wasn't. She heard his laughter then for the first
time, a light, mirthful enjoyment in deep tones, before he
ended, "I'll see you at one o'clock, then."

When she'd wished him good-bye, she fell back into her
swivel chair, linked her fingers and hung her palms on the top
of her head. This was ridiculous. She was becoming paranoid,
looking for faults in him even before she met him, hoping to
hear an effeminate tone in his voice, poor grammar, a lisp . . .
something!

Scott, get your ass going! she chided, and jumped to her
feet. He's not Jason, and he's not going to move in with you,
so call a sand-and-gravel company and get a promise of free
sand in exchange for free publicity shots of their operation or
free photos of the owner's grandchildren or whatever it takes
to get that sand up here. But get your mind off Rick Lang!

The following afternoon, Rick Lang entered the door of
Photo Images to find a woman with her back to him, talking
on the phone. She was tilted far back in an ancient oak swivel
chair, the high heel of one brown leather boot propped high
onto a frame of a huge wall of windows, the other ankle
crossed over her knee. Spicy brown hair hung to her shoulder
blades, held behind her ears by a pair of oversized sunglasses
pushed onto the top of her head. His eyes followed the taut

blue jeans on the outstretched leg, took in a bulky gray sweater and a coordinated woolen scarf wrapped twice around her neck. Suddenly she gestured at the ceiling like an Italian fruit vendor haggling over the price of an apple.

"But what if I sign up and get the bends or something, can I get my money back?" She gestured again, more exasperatedly, and the foot that rested on the knee started tapping the air sideways. Rick stood there, smiling, listening. The foot stopped tapping, the chin came down. "Oh, you can't?" she asked. "Not in a swimming pool?" She lowered the sunglasses to their proper place, and her voice turned innocent. "Well, to tell the truth, I really don't want to learn to scuba." She scratched the blue denim on her knee, nervously. "I just needed to use the gear for a couple of days for a photo project I'm planning and—"

She yanked the phone away from her ear, while across the room Rick heard snatches of a man's angry reply. "Lady . . . every curious . . . try diving . . . out of business . . . no time . . . want lessons."

The chair rocked forward, and her boots hit the floor with a slap. "Well, you don't have to get so—" She stopped, cut off, listened a moment longer, then spit, "Mister, I'm not after free—" Again she listened, then abruptly slammed the receiver onto the cradle in her lap, made a most obscene gesture at it, crossed her arms belligerently, and hissed, "That's for you, sweetheart!"

Rick Lang smiled widely, carefully wiped the expression from his face, and quietly said, "Excuse me."

The chair whirled around so fast, her sunglasses slipped down her nose, and the receiver flew off its cradle. She caught it by the cord, set the whole thing on her desk, and came to her feet, blushing a deep crimson.

"How long have you been standing there?" she snapped.

"A while." He watched the color flood her face, her lips compress, and studied the oversized lenses that hid her eyes. "Sorry, I got here a little early." He smiled as he came forward, hand extended. "Rick Lang," he greeted simply.

"Allison Scott," she returned as his warm palm enfolded hers, pumped once, then disappeared into the pocket of a misshapen garment that had once been a letter jacket.

"You wanted to look me over." He stood back, absolutely at ease, weight on one foot, not so much as a hint of nervousness while that easy smile turned his mouth to magic and Allison had the distinct impression that if anyone was being looked over, it was she.

"Yes ... I ..." Her cheeks were positively hot. "Listen, I ... I'm not a dishonest person." She gestured toward the phone, certain he'd seen her rude, unladylike gesture at the end of the conversation. "You heard me tell him I didn't really want to take scuba lessons, didn't you? I don't con people out of things, it's just that it's kind of tough to come up with props for pictures sometimes, and I need scuba gear for a project I'm planning, so I ... I thought I just might give scuba diving a try if it'd get me the gear and they'd let me have my money back after lesson number one, but the guy got nasty and I ... I ..." She suddenly realized she was blubbering to hide her embarrassment, so fell silent. Being at a disadvantage was something new to Allison Scott, and letting it show was even rarer.

Rick laughed engagingly, managing at the same time to admire her upbeat look, the sleek jeans and body sweater ending nearly at her knees, and her face, now pink and flushed with embarrassment.

"I'm not here to judge you, you're here to judge me, so forget I even heard it."

She told herself to cool down, that he was just another handsome face, another ego, another Jason. Yet even at first glance she sensed a difference. The cocky self-assurance was absent. Even his clothes were unsensational. He was dressed as Mattie had warned he might be—that seen-better-days jacket with the collar worn absolutely threadbare, faded jeans; a pair of scuffed, well-traveled almost-cowboy boots. The jacket was partly unsnapped. Beneath it she saw a purple sweatshirt bearing a white number 12. Her eyes moved from it to his face, which again affected her like a 110-volt shock.

Ruddy skin, bitten to a becoming pink by the wind outside, but smooth and unblemished; nose straight and shining from the cold. His hair had been styled by the feckless whims and guileless artistry of the January winds. That hair was, indeed, blond, a rich color that seemed a gift in the middle of this snowbound January, when most people bundled beneath warm caps. The lightly curled strands of hair were blown about his ears, temples, and forehead in engaging disarray. To comb it would be folly, she thought.

She suddenly realized she'd been staring, and looked away. He was, beyond a doubt, even better than his pictures.

"Did the agency tell you what this assignment is?" she asked.

"No, just that I should contact you to find out." He glanced across the studio—full gunny sacks resting against the front of an old, beaten desk; an ancient refrigerator; rolls of back-drop paper hanging from between the pipes on the ceiling; an assortment of chairs, stools, artificial plants, pillows, and cream cans in one corner; cameras on tripods, umbrella reflectors, strobes, a variety of photographic equipment. But mostly space—lots of space—and bright afternoon light flooding the place through the frost-laced windows. The corner where her desk stood was her "office," separated by two metal file cabinets against the wall, to one side. A nearby door led to a windowless room, but it was dark inside, and he couldn't tell what it was used for.

While he studied the studio, she studied him, wishing he were wearing a deep-necked shirt so she could see if there was hair on his chest. She wasn't quite sure how to ask him if there was. His eyes wandered back to hers, and she felt the color rise along her neck again.

"It's a book cover, and they need two poses, one for the front, one for the back."

"What kind of book?"

"A romance."

His eyebrows rose briefly, speculatively, then he shrugged and nodded.

"Have you ever posed with another model?"

"A few times."

"A woman?"

"Once."

"What was the ad for?"

"His and hers jogging suits or something like that."

She'd guessed right when studying the black-and-white glossy. He had the most utterly mobile mouth she'd ever seen and brows that expressed his mood almost before the words were out of his mouth.

"Will you do something for me?" Allison asked.

"If you'll do something for me." His eyes stopped roving and stared at his own reflection in her sunglasses. "Take off the glasses so I can see you."

"Oh!" She pushed the glasses up to rest on her hair. "I didn't realize."

"Better. Now where were we?"

"You were going to do something for me."

His hands came out of those drooping pockets, palms up. "Name it."

She moved from behind the desk to stand several feet before him, her hands slipped into the tight front pockets of her jeans, her shoulders hunched while she assessed him.

"Look angry," she ordered.

Again came the magic. In a split second his brows lowered, curling just enough to gain a viewer's sympathy yet not enough to make him look mean.

"Wily," she shot at him.

"What?"

"Look wily," she demanded, pointing a finger at his nose.

Immediately his gaze shifted until he peered from the corner of his eye at the refrigerator, as if it were there to thwart him but he had the goods on it.

Allison smiled, clapped her hands once in delight, then ordered, "Tired!"

His lips fell open slightly, a droop tugged the corners of his mouth down, and the sparkle disappeared from his spiky-lashed eyes, which he cast disconsolately at the floor between them. . . . Perfect, she thought.

Her heart went tripping over itself in delight. He was a natural! She went into a semi-crouch, hands grasping knees as if she were a lineman on a football team.

"Give me belligerent!" she threw at him.

The beautiful lips puckered up like a drawstring bag. The eyes scowled. The skin seemed to stretch tight over the sculptured cheekbones. She forgot his name, age, coloring, handsomeness, and saw only magic happening before her eyes. And while she was intensely captivated, caught up in discov-

ering him, she didn't realize how her own eyes danced, how
her face took on life, mirroring the responses he effortlessly
brought forth with each new order she issued. No matter what
it was, his face changed with each brusque command.
"Threatened . . . amused . . . puzzled . . . pleased. . . ." As fast
as she snapped out the words, he expressed them.

"Ardent!" she threw out.

For the first time his eyes settled on hers, remained on
them, in full, while he leaned toward her as if only the merest
thread of restraint compelled him not to touch. His eyes spoke
poems, his lips hinted kisses, and his stance was so questing
that she actually straightened and took a quick step backward.

Immediately he dropped the pose and took up his own lazy,
loose-boned stance again, his eyes asking how he'd done.

The breath she expelled lifted wispy Pekingese bangs away
from her forehead and temples, then she laughed, a bit nervously, but enormously pleased.

"Hey, do you do this all the time?" she asked.

"What?"

"This . . . this immediacy!"

He looked surprised. "Am I immediate?" He laughed a
little.

"Immediate!" She became animated, pacing back and forth
before him, boot heels clicking on the floor. "You're as immediate as electricity! Do you know what it sometimes takes to
pull those kinds of responses out of models?"

"I never thought about it much. I haven't been in this
racket very long. I just did what I was told."

"Yeah, you sure did." She came right up to him, smiling
now, shaking her head in disbelief. Involuntarily, she took two
steps backward.

Holy Moses! He didn't even know what he had. It was
more than looks, more than bone structure and vibrant skin
and come-hither eyes. It was . . . charisma! The kind photographers search for and rarely find. He quickly grasped each
mood she sought to create and portrayed them not only with
facial expression but with body language so poignant and natural that she hardly sensed him changing from one pose to the
other until his mood caught her in the gut and telegraphed
itself.

Suddenly realizing she was standing there clasping the top of her head as if trying to hold it on, she let her hands slide down and moved toward her desk, crossed her arms, and stared at the windows while stammering, "The . . . there's one other thing I have to ask you to do, and it may be rather unorthodox, but . . . I . . . I . . ."

He noted the defensive way she turned her back and crossed her arms. "You haven't seen me running yet, have you? So what's next?" He smiled.

She glanced back over her shoulder. "Take off your jacket."

"It's off," he claimed, snaps flying open even as he spoke. He dropped the jacket nonchalantly across one corner of her desk.

His arms and chest filled out the jersey beautifully. She took a gulp and reminded herself he was just a model.

"Now the jersey."

That one slowed him down for a fraction of a minute.

"The jersey . . . sure." It came off, but a little slower than the jacket.

He was now in a white V-neck T-shirt, the jersey bunched up in one uncertain hand as if he were getting ready to pitch it at the first thing that threatened.

"The T-shirt, too," she ordered.

He illustrated "suspicious" without being ordered to. His magnificent eyes skittered to her, to the desk top, to the wall where a few totally unobjectionable samples of her work were displayed. Finally, frowning, his eyes came to rest on her. "Hey, lady—"

She spun to face him fully. "The name is Scott, Allison Scott."

"Okay, Ms. Scott, I don't do any of that kinky stuff that I've heard—"

"Neither do I, Mr. Lang!"

"Well, just what kind of book is this, anyway?"

"It's not pornography, if that's what you're thinking. But if you're scared to take off the shirt, I've got a file full of faces that'll suffice just as nicely as yours!"

"I guess I'd like to know why first."

"I told you, it's a romance. It takes place on Sanibel

Island." Why was she being so defensive, she wondered. Because suddenly, when confronted with such an impressive physical specimen, she found she was wondering what he looked like bare-chested—and wondering out of mere female curiosity, not just artistic professionalism. Immediately she realized her mistake—it was amateurish and childish to be hedging the issue. She should have asked him immediately and avoided all mystery. Allison decided to be honest.

"All I need to know is if you have hair on your chest, but I felt a little silly asking."

Without another word the T-shirt came off. He stood before her in those tight, washed-out blue jeans, the nipples of his chest puckered up in the old icebox of a building, while zephyrs of too-fresh air sneaked along the floors. His was the first naked chest she'd seen since Jason departed, and Allison found she had to force her thoughts into structured paths while viewing it. But it was difficult to disassociate herself from the fact that he was—masculinely speaking—superb. Allison felt her body radiating enough heat to melt every shred of ice off those windows while he stood before her, shivering, letting her study him.

He looked down his chest, then back up at her. "Enough?" he asked.

For a moment she felt like a curious teenager peeping at the boys through a knothole in the changing-room wall, while he stood before her thoroughly at ease.

"Yes," she answered, and immediately the shirts started coming back over his head. From inside the first he asked, "So what am I going to wear for this picture?"

"Bathing trunks. Have you got any?"

"Sure." His head popped out, hair tousled in gamin boyishness that belied the mature, well-proportioned body she'd just assessed.

"What color are they?" she asked, moving back around the desk.

"White."

"Perfect, since we'll be shooting at night and they'll show up more."

His eyebrows curled and again he watched her warily as she moved, businesslike, to pick up pencil and clipboard, making a note while asking, "Do you have any scars on your legs or back?"

"No." He tossed the jersey on, shivering visibly now.

"Do you have any objections to kissing a stranger?"

With one arm half drawn into his jacket sleeve, he stopped, as if struck dumb.

"Kissing a stranger?"

"Yes." She raised serious eyes to his, making a desperate effort to appear calm.

"Who?"

Allison plucked the photo of the chosen female model from the pile on her desk and handed it to him. "Her."

He gave it a cursory glance. "The other subject in the photo, I take it?"

"Yes, if her coloring turns out to be right when I see her."

He turned it over and read the name on the back. "Vivien Zuchinski." He laughed and shook his head, lifting some of the tension from the room. "With a name like that she'd better know how to kiss!"

It broke the ice. Their eyes met and he chuckled first, followed by her mellow sounds of mirth.

"I feel like an ass," she admitted, relaxing even further, at last able to look him in the eye again.

"Well, I was a little uncomfortable there for a minute myself."

She ambled past the windows, toward the back of the studio, away from him. "I've never hired anybody for this kind of assignment before. I went about it all wrong. I apologize for making you feel ill at ease." She turned a brief glance back over her shoulder. He was still beside the desk.

"It's okay . . . as long as I get to kiss . . ." He checked the back of the photo again, "Vivien Zuchinski," he finished with a grin. He tossed the photo back onto the desk and followed Allison along the length of the studio.

"Do you mind my asking *you* a few things?" Rick Lang queried.

"No, ask away."

"Well, for starters, why are we shooting at night?"

She couldn't help smiling. "I can see you're still suspicious, Mr. Lang."

"Well, you have to admit it sounds a little fishy."

"Not when you want a nighttime effect. It's going to be a beach scene with a fire. I'll need total darkness outside so I can control the lighting. As you can see, the place is solid windows." She waved a hand at the glass wall and scanned the length of the studio before her eyes came to rest on him.

"A fire?" he repeated dubiously.

"Yup." With her hands in her pockets, one eyebrow raised slightly higher than the other, she looked a trifle smug.

"In here?" he asked skeptically.

"In here. You don't believe I can do it?"

He shrugged. "It'll be a good trick if you do. How many shots are you planning to take?"

"Oh, sixty-five maybe . . . of each cover, front and back."

He whistled softly. If she took that many shots, she was serious, dedicated, and thorough. He glanced around, obviously searching for a beach.

"Trust me," she said. "When you come for the session there'll be a beach. And all you have to do is wear a bathing suit and kiss a pretty girl. Is that so tough?"

"Not at all."

"Then do you want the job or not, Mr. Lang?"

"This is really on the level? Nothing kinky?"

"Honestly, you *are* a skeptic, aren't you? I admit the poses will be sensual. There'll be body contact—after all, it is a romance. But the final result will be tasteful."

A teasing light came into Rick's eyes. "Hmm . . . it's beginning to sound like more fun all the time."

"Then you'll do it?"

"When do we shoot?"

"Thursday night, if things go right. I've got to create the set first, and this one might give me a little trouble."

"The scuba gear?"

"No, not that. That's for the next series I'm doing. I was just planning ahead. It's the beach that's going to give me trouble on this one. I'll face the scuba gear later."

"Would it help you out if I borrowed some from a friend of mine?"

Her face registered pleased surprise. "Could you really?"

He glanced at the snowy city below. "I really don't think

he's putting it to very hard use right now, do you?"

"And I wouldn't have to take scuba lessons and get the bends?" She feigned great relief, then added seriously, "Taking the pictures is often the easiest part. It's setting them up that makes my hair turn gray sometimes."

"I hadn't noticed." He raised his eyes to the top of her head, then let them drift back to her face, an easy smile on his lips.

Immediately she was on her guard. It was the kind of remark Jason might have made, that sly, flattering brand of innuendo that had broken down her barriers and made her break her one basic rule of thumb: never get personal with the male models.

Though it was meant as banter, not flattery, the moment the words were out of Rick Lang's mouth he noticed how she crossed her arms tightly across her ribs. She was a classy-looking woman, particularly when she let her guard down. But often she set up unconscious barriers—the crossed arms, the lowered sunglasses, jumping behind the desk. He couldn't help but wonder what made her so defensive.

"I'll drop the gear by some afternoon."

"Oh, you don't have to do that. I can pick it up, wherever he lives."

"It's no trouble."

"I appreciate it, really. And thanks."

"Think nothing of it." He opened the door, turned with a grin, and finished, "As long as I get to kiss Vivien Zucchini."

"Zuchinski," she corrected, unable to stop the smile from spreading across her lips.

"Zuchinski."

Then he was gone.

Allison's arms slowly came uncrossed. She stared at the door, picturing his face, his form, his too-good-to-be-true physique. Unconsciously she slipped one hand through her long hair, kneading the back of her neck where pleasant tingles displaced common sense.

Haven't you learned your lesson yet, Scott? He's just another pretty boy out to make a score, and don't forget it!

CHAPTER

Three

VIVIEN ZUCHINSKI TURNED out to have exactly the right color
and length of hair. Her face wasn't quite as long as her publicity photo made it appear, but she had flawless skin, still clinging to most of last summer's tan, and a mouth that could be
called nothing but voluptuous. Her eyes were a stunning blue,
as big as fifty-cent pieces, eyes, Allison knew, that would
photograph beautifully, for they were fringed with sooty
lashes so thick it seemed they'd weigh her down. Her breasts,
it seemed, threatened to do the same. Oh, Vivien Zuchinski
had all the qualifications, all right. Her main shortcoming,
Allison could tell immediately, was that the girl was stupid,
which—thankfully—would not show in a photograph. She
chewed gum like an earth-breaking machine, had a fixation
with lip gloss, which she constantly pulled out of her shoulder
bag and painted on her pouting lips, whether in the midst of
conversation or not. Her favorite word, which made Allison
grimace, was "nice."

"Hey, *nice* studio," Vivien said immediately upon entering.
"Hey, *nice* boots! Wheredja get them? I got a pair's kinda like
them but not as nice. Those're really nice."

Allison cringed. Most of the models she worked with were
intelligent, upbeat, many of them students on their way to
professional careers in another field, helping themselves
through college with the money they earned modeling. Vivien
Zuchinski was definitely the exception to the rule.

"Hey, ah, what's the guy look like? Is he a fox, I mean, you know, ah, has he got a nice bod?"

"Very nice," Allison answered dryly. "Almost as nice as yours, Vivien."

"Hey, really? I like a guy with a nice bod."

It was all Allison could do to keep from rolling her eyes. "Have you got a bathing suit?"

"Oh, yeah, sure, got a bunch of 'em, nice ones, too."

"Would you mind bringing them along when you come?"

"Sure, you bet."

"The girl in the book wears a blue bikini."

"Hey, no sweat! I got this really nice blue bikini, bought it last summer when this lifeguard up at Madden's kinda started givin' me the eye, you know? And I figure I'd just put on a little show for him and come out on the beach with a different bikini every day, but I only had five and I was gonna be there for six days, so, gol, what was I s'posed to do?" She flipped her palms up at shoulder height, hopelessly. "So I find this nice blue bik—"

"Vivien, bring them all, would you?"

Vivien was too much of a stereotype to be believable. She hung a hand on one hip, threw Allison a wide-eyed look of innocence, and answered, "Oh, sure . . . yeah, sure thing."

"Then I'll see you Thursday."

"Yeah, sure. Where'd you say you got them boots again?"

By the time Allison had gotten rid of Vivien she wondered if she'd made a mistake hiring her. Allison stood with hands on hips, shaking her head at the door through which Vivien had left, then glanced down at her own high-heeled boots and said to herself, "Nice boots, hey."

The following afternoon Allison was standing disgruntledly with a broom and dustpan in her hand, spilled sand around her feet, when Rick Lang showed up with air tanks, flippers, hoses, and pipes.

"Hi."

She looked up, surprised, realizing in a flash how glad she was to see him again. "Oh, hi . . . oh, you brought them!" She dropped the dustpan, wiped her hands on her thighs, and came eagerly toward the door.

"Where do you want this stuff? It's kind of heavy."

She motioned toward the wall, sighed, and ran a hand through her hair. "Thanks. At least that's one thing that's gone right today."

"Have you got troubles?" He noted the sand, then her disgusted face. She noted his same old jeans and letter jacket, not at all the kind of clothing a guy wears to turn a girl's head.

"Have I ever." She glared at the mess. "I'm thinking about flying us down to Florida to do these shots! Except I think Vivien Zuchinski would drive me crazy before we got there."

"Vivien didn't turn out to be what you wanted?"

"Vivien's . . ." Allison searched for the proper word and turned a sardonic smirk his way. "Vivien's . . . *nice*."

He eyed the upward tilt of Allison's lips as she enjoyed some private joke. When she smiled, her eyes smiled with her mouth. She was dressed in off-white corduroy trousers with some kind of stylish, little army-green rubber shoes with bumpy white soles and long tongues and laces. They looked like something a socialite might wear duck hunting. Cute, he thought, taking in her modish hooded jacket and turtleneck sweater. Again she wore the sunglasses, pushed high up on her head.

"What's wrong with Vivien?"

"Nothing!" But there was a smirk of sarcasm in the quick word as she flipped her palms up innocently, then repeated, "Nothing. She has a terrific face and a very nice body."

"Good for me," he teased. "When can I kiss her?"

"Anytime you want . . . I'm sure she'll make that abundantly clear. You see, Miss Zuchinski has already pointed out the fact that she likes a guy with a, quote, 'nice bod,' unquote. Also, she likes her men foxy."

He laughed, leaning back, but it had a nice, easy sound, uncluttered by ego. "Need a hand?" he asked.

"I thought you'd never ask. The damn gunny sacks weigh a ton, and the first one came open halfway across the floor, which is not where I wanted to build my beach."

Already he was shucking off his frowsy letter jacket, laying it across the top of the refrigerator. "Just show me where."

She pointed to the area where the backdrop paper hung in huge rolls from the ceiling, then led the way, rolling aside some tall strobe lights on stands while he grabbed the ears of the closest gunny sack and dragged it over. She went to work cleaning up the loose sand while he moved the rest of the sacks. Covertly she watched the play of his back muscles as he lugged the bags.

"Do you go through this with every job you do?" He grunted, letting the first sack roll to its resting spot.

"Sometimes. I do what has to be done, get whatever props are necessary. You'd be surprised where trying to find them sometimes leads me."

"So I guessed when I walked in here the other day."

"A gentleman would tactfully refrain from mentioning the other day," she stated, her eyes on the broom while she swept. "Now the sand . . . I got it from a sand-and-gravel company, even got them to haul it up here free. In return I'll do a series of free shots of their operation when it's in full swing next summer. The kind of thing they can use on their Christmas calendar or whatever."

He glanced around the studio. "I never realized how much went into your kind of photography. In my kind the settings are already made for me."

"You're a photographer, too?" she asked, surprised.

"No, I'm a wildlife artist, but I paint from original photos."

She couldn't have been more surprised had he said he moonlighted as a fat man at the fair.

"An artist?" Yet the clothes fit, the lack of guile, of style.

"It's not a very lucrative business until you make a name for yourself. I only do the modeling to pay the bills."

"Like my school pictures."

"Your what?"

"I take school pictures . . . you know—little kids, stool, string-to-nose, smile and say *gravee-e-e!*" She made a clown face, tipping her head to one side, hands spread wide beside her ears, while the broom handle rested against her chest. "It pays the bills here, too."

"I thought that, working with publishers from New York, your career was going full swing."

"Not yet it isn't, but it will be," she stated, then set to work sweeping determinedly. "I had a good start once, but . . ."

Suddenly her face closed over, and she bit off the remark abruptly. He waited, studying her as she again attacked her sweeping, this time too intensely.

"But what?" he couldn't resist asking.

"Nothing." Suddenly she dropped the broom and turned toward her files. "Hey, wanna see some of the things I've done for local ad agencies?"

"Sure, I'd love to," he answered agreeably, following her.

It took no more than thirty seconds of viewing her work for Rick Lang to see she had enormous talent. "You're good," he complimented, scarcely glancing up as he studied her work. "Your concepts are fresh and vital." It was true. Still objects seemed to have motion, moving objects to have speed, scented objects smell, and flavored objects taste. He noted that she had two favorite models—one male, one female— whom she'd used predominantly, as was the case with most commercial photographers.

"Thanks. I love the work, absolutely do."

"It shows." He glanced up, but she was staring at the top photo, one of the favorite male model. The man wore a textured shirt and was posed against a background of bleached barn boards and a rich, rough stone foundation. The ancient building created the perfect foil for the man's handsome face and classic clothing. This was no manufactured set. She'd taken the shot when the sun was low in the sky, either early morning or sunset, for the shadows, even on the rocks and boards, were dark, rich, and intense. Shot after shot showed an artist's soul, an enviable talent behind the viewfinder.

While Rick Lang leafed through the matted enlargements, Allison saw Jason's face flash past time and again. She felt a sense of loss as keenly as ever, this time a professional loss, for the works featuring him were the best of the lot. Oh yes, she'd lost much more than a lover when she'd lost Jason Ederlie.

Rick looked up and caught an expression of unconcealed pain on her features. Realizing he was studying her, a tinge of color stained Allison's cheeks before she quickly reached to flip through the pictures to one she particularly liked. "I sold this one to *Bon Appetit* magazine." It was a photo of freshly sliced apples and cheese viewed through a bottle of pale amber wine.

"Mmm . . . you make my mouth water," Rick said.

She shot him a censorious look, but he was only studying the photo. How often Jason had said things like that—glib, quick, thoughtless compliments, laced with his irresistible teasing grin that were meant to do a snow job on her emotions while together they worked up an impressive portfolio of fashion shots on him alone. And, like a fool, she'd believed it all when he strung her along.

She swallowed now, trying to forget. Abruptly she lowered the sunglasses to cover her eyes, squared her shoulders, slipped her palms into her hip pockets, and walked away.

"Listen, thanks a lot for helping me haul the sand to where it belongs," she said. "I really appreciate it." The cool dismissal was unmistakable. It chilled the studio like air currents blowing across an icy tundra. Taken aback at her swift change, Rick's eyes narrowed, but he moved immediately toward his jacket.

"Sure. Anything else I can do before I leave?"

"No, I'm just about to close up here for the day."

"How about a cup of coffee? It's colder in here than it is outside."

"It always is, even though I crank up the radiators till they clank like a rhythm section. I'm used to it by now."

He waited, realizing she'd artfully glossed past his invitation without either accepting or rejecting it. "Maybe I'd better find one of those old-fashioned bathing suits, the ones shaped like long underwear, if it's always this cold in here."

"Oh, don't worry. Vivien will warm you up."

"You know, you've really got me wondering about this Vivien."

He managed to make Allison smile again, but her gaity seemed to have seeped away. Her lips turned up, but this time the smile seemed forced.

"Oh, I never should have made any comment about Vivien. She's just a little . . . inane, that's all," Allison noted apologetically.

"Which is a polite way for saying she's not too bright."

"Who am I to say?" She hadn't been too bright herself, falling for Jason's line all those months. Maybe it was better to be like Vivien Zuchinski and look for a man with a nice body, have a good time with it for as long as you both were willing, and forget in-depth relationships.

Rick Lang had snapped up his old jacket, and stood now with his hands lost in its pockets.

"How come you hide behind those glasses like that all the time?"

"What? Oh . . . these!" She flipped them up with a false laugh. "I didn't even realize I had them on."

"I know."

Their eyes met, serious now, his gaze steady, blue, and determined. He stood between Allison and the door.

"A minute ago I asked you if you wanted to have a cup of coffee. I thought maybe you were hiding so you wouldn't have to answer."

She experienced a brief thrill before quelling it to wonder why he asked. Goodness, he was nice enough—Vivien's word, but apropos at the moment—and handsome enough to land any woman in the city. But no matter how inviting it sounded, Allison had learned her lesson.

"Thanks, but my work's not done for the day. I still have to find a log."

He shook his head slightly, as if to clear it. "A what? You lost me somewhere."

"A log. I need a log for the beach, and I've kept putting it off and putting it off because it's been so cold, and I have to go out in the woods somewhere—if I can find a woods—and haul a log in here."

He gestured across the room. "You couldn't haul those bags of sand across the floor, yet you're going to haul a log out of the woods, into your car—"

"It's a van."

"Into your van, up the freight elevator that works whenever it feels like it, down the hall, and in here, all by yourself?"

She shrugged. "I'm going to try."

"No, you're not. You'll slip a disc, and I'll never get to kiss Vivien Zucchini."

Without warning she spurted into laughter. "Zuchinski,"

she corrected, "and I'm not too sure it would be such a great loss if you missed the chance."

"Oh yeah? Let me be the judge of that. I'm helping you do the logging because Miss Zucchini sounds like something mighty delicious. Maybe I like women with nice bods, too, and foxy faces." But his eyes were filled with mischief. He stood there in those raunchy old boots and that shapeless old jacket, with his hair all messed, for all the world as ordinary as any plumber or grocer or accountant. And dammit! she liked him. Not just because he had a face fit for the silver screen, but because he managed to be persuasive without being pushy, had a swift sense of humor, and was the first man who'd invited Allison out for coffee in over a year—and that included Jason Ederlie, who'd only drunk hers and never even washed his cup!

"Maybe we could pick up a cup of coffee and take it with us in the van," she suggested, then admitted, "I *am* freezing, and we're running out of daylight if we expect to come up with a log."

He smiled—not big, not phony, not even at her—and gestured with a shoulder. "Let's go." From the coat tree behind the door she grabbed her jacket, but he plucked it from her hands and helped her put it on. It was something Jason had never done. Thinking back on it, in that passing instant, Allison realized there were actually times when *she'd* held *his* sport coat while he slipped flawless shirtsleeves into it. Often, afterward, she hugged him from behind, using the jacket for an excuse to touch, to caress.

She'd forgotten how it felt to have a man help her into a coat. It made her more conscious than ever of Rick Lang as they rode down in the clanking old freight elevator together. She stared at the brass expansion gate, then at the ancient floor indicator, ill at ease as she sensed him studying her.

When they reached her van, he surprised her by following her to the driver's side, taking the keys from her gloved hand, removing his own gloves and unlocking the door. She found herself staring in disbelief. Did men actually do these things anymore?

He smiled, handed her the keys, waited for her to climb in so he could slam the door, then jogged around to the other side. He climbed in, hunched up, and chafed his arms.

"Not many guys do that anymore," she noted.

"Do what?"

"Help with coats and car doors and things."

"My mother used to cuff me on the side of the head if I forgot. After about the twenty-ninth cuff, I managed to remember. After that it kind of stuck with me. Guess I still think she'll manage to get me if I forget."

She couldn't help laughing. The story made him seem infinitely more human.

"God, but it's cold." He shivered, then pointed out the windshield and peered through the frosty glass as the engine chugged to life. "Go south and take Highway 12. I'll show you a place right in the middle of the city limits where we can get you your log."

"In the middle of the city?"

"Well, almost. Theodore Wirth Park."

"Theodore Wirth! But it's public land! It's against the law. If they catch us, we'll get fined."

He grinned, all lopsided and little-boyish. "Guess my mother didn't cuff me quite enough. Sounds like fun, trying to put one over on the law. Course, it's up to you . . . I mean, I don't want to be the one responsible for getting your name on the FBI's Ten Most Wanted List."

She laughed again. "You do that, and I'll personally see to it you never kiss Vivien Zucchini."

"Zuchinski," he returned with a smile coming from deep inside his turned-up collar and hunched-up shoulders. "And you'll have a tough time of it from behind the walls of the state pen."

They were thoroughly enjoying each other as the van headed toward Theodore Wirth Park. Allison stopped at a sandwich shop and Rick jumped out, returning a few minutes later with cups of hot coffee. The late-afternoon sun lit the clouds around it into crazy zigzags of aqua blue and vibrant pink. But suddenly Allison didn't mind the frigid temperatures.

Rick handed her a cup of coffee, watching appreciatively while she caught the fingers of her gloves between her teeth and yanked them off. He grinned broadly at the sight of her in the worst-looking bobcap he'd ever seen, pulled so low that her eyebrows scarcely showed.

"Forgot to ask if you like cream or sugar," he said.

"Sugar, usually, but I'd drink it any way today."

"Sorry. I'll remember next time." He sipped, looking around. "Nice van."

"Yup, it is, isn't it? Only another year and a half and it'll be paid for. I need it. I'm always hauling junk back and forth from the studio. Buying a van was the smartest move I ever made."

"I'm not big on vehicles," he offered. "Don't really care if I have a tin lizzy or an XKE—as long as it'll get me there, that's all that matters."

It had always been Jason's dream to have a sleek, silver Porsche, one that would set off his looks with a touch of panache. How refreshing to find a man whose values were so different.

"Would you look at that sky," Rick Lang said admiringly, almost as if reading her mind.

"Beautiful, huh?" They fell into comfortable silence, driving westward, squinting into the lowering sun against which every object became bold, black, and striking. Even the telephone lines, power poles, and road signs became artistic creations when viewed against the brilliant sky.

How long had it been since she had enjoyed a ride through an icy, stinging wintry afternoon and not complained about the cold? Allison wondered. Now she found herself noting the silhouettes of oaks standing blackly against their backdrop as she turned the van onto Wirth Parkway and entered the sprawling, woodsy park.

Children were sliding down the enormous hills between sections of wooded land. Skiers were out on the runs in gaily colored clothing. Even a sweatsuited jogger could be seen, his breath labored and hanging frozen in the air.

The road wove into the heart of the public land, past frozen Wirth Lake, the ski chalet, the ski jump, and acres of untouched woodland, which surprised and delighted Allison, situated as it was in the center of the teeming city. The van moved in and out of shadows as the late sun rested lower and lower in the west, behind the trees, making long, skinny shadow fingers across the road.

Rick directed Allison up a steep incline at a sign that read Eloise Butler Wildflower Garden and Bird Sanctuary.

"Anybody who's looking for wildflowers today is going to be disappointed," he commented. "I think we can steal our log up there without getting caught."

At the top was a paved parking lot the plows hadn't bothered to clear. Tracks left by cross-country skiers showed that only they had disturbed the snow here.

"You gonna be warm enough?" Allison asked as Rick opened his door.

"Yup!" He produced warm leather gloves from his pocket, yanked his collar higher for good measure, and got out.

It was getting dark quickly as they entered the woods, following the foot trails whose wooden identification signs now wore caps of snow. The trails were easy to follow, and when Allison and Rick were scarcely twenty-five feet from the van, they spotted a long, oblique lump beneath a thick coat of snow. Rick brushed it off, revealing a four-foot section of tree trunk.

"How's this?" he asked, squatting beside it and looking up.

She glanced measuringly from the log to the van. "Close, but too heavy, I think."

He walked to the end, kicked around in the snow, knelt, and boosted it up from the ground. "Must be half-rotten, just the kind we need so we can run fast when the posse comes."

"Think I can lift it?" she asked.

"I don't know. Give it a try."

She shuffled through the snow to the other end of the log, rummaged around to find a handhold, grunted exaggeratedly, and hoisted up her end. "I did it! I did it!" She staggered a little for good measure.

Rick trained his eyes on a spot behind her shoulder and said with grave seriousness, "Oh, officer, it wasn't me! I was just coming to turn in this lady for stealing this rotten log. Ninety-nine years should certainly be fair, yes, whatever you say."

Allison gave a giant shove, and the log rammed Rick Lang

in his beautifully muscled belly like a battering ram, then thudded to the earth at his feet as he dramatically clutched his gut. He staggered around as if he'd just had his lights punched out, hugged himself, and grunted, "I . . . I take that back . . . off . . . officer, let her go. I'll pay for the damn log!"

She affected a wholly superior air and joined his farce. "Officer, all this man's done all day long is talk about kissing girls. Can you blame a woman for grabbing the first thing in sight to protect herself with?"

Rick raised both gloved hands as if a gun were pointed at his chest. "Oh no . . . oh no, no, no, I'm innocent. Furthermore, after this display, you can put your damn log in your van by yourself! I'm going for a walk!"

He turned and continued along the trail, leaving her standing up to her knees in snow, laughing.

"Hey, no fair, you've got high boots and my shoes only go up to my ankles. . . ." She paused to check for sure, lifting one foot. She raised her voice and called after him, "Not even that high!"

"Come on. I'll make tracks," he said without pausing, dragging his feet to plow a way for her. It was somewhat better, but certainly left plenty of snow for her to trudge through. With high, running steps she hurried to catch up with him.

"Hey, wait up, you crazy man!" she hollered.

He paused, only half-turned to watch her over his shoulder. When she was close behind, he headed again along the footpath, with her at his heels.

It had been years and years since Allison had been in the woods at this time of day. The sky turned lavender as the sun sank. Snow blanketed everything, muffling sound, softening edges, warming—in its own way—all that lay around them.

Suddenly Rick stopped short and stood with his back to her, stalk still. Automatically she stopped, too. Sparrows tittered from branches above their heads, the notes crisp in the clear air. Wordlessly, Rick pointed. Allison's eyes followed. There on the snow beneath a giant tree sat a brilliant red cardinal.

"That's the kind of stuff I photograph and paint," he whispered.

The cardinal flitted away at the sound of his voice. Allison watched it flash through the trees. Suddenly she felt curiously refreshed and renewed. She turned in a circle, gazing at the white-rimmed branches overhead. "It's hard to believe we're in the heart of the city."

"Haven't you ever been here before?" He still faced away from her, and she looked up at blond hair curling over his upturned collar, then scanned the peaceful woods again.

"No. Not up here. I've been through the park, but I never bothered to come up here and see what was at the end of the trail."

He stood in silence, studying the sky, his head tipped sharply back. After a long time he said, "It's peaceful, isn't it?"

"Mmm-hmm." Even the birds had stopped twittering. She realized she could actually hear Rick Lang's breathing. They fell silent again, two people whose busy lives afforded too little of such elemental joys as this. There came a faint popping, as if bark were stretching in its sleep, growing restless for spring.

"This is what I miss about not living where I was born and raised."

"Are you a country boy?"

"Yup." Suddenly he seemed to grow aware of how long they'd been standing motionless, knee-deep in snow. "Your feet must be frozen."

"It's worth it," she replied, and found it true.

"Better get you back though, and steal that log if we're going to."

"I guess." Still, she was reluctant to return to the highway, to the sound of cars that was totally absent here, to the road signs instead of boles and branches.

"Can you even feel your feet anymore?"

Grinning, she looked down, then back up at him. His face was almost obscured by oncoming dark. "What feet?"

He laughed. "Just a minute, stay where you are," he ordered, then jogged off the path, circled around her, hunched over, and said, "Climb on."

"What!"

"Climb on." His butt pointed her way. "I got you into this mess, I'll get you out."

"Won't do you a bit of good. They're gone. The feet are gone. Can't feel a thing down there," she said woefully, staring at her hidden calves.

"Get the hell on, you're making me feel guiltier by the minute."

"Oh, lord, if I do, you'll be the one with the slipped disc."

"From a willow whip like you? Don't make me laugh."

So she clambered aboard Rick Lang's back, and he clamped a strong arm around each leg. She found herself with her cheek pressed against the back of his jacket, gloved hands clasped around his neck as she rode piggyback to the parking lot. Childish, foolish . . . fun, she thought.

He smelled of cold air and slightly of something scented, like soap or shaving lotion. Bumping along, she tried to think back to how she had managed to end up in such a spot. She could scarcely remember. Only that it had been painless, fun, and that somehow he'd managed to make her laugh again.

At the van she slipped off him and they loaded the log without mishap, but by that time Allison was shivering like a wet pup.

"Do you want me to drive back?" Rick asked. "You could stick your feet up underneath the heater and start thawing out."

"No, they're too cold. If I thaw them out that fast I'll lose 'em for sure."

"Minnesota girls!" he exclaimed in disgust. "Never know how to dress for the weather, even though they're born and raised in it."

"How do you know I was born and raised in it?"

"Were you?"

"Nope, South Dakota."

"Hey, you wanna talk all night or get back to town so you can thaw out?"

When they were halfway back to the city, the headlights picking the way through the dark, she asked, "Are you always this way?"

"What way?"

She shrugged. "I don't know . . . amusing."

She felt his eyes scan her for a moment before he turned away and answered, "When I'm happy."

Memories of Jason came flooding back, warning her again
of how sweet words such as these had hurt her once before,
led her into a trap that had been sprung with such suddenness
that she hadn't yet healed. This man was too new, too irresistible, too perfect. She was reacting to the loss of Jason, spinning Rick into a fanciful hero of her liking.

They parked the van on the nearly deserted downtown
street and unloaded the log. Carrying it down the hall of the
Genesis Building, they met the night watchman. As congenially and off the cuff as if the enormous log were only a
toothpick he'd been picking his teeth with, Rick nodded to the
curious old man, asked, "Hey, how's it going?" and marched
on past without so much as a snicker.

After they'd gotten into the ancient elevator and propped
the ungainly log in the corner, between them, they turned
around to see the gates closing on the night watchman's suspicious face.

Allison and Rick looked at each other and crumpled against
the sides of the elevator in laughter.

"He's probably still standing there with his tonsils showing," she managed at last.

"This is probably the most intrigue he's had since he got
the job. We'll keep him wondering for months what we did
with a log this size on the sixth floor of a downtown office
building."

They were still in stitches as they lugged the clunky log
down the hall and into the studio, stumbling under its weight,
which was far more appreciable the farther they went. When
they'd deposited it inside, near the sandbags, Rick dropped
down heavily on it, puffing.

"When I took this modeling job, I had no idea what else it
would entail."

"Listen . . . thanks. I realize now I'd never have been able
to do it alone."

"Any time."

The room grew quiet. Somewhere in the hall the elevator
reverberated as it moved in the silent building.

"Probably the night watchman coming up to see what those
two crazy people are up to," suggested Rick.

"I'll explain to him someday."

Rick clamped his hands to his knees and lunged to his feet.

"Well, I've got an appointment on a log with Vivien Zucchini Thursday night. I'd better get home and get my beauty rest."

Allison led the way to the door, switched out the lights, locked up, and walked with Rick to the elevator. The night watchman was standing there again, studying them with a curious look on his face.

As the cage was cutting him off from view, Rick waved two fingers at him. "G'night."

Unable to resist, Allison did the same.

"He has the master key. How much you wanna bet he goes into the studio and figures it all out?"

There seemed little more to say. Allison felt a strange reluctance to leave Rick. He walked her to the van and opened her door again.

"Well, thanks for the ride," he said.

"Same to you." She smiled.

He grinned, slammed the door, gave a good-bye salute, and sent Allison on her way wondering again where his hidden flaw was. Surely it would show up soon. The man was too good to be true.

CHAPTER

Four

THE FOLLOWING DAY Allison had an argument with a stubborn fool at the Anderson Lumberyard who refused to deliver a partial pallet of bricks because its value was under fifty dollars. When she explained her situation, he became even more belligerent, his raspy voice taking on an insolent tone. "Lady, we don't deliver bricks to no sixth floor of no office building. If we can't unload 'em with a forklift, we don't unload 'em at all. You want your bricks up there, you carry 'em up yourself!"

"But—"

The dead wire told her she was talking to nobody. She slammed the receiver down and kicked the corner of her desk, angered as she so often was by things beyond her control.

The phone rang and without thinking she jerked it to her ear and bawled into the mouthpiece, "Yaa, hullo!"

A few seconds of surprised silence passed, then a man's voice said, "Oh, I must have the wrong number."

Realizing how rudely she'd answered, she clutched the phone and put on a far more congenial voice. "No . . . wait, sorry, this is Photo Images. What can I do for you?"

"Ms. Scott?"

"Yes, who . . . oh God, is this Rick Lang?"

"You guessed it. Caught you being nasty on the phone again."

She sank into her swivel chair and hooked her boot heels

on the edge of the desk. "Listen, I'm sorry. You must think I'm a real asp, but sometimes I get so mad at . . . at . . . well, at men!"

"Hey, what'd I do?"

"Oh, it's not you, but do you mind if I blow off a little steam? I mean, all I asked for was a little partial load of bricks, and you'd think that damn fool could tell his truck driver to pull his truck up in front of the building and deposit them on the sidewalk or something! I mean, I wasn't asking to have them hand carried up six flights! But no, the load isn't worth enough for them to waste the gas. If they can't take it off with a forklift, they won't take it off at all!"

From his end Lang heard an ending sound like the growl of an angry bear while she worked off her frustration.

At her end, Allison felt slightly sheepish when his understanding laugh came over the wire and he asked good-naturedly, "There, do you feel better now?"

"No, dammit, I'll have to carry those bricks by myself . . . yes, kind of . . . oh hell, I don't know!" she blurted out in exasperation. But a minute later, Allison found her anger losing steam and finally disintegrating into self-effacing laughter. "Hey, I'm really sorry I took it out on you. It's not your fault. And what if you'd been a paying customer wanting to hire me? I'd have alienated you with the first word."

"How do you know you didn't? You still don't know what I called for."

Allison dropped her feet to the floor, crossed her legs, leaned an elbow on the desk, and affected a sultry, ingratiating feminine drawl. "Good mawnin' dahlin', this's Photo Images —hot coffee, hugs of greetin', and free makeup with every sittin', honey, so y'all come back, heah?"

She was twisting a strand of hair coyly around an index finger as Lang's full-throated laughter came over the wire, and she pictured him as he'd been last night in the woods, goofing around with the log, giving her a piggyback ride.

But now he reminded Allison, "Hey, I didn't get any hugs of greeting, and if I remember right, I'm the one who bought the coffee."

"But you'll get free makeup when I take the shots, and I'll buy you a cup of coffee then, so we'll be even."

"What about the hug?"

Something fluttery and warm lifted Allison's heart. She knew she was engaging in mild flirtation and shouldn't be. She searched for a glib answer, leaning back and gazing at the ceiling. "Mmm, what about when you gave me that piggyback ride? What would you call that?"

"You're too quick, Ms. Allison Scott. I'll let you off this time. What I called for was to check on your health today after last night's frostbite in those flimsy little duck shoes of yours."

"No worse for wear."

"Not even a head cold?"

"Not even."

"Well, good, at least I didn't add another item to your list of grievances against . . . men."

Allison smiled, toying now with the dial on the phone, warmed by his thoughtfulness, though she didn't want to be. But it had been a long time since anyone other than Mattie had been concerned about her welfare. Certainly Jason had never been. With Jason it was always her catering to him.

"Listen, what's all this about the bricks anyway? Can I help?" he offered.

"No, it's not your problem, it's mine. I need them to weigh down the plastic so I can build a lake."

"You're kidding!"

"No, I'm not! Have you ever heard of a beach without a lake?"

"Wouldn't it have been easier to take the pictures in the summer and use a real lake?"

"No challenge in that."

"Oh, you like a challenge, do you, Ms. Scott?"

"Rather. Besides, contracts like this don't always accommodate the seasons. I knew when I accepted that it would present problems, but it was just too good a chance to pass up. This cover will be for a new line of books coming out next year, and if I give them what they want, chances are I'll have my foot in the door. It'd be wonderful to know where my next month's grocery money was coming from . . . and the next, and the next."

"I know the feeling well and I admire your guts, but I'll

still have to see it to believe it—a lake, a beach, and a bon-fire?"

"Do you doubt me, Mr. Lang?"

"I have the feeling I shouldn't, but I do. It sounds impossible."

"Nothing is impossible if you want it badly enough, and I want this to be the best damn cover Hathaway Romances sees between now and June, so they beat my door down to get me to do a hundred more."

Rick Lang was beginning to admire the lady more and more. He couldn't wait to see how in the world she would build that lake. "So what about the bricks? Could I help? I haven't got a forklift, but I've got two good hands."

"Listen, you've done enough already, helping me get that log up here. I can handle the rest myself. The only thing is, if it takes me longer than I thought, we might have to delay the shooting for a day. But I'll call you and let you know when the set is ready. If we can't shoot Thursday, could you make it Friday instead?"

"Sure . . . whenever."

There was a pause in the conversation, and Allison suddenly felt reluctant to end it. Rick Lang was turning out to be one of the most congenial and warm men she'd ever met.

"Well . . . thank you again for checking on me, but as I said, there's no need to start cooking chicken soup."

"My pet hen will be glad to hear that."

They laughed together for a moment, and the line seemed to hum with expectancy.

"I'll call," Allison promised. "See you either Thursday or Friday night, six o'clock."

"Right. Bye."

But after the word was spoken Allison waited for a click, telling her Rick Lang had hung up. A full ten seconds passed, and she heard nothing. A curious throat-filling exhilaration tightened her skin, like back in high school when the boy you had a crush on stared at you across the classroom for the first time. Five more seconds of silence hummed past, and at last Allison heard the click. As if the phone had turned hot, she dropped the receiver onto the cradle, jumped back, and jammed her hands hard into her pants pockets, staring at the instrument with her heart hammering in her temples.

Scott, you're a giddy fool! she harped silently. Go get your
load of bricks!

She drove the van to the lumber yard, where she bought a
roll of strong, black plastic and the partial pallet of bricks.
When she started loading them single-handedly, the men at the
loading dock felt sheepish enough to lend a hand.

Back at the Genesis Building it took almost two hours to
round up the head janitor and locate a freight dolly, and by
that time Allison's temper was flaring again. At this rate she
might as well wait and shoot the scenes at Lake Calhoun,
come summer!

By four o'clock in the afternoon it was cold and windy in
the canyons between the tall buildings as she backed the van
up to the dock platform. The alley was dismal, foreboding,
and the cold was no palliative for her temper. Allison shivered, then pulled on leather gloves and began the arduous task
of transferring the bricks two at a time from the van to the
wide, flat dolly. According to the radio, the windchill had sent
the temperature down to minus forty. Allison tugged the thick
knit cap lower over her ears and forehead. The icy air caused a
pain smack between her eyes. As she bent and stooped, the
wind seemed to swirl and chill and find every hidden path into
the breaks between her layers of clothing.

Damn that stingy lumberyard! she cursed silently, thunking
down two bricks and turning back for two more. Allison's
nose was drippy, and her fingers had turned to icicles. She
looked like a disgruntled kodiak bear, bundled up in an ugly
old army-green parka with her hat covering her eyebrows.

"Ms. Scott, you're going to give yourself a hernia if you
don't slow down."

Allison spun around, a brick in each hand, and peered from
the depths of the van to find Rick Lang lounging against the
doorway beside the freight dolly, smiling in amusement. The
ugly, utilitarian bobcap had slipped so far down it now almost
covered her eyes. She had to tip her head way back to peer at
him from under it. At that moment, to Allison's horror, she
felt a trickle of mucous run warmly from her nose down to her
lip. Sniffing frantically, she thought, Oh no! Oh dear! I look

like the abominable snowman! And damn, why did my nose have to run right now?

"Oh God, how did you find me here?" she wailed.

"The studio was unlocked and the lights were on, so I figured you must be unloading bricks—I thought you'd be at the loading dock."

Before she could hide or run, he was pulling on thick leather gloves and bounding onto the back of the van. Automatically she bent over and covered her head with both hands. From the muffled depths came the wail, "Ohhhhhhh, hell! I look like the wrath of God."

He answered with a wide-mouthed laugh, then she felt a hand rough up her bobcap teasingly and push her face momentarily farther toward her knees.

"Hey, you look like an honest working woman, so let's get to work."

When spring comes, she promised herself, *I'm gonna bury this ugly cap in the garden!*

She stood up, knowing her face was beet red, thankful he couldn't see much of it in the dim light of the dock area. She peered up into his smiling blue eyes, sliding the bobcap farther back on her head. Immediately it slid back where it wanted to be, and any lingering delusions Allison might have had about her appearance vanished. She must be about as appealing as a seven-year-old boy after an afternoon of sledding. Horrified, she felt her nose dripping again. Rick Lang just stood there and boldly laughed at her, a pair of bricks in his hands.

"Hey, your nose is dripping," he informed her merrily.

She sniffed loudly, leaned farther back, purposely exaggerating her snot-nosed, childish appearance, swiped at her nose with the back of her gloved hand and pouted, "Well, I don't have a tissue, smarty! And if you were any kind of a gentleman whatsoever, you would politely refrain from mentioning it!"

He chuckled and dropped one brick. "It's rather hard to pretend when it's running right down." Leaning sideways, he fished in a hind pocket and came up with a crumpled white hanky. "It looks like it's been used, but it hasn't," he informed

Allison. "I do my own laundry and ironing isn't really one of my favorite pastimes."

"Beggars can't be choosers," she returned, yanking off a glove and turning her back while she buried her nose in his hanky and honked. To the best of her knowledge it was the first time she'd ever used a man's hanky.

"How come in the movies when this happens to girls they are somehow always daintily indisposed, with clinging tendrils of hair coming seductively loose from their topknot?" she grumbled.

"I think I see one now." Behind her she felt a tug as he lightly pulled a frowsy chunk of hair that must have been hanging from beneath her cap.

Never in her life had Allison felt more like an unfeminine klutz!

Rick Lang didn't mind one bit. He thought she looked delightful, bundled up in that ugly war-surplus parka, red nose running, scarcely an eyelash visible underneath that unflattering bobcap. She finished blowing her nose, turned, offered him the hanky, realized her mistake, and withdrew it with a snap. "Oh, I'll wash it first."

He unceremoniously yanked it out of her hand and buried it in his pocket. "Don't be silly. Let's load bricks."

He set to work with a refreshing vigor, unlike what she might have expected from a man with a cushy job like modeling. Somehow, when she'd first laid eyes on his snapshot, she'd visualized a self-pampering hedonist, but she was learning he was no such thing.

They had little breath for talking while they transferred the bricks from van to dolly. Their breath formed white puffs in the air as they worked. When they were finished, he ordered, "Toss me the keys. I'll pull the van in the lot, but wait for me. We'll take that dolly up together. Don't try to push it yourself."

He disappeared around the front of the van, and Allison lowered the big overhead door, evaluating Rick Lang anew. It was wonderful to have a man offering to help with the heavy work. She had done it alone for so many years, she never thought much about it anymore. But a warm glow spread through her at his admonition to wait for him.

He came back in, handed her the keys, and took up his place at the far end of the dolly, gesturing toward the other end. "You steer, I'll push."

"Aye, aye, sir," she replied with a grin.

The dolly filled almost the entire area of the freight elevator. When they'd eased it on, Rick sat down on top of the bricks and indicated a place beside him. "Your chariot awaits," he quipped.

Allison laughed and plopped herself down beside him, Indian fashion, for the ride up to the sixth floor. From the corner of her eye she saw him turn his gaze from the floor indicator to her. Self-consciously she realized she was wearing the most ridiculously ugly pac boots ever manufactured. Resolutely she kept her head tilted back, eyes trained on the numbers above the door.

"That's a damn nice cap," he teased.

Without taking her eyes off the numbers, she pulled the disreputable hat even farther down over her forehead, until only a slit of eyes remained visible beneath the turned-back brim.

"For a stupid South Dakota girl who doesn't know how to dress for the weather, it ain't too bad." She flashed him a smart smirk and a brief glimpse of the corner of one eye as it angled his way.

"I'll take that back when I see a beach, a lake, and a bonfire on the sixth floor."

"Doubting Thomas," she scoffed, and grinned.

They arrived at the sixth floor, and she leaped off the dolly and opened the clanking brass gate, then together they worked the ungainly vehicle into the hall. Wouldn't you know, the night watchman had just come on duty. He rounded a corner of the hall and saw the two of them maneuvering a load of bricks off the elevator.

Rick raised a hand in greeting and informed the wide-eyed fellow, "Just takin' my girl for a ride is all." He swept a theatrical bow toward the bricks, and Allison played along, clambering on board to again sit Indian fashion in snow boots, parka and bobcap, while Rick pushed her down the hall to the studio door.

When they got inside they closed the door, looked at each

other, and burst into laughter, as it seemed they were doing with increasing regularity. Rick dropped down onto the dolly. Allison leaned against the door, holding her sides, filled with rich amusement such as she hadn't shared with anyone in years.

"Oh, you were so glib, I think he believed you!" she managed to get out, quite weak now, reaching a tired hand to doff the cap from her head, leaving behind a mop of hair as disheveled as a serving of spaghetti.

"So were you—climbing on, sitting there like some Indian princess on her way to a fertility rite. You were superb!"

"I was, wasn't I?" she preened.

Immediately he reconsidered, scanning her from head to foot. He shook his head in mock despair. "I think I take that back. You're the biggest mess I've ever seen in my life."

"How would you like a brick implanted in the middle of your forehead?" She picked one up and threatened him with it.

"Hey, come on." He raised his arms protectively above his head. "Take a look in the mirror."

"*You* take a look in the mirror! Your hair looks like somebody styled it with a cattle prod, so don't point fingers at me." She deposited the brick and turned toward the doorway, across the room. Rick saw a light come on as she moved inside, and the next minute he heard a blood-curdling shriek.

He got up off the dolly and ambled over to the doorway, where he stood smiling. The well-lit room was apparently a dressing room, and Allison stood in front of a mirror, sticking her tongue out at herself.

"See? I told you," he nettled.

"Yep," she agreed dryly. She found a comb in a nearby drawer and dragged it unceremoniously through her hair.

He stood watching, noting the way the winter air had tinted her nose a becoming pink, the way her feminine shape was lost inside the enormous parka, which now hung unzipped, dwarfing her shoulders.

At that moment a furious pounding sounded on the studio door, followed by the concerned voice of the night watchman. "Hey, you all right in there, miss?"

Allison's and Rick's eyes met in the mirror, and they giggled.

"The night watchman. Thinks you're being assaulted in here."

"You'd better stop making fun of my appearance or I'll tell him it's true." She gave him a warning glance.

"Hello in there!" came another shout from the hall.

Allison hot-footed it around Rick Lang, opened the hall door, and confronted the frowning, grandfatherly man who peered past her to the pallet of bricks, the log at the far end of the room, and Rick lounging against the doorway of the dressing room. "Everything all right in here?" he asked. "Thought I heard somebody screamin'."

"Oh, that was me." She pointed over her shoulder. "He tried to get fresh, but I've got a black belt in karate. Thanks for inquiring, but I can take care of myself."

The watchman turned away, shaking his head and muttering to himself.

In the studio, Rick threatened, "If he sics the law on me, I'll tell 'em about the log you stole from a public park."

"I didn't steal that log, *you* did!"

"Oh yeah? Then what's it doing in your studio?"

She shrugged innocently. "Don't know. It just showed up here uninvited, like you."

Rick lazily pulled his shoulder away from the door frame, pulling on his gloves while he sauntered to the dolly and ordered, "Get your butt over here and help me unload these bricks, lady, before I take offense and leave you to do it yourself."

They worked companionably for the next two hours, placing the bricks in two roughly concentric circles on the floor at the far end of the studio. While Rick returned the dolly to the loading area, Allison unrolled the black plastic and sliced off an enormous piece to act as their lake bottom. When Rick came back, the two of them arranged the plastic, draping it over the inner circle of bricks, then weighing it with the outer circle. They crawled back and forth on their hands and knees in their stocking feet so they would not puncture the plastic, taking up slack, gauging how big the makeshift puddle of water had to be to produce an adequate reflection from the fill light that would simulate the moon shimmering upon the lake.

Next they worked with the sand. Allison was grateful to

have Rick there to lug the clumsy sacks around the edge of the "lake." As they emptied them one by one, covering the brick-work, the setting slowly took shape, appearing less and less artificial. The last item to be positioned was the log. Together they hefted it, placed it in the foreground where Allison indicated, then stood back while she formed a square with her palms to confine the view the camera would see and to judge the results of their labor. She hadn't yet set up a camera on the tripod, but she asked Rick, "Will you sit on the log for a minute so I can get a general idea of how we did?"

"That's what I'm being paid for." Obligingly he sat on the log, his arms draped loosely over his knees while she studied the composition as best she could without everything in it.

He watched her kneel, her face serious now as she peered at him from about hip level, where the camera would be come Thursday night. Again she was all brisk self-assurance, a stu-dious expression on her face as she did what she loved doing best. She had removed the army parka a while ago and now wore a white sweatshirt and blue jeans. As she bent forward, her hair fell across her cheek, but she seemed totally unaware of it, of anything but her work.

Suddenly she stood up, biting her upper lip while deep in thought. She glanced at the darkened strobes standing around the edges of the room, thought for a moment longer, abruptly smiled, clapped her hands, and declared, "Yup! It'll work just fine."

"Good," he returned, then sighed. He looked at his watch and reminded her, "Do you know what time it is? It's eight-thirty, and I haven't had any supper. Neither have you." He heaved himself to his feet, gestured with a sideward quirk of the head as he passed her, and led the way to the front door. "Come on, let me buy you a hamburger."

Walking toward their jackets, piled on her desk, she scolded, "Oh no, not after all the help you've given me. It's me who'll do the buying."

He automatically picked up her parka first and held it, waiting for her arms to slip in. "I asked first."

"I buy or I'm not going," she declared stubbornly. "It's the least I can do."

"Are you always this obstinate?"

"Nope. Only when guys come along and save my discs."

"All right, you win." He shook the jacket slightly. "Come on, get in, I'm starved."

At last she complied, buttoning up, retrieving her bobcap, and pulling it clownishly low over her forehead again while he slid his arms into his jacket and snapped it up.

"My car or yours?" he asked as they walked toward the elevator.

"How 'bout both of ours, then we can just hit for home after we eat."

"Right."

On the first floor he turned toward the front of the building, she toward the rear, having agreed upon where to meet. But when Allison got to her van she realized, chagrined, that she was almost flat out of cash. She counted the money in her billfold and her loose change. She had a single one-dollar bill and hardly enough change to make up the price of two hamburgers, much less drinks to go with them.

God, how embarrassing, she thought, and frantically started the van, thinking of her checkbook at home on the kitchen cabinet. The city streets were almost deserted. She had no idea what Rick's car looked like, so she had no recourse but to drive to the appointed restaurant and wait in the parking lot for him to arrive.

When she saw his face behind the window of a Ford sedan, she jumped from the van, left it idling, and was waiting when he came to a stop. She tapped on the window, and he rolled it down. She plunged her hands into her jacket pockets and looked up sheepishly.

"I feel like a real dope, but I haven't got enough money with me after all, so would you settle for an omelette at my place?"

"Sounds good."

"It's not far. I live on Lake of the Isles."

"I'll follow you."

She shivered, ran back to her van, and twenty minutes later the headlights of his car followed hers into the driveway between the high snowbanks.

When she emerged from the depths of the dark garage, he was waiting to lower the door for her, and once again Allison was struck by his unfailing good manners. He performed each courtesy with a naturalness that most men seemed to have long forgotten in this day of women's independence. Allison felt special when he treated her in this gentlemanly way. Inwardly she chuckled as she led the way up the stairway to her apartment, realizing she was dressed more like a combat soldier than a lady. Yet he still afforded her chivalry at every opportunity. And he did it in so offhand a manner as to make her feel foolish for giving it a second thought.

They stamped the snow off their boots and walked into her gaily decorated apartment. He was already pulling off his boots before she could turn around to protest, "Oh, you don't have to."

But he tugged them off anyway, then stood looking around the room while she removed her jacket and waited for his.

"Hey, this is like a touch of summer. You do all this yourself?" he asked.

"Yes. I like green, as you can see."

"Me too." His eyes scanned the room, moving from item to item while he shrugged from his jacket and absently handed it to her. "You have a nice touch. Looks to me like if you ever wanted to give up photography, you could take up interior decorating."

"Thank you, but you're making me blush. Please, just . . . just sit down and make yourself at home."

One brow raised, he glanced back over his shoulder with a grin to see if she was really blushing, but she was busy hanging up their jackets in a small closet behind the door.

She turned, caught him grinning at her, and gave him a little shove toward the living room. "Go . . . sit down or something. I'll be right back."

While she was gone, he walked around the room, noticing the tape player, the healthy plants, the daybed out on the closed-off sun porch. The main room was marvelous, full of light and color, its rich wood floor gleaming, tasteful art prints in chrome frames hanging on the walls. A decorator easel stood in one corner, and he wondered why it was empty. Hands in pockets, he ambled over to the opposite corner and was gazing at the ceiling hook that held up the suspended chair when she returned to the room.

"Doubting Thomas?" she inquired archly.

He glanced over his shoulder. She had put on some lip gloss and combed her hair. On her feet were huge, blue fuzzy slippers. "You read my mind so easily, do you?"

"Everybody who comes in here goes over to that chair, looks up, and asks 'Will this thing really hold me?'"

"Not me. I didn't ask."

"No, but you were about to."

"No, I wasn't."

She went to the kitchen end of the room and opened the refrigerator, in search of eggs. Funny, she had an inkling he'd ask it, even before he asked it.

"Hey, will this thing hold me?"

But he was already inserting himself into the almost circular basket, but very, very gingerly, as if it were going to drop him the moment he settled his full weight in it.

"Nope!" she answered.

He laughed, crossed his hands over his belly, pushed gently with his heel, and called across the room, "Hey, I want an under-duck."

"A what?" she asked, popping her head up from the depths of the cabinet where she was searching for a bowl.

"An under-duck. You know . . . when you were a little kid and you got pushed on a swing, didn't you call it an under-duck when they'd go running right under you?"

"Oh, *that!*" She laughed, cracked the eggs into the bowl, and remembered back. "No, I think we used to call it . . ." She screwed up her face, trying to remember. "Would you believe I can't think of what we used to call it."

"Shame on you. How will you teach your kids those all-important things if you forget them yourself?"

"Haven't got any kids."

From the depths of the basket chair Rick studied her while she beat the eggs with a wire whisk. The movement made her shining hair bounce at the ends, and inside her baggy sweatshirt he could make out the outline of her breasts bouncing, too. He let his glance rove down to her derrière—tiny, shapely buns . . . trim hips . . . long, supple legs.

You will have kids, he decided, admiring what he saw. "Do you plan to have kids?" he asked.

"Not for a while. I've got a career to establish first. I'm

just getting up a good head of steam."

He liked the way she moved, brisk and sure, taking a moment to wipe her palms on her thighs before reaching into the cabinet for a salt shaker.

Allison was conscious of his eyes following her, though she wasn't even facing him. It was disconcerting, yet welcome in a way, too. She was standing uncertainly, gazing into an open cabinet as she admitted, "This is awful, but all I have to put in an omelette is tuna fish."

She turned apologetically to find him six inches behind her. Startled, she drew back a step.

"Tuna-fish omelette?" he repeated, grimacing. "You lured me up here for a tuna-fish omelette?"

"I didn't lure you up here, and besides, experimentation is the mother of invention."

"I thought that was necessity."

"Well . . . whatever." She gestured haplessly. "Right now it's necessary for me to experiment, all right?"

"Okay, tuna-fish omelette. I'll grin and bear it, but we could have had a perfectly good hamburger and french fries if you hadn't been so stubborn."

"I get that way sometimes . . . female pride or something like that." She turned her back on him and rummaged for a can opener, her heart fluttering giddily at his nearness. When the tuna can was open, he reached around her, took a pinch, and popped it into his mouth. "Sorry," he offered, without the least note of contrition in his voice, "but I'm starving, and I thought I'd get at least one good taste before you ruin it."

"Would you rather have a tuna sandwich?" But immediately she waggled her palms. "No, forget I asked that. I just remembered I'm out of bread."

"There's one thing a person can't accuse you of, and that's trying to finagle your way to a man's heart through his stomach." He turned away and wandered to the tape deck, squatting down on his haunches to scan the titles on the shelf below. "You like The Five Senses, huh?" he noted.

At his question something tight and constricting seemed to settle across Allison's chest. A lump formed in her throat as she stared, unseeing, at Rick's back.

He swung around on the balls of his feet to look at her, and immediately she whirled to face the cabinet. "Yeah," she said, so crisply the word held an edge of ice.

Immediately he sensed he'd touched a nerve. She exuded defensiveness that chilled him clear across the room. "Do you mind if I put something on?"

She stared at the frying pan, seeing Jason Ederlie instead, wondering how she'd react if Rick happened by accident to put on the wrong song. Yet she'd just said she liked The Five Senses, so how could she possibly say what she was thinking: *anything* but The Five Senses.

"Go ahead," she answered lifelessly, leaving him to wonder what motivated her quicksilver change of mood.

She busied herself with the omelette, and a few minutes later the music of Melissa Manchester drifted through the apartment. Relieved, she cast him a quick glance to find he was standing by the stereo, studying her across the room.

Don't ask, she begged silently. *Don't ask, please.* Thankfully, he didn't, but went to sit on the davenport and wait to be called to the table. He stretched out, crossed his feet at the ankles, threaded his fingers together, and hung them over his belly, watching her covertly as she put the food on the table and wondering what had caused her sudden defensiveness.

A guy, he supposed. When it involved music it was usually a guy and some song the two of them had considered special. He made a mental note never to play any of The Five Senses tapes if he ever got up here again.

"It's ready," she announced soberly, standing beside the table with a long face.

He eased slowly to his feet, walked across the room, and stood by a chair next to hers. "Listen, I'm sorry for whatever I said that upset you. Whatever it was, I'm sorry."

Her lips parted slightly, and for a moment she looked as if she might cry. Then she slipped her hands into her jeans pockets, her throat working convulsively. "It's not your fault, okay?" she offered softly. "It's just something I have to get over, that's all."

His sober eyes rested on her questioningly, but he asked nothing further. Wordlessly he leaned across the corner of the table to pull out her chair. "Agreed. Now sit down so I can, too."

She gave him a shaky smile and sat, but the gaity had evaporated from the evening. They shared their meal in strained silence, as if another presence were in the room separating them.

Allison avoided Rick's eyes as he intermittently studied her, the downcast mouth, the forlorn droop of shoulder. His eyes moved to her left hand—no ring. Covertly they moved around the room in search of evidence of a man sharing the place or having shared it. There were no pictures, magazines, articles of any kind intimating a male presence in her life. His gaze moved to her again, to her shapely mouth, breasts, fine-boned jaw, shell-like ears, downcast eyes, and slender hand picking disinterestedly at the omelette. He leaned toward her slightly, resting his forearms on the edge of the table.

"Stop me if I'm stepping on hallowed ground," he began, "but are you committed to someone?"

Her head snapped up, and a shield seemed to drop over her eyes.

"Yes." She dropped her fork, giving up all pretense of eating. "To myself."

A brief flare of anger shone in his eyes. "That's not what I meant, and you know it. Is there some man in your life right now?"

Her heart began to beat furiously, but immediately memories of Jason came to quell it. "No," she answered truthfully, "and I don't want one."

He scrutinized her silently for a moment, his lips compressed. "Fair enough, but I had to ask. I enjoyed myself tremendously the last two evenings." He watched her carefully while relaxing back in his chair, leaning his elbows on the chrome armrests.

She propped her elbows beside her plate, entwined her fingers, and rested her forehead against white thumb knuckles. A shaky sigh escaped her lips. "I did too, but that's as far as it goes."

"Is it?"

"Yes!" she snapped, but her eyes remained hidden while her lips trembled.

"Somebody hurt you, and you're going to make damn sure nobody does again."

"It's none of your business!" Her shoulders stiffened, and her head came up.

"We'll see," he said with disarming certainty, not a flicker of doubt in his unsmiling countenance.

"I make it a practice never to get personally involved with my models. I'm sorry if you thought . . ." Her eyelids fluttered self-consciously before her gaze fell to her plate. "I mean, I never meant to lead you on."

"You didn't. You've been a lady every inch of the way, all right?"

Her eyes met his again—unsteady brown to steady blue. Against her will Allison was struck again by his flawless handsomeness, even as it filled her with mistrust. She wanted to believe he was sincere, perhaps for a moment. His face wore a look of quiet determination, warning her that he wouldn't back off without a fight.

She swallowed. "It's been a long day—"

"Say no more, I'm gone." Immediately he was on his feet, plate in hand, heading for the sink.

She felt small and guilty for giving him such an obvious brushoff when he'd been a perfect gentleman. But since Jason her instinct for self-preservation was finely honed. The faster she got Rick Lang out of here, the better.

He padded over to the entry, picked up a boot, and leaned his backside against the door while pulling it on. From the closet she retrieved his coat, and before she realized what she was doing, held it out as she'd often done for Jason. A surprised expression flitted across Rick's face before he turned, slipped his arms in, and faced her once more, slowly closing the snaps while she waited uncomfortably for him to finish and leave.

She trained her eyes on the frayed collar, afraid to raise them further, for she knew he was studying her while the sound of the snaps seemed to tick away the strained seconds.

His hands reached the last one, and he leisurely tugged his gloves from the jacket pocket, slowly pulled them on while she stared at them, knowing no other place to safely rest her eyes. He jammed his spread fingers into the gloves, all the while studying her averted face.

He was dressed for outside, ready to go, yet he stood there

without making a motion toward the door.

"I heard what you said before. I know what you were telling me," he said in a low voice. "But I just have to do this..."

She had a vague impression of the scent of leather while his glove tipped her chin up. Soft, warm, slightly opened lips touched hers. A tongue tip briefly flicked. Two strong gloved hands squeezed her upper arms, pulling her upward, forcing her to her toes momentarily, catching her totally off guard. Almost as if it were a harbinger of things to come, the kiss ended with a slow separation of their mouths. He lifted his head, studying her eyes for a brief moment, then dropped his gaze to her surprised, open lips.

"Nice," he said softly. Then he was gone, leaving behind only a rush of cold air and a trembling in her stomach.

CHAPTER
Five

ALLISON HALF EXPECTED Rick to call the following day, Wednesday, but he didn't. She wondered what he'd say when he walked into the studio Thursday night. She wondered how to act, then decided she would act no differently than she had all along. Maintaining the same light, teasing banter would be the best way to remain at ease and keep their relationship on a nonpersonal level.

One of Allison's Wednesday chores was to talk her landlord out of a garden hose and lug it up to the studio in preparation for filling the "lake." Then she made a trip to get firewood and a piece of asbestos for under it, so the heat wouldn't raise the linoleum off the studio floor. If that night watchman found out she was going to start a fire in the middle of the building, she'd be out on her ear. Thankfully the building was such a relic it had no smoke alarm or sprinkler system.

Thursday she filled the pool, checking to make sure there were no leaks, then set up her lights, deciding how many she'd need, the general positioning of both key light and fill lights, and what color filters to use on each. She cut out a circle in the backdrop paper, inserted an orange filter on one of the strobes, and positioned it to simulate the moon, which would appear only as a hazy, out-of-focus orb in the finished photograph, its reflection on the water being the chief reason she needed it at all.

By five o'clock she was loading her camera with nervous fingers, telling herself this was stupid, this was business, and Rick Lang was only a model.

Then why was she shaking?

She secured the camera on its tripod, coiled up the hose, disconnected it from the bathroom faucet, then cursed softly to find it had left a trail of water across the floor. Mopping up the spill, she suddenly remembered she hadn't asked the janitor for a wet vac to have on hand in case of an emergency, and ran to do so.

Returning to the studio, pushing the clumsy machine, Allison found Rick standing in front of the set, studying it.

He looked up as she entered and smiled.

"Hi," he said simply.

Something joyfully warm and appreciative crept along her veins at the sight of him. It was impossible to forget his brief parting kiss.

"Hi."

"You did it." He grinned, glancing at the lake, the sand, the bonfire ready for lighting.

"I told you I would." She sauntered over to the edge of the set.

"Clever lighting, with the moon—I presume—reflecting across the water." He turned to indicate the strobe showing through the backdrop, the low positioning of the camera on the tripod.

"Let's hope so. We haven't taken the shots or seen the results yet."

"How did you get that lake filled up?"

"With a garden hose."

"And you're going to suck it up with that when you're done?" He indicated the wet vac.

"Yup." She flipped her palms up and gave him a plucky smile. "Simple."

"Don't underrate yourself. It's more than simple, it's ingenious." Glancing at the set again he commented, "I see you made another trip for firewood."

"Yup."

"Who carried you out this time?" he teased.

"I wore my boots like a good girl. How 'bout you? Did you bring your bathing trunks?"

"Yup!" He pulled them out of a pocket, rolled up tight. "Got 'em right here, but I'm not anxious to put 'em on. It's like a meat locker in here, as usual."

"Don't worry, the fire will warm you up."

"Oh, I thought Vivien Zucchini was supposed to do that." He grinned down at Allison, hooked his thumbs in the pockets of his letter jacket, and watched her swing away.

"Zuchinski," she corrected without turning around.

Rick grinned in amusement, watching her trim hips and thighs take no-nonsense steps. Her hair swayed. Her backside was firm and athletic as she strode toward the dressing-room doorway, reached inside, and flipped the lights on. Slipping her hands into the pockets of her slacks, she turned and leaned one shoulder against the dressing-room doorway like a model in a chic shampoo ad. He scanned her long-sleeved khaki safari jacket, which was belted and had epaulets at the shoulders, his eyes lingering only a fraction of a second on the breast pockets with their button-down flaps. Matching trousers were tucked into thigh-high boots. Her hair was again held behind her ears by the upraised sunglasses, though night had fallen outside and inside the lights were dim.

"I've had the door to the dressing room closed so it would warm up in there," she said. "I don't want you to freeze and break in half before we get you posed and the fire started."

"Where's Miss Zucchini?"

She laughed, hands still in pockets, bending forward at the waist, then peering at him with mock admonishment. "If you say that one more time, she's going to walk in here and I'm going to pour tomato sauce over her instead of oil!"

Rick leaned back and laughed appreciatively while Allison checked her wristwatch. "She's due any minute. If you want to use the dressing room first, we can get started oiling you."

The oiling was news to him, though it was common practice to oil skin to simulate wetness and bring out highlights on the skin.

But at that moment the door opened and in came a stunning blue-eyed brunette bundled up to her ears in fake fur. In an affronted tone she said, "I hope it's warmer in here than it was the other day, or my unmentionables will shrivel up like raisins."

Both Rick and Allison burst out laughing. The woman gazed at them with wide, innocent eyes, as if she had no idea she'd made a graceless, tasteless opening remark.

"Rick Lang, I'd like you to meet Vivien Zuchinski." It was all Allison could do to hold a straight face and get the name right. "Vivien, this is Rick Lang, the man you'll be posing with."

Rick extended his hand.

In slow, sultry motion, Vivien's came out to meet it. She wrapped it tightly in long, shapely fingers with long, shapely nails of a ghastly vermilion that looked surprisingly right on her. Sweeping her spaghetti-length lashes up and down Rick's body, Vivien cooed, "Ooooo, *nice*."

Rick laughed good-naturedly, playing along when Vivien refused to relinquish his hand. "Likewise, I'm sure, Vivien," he said congenially. "I'm happy to share a book cover with a pretty face like yours."

She teased the hairs on the back of his hand with a tapered nail and widened her devastating eyes on him. "Heyyyy, no . . . lisssen, I'm the one that's really knocked out. I mean, you're really somethin', Rick. I'm already forgetting how cold it is in here."

Allison cleared her throat, and Vivien turned to find her leaning against the doorway to the dressing room, one foot crossed in front of the other, with a toe to the floor.

"Mr. Lang has been complaining about how cold it is in here, too, so maybe the two of you can warm each other up, huh?" Bringing her shoulder away from the door frame, Allison gestured Vivien into the brightly lit dressing room. "Would you like to be first, Miss Zook—" She caught herself just in time and finished, "Miss Zuchinski?"

Vivien swooped into the dressing room, shedding her coat and looking around. "Heyyyy, *nice*. Lots of good light for putting on makeup."

"Yours looks great already, so don't change a thing. Just put on your suit, and I'll give you a bottle of baby oil. Is your hair naturally curly?"

"What?" Vivien momentarily gave up studying her pouting lips in the mirror.

"Your hair—is it naturally curly? I'd like to put baby oil on it, too, to create the illusion of wetness."

Vivien patted her tresses with deep concern. "Oil! On my hair? I'd rather not."

"How about just on the ends then, to make it look like you've been in the water?"

"Well, you're the boss . . . but, gee!" She looked crestfallen, her face much more expressive than her vocabulary.

"Why don't you change first, then we'll experiment a little," Allison advised.

Vivien closed the door all but a crack, through which she waggled two fingers at Rick before closing it the rest of the way. Allison bit her lip to keep from laughing, but she couldn't resist glancing Rick's way to check his reaction. When their eyes met, he feigned a wolfish grin and rubbed his palms together in anticipation. "Hey, I can't wait," he teased in a whisper.

"I'll just bet you can't."

The door opened a short time later, and Vivien appeared, clad in a minuscule two-piece bathing suit that showed off every voluptuous hill and valley to great advantage. Out she came, hands thrown wide. "How's this?"

"Wow!" Rick exclaimed exuberantly.

"Nice," Allison commented dryly.

"I'm ready for oiling," Vivien declared.

"Let me get the tomato sauce, and I'll get you started," Allison quipped.

"The wha-a-a-t?" Vivien questioned, a puzzled frown on her face, dropping her hands to her hips.

"Rick, go ahead and change," Allison suggested. "It's just an old inside term, Vivien. Come on."

Allison felt rather small, having resorted to such catty tactics with Vivien. It wasn't like her at all. What in the world had she been thinking to say such a thing? Vivien was here as a professional, and if anyone was acting unprofessional, it was Allison herself. The truth was, Vivien Zuchinski was a beautiful woman with impressive proportions. Allison was abashed to find herself slightly jealous.

In two minutes the changing-room door opened again. "Hey, come on in, ladies, it's warmer in here."

Standing behind her desk, Allison lifted her eyes, and her mouth went dry. Rick stood in the doorway, barefooted, bare chested, bare legged, only that tight white suit striping his midsection, dividing his dark skin. Unlike Vivien, he didn't flaunt his assets, but just appeared at the door, invited them in, then stepped inside himself.

"Heyyyy, sugar, I'm comin'!" Vivien giggled.

There was an awkward moment when Allison stepped to the door and handed Rick a full bottle of baby oil. Her eyes had lost all hint of teasing. He was magnificent! Sparkling golden hair covered not only his chest, but also dove in a thin line down his belly, covering his legs and arms lightly. He turned to face the mirror and poured a modicum of oil into his palm, then began applying it to his shoulders while Allison saw his back for the first time. Her eyes drifted from wide shoulders to narrow hips, taking in firm skin and fine-toned muscle. His derrière was flat, his legs well shaped without the bulging muscles that ruined the male form when it came to photographing it. Truly, his body was an artist's concept of beauty.

In the mirror Allison caught his eye and knew he'd been watching her assess him, but he only looked away and continued applying oil briskly. Unlike Jason, who used every such opportunity to smirk and flaunt and tease with his eyes, Rick accepted his physical assets with dignity, but not ego. He radiated no sexy innuendo, but merely turned to the mirror and vigorously continued what he was doing.

Vivien sat on a chair and hooked her shapely toes—vermilion, too, Allison noted—on the edge of the vanity, squirting a line of oil up a perfect leg. Spreading it, she kept her eyes on Rick.

"I'll put some on your back," Allison offered, moving behind Vivien, who swiveled sideways a little on the chair.

It seemed Vivien had dreams of becoming a Playboy bunny, and she prattled on about a trip she had taken to the Playboy Club in Chicago, all the while scouring Rick with admiring gazes.

"I think we'll need some oil on the ends of your hair anyway, Vivien. Do you want me to put it on?" Allison asked.

"Do we have to?" Again Vivien appeared devastated.

"Unless you have some other suggestion as to how we can make it appear wet."

Vivien stood before the giant mirror beside Rick, leaning forward while she concentrated on the monumental decision, then began applying carefully controlled amounts of oil to selected strands of hair.

"Will you help me with my back?" Rick asked Allison, offhandedly passing the bottle of oil over his shoulder and catching her eyes in the mirror.

She was suddenly reluctant to lay a hand on him. She had little choice, however, and accepted the bottle from his slippery fingers. Thank God he didn't grin or tease, just handed the bottle over and waited. Allison poured oil into her palm, thinking: This is how it all started with Jason.

She went at it energetically to hide the fact that her hand shook when she touched Rick's bare skin for the first time. She was unaware of how she glowered or that behind closed lips she held the tip of her tongue tightly between her teeth. Sensations of touch came flooding back to her, filling her memory and her body at this first touch of a man's flesh since Jason's. How many times had she done this for him? How many times had he done this to her? How many times had their oiled skins delighted each other?

Don't think about Jason. Don't think about the fragrance of the oil. Don't think about all the times he was sleek and slippery and seductive.

But Rick's flesh beneath Allison's hand was warm and firm, and her palm slipped over it, conforming to its strong, sleek lines. The shoulder was tough, the shoulder blade hard, the neck unyielding with a tensile strength. Her fingertips inadvertently touched Rick's hair and learned its fine softness, so different from the hardness of his muscles. The contrast jolted her, and she raised her eyes to the mirror to find Rick studying her solemnly.

She was suddenly swept with the awkward feeling that he'd read her mind. Immediately she dropped her eyes to his back again. Taking more oil, she worked it down the warm center of his back to the waistband of his trunks. The memory of his light, undemanding kiss came back to her, and his words, "I just have to do this." With her hands on his skin he somehow became all mixed up in her mind with Jason. Love, hurt, sensuality, and bitterness welled up within Allison, leaving her confused. Then her fingertips slipped over Rick's ribs, and he flinched and tipped guardedly sideways.

Allison came back to the present, realizing it was Rick, not Jason. Their eyes met in the mirror.

"I'm ticklish," he informed her, and the spell was—thankfully—broken.

"I'll remember next time." She handed him the bottle, said, "Excuse me," and reached around him for a roll of paper towels on the vanity.

"Your hair, too," she instructed, brushing alarmingly close to his chest as she reached.

"What?"

Wiping her hands gave her an excuse not to look up at his reflection in the mirror. "Oil your hair, too. How're you doing, Vivien?"

"Can't say I like getting all greasy like this, but I hear oil makes the hair healthy, huh?"

"As soon as you two are done, come on out to the set. I'll get the lighting started."

Outside the wide wall of windows it was totally black. Inside, the only light came from the dressing room. Allison shook off thoughts of Rick Lang and set to work, adjusting the direction of the strobes, firing them time after time to see the effect they created on log, water, sand. Working with a light meter, she took readings from various points, adjusting the rheostats on individual strobes, which were all connected to a single triggering device that would fire them simultaneously with the shutter release when connected to the camera.

Rick and Vivien padded out, barefoot and shivering, to find Allison's shadowy form darting back and forth amid the equipment.

"Oh, good, you're ready. Listen, this sounds like a joke, but I have to crack a window a little bit to let the smoke out once I start the fire. But the room should warm up as soon as the fire gets going. I'm really sorry about the chill in here, but bear with me, okay? I didn't want to strike the match until you two were out here, because I don't want that fire going any longer than necessary.

"Okay, Rick, I want you on the log, Vivien laying on the sand below him, facing him and rather leaning up onto his outstretched leg, gazing up into his face. For now, take the general positions, but don't strain yourselves to hold them. Just relax and I'll light the fire and do a final metering on all the strobes once the flame is going."

A shivering Vivien moved toward the set, rubbing her goose-pimpled arms.

"Step lightly on that sand," Allison warned, "and move slowly across it so it doesn't get spread out any more than necessary." Vivien's teeth were chattering. "Rick, why don't you sit down on the log first?" Allison continued. "Maybe Vivien can lean against your legs for a minute and keep warm." There was no joking now in Allison's voice. As Vivien picked her way gingerly across the sand, Allison touched a match to the hidden chunk of Dura-Flame log that gave a clean, smokeless *pouff* before the small twigs caught. Immediately Allison was moving about, taking readings, firing the strobes time and time again, resetting the angle of the camera now that she had bodies to compose in the viewfinder. Crouching, she peered into the camera to assess the angle of the moon's reflection on the water, firing the strobes repeatedly, making minute adjustments.

The oil caught the gleam of the strobes and sent it shimmering to the eye of the camera, creating precisely the illusion of wetness Allison was aiming for. She decided it would not be necessary to further discomfort Rick and Vivien by sprinkling water on their already shivering skin. In the night light the oil was all that was necessary.

The key light had a blue filter to simulate moonlight. When Allison fired it, Rick's hair took on a life of its own, haloed to perfection in all its glorious disarray. Vivien's, too, became a moonlit nimbus about her head, the oiled ends perfect.

By using fill lights with orange filters, Allison had eliminated shadows that were too stark, tempering them with simulated firelight at each flash.

"Okay, all set," she declared, moving toward the set now, standing just beyond the sand, leaning over with hands on

thighs, giving orders. She positioned Rick with his far knee
raised slightly, the near leg stretched out with only its heel
resting on the sand. Touching his shoulders, she ordered,
"Turn . . . no, not so much . . . good. Now tip that head down,
and Vivien, I want you to look like you want to crawl right up
his body. Roll onto your far hip just a little . . . a little more, let
me see just a hint of tummy. Good, now brace on your left
hand any way you can to keep from falling over, and put your
right hand on his chest." There followed a single reflex drawing apart as Vivien's biceps inadvertently came up against
Rick's vitals, for she lay in the lee of his legs now. But the
two of them reverted to faultless professionalism in an instant,
settling into the pose again.

Allison produced a small jar of petroleum jelly, touched a
spot of it to the corner of Vivien's mouth, produced a comb
from her pocket, and tugged free a strand of Vivien's beautiful
hair to fasten to the corner of her lips. Perfect!

"There . . . don't move," Allison breathed, backing away.
Immediately she returned, touched the comb to a few way-
ward strands of hair at the back of Rick's neck, flicked it
through a lock above his ear to partially cover the top of it,
then stepped to the camera to evaluate the composition in the
viewfinder. Immediately she saw sand where it wasn't supposed to be, produced a small, soft barber's brush and
whisked it off the top of Vivien's leg. Another check in the
viewfinder, a flash of strobes, and she found the stunning fire
glow had created exactly the skin effect she wanted. But the
sand that she'd found distracting on Vivien seemed lacking on
Rick. Quickly she stepped around the tripod, picked up a
handful and threw it at his near shoulder.

This time the scene in the viewfinder was flawless.
Another quick check of all the strobes, firing them six times in
quick succession before connecting them to synchronize with
the camera.

Allison's voice became silk as she stepped behind the camera, crouching low, ready to shoot.

"All right, I want you to think about that skin you're
touching . . . sleek, desirable . . . wet those lips, come on."
Their tongues came out, leaving lips glossy in the firelight.
The strobes flashed as the shutter opened for the first time,

capturing the image on film. Allison's heart hammered with excitement. They were perfect together!

"Ease up a little higher, Vivien, and droop those eyelids just a li-i-i-i-tle more . . . more . . . no, too far, lift your chin now, think of how much you love him."

Flash!

"Great!" Exhilaration filled Allison as she moved deftly around the camera, giving sharp orders at times, soft compelling orders at others.

"Rick, I want a long, caressing thumb touching the hair that's caught in her mouth, but don't cover those beautiful lips of hers . . . let my camera see them . . . good with the thumb, now closer with your lips . . . think about tongues . . ."

Flash!

"Let's see the tip of your tongue, Vivien, and ease up with that hand on his chest. You're caressing it, not hanging suspended from it."

The perfection broke and both Rick and Vivien laughed, falling out of their poses momentarily.

Allison waited only briefly before saying, "Okay, back at it, lovers. Let's get messages going between those eyes, and Vivien, I want that tongue peeking out . . . open the teeth only slightly . . . good, good."

Flash!

"All right, Rick, spread those fingers and bury them in her hair . . . you love that magnificent hair, you're lost in it . . . not so deep, we're losing those beautiful fingers of yours, gently . . . gently."

Flash!

"You have wonderful hands, Rick. Let's use them some more, give me sensuality with your hands . . . wing it, fly with it, Vivien, respond to his every touch . . ."

Rick relaxed, curled his fingers, and lay the knuckles gently against the crest of Vivien's cheek. At his touch she turned her head slightly as if to take more, lips falling open, eyelids drooping with sensuality.

Flash!

"Now you, Vivien, what can you do with those delicate fingers . . . touch him where he wants to be touched, turn him on, tell him with your fingertips what's on your mind. . . ."

Vivien's hands slid down to Rick's bare thigh, and immediately his face reacted. His shoulders and arms spoke to the camera of wanting to express more than the photograph would allow.

They continued for a series of twenty-four shots, and during that time Allison all but forgot who Vivien Zuchinski and Rick Lang were. She moved with an unconscious purity of purpose and saw her subjects with uncanny acuity, missing not one hair that needed straightening or messing. Halfway through the first roll of film she repositioned Vivien, raising her farther up until her head rested against Rick's chest. Ordering Rick to place his hand almost on the side of Vivien's breast, hers on his hip, she received immediate, professional response, then hustled back to the camera.

Rick and Vivien were subjects, integral parts of the art she created, nothing less. Allison's vitality and enthusiasm brought out the best in them, and her businesslike attitude put both Rick and Vivien at ease in a situation that otherwise might have been embarrassing.

When it was time to change film, Allison straightened. "Okay, stretch for a minute, but watch that sand—don't get it anyplace I don't want it."

She fetched fresh film from the old refrigerator and in a matter of minutes had reloaded. A quick check of the fire, another stick on it, and it was back to work.

They resumed shooting, with Allison issuing rapid-fire orders that immediately brought changes of pose, expression, and body language. With the next change of film came a change of camera angle. This time Allison posed Rick and Vivien hip to hip, facing each other, creating sensuality not only with near kisses, but with hands on each other's ankles and calves. Another pose had Rick leaning across Vivien's lap, his lips just above the fullest part of her breast while her head hung back in abandon.

As the session moved on, the models' muscles grew stiff, and, quite naturally, their facial expression and body language did, too. Allison worked quickly, efficiently, noting the first times Rick and Vivien sighed wearily, understanding that cramps and outright pain were very real afflictions for models.

But when Vivien suddenly jumped and raised her backside

sharply off the sand, ruining a shot, Allison's head popped out from behind the camera.

"Tired, Vivien?"

"No, something bit me." She scratched the underside of a thigh, then settled back into the pose again.

But just as Allison pushed the shutter release again, Rick twitched, ruining a second shot.

"You two need a break?"

"No," they answered in unison.

"Let's keep going and get finished," Rick advised. "All right, Vivien?" He gave her a considerate glance.

"Sure, this sand is . . . ouch!" This time Vivien leapt to her feet.

Now Allison became concerned. What was troubling Vivien?

"You too?" Rick questioned, suddenly getting to his feet and straining around, twisting at the waist in an attempt to see the backs of his thighs. "I could swear something's been having me for dinner, but I didn't want to say anything."

"Honey, you and me both!" Vivien seconded, scratching her legs now, lifting one foot to rake her nails on the back of an ankle.

Allison stepped to the light switch. A moment later the room was flooded with light while she knelt at the edge of the fake beach, studying the sand. She could see nothing. She fetched a large white sheet of paper and laid it on the sand, stooping again to watch carefully. A moment later she saw a tiny black dot hit the paper and disappear so fast her eyes couldn't follow.

Horrified, she stood up, biting her lip. "I hope you two have a good sense of humor, because it looks like sand fleas."

"Sand fleas!" Vivien yelped. "Eating *me?*"

"I'm afraid so. They must have come to life when the heat from the fire thawed them out." Immediately Vivien began scratching harder. "I'm . . . I'm really sorry about this," Allison apologized, more than a little embarrassed. Lord, what next! she thought. How was she going to control the insects and finish the rest of the shots? There was no bug spray in the studio. Crestfallen, Allison added, "I don't have anything to get rid of the pesky things. I guess we'll have to stop shooting and go with what we have. Hey, I'm really sorry."

"How many shots do you have left on that roll?" Rick inquired.

Allison checked. "Thirteen."

Rick turned to Vivien. "Well, I can stand it for thirteen more if you can. What do you say, Vivien?"

Suddenly Vivien grinned, and with a rueful gesture said, "Ah, what the heck. Fleas have to eat, too."

To Allison's surprise, they resumed their places and suffered through the rest of the shots with the best of humor.

"Ah, that one likes his steak rare," Rick joked.

"I would too if I could take a bite out of the back of your leg," Vivien countered.

"Do you suppose we should demand to see a certificate from the local exterminator before setting foot in this place again?"

"To say nothing of the fire marshal."

"I think maybe an extra life-insurance policy is in order before taking a job at Photo Images. How about you, Vivien?"

"Why, whatever makes you ask? I have a bad case of pneumonia, slivers in my back from this log, flea bites, and my feet are scorching!"

"All right, you two ... that's it!" Allison announced, ending the session.

By this time it was almost ten o'clock, and they were all grateful to stretch and bend. As the overhead fluorescent lights came on, Allison rejoiced, "A hundred and fifty-four shots, and you two were fabulous!"

"I think she's soothing our egos in hopes we won't sue for damages," Rick kidded as he and Vivien hurried off the sand.

"Damn pesky things!" Vivien exclaimed, dancing, scratching again.

"I really am sorry, and I mean that. You were both ..." Allison searched for the proper word. "Intrepid!"

Vivien, looking puzzled, turned to Rick and asked, "Is she sayin' I didn't do so hot?"

They all laughed. "You were great, and I mean that sincerely," Allison clarified. She had gained a new, healthy respect for the girl who—true—might not be exceptionally bright. But she had a glow that looked wonderful through the viewfinder and, more important, a willingness and tenacity, even under less than ideal conditions. Allison had worked with lots of models who grew increasingly irritable as their muscles tightened and the hours passed. Who knew what would happen if they were asked to pose in a nest of sand fleas! But throughout it all Vivien had remained adamantly good humored and uncomplaining. "I know a lot of models who *would* sue!" Allison commented.

"Only thing that'll make me sue is if you don't let me get this oil off. I feel like a regular grease ball!" Vivien complained volubly, now that the session was over.

"Go ahead, you deserve it," Allison said. "Straight through the dressing room to the shower. There are clean washcloths and towels back there and plenty of soap."

Vivien disappeared through the dressing room, and Rick watched Allison remove the camera from the tripod, rewind the final roll of film, then begin disconnecting cables, pushing lights aside, seeing to the equipment.

"Can I help?"

"Absolutely not. You've done enough already." She placed a lens cap on the camera. Looking up, she found him carefully scrutinizing her. Immediately she dropped her eyes to her work. Now that the camera was no longer before her eye, it was too easy to view Rick Lang as a man instead of a model.

Just as Allison had gained a healthy respect for Vivien, Rick had gained the same for Allison. She was a true professional, with an attitude and ability that made working with her a rewarding experience.

"Hey, you're shivering," she said, and Rick snapped out of his reverie. She was wrapping an electrical cord around her arm with brisk, efficient movements.

"Am I?"

"Yeah. Why don't you see if you can find a robe in the dressing room until the shower's free?"

Instead he moved across the space between them, taking the cord from her arm while she protested, "Hey, I can—"

"So can I. Don't be so bullheaded and independent."

"But you must be tired." Somehow she acquiesced without realizing it.

"Yup, I am tired. How about you?"

"In a way, but whenever I finish a session that's gone particularly well, like this one has, I'm so high I can't come down for hours. I'll go home and feel like I'm falling off my feet, but when my head hits the pillow it'll take forever to fall asleep."

"You do love it, don't you?"

Suddenly their eyes met, and they forgot what they'd been doing. Allison's hands fell still.

"Yes, I do," she said, almost reverently. "There's no feeling like it in the world . . . not for me. Tonight was . . ." She glanced at the set, the shrouded equipment, the cable release in her hands. Finally her eyes came back to his. "It was unadulterated joy for me," she finished solemnly.

"You're damned good, Allison, do you know that?" He spoke quietly, admiring the strong sense of purpose she emanated. Her love of work seemed to radiate from her glittering, eager eyes.

The softly spoken compliment went straight to her heart. She smiled, and her eyes fluttered away. He had never called her Allison before. It warmed her almost as much as his opinion and the ungushing way he'd voiced it. In all the months she'd worked with Jason, he'd never once come right out and said as much. He'd glanced at the finished products with an eyebrow cocked. But if he admired them, it was always with a hint of egoism that left Allison feeling slightly empty.

She studied Rick now, comparing him to Jason, finding him totally opposite—warm, sensitive, considerate.

"Thank you," she replied quietly, giving him the rare gift that to some comes so hard—accepting a compliment at face value, thereby lending it a value of its own. "So are you," she added softly.

Their eyes lingered on each other, and at last, unsmiling, he replied, "Thank you."

Just then Vivien came bouncing out of the dressing room, swaddled in her fake fur and looking considerably revived. "Shower's all yours, honey!" she announced, perkily strutting over to Rick. "But before I lose you, I want one real honest-to-goodness kiss out of that hundred-dollar-an-hour mouth of yours. I deserve it after all the suffering I've been through resisting it while it was half an inch away from me for four hours."

Boldly, Vivien slipped her fingers around Rick's neck and pulled his head down for an unabashedly lingering kiss.

He was taken off guard, and though Allison had a brief impression of his surprise, he acquiesced gracefully while Vivien audaciously demanded a full-fledged French kiss, holding his head until she'd received what she was after.

Looking on, Allison felt a little red around the collar, and again was bothered by a faint twinge of jealousy at the impudent woman who had no compunctions whatsoever about being so outlandishly forward.

Backing away, finally, Vivien gave Rick a sultry once-over. "You are *reeeeeally* something. You ever want to get together where there's no camera lookin' on, you just give li'l Vivien a call, okay?"

Rick laughed into her upraised face, his hands resting on her waist. "Vivien, I just might take you up on that. Maybe we can compare fleabites," he managed, ending the touchy moment gracefully, with exactly the proper touch of humor.

Vivien socked him playfully on the shoulder. "Hey, I like that. I like a man with a nice bod and a good sense of humor. You're a real fox, fella." She flitted out of his arms with no more compunction than she'd flitted in. "Well . . . gotta run."

Allison, discomfited by watching Vivien's dauntless, straightforward display, turned her back on Rick as she gave the woman a one-armed hug and walked her toward the door.

"Vivien, you're marvelous to work with, and I'd like to do it again." She meant it. In spite of the past sixty seconds, which had been embarrassing, Allison meant it.

CHAPTER

Six

WHEN RICK EMERGED from the dressing room, Vivien was gone. Allison had wet down the coals and was scooping the sodden lumps into a metal garbage can. She heard the door open and watched him cross the long, open length of the room. She attended to her chore, conscious of his eyes on her while he stood nearby with his hands in his pockets, conscious, too, of the flustering memory of Vivien's mouth demanding his to open. Throughout the shooting Allison had managed to keep her thoughts separate from her personal feelings, but with Rick standing beside her in street clothes, and after Vivien forcing that impromptu, final pose on him, Allison was suddenly at a loss, searching frantically for something to say. Her hand trembled as she dumped the last dustpan of coals and clapped the cover over the garbage can. As the tiny clang drifted away into silence, she looked up at last.

"Vivien's gone," she said inanely. Rick's hair was damp, clinging to his temples, coiling about his ears. The overhead lights reflected off his fresh-scrubbed forehead and nose, highlighting his skin.

"I know. And I'm sorry about what happened. I didn't mean to embarrass you."

Her cheeks flushed. "Oh, that's okay, it's none of my business." She frantically tried to appear busy, to disguise her discomposure. She wiped her hands on her thighs and looked around. Everything was done. "I'll clean up the rest tomorrow." She checked her watch. "Goodness, it's late! I'll get your check so you can go."

She escaped to her desk, picked up the check she'd made out while he was in the shower, and handed it to him, extending, too, her other hand in a gesture of good will.

Without taking his eyes from hers, he accepted the check with one hand, her cold palm with the other. But instead of shaking it, he held her hand firmly, refusing to relinquish it when she tugged away. She flashed him what she hoped was a dismissing smile and reiterated, "I really meant it when I said you were wonderful to work with. As soon as the transparencies come in, I'll give you a call so you can see them."

"Fine," he replied, obviously not giving a damn about transparencies as he still refused to release her hand.

His touch sent paths of fire up her arm, and she frantically raked her mind for something more to say. "M . . . maybe I'll get some extra color stats of the cover when it has the title and copy on, so you can see what the finished product looks like, too."

"Fine," he agreed disinterestedly, brushing a thumb against the back of her hand. His eyes remained fixed on hers. She knew instinctively it would not bother him in the least if he never saw the finished photos. It was becoming increasingly difficult to dream up things to say. Finally she stammered, "I . . . I'll call when the stats come in."

"And how long will that be?"

She forcibly pulled her palm from his. "Oh, maybe three months."

"Too long." He folded the check in half and creased it with his thumbnail without removing his eyes from her face.

"I'm afraid that's entirely up to New York. After the transparencies leave here, my part is done."

"That's not what I meant." With unnerving slowness he pulled a billfold from his hip pocket, inserted the payment, then tucked the billfold away again. "Thank you, though it doesn't seem right taking money for a job I've enjoyed as much as tonight's."

Common sense told her this was no time to make jokes about Vivien or fleas or pneumonia. "You earned it, Rick," she said simply, gesturing nervously, then twisting her fingers together.

He shrugged, dropped his eyes to her desk, and still didn't move. He stood there, his weight on one foot, considering the clutter of photos, bills, lenses, filters. The old building emitted faraway nighttime sounds—the soft clang of a radiator pipe, the hum of a clock, a janitor's pail way off in the distance.

Finally Rick looked up. "I didn't have any supper, did you?" he asked.

"No." Her eyes met his, then flitted away. "But I'm all out of tuna and eggs."

A long silence followed while Allison commanded her eyes to stay off Rick, who seemed to be considering deeply as he stood before her.

"I don't want any of your damn tuna and eggs. I want to go somewhere and talk to you and get to know you."

Her startled eyes flew up. "I told you—"

"Hey, wait." He pressed open palms against the air. "A sandwich and a cup of coffee and some talk, okay? No commitments, I promise. You said yourself you're so keyed up you won't sleep if you do go home, so let me do the buying and you can bubble off your enthusiasm on me, okay?"

"Thank you, Rick, but the answer is no."

A slow grin climbed one cheek. "Would you reconsider if I threatened to sue for the fleabites?"

A quavering smile tipped her lips up, but a warning fluttered through her heart. Afraid of eventualities, afraid of letting anyone close again, afraid of being hurt as before, she drew in a sharp breath, stifling the sweet enjoyment she felt being with him.

"I think I'll have to call your bluff, and just hope you won't."

"Then just come because I ask, and because I can't sleep if I go straight home, either."

Uncertainly she stood before him, pressing her thighs hard against the edge of the desk, as if its solidity might anchor her to earth when she was so tempted to drift above it at his invitation.

His eyes fell to her tight-clenched hands, then rose to her

face again. He moved around the side of the desk, captured one of her wrists, turned and towed her toward the door, affecting an injured tone. "Hey, you owe me. After I helped you lug six tons of bricks up here for that set, not to mention one illegal log, which put me in jeopardy with the law, and after almost getting pneumonia from the cold in here, as well as a bad case of fleabites. You can't put a man through all that, then refuse to have a cup of coffee with him."

"Rick, listen—"

"Listen, my ass, I'm done listening. You're coming with me." He moved decisively, retrieving her jacket from the hat tree and turning again to face her with the garment held wide, waiting.

With a sigh of resignation, she turned to slip her arms in. As she buttoned up, he hit the light switch, plunging the room into darkness, except for the vague light from the hallway, which fell through the old-fashioned glass window of the door.

He stood close behind her—too close for comfort—so, rather than turn again to face him, she reached for the doorknob. His hand moved quickly to cover hers and prevent her from turning it. Immediately she yanked free of his touch, burying her hand in a pocket. But his palms fell lightly on her shoulders, turning her to face him once more.

His fingers circled her neck, under the jacket hood, pressing on her collarbone, the thumbs pushing the wool fabric lightly against her throat. A spill of brightness from the hallway washed one side of his face, leaving the other in shadow, and Allison experienced an unruly wish to photograph him this way, for his profile was pure, sharp, perfect, the sober expression in his eyes accentuated by the fact that one eye was thrown totally into shadow.

She was conscious of the scent of soap lingering on his skin and of the warmth from his hands seeping through her coat to circle her neck.

"For some reason you don't trust me," he said softly. "I can tell it. Yet I think you enjoy being with me, and I know I enjoy being with you. I won't push—that's a promise—but neither will I give up on a relationship with definite possibilities."

"I . . . I'm not looking for a relationship. I already told you that."

"Hey." He shook her gently, cajolingly. "People don't look for relationships. They just happen, Allison, like heaven-sent gifts, don't you know that? Afterward, the two people can work on them. But meeting is the accident."

"No, I don't know any such thing." She herself had spent years, it seemed, always *looking* for a relationship, only to be wounded when she found it, and it ended just like the one before, against her wishes.

His gaze was intense as he studied her face, half-lit from the hall. She found it impossible to pull her eyes away. "What are you afraid of?" he asked, his voice gone slightly gruff.

"I'm not afraid. I just view things . . . people . . . more cynically than you do. Besides, heaven has never sent me a gift that turned out to be worth two cents, so you'll pardon me if I don't take a very optimistic view of heaven."

"Maybe I can change your mind," he ventured.

"I doubt it."

"Do you mind if I try?"

"That depends."

"On what?"

"On what you want from me."

"Why do you think I want something?"

"Everybody wants something." She swallowed. "Only they usually want it for nothing."

"Who was the last person who wanted something from you for nothing?"

"Nobody!" she retorted too sharply. Then quieter, "Nobody."

His eyes assessed her, carefully tracking the defensive expressions across her face with its downturned mouth. "You're lying," he said softly. "Somebody hurt you and left you distrusting the rest of mankind, and left me with the job of proving to you that not everyone in this world is a rat."

"You'll have a tough time doing that during the course of a quick cup of coffee."

"I believe I will," he agreed amiably, leaning around Allison to open the door. "It may take more than just tonight, but you'll find that I'm a very patient fellow." Waiting for the elevator, he asked, "Would you like to ride in my car?"

Again she watched the changing numbers above the door, knowing he was studying her. "No, I'll take the van and meet you."

"Where?"

She eyed him sideways. "Wherever we're going for coffee."

"Where would you like to go?"

She shrugged, caring only that it wasn't too dimly lit or intimate.

"Do you like big, fat, juicy hamburgers dripping with cheese and crisscrossed with bacon srips and sour pickles and fries?" He sounded like an ad for a fast-food hamburger place.

She couldn't help grinning. "I think I'm being prompted. Do *you* like big, fat, juicy hamburgers dripping with cheese and crisscrossed with bacon and dill pickles and fries?"

His eyes lit up merrily. "How'd you guess?"

"Go ahead, name it."

"The Embers—my favorite."

"And what if I said no, I don't like big, fat, juicy hamburgers, that I want a . . . a bowl of chili and a corn dog?" She pursed up her mouth in mock petulance.

"I'd say, tough! I said first, and I said hamburger. So whaddya make of it, huh, lady?" The elevator arrived and he punched her arm playfully, dancing through the open doors on the balls of his feet.

She fell back convincingly against the elevator wall. "I give!" Her hands reached for the sky. "I love hamburgers, I swear I love 'em!"

He shadowboxed his way to her, stopping close, playfully raising her chin with one gloved fist. "Yeah?" He grinned into her eyes. "Well, youse is one smart broad if youse already learned not to cross me when I want hamburgers."

By now she was laughing out loud, her shoulders shaking as she leaned against the elevator wall. He was incorrigible. If he couldn't get her one way, he got her another. It was becoming harder and harder to resist him. She found herself smiling all the way to the restaurant. Entering and scanning the booths, she found she'd arrived first.

When Rick came in minutes later, he sauntered up to her

booth, leaning negligently against the backrest across from her, looked around shiftily, and asked, "Hey, ah . . . lady, ah, you're a pretty good-looker. You got anybody in particular hidin' in the men's room or somethin'?"

"That'd be tellin'," she replied in her best gun moll's accent. "With me you take your chances, bud."

Smiling, he slipped into the booth, across from her. They talked for two hours. During that time he learned she was from a small farming town in South Dakota, where her family still lived, that she'd come to Minneapolis to attend school at Communication Arts, and had stayed because the city offered opportunities for an aspiring young photographer that couldn't be found in Watertown, South Dakota. Her ambitions were to own a Hasselblad camera and to sell a fashion layout to *Gentlemen's Review* magazine.

"Why *Gentlemen's Review*?" he asked.

"Why not? It's the epitome of prestige to be published in *GR*, so why not set my goal as high as possible?"

"But why a man's magazine?"

Without thinking, she answered, "Because I'm good with men."

"Are you now?" he purred. His eyelids drooped to half-mast, and he picked up his cup, smirking as his lips touched its rim.

She colored and stammered, "I . . . I mean with a camera, of course."

"Of course," he agreed, clearing his throat, again hiding behind his cup.

"Quit smirking and get your mind out of the gutter," she scolded, sitting up straighter. "I can see you leering behind that cup. It's the truth, I *am* good with men. I have a good eye for men's clothing and for backgrounds that flatter masculine features and for bringing out ruggedness, suaveness—whatever. I have to work much harder to achieve those things with women." She toyed with her cup. "I suppose that sounds egotistical, but it's imperative in my line of work to recognize where my strengths lie and pursue that direction."

"You're forgetting, I'm an artist, too. The same is true with my work."

She leaned forward eagerly, caught up in the subject she

loved best. "It's disconcerting sometimes, isn't it, having your work so . . . so *visual!*" She gestured at the table top. "I mean, whatever we produce is right there for the world to judge us by."

They talked on about the common interest they shared. Her cheeks grew pink, her eyes excited, body language intent, and he absorbed it all with growing enjoyment.

"Do you know you become vibrant when you talk about your work?" he asked.

"I do?"

"Your cheeks get pink, and your eyes dance around, and you get all animated and turned-on looking."

She leaned back, retreating into the booth. "I guess I do. It exhilarates me."

"Like nothing else can?" The implication was clear in his voice. The memory of his kiss came back vividly, and she dropped her eyes from his carefully expressionless face. She thought it best to lighten the atmosphere. "There's one other thing that does as much for me."

"And what's that?"

"The mere thought of working with a Hasselblad." She shivered, pressing folded hands between her knees as if even the word itself were sensual.

He lifted his cup, took a sip, mentioned casually, "I own a Hasselblad."

Her eyes grew wide. Her back came away from the booth. "You do?" She gulped.

"Is that covetousness I see gleaming in your eye?"

"Is it ever!" She rolled her eyes toward the ceiling. "Oh, those enormous two-and-a-quarter-inch negatives!" she swooned. "Oh, those lenses! Oh, the dream of owning the camera the astronauts took to the moon!" She sank back as if overcome, then pressed a hand to her heart. "I'd sell my soul for one of those things."

"Sold!" he put in quickly.

"Figuratively speaking, of course. You actually own one? You're not kidding?"

"I worked one whole summer on a road-construction crew and saved every cent I possibly could, and by fall I had enough to pay for the camera."

Her face became clownishly sad. "Somehow I don't think a road-construction crew would hire me on to drive a cat."

"Don't bother applying. You can try my camera any time."

Again she sat up, surprised, a new look of fire in her eyes. "You mean that? You'd actually let me?"

He gestured nonchalantly. "I mostly use the thing when I make trips up north to Emily, where my folks live. They have a cabin on Roosevelt Lake, too, and I do most of my photography around the lake and in the woods up there. I stay in the city because the modeling pays for the wildlife art, which doesn't pay for itself yet. But, like I said, the camera's yours whenever you'd like to try it."

"You mean it, don't you?" she said, flabbergasted.

"Of course I mean it." He leaned back, crossed his arms over his chest, and hooked a boot on the seat beside her. "But I didn't offer to give it to you, just to let you try it."

She smiled, overjoyed. Her nostrils flared slightly as her eyes drifted shut for a moment. She opened them to meet his, a hint of naughtiness about her lips while she made circles around the lip of her coffee cup with an index finger.

"I might abscond with it."

They leaned back lazily, playing teasing games with half-shut eyes.

"Then I'll have to make sure I stay very close to it . . . and to you, won't I?"

Allison was suddenly very aware of his foot propped on the seat, almost touching her hip. And of how incredibly handsome he was, lazy that way, almost as if he were half asleep. And of the dancing eyes that told her he was far from asleep. And of the fact that, when the waitress asked, he had remembered she liked sugar in her coffee. And of the fact that she had laughed with him more in the last couple days than she'd laughed with Jason during all the months they'd lived together. And of the dawning realization that she and Rick Lang had an incredibly lot in common.

It was well past midnight when Rick paid their bill. Allison stood behind him, watching him shrug as he dug in his tight jeans pocket for change. His hair was flattened where he'd leaned his head against the booth. The collar of his old jacket

was turned up, crinkled leather touching the back of his head.
Without warning she itched to touch it, too.

Allison shook off the thought, buttoning her jacket up high
and twisting her scarf twice about her neck.

"All set?" Rick asked, turning.

She nodded and moved toward the door. He reached
around her, almost brushing her arm as he pushed the heavy
plate glass open for her to pass through. Outside, crossing the
parking lot, she was too keenly aware of the fact that he
walked very near, just behind her shoulder, pulling leather
gloves on while she buried her chin in her scarf, hands in
pockets.

She stopped in the middle of the snow-packed parking lot
and turned toward him. "Well, my car's over here."

He gestured in the opposite direction with a sideward bob
of the head. "Mine's over there."

An uncertain pause followed, then, "Well, thanks for the
hamburger. It was good, after all."

"Anytime."

It was quiet, late. All that could be heard were the exhaust
fans on top of the restaurant humming into the neon-lit night.
Allison looked up at Rick. His breath came in intermittent
white clouds on the chill air. He stood before her, not a hint of
smile on his face, pushing his gloves on tighter, tighter, while
perusing her in the night light that turned her face pink.

"Well . . . good night," she said, hunching her shoulders
against the cold.

"G'night." Still he didn't move away, but stood there
studying her until she became giddily aware of how fast he
was breathing. There was no hiding it, for each breath was
broadcast by its spreading vapor cloud. Reactions spread
through her in a warm drift of awareness. Her heart seemed to
be beating everywhere at once. Then common sense took
over, and she turned quickly toward the van, only to find him
still following behind her shoulder. He slipped a gloved hand
on her elbow, squeezing tight as they picked their precarious
way along the icy footing. Though his touch was far from
intimate through layers and layers of winter clothing, it sent
shivers up her spine.

At the van she reached to open the door, but he beat her to

it, reaching easily around her, then standing back, waiting,
with his glove on the handle.

She turned to give him a last brief glance over her
shoulder.

"Well, good night and thanks again."

"Yeah," he tried, but it came out cracky, so he cleared his
voice and tried again. "Yeah." Clearer this time, but low, soft,
disconcerting.

Just as she was about to raise a foot and climb into the van,
his hand captured her elbow once more, tugging her around.

"Allison?"

Her startled eyes met his as he circled both of her elbows
with gloved hands. They stood in the narrow space between
the open door and the vehicle as Rick's hands compelled her
closer. The freezing night air seemed suddenly hot against her
skin. He pulled her closer by degrees, his head tipping to one
side, blotting out the lights behind him as his lips neared.

"Don't," she demanded at the last moment, turning aside
and raising her palms to press him away, though her heartbeats
were driving hard against the hollow of her throat.

The pressure on her elbows increased. "What are you
afraid of?"

"You promised you wouldn't push."

"Do you call one kiss pushing?" His breath was so close it
brushed her cheek, sending a cloud of warm air over her skin.

"I . . . yes," she managed, refusing to look up at him.

"Why don't you try it and see if I push any farther?" The
hands commanded her again until their bodies were so close
that their jackets touched. Again Allison's eyes met Rick's,
which were shadows only, though his hair, forehead, and nose
were rimmed with a pinkish glow from the lights of the parking lot. "One kiss, all right? I've been thinking about it ever
since the shooting session, watching you all fired up behind
your camera. We were sharing something together then, I
thought. Something that caught both of us up and exhilarated
us, excited us. Don't tell me you didn't feel it. I thought
maybe that common ground was reason enough to end the
night with a simple kiss."

"I told you, I'm not looking for a relationship."

"Neither am I. I'm looking for a kiss—nothing more.

Because I like you, and I've enjoyed being with you and working with you, and kissing is a helluva nifty way of telling a person things like that."

There was little she could do—and in another moment, little she wanted to do—to combat him. He lowered his lips the remaining fraction of an inch, touching her mouth lightly with warm, warm lips, made all the more warm by the contrast of his cold, cold nose against the side of her face while he held her by her upper arms. Her eyes slid closed, and her guard grew shaky while the gentle pressure of his mouth lingered, growing more welcome as the seconds passed. Without removing his lips from hers, he pulled her lightly against him, guiding her resisting arms around his sides, then clamping them securely with his elbows. When he felt her stiff resistance melt, he slowly, cautiously moved his hands to her back, wrapping her up, tightening inexorably while he started things with the sensuous movement of his head—nudging, now harder, now softer, back and forth, while she felt the warm proddings of his tongue. The warning voices, reminding Allison of Jason and the hurtful past, echoed away into silence. Only the thrumming of her own heart filled her ears as her hands rested on the back of his jacket, holding him lightly. Her lips parted, and his tongue came seeking. She met the warm, wet tip with her own and felt the heart-tripping thrill of wet flesh meeting wet flesh in a first seeking dance.

Behind her she felt his hands moving brusquely and wondered what he was doing as the motion jerked his mouth sideways on hers momentarily. The next moment she knew he'd removed a glove, for she felt his bare hand seek her warm neck, under the cascade of hair, nestling in under the twist of scarves, massaging the back of her neck and head, commanding it to tip as he willed it, holding her captive though she no longer sought escape.

Her heart hammered everywhere, everywhere as she drifted beneath his warm, wet tongue while it slid along the soft, velvet skin of her inner lips, drew circular patterns around her own before he softened the pressure of his entire mouth, nibbling at the rim of her lips, making the complete circle before widening again, the kiss now grown wholly demanding.

Their jackets were waist length. He held her around her hips with a strong arm, and she felt his body spring to life with hardness as he pressed the zipper of his blue jeans firmly against her stomach, and before she knew what she was doing, she was moving in afterbeats, making circles with her hips that chased those he made with his.

As if realizing he'd taken the kiss farther than he'd intended, Rick closed his fingers around a fistful of Allison's hair, tugging gently, gently as he dropped his head back and swallowed convulsively.

Their breaths came strident and rushed, falling in blending clouds of white as she leaned her forehead against his chin.

Rick's eyes slid closed while he bid his body to slow down.

"Wow," he got out, the word a guttural half gulp.

She chuckled, a high, tight sound of unexpectedness before two strained, little words squeezed from her throat. "Yeah . . . wow."

Her hips rested lightly against him. She waited for her body to cool down and be sensible, but against her she could feel the difficulty he, too, was having talking sense into his body.

"One kiss," he managed in a gruff voice. "That's what I promised, and I keep my promises."

Seeking to control emotions that seemed to be running away like horses with the bits between their teeth, she teased, "Would you believe I did that so convincingly just so I could get my hands on your Hasselblad?"

He laughed, raised his head, and answered, "No."

She disengaged herself from his arms, and Rick complied without further resistance.

"Well, I did," she teased, jamming her hands deep into her pockets and backing a step away. "I told you I'd sell my soul for one of them."

He smiled, his eyes on her upturned face as he drew his glove back on. "You keep that up and you might end up doing exactly that."

For a moment she had the urge to step into his embrace and try that one more time. But if she did, it might be more than his Hasselblad she wanted to get her hands on.

While she pondered, he indicated the van with an upward

nudge of chin, ordering, "Get the hell in, do you hear?"

Obediently she turned and climbed aboard.

"I'll call you," he said tersely, as if trusting himself to say no more at the moment.

Then the door slammed shut, and he stepped back, feet spread wide, moving not a muscle as he watched the van back up and drive away. In the rear-view mirror she saw him as she rounded the corner. He hadn't moved from the spot.

CHAPTER

Seven

THE PHONE RANG exactly six times the following day. Each time Allison expected to hear Rick's voice but was disappointed. Neither did he call all weekend. During the following week Allison grew more and more impatient for the sound of his voice on the other end of the line. But he didn't call.

The transparencies for the book cover came back from processing and she tried calling him but got no answer. Vivien came to see them one afternoon, gushing in her own inimitable way that the shots were *"re-e-eally* nice." Then she asked for Rick Lang's phone number.

After giving it to her, Allison wondered if Vivien called men and asked them for dates. Probably. Remembering the freewheeling kiss Vivien had laid on Rick, and the kiss she herself had shared with him, Allison couldn't say she blamed Vivien one bit.

Friday night and Saturday seemed to crawl by, and still he didn't call. Sunday morning Allison was up early and in the shower when the phone rang.

She burst from the spray stark naked and dripping, flying around the corner of the hall into the living room, skittering on the slick floor in her bare feet.

"Hello!" she exclaimed breathlessly.

"Hi." One deep-voiced syllable turned her heart into a jackhammer. "Did I wake you?"

"No. I was in the shower."

"Oh! Why don't I call you back in a few minutes?" he returned apologetically.

"No!" she almost yelped, then consciously calmed her voice. "No, it's all right." There was a puddle on the floorboards at her feet. Her breasts were covered with goose pimples, which also blossomed up and down her belly like the curried nap of a carpet. Wet hair was dripping into her eyes and streaming into her mouth. She pushed a straggly strand away from one eye as she lied, "I wasn't really in the shower. I was all done."

"Are you sure?"

"Sure I'm sure. You should see me—all bright eyed and bushy tailed." She glanced at her naked, shivering body and controlled an urge to laugh out loud.

"It's been over a week," he reminded her unnecessarily.

"Oh, has it?" Allison was shivering so badly she covered her breasts with one arm and hand, trying to keep warm.

"Very funny—*has it,*" he repeated dryly, "as if I haven't been counting off every damned day."

"Then why didn't you call?"

"I was up north taking winter shots while there's still some snow left, getting last dibbs in on my Hasselblad before somebody else gets her hands on it. I just got back."

"Just? You mean just now?" She checked the kitchen clock. It wasn't quite nine yet. Emily was a three-hour ride from here.

"Yes. I wanted to leave yesterday, but my mother insisted on cooking my favorites for supper last night—a convenient ruse to keep me another day, so I just pulled in."

"And?" she prompted innocently.

"And can I see you?" Beneath the hand that cupped her naked, wet breast a rush of sensuality tingled the nerve endings of her flesh. She closed her eyes and pretended it was Rick's hand.

"I have the transparencies here to sho—"

"Screw the transparencies! When can I come?"

"I have to do my—"

"When?" he demanded, then decided for her. "Never mind answering that. I'll be there in fifteen minutes."

"Fif—hey, wait!"

But it was too late. The line had gone dead. She flew back to the bathroom, stubbed her toe on the corner of the vanity, cursed volubly, and flung a towel over her hair. Frantically rubbing, she wondered which to do, hair or makeup? There wasn't time for both. Oh God, he was going to walk in here and she would look like she had just had a Baptist baptism! She flung the towel aside just as the phone rang again.

"Yes, what is it?" she demanded impatiently.

It was him again. "Have you had breakfast?"

"No."

"Well, don't!" The line went dead in her hand again, and she stared at it a moment, smiled then flew back to the bathroom. When the doorbell rang less than twelve minutes later, she was sure it was him.

"Oh, *no-o-o!*" she wailed at her reflection in the mirror, her face sans lip gloss, blush, mascara, or even dry hair. Only one eye had pale mauve shadow above it. Like a half made-up clown she opened the door to find Rick standing on her landing hugging a grocery sack in both arms.

"Hi," he said quietly, a slow smile spreading over his face.

"Hi." A beguiling fluttering began just beneath her left breast as they stood in the cold morning air, measuring each other while the draft swirled into the apartment.

"Can I buy you breakfast?"

She couldn't seem to take in enough of him at once as her eyes wandered over his face, freshly shaved and shining, while he let his gaze roam over her half made-up face.

She nodded mutely, forgetting to step back and let him in. Still holding the brown paper bag, he reached one gloved hand out and captured her neck, pulling her half outside while he leaned down to kiss her, the zigzagged edge of the crackly bag cutting into her chin. His lips were warm and impatient as his tongue slipped out to touch her surprised lips. Then he straightened, released her, and smiled sheepishly.

"Oops, I'm sorry. Here I am letting all the warm air out while your hair turns to icicles." He moved inside and glanced down her legs. She had whipped on a pair of faded jeans and a plaid cotton shirt but hadn't had a chance to put her shoes on.

Self-consciously she tried to cover the bare toes of her left foot with those of her right.

His eyes moved to her wet, straight hair, and from her left eye to her right. Next he caught sight of the puddle of water on the living room floor, by the telephone.

One eyebrow lifted skeptically. "All bright eyed and bushy tailed, huh?"

"Well, sort of." She flipped her hands out only to realize she still held the brush from her eyeshadow.

The room was flooded with bright morning sunlight, cascading across the yellows and greens, dappling the gleaming hardwood floors where the plants cast leaf shadows. Rick's glance moved around, lingering longest on the puddle before returning to her face.

"Should I have waited until later to call?" he asked.

Her heart threatened to explode in her chest as she admitted, "No, I'd have gone mad waiting another hour."

The brown paper bag slid down his leg and landed on the floor with a thump. Rick's eyes devoured Allison's face while he reached out and brought her up hard against his chest, lifting her completely off the floor while he kissed her thoroughly. His tongue sought her mouth, and hers eagerly waited to meet it, moving in wild, eager greeting as if these last eight days had been agony for each of them. His teeth trapped her bottom lip, but she neither knew nor cared when she tasted the faint saltiness of blood. He fell back against the door, taking her with him, letting her body slide back down until her toes touched the floor. And in passing she realized he was hard, aroused, and marveled that she could make him so even while her hair was wet, her makeup still in its plastic cases. His hands disappeared from her back, and she began to pull away, only to be stopped.

"No, wait, don't go," he said, close to her ear, "I just want to get my gloves off so I can touch you." Behind her she heard the gloves hit the floor, then his hands pulled her close again, and she clambered right up on top of his boots with her bare feet, leaning willingly, feeling the welcome length of his body against hers. His palms slid to her buttocks to draw her harder, harder against him. She circled his neck with both arms, straining toward his lips, tongue, chest, and hips while desire flared in her. His cold palm slid beneath her shirt. When it brushed the skin just above her waistband, she flinched and shivered.

He pulled back, looking down into her eyes. "What's the matter?" His voice was deep and ragged.

"Your hands are like ice."

"Do you mind?" he asked with gruff tenderness, one cold hand already warming on her soft, willing skin.

She searched his eyes, her own gone somber, her lips fallen open, slightly swollen and glistening with moisture from his tongue.

"No." It was difficult to speak, her heartbeats were so erratic. She had missed him incredibly, found herself undeniably eager for more of his lips and hands on her. Those hands now spread wide over her ribs, which rose and fell in sharp gusts while the driving thrum of her heart seemed to lift her from his chest and drop her back against it heavily.

And then his face was lost in closeness as he kissed the side of her nose, her colored eyelid, her uncolored eyelid, her temple, and after that impossibly long wait—her mouth. He took it with tender, demanding ease, playing with her tongue, nuzzling even as he tasted, tempted, tried. His hand rode up her ribs until one thumb rested in the hollow beneath her left breast, where it gently stroked. Surprised when he found no bra, he lifted his head, smiled, and murmured, "Mmmm?"

Her arms still looped about his neck, she replied, "Well, you only gave me ten minutes." Then she reached to catch his upper lip between her teeth and tugged him back where he belonged. His kiss grew ardent and searching while his hand at last filled itself with her naked breast, its nipple puckered tight with desire.

Into his open mouth she whispered throatily, "Rick, what did you do to me in these last eight days?"

"Exactly what you did to me, I hope—drove me crazy."

"But I don't want you to think I just . . . just fall against every man who walks through that door with a grocery bag in his arms."

"How many have walked through it that way?"

"One."

"Hell, one's not too many. Your reputation's safe." But he backed away, grinned into her eyes, and added, "For the time being."

And she knew her days—maybe hours—of celibacy were numbered. She was falling for him more swiftly than she'd fallen for Jason, and more surely, for while she had learned to love Jason, she'd never really liked him. But she had liked Rick Lang even before falling in love with him.

Restraining his desires, he smiled down into her eyes. "Hey, lady, did you know you have purple stuff above one eye and not the other?"

"It's mauve, not purple, and it's eyeshadow, not stuff, and I was hoping you'd be so overcome by me you wouldn't notice."

"And what about that mop of hair? You intend to leave it that way or do you want to dry it while I cook us a *real* omelette?"

"Inferring that the one I fixed us was not a real omelette?" she returned in an injured tone.

"Exactly. Mine will have ham and green pepper and onion and tomato in it, and it'll be topped with cheddar cheese."

"I can't stand green peckers," she stated tartly.

"Green *whats!*"

Immediately she colored. "Oh, Rick, I'm sorry. I . . . I . . ." She turned her back, horrified to have let the familiarity pop out unrestrained. It was an old joke between her and Jason.

"Go dry your hair. I'll holler if I can't find everything I need."

In the bathroom she glowered at her reflection in the mirror.

"Stupid twit!" she scolded her reflection.

To turn the odds in her favor, she made her bed, put on a bra, and took extra pains with her hair, styling it with the curling iron until it fluffed about her collar in wispy tendrils that bounced on her shoulders.

The sound of the stereo came to her. Smiling, Allison glanced toward the doorway, then began humming as she turned toward the mirror again.

Her makeup was subtle and iridescent, applied with a light but knowledgeable hand, for she'd made up many models in her day. As an afterthought she placed light touches of perfume behind each ear, on each wrist, then on impulse snaked a hand beneath her shirt and touched the valley between her breasts before bending to touch each ankle, too.

Straightening up, she turned to find Rick leaning indolently against the bathroom doorframe, grinning as he watched her. He let his head tip speculatively to one side while teasing, "So that's where you women put perfume, huh? I counted—there were seven places." He pulled his shoulder from the door and turned away. "Your breakfast is ready, Cleopatra."

Allison could have died on the spot.

She might have felt self-conscious meeting his eyes when she took her place at the table, but he put her at ease with his teasing. Swinging around, bearing two plates with enormous, fluffy Spanish omelettes, he unceremoniously plopped them on the table, advising, "Eat up, skinny, you look like you can use it."

"Oh, do I now? I didn't hear any complaints a few minutes ago when you came in."

"You may not have heard them, but you may recall I had a hand on your ribs, and you're about as fat as a sparrow's kneecap."

She smiled. "You sound just like my mother. Every time I go home it's, 'Allison, eat up. Allison, you just don't look healthy. Allison, have a second helping.' It drives me crazy. Why is it that mothers and grandmothers think a woman isn't healthy unless she's at least twenty pounds overweight?"

"Probably because they love you and mean the best for you. If they didn't they wouldn't bother to notice. I get the same thing from my dad when I go home, only about being single. 'Rick, you know that Benson girl moved back home and got a job in Doc Wassall's office. Didn't you used to date her when you were in high school?'" Rich grinned sardonically. "That Benson girl probably weighs a hundred and eighty now and wears support hose and orthopedic shoes. Besides, I don't think Dad would believe it if I told him I can actually cook an omelette. He's never cooked one in his life. Mom's always there to do it for him . . . *and* his laundry, his housecleaning, and reminding him when it's time to pay the electric bill. That's their way of life. If they try to force it on me, I understand it's because they want me to be happy. So I just grin and tell Dad maybe I'll give old Ellen Marie Benson a call before I leave."

"And do you?" Allison peered up at him, suddenly curious about the women he'd dated.

"Occasionally . . . oh, not Ellen Marie, but a couple of others my folks don't know about."

"Anyone in particular?" she inquired, watching his expression carefully.

It remained noncommittal. "Nope," he answered shortly and took another mouthful of eggs.

"Speaking of calling girls, you're going to get a call from one."

"Who?" He looked up over the rim of his coffee cup.

"Vivien. She asked me for your phone number."

He chuckled. "Oh, *Vivien.*" He drew out the name and followed it with a salacious grin.

Allison leaned an elbow on the table, smirking. "Do girls actually do that, I mean, call guys and . . . and boldly . . ." She stammered to a halt.

"And boldly what?"

"And boldly . . ." Allison gestured vacantly. "I don't know. What do girls boldly ask when they call guys? I've always wondered."

"Meaning you've never done it yourself?"

"Hardly. It's not my style."

His eyes danced over her pink cheeks, and he leaned his elbows on either side of his plate, a coffee cup in one hand. "I'm glad."

"You are?" Her eyes were wide and innocent now, meeting his over the cup.

"Yes, I am. Because I'm one of those guys who still wants to do the pursuing as if women's lib never came along and gave women the idea of doing it themselves."

"Judging from the kiss Vivien treated you to, I'd say you're in for some mighty diligent pursuing from that quarter."

He lifted his chin and laughed lightly, leaning back in his chair. "Oh, that Vivien, she's incorrigible." Yet he didn't fawn over the fact. Instead he made light of it, suffering no bloated

ego, which pleased Allison. All of a sudden the corners of his
mouth drifted down into a placid expression as he studied her.
His eyes moved over her hair, ears, mouth, cheeks, and came
at last to her wide brown eyes. "Your hair is very pretty," he
said quietly.

A stab of warmth flooded her cheeks, and her eyelids fluttered down momentarily. He crossed his hands over his stomach and continued studying her pink, flustered cheeks and the
self-conscious way her eyes cast about for something to settle
on. They came to rest on his knuckles. "And so is the rest of
you," he added.

A warning signal went off in her head. Was this his line? It
was different from Jason's, which never included compliments
quite this simple, but rather effusive hosannas on how she
"turned him on." Remembering them now, Allison told herself
to slow down, beware, things were going too fast.

But she experienced a heady feeling of pleasure in being
the object of his admiring scrutiny as he leaned back in his
chair with casual ease, his voice coming softly again. "You
have butter on your top lip." Her hand reacted self-
consciously, grabbing the paper napkin from her lap and lifting it toward her mouth. Halfway there, his came out to stop
it. He leaned across the corner of the table while her eyes flew
up in alarm.

"Would you mind very much if I kissed it off?"

His eyes remained steady on Allison while her throat muscles shifted as she swallowed. Her brown gaze held a startled
expression. Her lips fell open in surprise while she sat as still
as a bird in deep camouflage, staring back at Rick.

"Would you?" he repeated so softly it was nearly a mur-
mur.

Her wariness fled, chased away by his soft, persuasive
question. The negative movement of her head was almost
imperceptible. Eyes locked with hers, Rick removed the napkin from her numb fingers, crossed her palm with his, in the
fashion of an Indian handshake, only gently, as if he held a
crushable flower. As he leaned by degrees across the corner of
the table, the pressure of his fingers increased, and he brought
the back of her hand firmly against his chest. She felt the
heavy thud of his heart as his eyes slid closed, and his lips

touched her buttery upper lip, lightly sucking, licking, moving across its width from corner to corner before he did the same to her bottom lip. Allison felt as if melting butter were rippling down the center of her stomach, ending in a fluttering delight between her legs.

He backed away a fraction of an inch so that only the tip of his tongue circled her mouth, which eased more fully open until her own tongue did his bidding, just its tip caressing the tip of his while beneath her hand the hammering of his heart grew almost violent.

He took his long, sweet time at it, tempting her with unhurried leisure, backing away an inch that made her eyes drift open to find his had done the same. He rested his forehead against hers, nudging softly, then backing away again so they could gaze into each other's eyes. His calculated slowness caused an insistent throbbing within the deep reaches of Allison's body. His eyes stayed on hers while he gradually brought her hand between their two mouths, opening his lips in slow motion, taking her thumb gently between his teeth, making miniature, caressing motions of gnawing, while his chin moved left and right, left and right, and his eyes burned into hers. He moved on to her index finger, biting its knuckle before straightening it with a flick of his thumb. She watched, fascinated and sensualized as it disappeared into the warm, wet confines of his mouth.

The gushing responses in her body were like nothing Jason had ever elicited from her, short of climaxes, which he had carefully regulated and often delighted in denying until she begged. Now, as Allison's finger was caressed by Rick's tongue, her body felt ready to explode. Gradually he slipped the finger from his mouth, then turned her hand over and gently bit its outer edge, his eyelashes drifting down to create a fan of shadow on his cheek while his labored breathing told her what this foreplay was doing to him, too.

He fell utterly still for a long, long moment, resting the backs of her fingertips against his lips, eyes closed as if in deep meditation. When he lifted his lids to study her, he spoke hoarsely, with her knuckles still touching his lips, muffling the words. "I didn't think I'd make it through these last eight days. You don't know how many times I went to the phone and stood there staring at it, wanting to call. But I remembered what you said about not wanting a relationship, and I was sure you'd say you didn't want to see me again."

His words sent a wild reverberation of joy through Allison.

"Are you for real?" she managed at last, letting her eyes travel over what she could see of his face behind their hands. "I mean, look at yourself. Look at your face and your . . . your form, and tell me why you should be worried about whether or not one girl wanted to see you again."

"Is that all you see when you look at me? A face and a . . . a form?" he queried.

"No." She swallowed, retrieved her hand, and picked up her coffee cup to have a reason for withdrawing from him. "But why me?"

"If you don't know, if you can't feel it, I can't explain. I thought what was just happening here a moment ago was explanation enough—that, along with some enjoyable hours we've spent together."

"Rick . . . I . . ." She quickly rose to her feet, taking their plates to the sink so she could turn her back on him. She heard his chair scrape back and knew he was standing directly behind her.

"You don't trust me, do you? You think I'm handing you a practiced line of bull."

"Something like that," she admitted. In her entire life no man had ever so effectively seduced her as he'd just done across the corner of a breakfast table, touching no more than her hand. He had to know his appeal—all he had to do was look in the mirror to see he was no Hunchback of Notre Dame. And he had a wooing, winning way that could easily turn a woman's head.

"You want me to act like an admiring monk, is that it?"

She rested the palms of her hands against the edge of the sink, staring straight ahead, not knowing what she wanted, afraid of things her body was compelling her to do.

"I don't know," she choked, near tears, so confused by her impulses to trust him, those impulses juxtaposed against past experiences that had always turned out disastrously when she too eagerly placed her trust in another person.

A heavy hand fell on the side of her neck, kneading lightly. "I'm sorry, Allison. I promised, didn't I?" Even the touch he bestowed so casually made her heart race. Silence ticked by for several seconds, then Rick said quietly, "But after what happened at the door when I came in, I thought—"

"My mistake, letting it happen, okay?" she quickly interjected, afraid to turn around and face him. "I *was* glad to see you, and you just caught me a little off guard, that's all."

"You feel you have to erect a guard against me, is that want you're saying?"

"I . . . yes," she admitted.

"Why?"

She refused to answer. His warm hand lowered to the center of her back and began stroking up and down. "I'm not him, Allison," he said in the gentlest tone imaginable.

The hair at the back of her neck bristled. Her shoulder blades tensed. "Who?" she snapped.

"I don't know. You tell me." His hands circled her upper arms and forced her to turn around.

"I don't know what you're talking about," she lied, staring at the floor.

"Neither do I. What was his name?"

Her lips compressed into a thin line. He watched her face for every nuance of truth while dropping his hands from her. He stepped back, crossing his arms, then his calves, leaning his hips against the edge of the kitchen stove behind him.

"Do you want to tell me about him?"

"Him! Him!" she spouted belligerently. "You don't know what you're talking about."

"The man who made you so defensive and jumpy and wary of me, that's who I'm talking about. What was his name?"

"There is no such man!"

"Bull!" he returned tightly.

Her eyes met his determinedly. *"There is no man in my life,"* she stated unequivocally.

"No, but there was, wasn't there?"

"It's none of your business."

"Like hell it isn't. If he's what's keeping you from me, it's my business."

"I'm what's keeping me from you! I'm cautious, all right? Is there any crime in that?" she shouted in a sudden display of hot temper.

Rick scowled, studying her with a hard expression about his mouth. "Boy, he soured you on men but good, didn't he? Made up your mind you'll never trust one of us again, is that it?"

"Trust is another thing that never profited me one damn bit in the end," she stated bitterly.

"And so you're done with it, no matter what your gut feeling tells you?"

She suddenly bristled, gesturing angrily with her hands in the air, storming away. "I don't have to stand here for this . . . this third degree! This is my house, and just because I let you come in and cook breakfast for me doesn't give you the right to assess my motives. I thought of you, too, during the last week." She swung around to face him. "Is that what you want to hear? All right, I did! And I knew before the second day was gone that I wanted to see you again. But don't probe into my past if you want to share any of my future, be it a day, a week, or a month, because I won't stand for it!" She was back before him, practically nose to nose, bristling with defensiveness, striking out at him because she was afraid of the overwhelming urges she felt to like him, to trust him, maybe even to fall in love with him.

He stared at her angrily for a moment, and she saw his eyebrows finally relax from their tightly knit curl, his mouth take on a less pinched expression as he made a conscious effort to quell the urge to argue.

"You're right. It's none of my business," he agreed, backing off, shelving the issue for the time being. "Peace offering, all right?"

He pulled away from the stove and dipped a hand into the brown paper bag that was still on top of the counter. The next moment he lifted a camera in a black leather case. He held it aloft in invitation, its wide, woven strap swinging in the sudden silence between them.

Her animosity fell away with amusing speed, to be replaced by excited surprise. "The . . . the Hasselblad?" she asked breathlessly.

"The Hasselblad."

She reached for it, but he pulled it back just beyond her fingertips. "Wait a minute. Aren't you the woman who said you'd sell your soul for a chance to use it?"

Here it comes, Allison thought, the proposition.

But he only grinned one-sidedly, leaning over from the hip to place his mouth within easy kissing distance. "I won't ask for your soul, just one little kiss to bring peace back between us."

She gave him the price he asked, a quick, fleeting smack, but he still refused to give her the camera. "Friends?" he inquired, grinning into her face.

"Friends," she agreed, and snatched the camera from his hand.

Behind her she heard a throaty chuckle as she whirled toward the sunny living room to sit cross-legged on the shag rug. He ambled over and joined her, sitting almost knee to knee with her. He produced a roll of film and smiled, watching as she loaded the camera, exhilarated now, all attention given over to the coveted piece of equipment.

"Here's the film advance." He pointed to a silver crank. "And here's the shutter release." Her face was a picture of radiance as she looked down into the magnified square to study the light falling through the long, narrow windows. She spun around on her derrière, then rolled to her knees, walking on them across the hardwood floor while scanning the room through the viewfinder, looking for a setting that caught her eye.

The camera fell against her tummy. "Over there!" she ordered, pointing.

"Where? What?" He played dumb.

She wagged a finger at the floor to an oblique square of morning sun. "Over there, quick! Just sit the way you are, only do it over there, and face the kitchen so your face is sidelit."

He complied, smiling, sitting on the floor in the warm wash of sunlight, drawing his knees up, crossing his arms loosely over them. Allison lay on the floor before him, flat on her belly with her elbows braced on the floor, directing the tilt of his head in this direction and that. The natural window light illuminated the side of his face, put highlights on one side of his thick hair, lit the top of an ear, and left a solid line of shadow beyond the ridge of his forehead, nose, lips, and chin. She took two shots, then popped up, dragged a schefflera plant across two feet of floor, and ordered, "Now, with the shadows of the leaves on your face . . . but no smiles, okay? Turn a little more toward the window and give me that handsome seriousness and let the mouth speak of thoughtfulness." The shutter clicked two more times, and her exuberant face appeared above the Hasselblad, a puckish smile on her mouth. "You're stunning, Rick Lang, do you know that?"

The camera freed her and let her natural impulses bubble out. With it around her neck, she felt totally uninhibited, released to speak what she felt. Only without the camera was she thwarted by the idea of getting involved with personal emotions.

"How about the basket chair?" he suggested next.

"Ahhh, perfect. Get in."

He pushed himself up off the floor and plopped onto the cushioned seat while she directed the chair opening toward the light source with an acute instinct for shadow effect and camera angle. She peered down into the viewfinder, checked the composition, lowered the camera, and looked around. She bounced across the room to drag a potted palm over, knelt down, and framed the shot with a spiky frond, making sounds of delight deep in her throat when she found the composition to her liking.

When she'd satisfied her artist's eye at that setting, she scanned the room, pointed to the French doors leading to the porch, and asked if he'd mind going out there where it was cold.

"What'll you give me?" he teased. "I work by the hour, you know."

She plopped a passing kiss on his mouth, hardly conscious of what she was doing, so caught up was she with the joy of photographing with the prized piece of equipment.

She framed him through the panes of the French door, adjusting the angle of the camera time and again in an attempt to create a well-composed photo without hiding his features behind the crossbars of the window frames.

"Hey, hurry up!" he complained, his voice coming muffled through the closed door. "My nipples are puckering up."

She laughed, snapped two quick ones, told him he could come back in, then admitted, "Mine, too," adding impudently, "they always do when I get turned on, and your camera really turns me on."

"Only my camera, huh?"

"I didn't say that, did I?"

"Well, let me know when you want to indulge in a little puckering. Maybe we can work together on it, without the help of porch or camera."

When she'd exhausted all the best possibilities the apartment offered for settings, she was still rarin' to go. "How about doing some outside shots?" he suggested. "There's a Winterfest going on at Lake Calhoun this afternoon, and I was planning to ask if you wanted to go over and fool around anyway."

"Fool around?" she repeated archly.

"With the camera, of course," he returned. "There's all kinds of stuff going on over there. What do you say we bundle up warm and check it out?"

He was irresistible, and she *did* want a chance to get to know him better. And she *did* want to work with the camera a little longer. And she *did* so enjoy being with him.

"Why not?" Allison replied, jubilant at the thought of spending a whole afternoon with him without having to talk her emotions into a state of equilibrium because privacy offered him a chance to kiss or touch her.

CHAPTER

Eight

SHE DONNED HER disreputable bobcap and scarf, and thigh-high boots lined with fur and a hip-length jacket belted at the waist. From the trunk of his car Rick dug out an enormous parka. He let the hood flop down his back, but the wolf-fur lining, framing his chin and jaw, set off his masculinity to great advantage. Even before they got in the car, Allison snapped a shot of him, having adjusted the f-stop to compensate for the blinding brightness of the snow outside.

It was a dazzling day, as bright as their spirits as they drove the short distance to Lake Calhoun. The Winterfest was already in full swing when they arrived, the activities taking place right on the frozen lake, which looked like a confetti blanket, its white surface dotted with multicolored wool caps and bright ski jackets. Wandering from event to event, Allison snapped random shots—two runny-nosed eight-year-olds angling for sunfish through a hole in the ice; the laughing face of a man who'd fallen onto his back like an overturned turtle during a game of broomball; a young married couple sculpturing an ice mermaid by wetting down snow and compacting it with mittens covered with plastic bags; a string of red-nosed youngsters at the finish line of an ice-skating race, their lips set in grim determination; a boy and girl kissing, unaware that Allison was snapping them because their eyes were closed; an ice boat with its orange-and-yellow sail furled by the breeze, its rider hanging over the edge at a precarious angle; Rick lying flat on his back, making an angel in the snow; the grand, old Calhoun Beach Hotel Building—which was a hotel no longer—standing across the road from the lake in majestic watchfulness while funseekers romped and played and totally disregarded the fact that the temperature was only twelve degrees above zero.

Rick brought hot chocolate from a stand that had also been on the ice. They sat on a snowbank, squinting through the steam rising from their cups, watching a judge measuring a ridiculously short pickerel with a tape measure while a small boy looked on hopefully. Allison felt Rick's eyes on her instead of on the fishing contest, and turned to meet his gaze.

"You're the neatest girl I ever met, you know that?"

Flustered, she looked away and hid behind a sip of cocoa.

"Don't hide, it's nothing to be ashamed of. You're game for anything—bundling up and clumping out here in this cold, taking pictures of stuff that to some would seem so ridiculously bourgeois they'd scoff at the suggestion of even coming here, much less recording the homey events on film."

"It's been fun," she replied honestly, then braved a look into his eyes, adding, "and I've had a wonderful day."

"Me too."

For a moment she thought he was going to kiss her. With her heart already fluttering greedily in her throat, she suddenly didn't trust her own common sense, so she put on a pained expression and informed him, "But my derrière is so damn cold there's no feeling left in it."

Abruptly he laughed. "How 'bout your nipples?" he teased secretively. "Anything happening to them?"

"None of your business, you dirty old lech."

He licked his lips, gave her a suggestive head-to-toe scan, and grinned. "Like hell it isn't."

She hauled herself to her feet and reached out a mittened hand to give him a tug. When he was on his feet, Rick bracketed her temples with gloved hands. Her heart went a-thudding in anticipation, but he only pushed her drooping bobcap up out of her eyes and teased, "Nice cap, Scott." Then he kissed the end of her icy nose, bundled her up against his side, and hauled her with him, pressed hip to hip while they walked to the car.

Pulling up in her driveway sometime later, she moved a hand toward the door handle. His glove crossed over her arm. "Wait," he commanded.

She listened to his footsteps crunch around the rear of the car, and a moment later her door was opened. She had to giggle at his gallantry when she was dressed in her urchin's outfit, totally unflattering and unfeminine.

He followed close behind her as they climbed the stairs in slow motion. At the landing, when she aimed the key for the lock, he took it from her hand and opened the door for her, then dropped the key into her mitten. He looked into her eyes and once more pressed his palms to the sides of her head and pushed the bobcap back where it was supposed to be. But he left his hands on her cheeks this time and said into her eyes, "I want to come in."

Her lips opened to say no, it was dangerous, their feelings were rioting too fast, they needed time to assess what was happening. But before she could speak he slowly lowered his mouth to hers and her heart fluttered to life and sent quivers to her breasts. As the kiss lingered, he released her face, taking her in his arms to pull her against his bulky jacket.

She pressed her mittened hands against his back, drawing close and moving her mouth languorously beneath his, opening her lips to invite his seeking tongue. It was hot, wet, tantalizing, seductive, and it stroked away the memory of Jason. His hands roved down the back of her jacket, then underneath it. Spreading his hands wide, he gathered her close against him, spanning her icy buttocks with warm, wide palms.

His lips left her mouth. He bent his face into the warm hair at her neck, burrowing deep to find skin inside the folds of scarf. "Allison," he murmured gruffly, "let me come in. I want to warm you up."

You already have, she thought, delighting in the feel of his palms against that intimate part of her body. He drew back, deliberately lifting first the hem of his parka, then her jacket, recapturing her buttocks to pull her against the long ridge of flesh inside his jeans, to let it speak for him as he pressed its heat against her stomach. He undulated his hips, grinding against her while on her backside his hands asserted themselves and controlled her.

He kissed her with a wild thrusting of tongues, rhythmically matching the strokes of tongue and hip before jerking his mouth aside and begging in a raspy voice, "Let me come in, Allison."

She knew what he was asking and was abashed to find she wanted to do his bidding, to invite him not only into her house, but into her body as well. But she pressed her hands against his chest, begging, "Please, Rick, please stop. It's too soon, too sudden."

"What are you afraid of?" he asked.

She swallowed, reached for his hands, and brought them between them, folding his palms between her own while looking deeply into his eyes.

"Me," she admitted.

He drew in a deep, shuddering breath, put a few more inches between their bodies, and asked, "So you'd turn a man away hungry?"

"Is it supper you want?" She knew it wasn't, not any more than it was what she wanted.

"I guess I'll have to settle for it, if that's the only way I can stay."

It seemed a reprieve. She wanted him with her yet, and supper was a plausible excuse to keep him a while longer.

"I have a pizza in the freezer. How does that sound?"

"Like a hell of a poor second, but I accept."

They moved inside, but when the door was closed and the lights snapped on, there was no denying that the sexual tension remained, as vibrant as before. She hung up their jackets and turned from the pursuit in his eyes, telling her heart to calm down. But it felt deliciously good, this business of being pursued. It was beginning to dawn on her why Jason Ederlie had eaten it up so.

Allison was halfway across the living room when she was swung around abruptly by an elbow. "What's the hurry?" he teased, swinging her against him, holding her loosely around the waist, leaning back so their hips touched.

"Are you about to extract payment for the use of your Hasselblad?" she asked, resting her hands on his inner elbows, striving to keep the mood light.

"Not at all. You can keep it awhile . . . unconditionally."

"God, how can you let a camera like that lay around in its case all the time, then lend it out to some girl who . . . who . . ."

"Puckers up at the sight of it?" he finished. "Well, if you can't make the girl pucker up at the sight of you, you do the next best thing, right?" His hand wandered to her breast to brush it testingly with the backs of his fingers.

"Rick, stop it. You came in here for pizza."

"Did I?" But the humor fell from his face as he reached to take the back of her head with both hands and pull her hard against his mouth. She forgot caution and flung her arms around his neck, a hand twining into the thick hair above his collar as he made sounds of frustrated passion deep in his throat. Stars and suns and moons seemed to flash across the darkness behind Allison's closed eyelids while she let her tongue and hips and hands respond to the plea in his eyes. He tore his lips from hers. They buried their faces in each other's necks, clinging, learning the scent of each other, the texture of skin, of hair, of clothing as his hands played over her hips, and hers over the taut muscles of his shoulders and back.

"Allison, this afternoon seemed like a year," he ground out, his voice gone low. His hand cupped the back of her head, losing itself in her hair. "I swear, woman, I don't know what's happening to me."

In an effort to control the body that threatened to burst its skin, she laughed—a throaty, deep sound that came out very shaky. "I think it's called hunger pains. Let me put the pizza in."

Reluctantly he released her, his eyes darkly following the sway of her narrow hips while she crossed to the kitchen, turned on the oven, and opened the freezer door. He turned away, unable to watch her and retain control. He ambled to the component set and switched on the radio, wandered aimlessly about the living room to find himself once again drawn near the kitchen, his eyes riveted to her backside while she leaned over to slip the pizza into the oven. The back of her jeans was faded to a paler blue in twin patches just below the pockets. His eyes roved over them and he inhaled a deep, shaky breath before letting his eyelids slide closed. He ran a palm down the zipper of his jeans and pressed it hard against his tumescence.

When he opened his eyes again, she was facing him. Her cheeks lit up to a fiery red, and she bit her bottom lip, then swallowed hard.

"It's no secret," he admitted gruffly, "so why pretend? I've spent the entire afternoon thinking about one handful of warm breast in the early morning when I came here today, and somehow it just hasn't been enough."

She backed up against the oven door, reaching behind her to grab the handle in both hands to steady herself. Her face was a mask of uncertainty, and her breath fell hard and heavy from her chest.

"Rick, I'm no virgin," she admitted, abashed, yet facing him squarely.

"Neither am I. So what?"

"I'm a woman, and we're the ones who have been taught since puberty that it's up to us to control situations like this. But I feel like I'm losing control, and I don't want you to think I'm easy." She suddenly covered her face with both hands and spun around, afraid to face the hour of reckoning she knew was at hand.

How long did she think she could play with fire? How long did she think she could string along a healthy, virile, and willing twenty-five-year-old man? And what was she going to do now that she'd backed herself into this corner?

"Rick, you were right, I'm scared."

"Of what?" he asked, close behind her. "Of me?" His hand touched her hair, smoothing it gently, without the slightest hint of force. "Allison, look at me . . . please. Don't hide from it. It's nothing to be scared of."

She turned at the gentle pressure of his fingers on her neck and lifted quavering eyes to his. A moment later her voice came, shaky, unsure, doubtful. "I don't think I like being a woman in this . . . this liberated age," she admitted. "I'm not very good at being a . . . a casual lay."

His hands bracketed her jaw, lifting her face so he could look deeply into her eyes. A thumb stroked the hollow of her cheek. "Thank God," he said softly.

She lunged against him, turning her cheek upon his chest, squeezing her eyes shut, wrapping her arms tightly about his sides. "Oh, Rick, what happened to the days when a man and woman went to the altar as virgins and learned about each other in their wedding bed and stayed in it for seventy-five years, forsaking all others? That's what I'm afraid of . . . It's not there anymore!"

She could hear the steady thrum of his heart beneath her ear, then the deep rumble of his voice as he spoke reassuringly. "Allison, I don't care if there's been someone else. It doesn't change how I feel about you. What you are now you wouldn't be if you hadn't lived your life as you have so far. Does that make any sense?"

"Nothing makes any sense when I'm near you. I try to think clearly, but everything goes blurry. The only time things aren't blurry is when I'm behind the camera. Then things are clear, uncomplicated, I can understand them. If I could . . . could turn a focus ring on my life and bring it into focus as easily as I can a picture, I'd feel I had control of my life."

"And if you let your defenses down with me, your life goes out of control?"

"Yes!" She pulled back, looking up at him with haunted eyes. "Don't you see? It's like turning it all over to you. That's what scares me."

"I don't want to control your life, Allison. I want to make love to you." Gently he drew her near, raising her chin while he spoke.

She studied him, wanting to believe but afraid to. "They're both the same thing," she said shakily.

"Not with the right person."

He kissed her left eyelid closed, then her right.

"Don't," she breathed.

As if she hadn't spoken, he wrapped his arms around her, pinning her arms to her sides in the strong circle of his own. He leaned to kiss her neck. Her eyelids remained closed as she dropped her head to the side.

"Don't," she whispered raggedly.

But his lips moved to hers while he held her with one arm, peering past her cheek as he turned off the oven. Continuing to control her movements with his own, he opened the oven door while pulling her two steps away to make room for its downward swing.

"Don't."

Keeping his arm around her, he leaned to pick up a pot-holder from the top of the stove, then bent her over half backwards, half sideways, while he got the pizza out of the oven and set it on a burner.

The heat on the backs of her legs was nothing compared to that springing through her body as she repeated weakly, "Don't."

He manipulated her at will, dipping to reach the oven door and close it again before marching her slowly backwards in his arms across the kitchen, kissing her all the way. He stopped to turn off the dining room light, but didn't stop kissing, only opened his eyes and peered across her nose to find the light switch and snap it down while she mumbled with her lips pressed against his, "Don't."

He danced her backwards with slow, deliberate pushes of his thighs against hers, kissing her now open mouth as they progressed across the dining area toward the living room. He released her arms, found them with his hands, and forced them up over his shoulders, still walking her inexorably backwards while her body tingled and strained against him with each step.

At the stereo he dipped again, punched a button, then let his eyelids drift closed, kissing her while his tongue delved deep into her mouth, all the while idly playing the radio dial across the scanner until he'd found something soft and vocal with a guitar background. Her arms were now looped around his neck without resistance, and her words were nearly unrecognizable, spoken as they were with her tongue pressed flat against his: "Don't . . . waste . . . so . . . much . . . time."

He smiled, devouring her mouth while his hands slid down to her buttocks, pressing their shifting muscles as he hauled her step by agonizingly slow step to the light switch by the entry door. After he'd fumbled for it behind her back, his hand returned to her buttocks. He held her firmly against him in the dark until neither of them seemed able to strain close enough against the other. His thighs pushed against hers again, and she took a faltering step back to feel something solid against her shoulder blades. Wedged between his warm flesh and the wall, her breath came in onslaughts as he pressed his hips against hers, moving in sensual circles until she responded, beginning to move, too. Her shirt went sliding out of her jeans as he pulled it up with both hands, easing away from her with all but his mouth, which continued plundering in welcome attack. Behind his neck she unbuttoned her cuffs. He sensed what she was doing, stopped kissing her, and leaned his forearms on the wall beside her head.

"Unbutton the rest of it for me," he begged, his voice gravelly with emotion while his breath whisked her lips. With scarcely a pause, her trembling fingers moved to the top button. He leaned his head low in the dark, feeling with his mouth to see if she was doing as he asked. When the first button was free, his lips pressed warmly against the skin inside, above the bra. She hesitated, lost in delight as the touch of his tongue fell on her flesh. Then, keeping his palms pressed flat on the wall, he bent his head even lower, nudging her fingers to the next button, which opened at his wordless command. This time when he pressed his lips inside he met the small embroidered flower at the center of her bra. He breathed outward gently, warming her skin beneath the garment, sending shivers of desire to the peaks of her breasts. When at last her blouse hung completely open, he ordered in a husky whisper, "Now mine," hovering so close his breath left warm, damp dew on her nose.

She reached out in the dark, exploring the front-button band of his shirt running down its length. When her hand reached the waistband of his jeans he sucked in a hard, quick breath and jerked slightly. With both hands she explored his hips, just above the tight cinch of waistband. He was hard, honed, not a ripple of flesh that shouldn't be there. When her hands reached the hollow of his spine, she slowly tugged his shirttails out.

"Allison." His voice was thick and throaty. "How I've wished for this."

"And how I wanted to wish, but I was afraid."

"Are you always this slow?" came his gruff question at her cheek, and in the dark she smiled.

"Mmm-hmm, I like it slow."

"Me too, but I can't wait any long . . ." The last word was swallowed up by her mouth as his came against it while he speedily loosened his remaining buttons.

He laid his warm hand inside the open neck of her shirt, caressing her throat before pushing the garment back from her shoulders to fall to the floor behind her. His arms slid around her ribs, fingers testing their way to the clasp of her bra. It came away in his hands, leaving her half naked, eager for the caress of his palm upon her bare flesh. He stepped back, taking the bra down her arms, and in the dark she heard a rustle as he tucked it into his hind pocket. She waited, breath caught in her throat, for the return of his touch, expecting a warm cupping of her breast.

But he, too, seemed to be hovering in wait.

She reached out a tentative hand, seeking texture, seeking warmth, remembering the look of him standing in the studio, straight, erect, with his shirt off, while she assessed his almost square chest muscles studded with lightly strewn hair as pale in color as a glass of champagne, the light refracting off them as if caught in champagne bubbles.

Her hands now found what they sought, sensitive fingertips fanning across the hard muscles, the soft hair, the firm skin that shuddered beneath her touch, surprising her.

"Richard Lang," she murmured, almost as if to remind herself she was here, that it was he whose skin had just reacted so sensuously to her touch.

An almost pained sound came raspily from his throat while he scooped her against him, coaxing her bare breasts to his half-exposed chest. His lips and tongue swooped down again, working their magic as he pulled her away from the wall and took her with him, this time stepping backwards himself, feeling her legs brush his as she followed his lead.

In front of the stereo he stopped, studying her face by the dim light radiating from the face of the dial. Scant though it was, Allison could make out the outline of his features, the points of light caught in his eyes as he wrestled his shirt off, then draped it across the top of the closed turntable. He stood away from Allison, reaching first to touch her eyebrows while her lids lowered and a shudder possessed her body. His fingertips trailed over her cheeks, touched her lips, then after what seemed an eternity, found her waiting breasts.

She opened her eyes languorously. His were cast down, watching his hands. She, too, followed his glance to witness long fingers gently adoring, caressing, exploring, while beside them a voice sang, "It was easy to love her, easier than whiling away a summer's day . . ."

He touched her with tentative reserve, almost a reverence, until she could stand it no longer and covered the backs of his hands with her own, pulling his palms full and hard against her, twisting repeatedly at the waist to abrade his palms with the side to side brushing of her nipples, all hard and eager and tightened into little knots of desire.

"Allison . . ." he uttered, and dropped to one knee, reaching his mouth up to cover the hardened peak with his lips and suckle it with his tongue. "You're beautiful."

She felt beautiful as his words washed over her and a strong forearm pulled her hips against the fullest part of his chest. Her head fell back weakly, a soft sound of abandon issuing from her throat while she undulated slowly against him, brushing, brushing, with light strokes that moved her in sensual rhythm. She ran languid fingers through his hair, lost in sensation, while he moved his mouth to her other breast and took its nipple gently between his teeth, tugging lightly before circling it with his tongue, sending shivers of desire coursing through her body.

The song on the radio changed, and as if to verify the softly uttered confidences of minutes ago, a feminine voice crooned about wanting a man with a slow hand.

And a slow hand it was, slow and sensual and arousing Allison's passions until her breathing grew labored and her limbs felt as if she were moving against swift water.

Rick was on his feet again, moving against her in the age-old language of rhythm and thrust, compelling her hips to seek a mate. He backed away, guiding Allison to the soft cushions of the wicker sofa, leading her by a wrist, then urging her down with the gentle pressure of his hands on her shoulders until she lay on her back while he knelt on the floor beside her.

A strong hand found the hollow beneath her jaw, while his

other one slipped behind her head, controlling the kiss that moved from mouth to nose to eyes, questing, testing. When Rick's mouth found hers again, his tongue slipped within, riding against hers in rhythm to the music, the song's sensual words underlining their feelings about this act they were sharing.

While his left hand remained buried in her hair, his right traveled down the center of her bare stomach, following the zipper of her jeans until he cupped the warmth between her legs, pressing, pressing, unable to press hard enough to satisfy either of them, exploring through tight, restrictive denim until she raised one knee and her hips jutted up, bringing her body hard and thrusting against his touch.

Lowering his mouth to her breast, he continued his exploration, pressing the heel of his hand against the mound of flesh hidden yet from him, delighting in her response as small sounds of passion came from her throat, and she strained upward with arousal and the need for more. He kissed the hollow between her ribs, burying his face in the wider hollow just above her waistband, feeling the driving beats of her breath as her stomach lifted his face time and again.

He raised his head. With one tug, the snap of her jeans gave, and she fell utterly still, not breathing, not moving, but waiting . . . waiting. The rasp of the zipper seemed to match the sound of Rick's strident breathing.

When his palm slipped inside, against her stomach, pent-up breath fell from Allison in a wild rush, and she flung one arm above her head while wholly giving over the control of her body to him. His hand slid lower, fingers delving inside brief, silken bikinis until they brushed flattened hair and moved beyond, contouring her flesh, seeking, finding, sliding within the warm wet confines of her femininity. Her ribs arched high off the cushions as he began a slow, rhythmic stroking to which her body answered.

She lowered the arm from above her head, seeking to know him in the dark, then rolled slightly toward him and found his hot, hard body, while he knelt with knees spread wide, ready. He made a guttural sound deep in his throat, and she caressed him more boldly, learning the shape of him through his jeans. He leaned to nuzzle her neck, and as his nipple touched hers she could feel the torturous hammering of his heart against her own.

The moments that followed were a rapturous swirl of sensation as they pleasured each other with touches. There no longer seemed a need for lips to join. Only their cheeks rested lightly against each other while they savored this bodily prelude and honed their senses to a fine edge.

He was so different from Jason, unrushed and sensitive to her every need. "You like that?" he whispered against her breast, laughing deep in his throat when she answered, "Yes, do it again." He washed the entire orb of her breast with his tongue again, wetting all of its surface until shivers radiated across the aroused skin.

He slid his lips to the corner of her mouth. "Lift up," he whispered, hands at her hips. And in the next moment, both denim and satin were down around her hips, then gone, whispered away from her ankles. His hands deserted her body, and she listened to the rustle, snap, and zip as he freed himself in like manner, found her hand, and once again led it to him.

He leaned over, burying his face in the warm hollow of her waistline as a shudder overcame him and he held her wrist, guiding her to stroke his velvet sleekness. Then they were lost in each other, in the moving, touching, and trembling. They reveled in the taking and giving of sensory delights while the darkness whispered their intimacies. Time had no limits as they explored with slow ease, thrilling to the realization that they had found each other. Somehow, in this wide world of countless souls, theirs had managed to meet and strike a chord of kindred need and compatibility.

They felt rich and blessed, at times awed that they should be this lucky. They were, in those minutes, open and unencumbered, hiding neither the passion to give nor the pleasure in taking, extending the anticipation of the final blending until their bodies writhed and burned.

But soon the heat and height grew too great for Rick. "Allison, stop . . . stop . . ." He grabbed her wrist and pinned it above her head, pulled in a deep, shuddering breath and lay his hips just beside hers. "I'm outdistancing you, darling," he whispered thickly, "but there's no hurry, we have all night." He kissed her eyelid, the side of her nose, continuing his silken arousal of her even while temporarily denying himself fulfillment. Again his mouth was at her breast, teeth, tongue, and lips sending ripples of impatience radiating everywhere. The tumult he'd started rumbled close to the surface—higher, higher, until Allison's head arched back, her body now moving to meet his velvet touches. Through clenched teeth she whispered a single word, "Please..." knowing he would stop, leaving her at the brink of that hellish heaven where her body would be exposed in its most vulnerable state.

But it was Rick, not Jason, who wielded the touch of fire in which she burned. And rather than withdraw it, he extended it as Allison had never known it could be extended, until her muscles went taut and the goodness lengthened and strengthened and took her tumbling into the world of sensation as her body became a choreographed dance of muscle and motion.

In the height of her passion, Allison's palms unknowingly pressed his mouth away from her nipples, which had suddenly gone sensitive while she shuddered and cried out in a half sob, half laugh.

When she drifted down to earth from the place of lush quickening, his hand was stroking her languid legs, his kiss etching its mark upon her damp stomach. Weakly she reached to lift his face back to hers. "I didn't mean to push you away. I'm sorry..."

His kiss cut off her apology. "For what?" came his throaty whisper. "Allison, that was beautiful. I never thought you'd be so... so free and open with me." He kissed her neck, his voice a loud rumble in her ear as a hand ran from her knees to her waist and back again. "God, Allison, that was more than beautiful. It was an accolade."

"It was selfish," she insisted, abashed at her total abandon.

"No... no," he assured her against her lips.

"But I forgot all about you in the middle of it." She lay a palm along his cheek and felt him smile as he chuckled.

"But I'm next, darling."

She rolled to her side, brushed her hand down his stomach to find him taut, silken, waiting. The next moment, she felt herself being tugged into a sitting position, insistent hands stroking her spine and urging her toward the edge of the cushions. He leaned away. Warm touches guided her to do his bidding. Her knee brushed his hard stomach as he parted her knees and settled himself between them. "Come here," came his voice thickly. Then he pulled her hard and tight against him and tilted her back with a gentle pressure of his palm upon her chest. There came a rustle in the dark, and she felt a cushion fill the void between her back and the sofa. His hands found her hips, moved sleekly down the backs of her legs to the hollows behind her knees. Then he was touching and kissing her everywhere. The sated feeling of moments ago slipped away to be replaced by renewed desire as he laced his brushing caresses with random kisses, dropping them along her darkened skin wherever they happened to fall—on a breast, an inner elbow, a hip, her stomach...

She tensed, tightened her stomach muscles, and held a pent-up breath, sensing his destination. She reached for his shoulders to stop him, but it was too late. His tongue touched her intimately, leaving her feeling utterly vulnerable and undeniably prurient.

"Rick...I..." His hand reached blindly to cover her lips while his lambent touches sent currents of sensation firing her veins with new life. Resistance fled beneath the onslaught of sensations, and she fell back, a strangled sound issuing from her throat, until at last he knelt to her, entering the silken front of sensuality with easy grace. When he clutched her hips and pressed deep, a soft growl escaped his throat, then the dark was filled only with music and breathing and the magnificence they shared as his body blended into hers.

He murmured her name, interspersing it with endearments, and somehow the beats of their bodies matched, became rhythm and rhyme as she lay back, remembering the sheen of these muscles the first time she'd rubbed them with oil, picturing his perfect face as vividly as if the room were not cast into darkness.

Her fingers flexed into the flesh of his shoulders as he moved within her, taking her beyond the point of no return. And when her nails unconsciously dug in, he jerked her wrists down, pinning them against the cushions while together they thrust closer...closer...closer.

His breath was tortured, her voice a ragged plea as she begged, "Let...m...my...hands...g...go." The pressure left her wrists, but her fingers remained clenched as she clung to his strong back while beat for beat she rode with him to their devastating climaxes.

Oh, it was good. Everything about it was good.

He, too, was trembling, trying to control it by pressing her hard against him, holding the back of her head with a widespread palm. They had slipped down, their bodies now wilting toward the floor. Finally they gave in to the inertia that dumped their sated limbs in a loose heap onto the shaggy rug.

The radio was still playing. It intruded now where before they'd been unconscious of it in the background. Side by side they rested, neither able to conjure up the strength to move, while tomorrow's weather was followed by a time check and a tuneful commercial for soft drinks. Then from the speakers came a guitar intro to a soulful melody and a man's voice singing into their intimate world: "When I'm stretched on the floor after loving once more with your skin pressing mine and we're tired and fine . . ."

The words broke into Allison's consciousness in an unwelcome reminder of the past. But this was Rick, not Jason! Yet he was lying just as the words of the song described, flat out on the floor, and the enormity of what they'd done together struck Allison. Committed. She'd committed herself to a man again by sharing the most intimate of acts. Almost as if it possessed a clairvoyance, the radio reminded her that once before she'd done this, trusted like this, only. . .

Rick's warm hand rested on the soft skin of her inner elbow, and slowly she eased away from his touch and left his side to search for her clothing in the dark.

"Allison?" She sensed how he'd braced up on an elbow, but she didn't answer, feeling along the seat of the sofa. Through the dark the song kept playing. Then a moment later she heard his heels thud across the floor toward the radio, and an angry hand slam against it, thrusting the room into silence. He found her again, but as his hand touched her shoulder, she ducked aside and evaded it.

"Allison, what's wrong?"

"Nothing."

"Don't lie to me." He touched her again, but she retreated to the sofa, curling up with her feet beneath her. The light switch sounded, and Allison flinched.

"Don't . . . don't turn the light on, please."

The light flooded over her shoulder from the table lamp behind her, revealing her strewn hair and withdrawn pose as Rick studied her.

"You want to talk about it?" he asked.

"Just . . . let it be." The only garment at hand was her jeans. She pulled them across her lap and slumped her shoulders as if to shield her naked breasts.

He leaned forward to touch her knee. "No, it's too important."

"Don't look at me." She huddled now, shivering while he hesitated uncertainly for a moment, then retrieved his shirt from the top of the stereo and draped it over her shivering arms and shoulders. He slipped into his pants, then returned to kneel on one knee before her, searching for words, for meanings, for reasons. But she remained closed against him as he tiredly rested an elbow on a knee and kneaded the bridge of his nose, waiting—for what, he didn't know. Insight perhaps, guidance, a hint of where to start.

"Allison, tell me about it. Tell me about him."

Her head snapped up. "It's none of your business. I told you, no questions. Just . . . leave me alone, Jas . . ." Realizing her slip, she cut the word in half.

"Is that his name . . . Jason?"

"I said don't probe, dammit! Don't try to ch—"

"Don't probe!" he shouted, coming to his feet, towering over her. "Don't probe?" He flung a palm angrily at the sofa cushions. "You just came close to calling me by his name and you say don't probe?" He laughed once, ruefully. "What the hell do you think I am, stupid? I heard your precious Five Senses song come on the radio, and I felt what it did to you. All of a sudden you weren't there any more. How do you expect me to react?"

"Please, I . . . I . . . we shouldn't have done this." She turned her eyes aside. "I think you should go."

She saw how he braced one hand on his waistband and locked his knees, his feet spread wide.

"I'll need my shirt," he stated coldly.

She waited, expecting him to yank it from her, dreading

the moment when she'd be exposed to him again. Instead his angry footsteps moved across the hardwood floor to her bedroom. She heard the closet door open, then he came back, stood before her with her blue robe clenched in his hands, and repeated tightly, "I have to take my shirt." A hand reached out, and she thought she saw it tremble before she clamped her eyelids shut, and the cool air covered her naked skin.

He glanced at her arms, crossed now protectively over her breasts. "I want to fling this thing at you and tell you to go to hell, you know that?"

Her eyes opened and met his. He was so totally honest—why couldn't she be that honest about her feelings? He dropped the robe in her lap, then donned his shirt, tucked it in, and stood contemplatively. He sighed heavily at last, ran a hand through his hair, and squatted down beside the sofa again, studying the floor. "We can't drop it here, you know. We have to talk," he said.

"Not now, okay?" she asked tremulously.

He nodded. His knees cracked as he stood up again. "I'll call you."

Still he didn't go, but stood above her, looking down on her hair, which stood out like a dark nimbus in the light drenching her shoulder as she fought to hold back the tears.

"Hey," he asked huskily, "you gonna be all right?"

She nodded jerkily, once, and he turned away. She heard him pause at the door to pull on his boots, heard the snaps of his jacket, and knew he was watching her through the long silent pause before the door opened, then quietly closed behind him.

At its soft click Allison flung herself around and fell across the back of the sofa, burying her head in her arms. And there in her loneliness and confusion she cried. For Jason. For Rick. And for herself.

CHAPTER

Nine

RICK LANG HAD left his Hasselblad behind. Guilt stricken at how she'd treated him, Allison at first declined to use it. He didn't call on Monday or Tuesday, and by Wednesday the shots of the Winterfest came back from processing—crisp, clear and breathtaking. After viewing them, she found herself staring at the phone, wanting terribly to call him, to apologize. But she had hurt him so badly . . . so badly. She stared out the studio windows, seeing only Rick Lang, whom she'd likened to Jason when he was nothing at all like Jason. He cared so little about his looks, he hadn't even asked to see the transparencies of the book cover.

She sighed and turned back to her work—a layout for a Tiffany diamond. The engagement ring nestled within the petals of an apricot rose to which she had applied a single drop of water with an eyedropper. Against a backdrop of lush salmon satin, the composition was stunning. She glanced at the Hasselblad again, weakened, picked it up, and was loading it a moment later.

The diamond, the rose and the camera again worked on Allison's conscience, and she promised herself she'd call Rick and apologize as soon as she got home. But before she finished the series of photos the phone rang, and Mattie said, "Prepare yourself, kiddo, I've got some news you aren't going to like."

"What?"

"Remember that series of shots you took of Jason last fall —the ones in the Harris tweeds?"

"Of course I remember."

"Well, get ready for a surprise—they're in this month's *Gentlemen's Review.*"

The shock set Allison in her chair with a plop. "What!"

"You heard me right. They're in this month's *GR.*"

"B . . . but that's impossible! He only stole them a few weeks ago."

"Apparently not. It appears he lifted them months ago and submitted them then. When did you realize they were missing?"

A sick feeling made Allison's stomach go hollow. "When he left, of course. I wasn't running to the files daily while he was living with me to see if his intentions were honorable or not."

"Well, the creep was about as honorable as Judas Iscariot! The photo credit lists the photographer as Herbert Wells."

"Undoubtedly with a post office box in some eastern city to which *GR* was instructed to send the handsome paycheck," Allison surmised bitterly.

"You're going to tell the police, aren't you?"

Allison sighed uselessly. "Without the negatives to prove the originals were mine?"

There was silence, then Mattie's sympathetic voice. "Listen, honey, I'm really sorry I had to give you the bad news."

"Yeah, sure," said the lifeless voice in the wide, drafty, echoey studio.

Allison hung up and shot to her feet, taking a defiant, angry stance as she stared unseeingly at the glittering diamond that seemed to wink hauntingly from the velvety folds of the rose. Two diamond-hard tears glittered from Allison's eyes.

Damn you, Jason, you bastard! Even while you were taking me to bed night after night you were lying all the time, using your body to get me to do exactly what you wanted. Well, you certainly saw me coming! You must've been standing on the sidewalk watching while this stupid little South Dakota farm girl came rolling off the turnip truck!

I fell for your line like some sex-starved ninny, while you

stole the one thing that meant more to me than even you. All those transparencies—my God!—all of them good enough for publication, while I never suspected. But you knew, didn't you? You knew and you used me. You picked my body and my files clean and made sure I'd know exactly how, by selling them to *GR!*

Where are you now? Laughing in some other woman's arms while you tell her about the ignorant little farm wench from Watertown?

It all flooded back, redoubling Allison's sick realization of how gullible she'd been—of all the times she'd fawned over his body, adored it, both in clothing before the lens and out of it in bed. What a fool she'd been not to see how one-sided her affection was. He took her every compliment as if it were his due while giving back nothing but his body. And that he gave with a hint of smugness, as if doing her a favor.

She cringed now at the memory of how openly she'd displayed her need, her desire, her love. For she *had* loved him. That's what hurt the most. She had. And Jason had fed off her, figuratively as well as literally, for she'd paid all the bills as long as he posed, posed, posed, while she collected the portfolio of photos he was systematicaly rifling all along.

She lived again the anguish and disbelief of that afternoon she'd returned to the apartment to find his message scrawled across the bottom of the picture on the easel. How typical of him to leave his parting message in that way, as if she were some adolescent groupie.

Allison sighed, deep and long, then dropped to her desk chair forlornly. Jason Ederlie had done it all to her, everything a man could possibly do to a woman. He'd taken all a man could take, left as little as a man could leave.

Well, she'd learned her lesson but good. She'd been taken in once by a stunning face and a talented body, but no man would ever reduce her this way again. Not even Rick Lang! Whether he doled out kisses like Eros himself, nobody was going to worm his way into her heart or her bed or her files again!

The telephone rang once more that afternoon. When Allison recognized Rick's voice, she told him this was the answering service and that she would have Ms. Scott return his call.

There followed a puzzled hesitation before he thanked her and hung up.

At home that night during supper Allison's phone rang twice. Later she lay in bed listening to its jangling insistence for the fourth time since she'd gotten home. Determinedly she buried her head under the pillow.

The following morning her answering service reported that a man named Rick Lang had been calling and was becoming abusive to the woman on duty, who could not make him believe they weren't withholding his messages from Ms. Scott.

Late Thursday Allison made the sudden decision to go to Watertown for the weekend. But she was restless and irritable even there, for the farmhouse felt confining. She wished she could talk to her mother about Jason and Rick, but her mother would never understand Allison's having had a sexual relationship with a man before marriage, much less having lived with him for the better part of a year. Sexual intercourse had never, never been a discussed subject at home, and Allison knew her mother would be extremely uncomfortable to confront it with her daughter, even now.

Allison's married brother Wendell farmed nearby, but they weren't close enough for her to seek his counsel either. Then, too, every time Allison's mother looked at her it was with a shake of the head as she declared, "Land, you're nothing but skin and bones, girl." At mealtime the woman invariably added another spoonful from each dish after Allison had already filled her plate.

Finally over Sunday breakfast Allison's irritation churned out of control, and she exploded, "Dammit, Mother, I'm twenty-five years old! I don't need any help deciding how many scrambled eggs to eat for breakfast!"

The stunned silence that followed left Allison feeling guilty and far less adult than she claimed to be. She returned to the city more discontent than ever, and bearing one more niggling burden of guilt.

She was sitting in her empty, silent apartment eating a TV dinner that tasted like plastic when the phone rang. She glared at it, dumped her unfinished food into the garbage can, and went to do her washing. The damn phone rang with extreme regularity through three loads of washing and the ironing, too. She was sure it was Rick, but refused to take the phone off the hook, and let him know she was home.

But the ringing finally raised her hackles beyond soothing. She yanked the receiver up and blared, "Yes, yes, yes! What do you want!"

There was a moment of silence, then his voice. "Allison?"

"Yes?"

"Just where in the hell have you been for three days!" he exploded.

"I went home to South Dakota."

"While you let me wonder if you'd dropped off the face of the earth!"

"I didn't want to see you or talk to you," she explained expressionlessly.

"Oh, well, that's just dandy! You didn't want to see me! Just like that! Did you happen to think I might be going crazy worrying about you while you traipsed off and ignored my calls!"

He was so angry the receiver seemed to quiver in her palm. Allison's hand was shaking too as she backed up against the wall, let her eyes droop shut, sighed, and slid down until her butt hit the floor. "No," she answered wearily, "no, I didn't stop to consider that. I'm sorry."

"Well, you should be, for crissakes," he raged on. "You don't just disappear into thin air to leave a man wondering if you're alive or dead or what the hell is going through your impossible female head. You were pretty damned upset when I left you the other night, you know. Did you think I—"

"I said I was sorry!" she hissed.

"Well, dammit, I was worried sick! I've been up to your apartment no less than eight times in the last three days, and all the people downstairs could tell me was that they hadn't seen you since some time Thursday morning, and they didn't know where you'd gone. And I couldn't get one damn thing out of your answering service except some catty little snoot placating me with 'I'm sorry, Mr. Lang, but we've given her all your messages.' So just what the hell kind of game are you playing!"

"It's no game," Allison assured him. "We had some laughs

together and took a few pictures and ended up making love, that's all. That doesn't constitute a commitment of any kind. It was just a . . . a mistake."

"Just a mistake," Rick repeated, thunderstruck, his voice now holding a sharp edge of hurt. "You call what happened between us a mistake? Who the hell are you trying to kid, Allison?"

"It *was* a mistake for me. It's too . . ." She stopped, drew a deep breath, and went on. "I can't see you anymore, Rick. I'm sorry, I'm just not as resilient as I thought I was. I can't forget that fast—"

"Forget what! Something I did or something *he* did? I'm not him, damn it, yet you're judging me as if I were! If you're going to judge a man, at least do it on his own merits and shortcomings instead of someone else's."

Damn him, he was right! But the full sting of Jason's duplicity was too fresh within Allison to allow her to feel unthreatened by the thought of committing herself to a new relationship. To commit was to become vulnerable again.

"So why are you wasting your time on me?" It hurt, it hurt, having to say those words to him. And even across the telephone wire she could tell they hurt him, too.

"I don't know. I felt what we did together *does* constitute a commitment, and I thought you were the kind of woman who felt the same way, but apparently I was wrong." A pause followed, then he muttered, "Oh, hell," and his voice grew persuasive. "I don't know how to say this, but you and I spent some hours together that were far, far above the ordinary for first times. We worked and laughed and learned we had a lot in common. And after such a great day last Sunday, the way we ended it was as natural an ending as . . . as . . . you know what I'm talking about, Allison. We're good together, so I kissed you and you kissed me back and we made love . . ." His voice had gone low and gruff. "And don't lie to me. It was like fireworks." She heard him swallow. "And then you ran, and I deserve some answers, Allison. I have a right to know why."

"Because I'm afraid, okay?" she answered truthfully.

"Tell me what Jason—"

"I don't understand why you're bothering. I'm not even a

very good . . ." But abruptly she gulped to a halt.

"Lover?" he filled in. "Is that what you were going to say? Because if it is, you might be interested in knowing that not every guy thinks of that first. Some people honestly look for the person inside the body first. Some people actually base their feelings on more than just superficial appearances." He paused. "And you are a hell of a good lover."

"Stop it! Stop it! You want to know why I'm afraid to trust you, I'll tell you why. Because I trusted Jason Ederlie and all I got for it was taken. We lived together and I paid his way. Like a stupid, lovesick fool I took him in and stroked his ego and let him live scot free off me, thinking all the time we were working toward . . . toward something permanent. He posed for me. Oh, did he pose! And he knew his charms very well. I laid my whole future on the line with him, and one day I walked into this house and found him gone—lock, stock, and negatives! You want to know why I'm afraid to commit myself to a man again? Open up this month's issue of *Gentlemen's Review* and find out. You'll recognize his face—it's the one from my files. They say a picture is worth a thousand words—well, in *GR* it's also worth about a thousand dollars and a fixed career, and there's a whole layout of them. Only the photo credit, you'll note, is not quite accurate!"

By now Allison was quivering, viewing the chrome legs of the dining room chairs through a blur of angry tears.

"All that doesn't change one thing that's gone on between you and me, Allison, because it's past. It's done. What about what we shared?"

"What about it?" she retorted, wanting to draw back the words, but unable to, hurting him, hurting herself.

First came stunned, hurt silence, then carefully controlled words. "Nothing—nothing at all. I've been talking to the wrong girl all night long. And I mean *girl!* Why don't you grow up, Allison, and stop blaming the rest of the world for one man's transgressions? Then maybe you'll find somebody *worthy* of your lofty attention!"

Without saying good-bye, Rick Lang hung up.

The days and weeks that followed were filled with the deepest despair Allison had ever known, deeper than that she'd suffered when Jason deserted her, for then she'd been fortified by justifiable anger. Now she had no blame to lay on Rick Lang and thereby assuage her own shortcomings.

Rick had done nothing to earn her callous rejection—nothing. Her own insecurity had caused her to treat him so cruelly. A hundred times a day she considered calling him, apologizing, telling him it wasn't his fault, that he was innocent of everything she had accused him of. But she was utterly ashamed of how she'd acted. And now, too, she felt unworthy of him.

The vision of Rick filled her thoughts as the days stretched into weeks. In her memories she no longer searched for flaws, for he possessed none, none with which he had ever sought to hurt her, to dominate her, even to bolster his own ego. Those were crutches Jason had used—Jason, not Rick. He had entered the relationship honestly; it was she who had hidden truths from him and disguised her fears behind a façade of wariness and distrust.

Ah, what a sorry human being she was. She deserved the hurt and the sense of loss she now suffered as the dreary days of February paraded past and she heard nothing from Rick Lang.

The photographs of their day at the Winterfest brought painful memories of what she had so carelessly cast aside. Leafing through them one day, she recalled a time she now longed for, a man she now longed for, who had treated her decently, honorably. In a spate of self-disgust she threw the pictures across her desk and lowered her head to her arms to cry again.

She was so tired of crying.

When she blew her nose and dried her eyes, she felt better. Resting her chin on a fist on the desk top, she scanned again the scattered scenes with their bright colors and bittersweet memories.

Call him, call him, a lonely voice cried.

He'll have nothing to say—you've hurt him too badly.

Apologize, came the taunting, haunting voice.

After the way you treated him? You have no right to call him.

Her head came up off her fist, and she collected the photos, sniffling still, and rubbed a wrist under her eyes and laid the collection in a row. Studying them in a series, she realized they were remarkably well-done, giving an overall effect of vibrant Minnesotans hard at play in the midst of an icy winter's day.

On a sudden impulse she dashed off a cover letter and jammed them into an envelope along with it, and put them in the mail to *Mpls./St. Paul* magazine.

To Allison's amazement, she received a call three days later from a man who wanted to buy the series for their April issue.

But the joy she would otherwise have basked in was dulled by the fact that she couldn't share it with Rick, who had been so much a part of that day. When Allison hung up the phone, she stood for long minutes, hands hugging her thin hips through tight jeans pockets as she stared at the phone.

Again she had the sudden urge to call him and tell him the news. But once more she felt guilty and undeserving and decided against it.

The Hasselblad was still here. She worked with it daily, realizing she must return it, afraid to call and tell him he could either come and get it or she would take it to his place.

On the first day of March she returned home to find an envelope with strange handwriting in her mailbox. Racing up the stairs, she flung off her cap and scarf, her heart warming, warning—it's from him! It's from him!

She curled her feet beneath her on the sofa, studying the writing. The envelope was pink. She began to rip it open, then suddenly changed her mind, wanting to keep it flawless and neat if it truly were from him. She found a knife in the kitchen and slit the envelope open carefully.

Back on the sofa she slipped the greeting card slowly from its holder. There came into view a hand-painted card done in pastel watercolors of a single stalk of forget-me-nots forcing their way up between an old brick wall and a weathered gnarl of driftwood around which wild grasses waved in dappled shadow.

Even before she opened it, Allison's eyes had filled with tears. She ran her fingertips over the rough texture of the watercolor paper, realizing it was the first of his work she'd seen.

A wildlife artist, he'd said, but she'd never asked once to see his work, never displayed an interest in it at all. Yet she'd heartlessly accused *him* of egoism! She was the egotist, so wrapped up in her own career she'd never bothered to ask about his.

Considering the sensitivity that radiated from the simple drawing, she realized an enormous truth—Rick Lang didn't give a damn about his physical appearance and did not feed off it, because it was wholly secondary to what was most important in his life—his art.

She opened the folded sheet. His writing, done with black ink and calligraphy pen, slanted across the page: *I haven't forgotten. Rick.*

Allison clamped a hand over her mouth, swallowing repeatedly at the sudden surge of emotion that welled up in her throat. His face came back, beguiling, entreating.

No, Rick, I haven't forgotten either, but I'm so ashamed, how can I face you again?

She sat there for a long time with her legs drawn up tightly against her chest, thinking of him, remembering, reliving all the enjoyable hours spent with him, their teasing and laughter, the disastrous omelette, their exuberant forays into the winter days, the night they'd shared that wonderful sense of oneness after the studio session, and, of course, the night he'd made love to her.

His words came back clearly. "I'm still one of those guys who wants to do the pursuing." She now wanted so badly to call him, but the memory of those words stopped her.

She glanced at the telephone and decided that if he wanted to see her again, he'd call.

In mid-March she sent him a brief note telling him she'd leave the Hasselblad at the North Star Modeling Agency, and he could pick it up there. She debated for a long time before adding, "I loved your card. You're gifted with a paintbrush." Debating again about how to sign it, she finally decided on, "Yours, A."

The last two weeks of March dragged past. The buds on the trees along Nicollet Mall were bursting with new life, ready to sprout greenery into the heart of downtown Minneapolis, which was vibrant with expectancy now that spring was just around the corner. In downtown bank plazas noontime fashion shows offered spring garments in an array of bright colors—short sleeved and breezy in anticipation of the balmy season ahead.

Allison bought a chic suit of pale yellow linen to take home to Watertown for Easter, which fell in mid-April. But the new suit did little to lift her spirits as day after day she hoped to find another letter in her mailbox from Rick. But none came.

She broke down in early April and tried calling him for three days in a row, but got no answer.

Carefully nonchalant, she went to North Star's office one day to ask Mattie if Rick Lang had come by to pick up his camera.

"Sure did," Mattie answered. "Said he was happy to have it back because he was going home, wherever that is, to get some spring shots for his files."

Depressed at the idea of his being miles away, in a town where she'd never been, Allison submerged herself in work, trying to put him out of her mind.

Hathaway Books called, saying they loved the cover concept and photography she'd done and offering her a contract to do two more. It should have elated Allison, but while she was happy, that ebullient feeling she'd expected to experience at a time like this was curiously absent.

In mid-April another envelope bearing Rick's writing showed up in the mail—a hastily scrawled pencil sketch of a fawn standing beneath a leafless tree. Inside he'd written, "I've been out of town, reevaluating. Just got back and saw the spread in *Mpls./St. Paul*. Congratulations! You, too, are gifted . . . with my Hasselblad. Yours, Rick."

The spirits that had lain unlifted by either the new spring suit or the two-book contract offer were buoyed to the heights by his simple message.

Again she considered calling him, but studied the word "reevaluating" and decided it was best to leave the pursuing to him, if he ever decided to see her again.

Easter came and at the last minute before leaving town on

Good Friday, Allison picked up an Easter card at the drugstore and addressed it to him, writing beneath the printed message, "I, too, am reevaluating. Yours, Allison."

Spending two days at home this time, Allison remembered Rick's analysis of her parents' motives and found herself less critical of them, enjoying her weekend immensely.

The winter wheat was already sprouting in the limitless fields around the farmhouse, and she took time for a long walk through them, evaluating not only herself but also Rick, their relationship, and the far too great importance she had put on the treatment given her by Jason Ederlie.

What was she afraid of?

The answer, she found now, was nothing! She wasn't afraid; she was eager. She wanted the chance to see Rick Lang again, to apologize, to laugh with him, make love with him if he would have her, and to prove that she was willing to judge him for himself alone, not by measuring him against a man who, during the past few months, had become only a vague recollection and whose memory had almost ceased to bring the hurt and despondency it once had.

No word came again until the first of May. A long, narrow, hand-painted card bearing a basket of mayflowers with a ribbon tied to its handle, streamers flying breezily in the wind.

Inside it said, "There's an old May Day tradition that if a girl likes a boy, she leaves a May basket on his step, rings his doorbell, then runs, in the hopes that he'll catch her and kiss her. I'm not sure if boys are allowed to do the same thing, but . . . Love, Rick."

Allison's cheeks grew as pink as the May blossoms on his painting, and a glorious smile lit her face. She felt as if a bouquet of flowers had burst to profusion within her very heart. Breathing became suddenly difficult, and she turned, studying the sofa in her bright living room where late afternoon sun now streamed through the windows of the sun porch, whose French doors were opened.

She remembered Rick here in his many poses and knew beyond a doubt that he would be here again . . . soon.

She would invite him over for supper, she thought, immediately tossing the idea out as too forward. Not here, not in this place where memories of the past might come to threaten. They needed neutral territory on which to meet and assess the changes they were sure to find in each other.

Unsure of what his message meant, she was still reluctant to be the one to call him. Rick Lang, pursuer, she thought with a smile.

She waited another day, and in the mail at the studio there arrived the answer to her quandary—the announcement of a two-day symposium and workshop at University of Wisconsin-Madison, at which the keynote speaker would be Roberto Finelli, a renowned instructor of photography from Brooks Institute in Santa Barbara.

Subject: Photographing People for Profit
Requirements: 35mm camera, colored film and a model
              of your choice
Dates: May 19–20
Registration Fee: $160.00
Meals: Available at the college cafeteria at student rates
Lodging: Not arranged for, hotels and motels available
           in vicinity near the campus

Odd how insignificant her lifetime dream of meeting Finelli suddenly seemed when offered beside the opportunity of seeing Rick Lang again, of working with him and in the process rectifying the mistake she'd made with him.

The hands of the clock seemed to creep by so slowly that at one point Allison actually called for correct time, verifying that it was her own eagerness and not some electrical malfunction that made the hours move so slowly. She could have called Rick from the studio, but for some reason she wanted to be at home when she did.

But when five o'clock finally arrived and Allison got home, she dawdled unnecessarily through a tuna salad sandwich, reaching for the phone three times while the heartbeats in her throat threatened to choke her. Each time she pulled back the sweating hand, wiping it on her thigh, turning around to pace the living room and work up her courage.

He wouldn't be home, she thought frantically. Or he might be home but have somebody else with him and not be able to

talk. Or maybe he would be able to talk but would refuse—
then what?

Chicken, Allison?

Damn right, I'm chicken!

Then don't call—spend the rest of your life wishing you
had!

Oh shut up, I'll do it when I'm good and ready!

Ha!

He would have called if he wanted to see me.

You're the one who threw him out, remember!

But he said he's old-fashioned about these things.

He's made it abundantly clear he wants to see you.

She grabbed the phone and dialed so fast she had no chance
to change her mind. Waiting while it rang, she wildly wished
he wouldn't be home, for she had no idea how to begin.

"Hello?"

She clutched the phone, but not a word squeaked through
her throat.

"Hello? . . . Hello?"

"Rick?" Was that her voice, so cool, so low, so controlled,
when her heart was thumping out of her chest?

A long pause, then his surprised voice. "Allison?"

"Yeah . . . hi."

"Hi yourself." The ensuing silence seemed to stretch across
light-years of time before he added, "I pretty much gave up
hope of hearing from you again."

"I gave up hope of hearing from you."

Silence roared along, carrying her thumping heart with it.
He began to say something but had a frog in his throat and had
to clear it to start again. "So how are you doing?"

"Better."

"Obviously, with the sale to *Mpls./St. Paul* and everything.
The pictures were really great, I mean that. I couldn't believe
it when I opened my copy and saw them."

"It . . . it was a surprise when they called to say they'd buy
them. I . . . well, I sent them off on kind of an impulse, you
know?"

"Lucky impulse."

"Yeah . . . yeah, lucky."

She shrugged as if he could see her and stared at the floor

between her feet, but neither of them seemed able to think of anything more to say now that that subject was exhausted.

"Oh, guess what!" she said, remembering. "Hathaway offered me a contract to do two more book covers!"

"Hey, congratulations! Now you'll know where next month's groceries are coming from, and the month's after that."

Old simple words from their past—did he forget nothing? —but the memories they conjured up were rife with other things she wanted them to say to one another.

Finally Allison remembered what she'd called for.

"Listen, are you still modeling?"

"Sure. It pays the bills, same as always."

"Would you like a job?"

"Sure."

"For me?"

To Rick she sounded uncertain, as if she thought he might say no when he found out who it was for. "Why not?" he asked.

"It's not the regular kind of job, you know—I mean, not the book covers again, but I figure we can both learn a little something if we do it together. I mean, it's a workshop and symposium down at University of Wisconsin called Photographing People for Profit. The guest speaker is going to be Roberto Finelli. I've . . . well, I've always wanted a chance to meet him." Her words tumbled out one after the other to hide her nervousness.

"When is it?"

"May nineteenth and twentieth."

"Two full days?"

She realized the implications of staying overnight and swallowed hard, wondering what he was thinking.

"Yeah," she finally answered, trying to sound noncommittal. He's going to say no! He's going to say no! she thought, her palms now sweating profusely, her cheeks already flushing with embarrassment.

"It sounds fun."

The sun burst forth inside her head with a blazing flash of wonder.

"It does?" Her lips dropped open, her eyes were wide with pleasant shock.

"Of course it does. Did you think I'd refuse?" She thought she detected a slight lilt of teasing in his question.

"I . . . I wasn't sure." She had clapped one hand over the top of her head to hold it on. You like to do the pursuing, she thought—you told me so!

"You'll have to tell me what kind of clothes to wear," he was saying, while she controlled her euphoria in order to settle the final details.

They made plans for her to pick him up at four A.M. on the appointed day. This settled, there came a lull in the conversation.

Allison was on her feet, pacing the length of the phone cord. She stopped and stared at the daybed on the sun porch, wondering if summer would find them on it. "Well . . ." she muttered stupidly.

Well, she thought . . . *well?* Is that all you can think of to say, *well!* Think of some bright, witty ending to this conversation, Scott!

He cleared his throat and said, "Yeah . . . well."

Silence.

Allison's palms were sweating. She wiped them on her thighs. "I'll see you on the nineteenth then."

"The nineteenth," he repeated. "Good-bye."

"Good-bye."

But Allison didn't want to be the first one to hang up. She stood in the sunset-washed living room, staring at the spot where they'd made love, hugging the receiver to her ear, listening to him breathe. After a long, long moment she lowered the receiver and pressed it firmly between her breasts, her heart racing, a feeling of imminent fullness overpowering her senses.

"Rick Lang, I love you," she whispered to the picture of him behind her closed eyelids, unsure if he could hear the muffled words or the crazy commotion of her heart, suddenly not caring if he knew the full extent of her feelings for him.

She lifted the receiver to her ear again and listened, but could not be sure if he was still there. At last she hung up.

CHAPTER

Ten

THE MORNING OF May nineteenth had not yet dawned when Allison Scott drove her Chevy van through the winding streets of the elegant old part of Minneapolis called Kenwood. Situated in the hills behind the Walker Art Center and the Guthrie Theater, it was once home to the city's oldest monied families. But in more recent years the founding families had moved to lake-shore estates, and Kenwood had been captured by young architects, lawyers, and doctors who'd brought new life, and children, to the staid, old sector.

Thick wooded hills and winding streets twisted through the area, making addresses hard to find. But Allison followed Rick's precise instructions through the sleeping hulks of old homes that in the daytime drew sightseers to admire cupolas, porches, bannisters, turrets, carriage houses, dormers, gables, and more, for no two homes in the area were alike.

Just off Kenwood Parkway Allison found the designated street and number, an elegant old three-story building of English Tudor styling buried beneath overhanging elms, its front door flanked by soldier-straight bushes trimmed to military precision. A sidewalk wound its way around to the back of the house, and Allison followed it beside a high wall of honeysuckle hedge that dripped dew, its full blossoms giving off a heady scent.

A light was on above a second-story door much like hers, and she took the steps with a queer sense of familiarity, of

144

coming home. He'd never told her he lived in a place so much like her own.

She paused, searching for a bell. There was none, but she clutched the tiny woven Easter basket in her hands, wondering if it was wise to give it to him after all. It was large enough to hold only one Easter egg, which it had when her brother Wendell's little daughter had given it to her Aunt Allison with beaming pride, declaring she had dyed the egg herself.

The basket now held two candy kisses and a tiny cluster of lilies of the valley that Allison had stolen from her landlady's garden and tied with a small pink grosgrain ribbon.

Allison drew a deep, deep breath, held it for an interminable length of time, let it gush out, then soundly rapped on the door.

She heard footsteps approaching on the opposite side, and her heart threatened to stop up her throat.

The door opened, and she forgot the basket, forgot the words she'd rehearsed, forgot the businesslike air she'd vowed to maintain, forgot everything except Rick Lang, standing before her in a pair of crisply ironed blue jeans with an open-necked white shirt underneath a flawless lightweight sport coat of muted spring plaid that gaped away from his ribs as his hand hung on the edge of the door.

Through Allison's tumult of emotions it struck her that he'd dressed up for her. His hair, she thought—he had combed his hair! How could she ever have imagined it would be folly to touch a comb to it? She'd never seen such a tempting head of hair in her life. It was blow-combed to a neat feathered perfection, covering the tips of his ears on its backward sweep, touching his forehead as it fell faultlessly forward.

Rick Lang neither smiled nor stepped back nor spoke, but studied her with an expression that told Allison little about what he was thinking.

At last she came to her senses. "Good morning." Her voice sounded pinched and squeaky.

"Good morning." His sounded deep and even.

Again Allison struggled to find something to say. Suddenly she jumped as if she'd just touched an electric fence and thrust the silly little basket forward.

"Here . . . for you." She added a quavering smile. "But I'm not running."

He looked down, smiled, and slowly reached out for the basket, hooking its tiny handle over a single index finger.

Immediately she clasped both hands behind her back.

He looked up with a grin. "Of course not. It's not May Day."

She felt herself blushing and cast about for a quick reply, but none came. Still clutching her hands behind her, Allison leaned forward from the waist, peering around him inquisitively. "Mmm . . . nice house. It reminds me of mine."

He stepped back quickly. "Mine doesn't have a sun porch, and somebody covered up all the hardwood floors with these ugly brown carpets, but it's roomy, close to town, and has all the conveniences."

"Yes, it's nice." *Nice,* she thought . . . you *ninny!* "It's really . . ." Allison stopped her examination of the premises. Realizing it had grown silent behind her, she turned to find his eyes following her with a hint of amusement in their expression.

"You were about to say?" he prompted.

"I . . . nothing." She ordered the blood to stop rushing to her head.

"We'd better get going if we're going to make it to Madison by ten." He turned away and headed toward a door leading off the opposite side of the living room. "Be right back," he called over his shoulder.

She scanned the room again, wishing she had hours to study it so that she might learn of him, his likes, his ways. An easel stood near a north window, but it was turned to catch the window's light, and she couldn't see what he was working on. There were deep leather chairs and a matching davenport and bookcases with hundreds of items other than books. His old, worn letter jacket lay across the back of one of the chairs. She walked over and touched it lightly.

"Ready?" he asked.

She jerked her hand back as if he'd caught her stealing.

"Yes."

He held a suitcase in one hand, a zippered clothing bag slung over the opposite shoulder, and in the buttonhole of his jacket lapel he'd stuck the cluster of lilies of the valley.

She pulled her eyes away from the flowers with an effort and came forward. "Here, I can take something."

She reached for the garment bag, but he said, "No, I'll get that, but you can take this." There was some confusion while he attempted to shrug a wide woven strap from his shoulder, but it got tangled in the ends of the hangers.

At last it was free and in her hands. "The Hasselblad?" she asked, looking up with surprise in her face.

"What else?" He smiled.

"But—"

"When she's working under Finelli for the first time, a woman ought to be really turned on, right?"

She beamed radiantly, hung the wide strap over her shoulder, and hugged the case protectively against her belly. "Thanks, Rick, I'll treat it like spun glass."

He stepped out onto the landing, set his suitcase down, and held the door, waiting for her to pass before him. "If I remember right," Rick teased, "that's where all this started."

As she crossed in front of him, she caught the intoxicating drift of lily of the valley, and it did little to still the heart that beat at double time, because she was with him again.

They stowed his gear in the back of the van. Rick slammed the doors shut and asked, "You want me to drive?"

"I'd love it."

She dropped the keys into his palm, and a minute later they were backing down the driveway, heading through the sleeping city toward the interstate.

"I've got coffee." She twisted around in her seat and dug out a thermos and chubby earthen mugs while he glanced sideways briefly, then back to the road, checking the rearview mirror as the scent of coffee filled the van.

"One black . . . one with sugar," he remembered, reminding Allison of the first time they'd shared coffee this way. But his eyes remained on the road as he reached blindly and she placed the mug in his hand.

The horrible uncertainty of her first moments with him were gone, spinning farther into the distance as the miles rolled away beneath the wheels. She slumped back in her bucket seat, resting one high-heeled boot against the corner of the dash, balancing the coffee mug on her stomach. Occasionally she sipped, but mostly she basked in a feeling of supreme well-being at going off with him alone, attuned to his nearness, covertly watching his familiar hand on the wheel, listening to him sip his coffee now and then.

Rick, meanwhile, glanced time and again at the blue denim stretched tightly over her upraised knee and occasionally at the coffee mug resting on her stomach. At first only the lights from the dashboard illuminated the outline of her legs, but within half an hour the first strands of dawn lit the eastern sky as they headed directly into the sunrise. It was one of those explosive dawns that splash across the sky in layers of blue, pink, and orange. As the sun slipped above the horizon, they crossed the border into Wisconsin.

Rick turned to find Allison's cup slipping sideways. He smiled to himself, turning lazy eyes toward her sleeping face. He had time for a longer, more intimate look as she slept trustfully beside him. He scanned her body with its chin settled onto a shoulder, that shoulder wedged at an uncomfortable angle in the corner of the seat, while her upraised knee swung indolently back and forth with the motion of the vehicle. The way she was scrunched up made her blouse buckle away from her chest. A shadowed hollow invited his eyes, and inside he saw a wisp of white lace. His eyes moved back to the road momentarily.

Her cup slipped farther askance and he reached to slide it from her fingers, but as it slipped away she jerked awake and sat up, looking sheepish.

"It's okay, go back to sleep."

"No, I'm not tired. I slept like a log last night."

He grinned and turned back to the road, making no comment while she wondered how he could possibly believe such a fat lie!

She sat up, entwined her fingers, and stretched her palms toward her knees, writhing a little, stiff-elbowed, and catlike.

"Looks like we're in for a knockout sunrise," Rick observed.

"Mmm . . . and I nearly missed it." She scanned the eastern horizon from north to south, her artist's eye appreciating this masterpiece the more for sharing it with him. She leaned forward, clasping her hands back to back between her knees, and savored being with him.

Wisconsin was devastatingly beautiful in its May costume. Fields of freshly tilled soil rolled along like flags waving in the wind, interspersed with blankets of budding forests where an occasional burst of wild plum blossoms could be seen in the distance. Immense promontories of sharp, gray rock loomed above the roadside, high and straight, their tops flat. They were awesome.

"It seems as if there should be an Indian on top of every one of them," Allison observed, "sitting there on a painted pony with a feathered lance in his hand."

"I've often thought the same thing myself."

Still they spoke of nothing personal. The remainder of the trip passed in companionable silence, but Allison knew they were only delaying what could inevitably not be delayed.

As they turned off the interstate at the Madison exit and followed Washington Avenue straight into the heart of the city, the dome of the state Capitol proudly guided them to its very center, seemingly built in the middle of the highway. They circled the Capitol grounds on quaint city streets arranged like a spiderweb around it.

The college town was bustling, its sidewalks swarming with students on bikes and on foot, bare armed, hurrying through the warm spring weather.

Allison and Rick found the correct building, parked the van and collected the Hasselblad, its equipment bag, and Allison's clipboard.

Finelli in the flesh inspired every photographer there with his opening speech and the narrative that accompanied a slide presentation of some of his most stunning work, many famous faces from film stars to politicians, cover girls to cardinals.

The lunch break came all too soon. Rick and Allison shared it in the campus cafeteria. Allison had difficulty coming down from the high inspired by the man who epitomized success in her chosen field.

Rick's voice repeated her name for the second time. "Allison?"

"Hmm?" She came up from her fanciful world where success was wholly achievable, pulling her eyes from her bowl of chili and grilled cheese sandwich to find Rick laughing at her.

"Hey there, dreamy, you haven't got Finelli's job yet. We have a workshop to attend and pictures to take. You gonna sit there and dream in your chili all day?"

She braced her chin on a palm and smiled dimly. "I will one day—have his job, I mean. Just you watch and see."

During the actual workshop cameras were set up in various lighting situations and personalized guidance given to the photographers, allowing them to experiment with newly marketed equipment and various techniques. Ideas were exchanged freely, live models wandered about, and the country's most noted teachers of photography gave advice and inspiration.

Allison looked up to see Rick approaching after having changed his clothes. He came striding toward her in a set of clothes the likes of which she'd never seen on him before. She was stunned. He was dressed in a thick-textured sweater of pale gray with a bulky collar; dress trousers of smooth navy gabardine, slightly pleated at the waist; a small-collared button-down dress shirt of pale smoky blue; highly polished black loafers; a gold identification bracelet with a large-linked chain; and a pendant bearing his sign of the zodiac—Aries—lying just below the hollow of his throat, nestled in the pale gold hair above his open collar.

"I'm ready," he announced quietly.

Wow, so am I! she thought, then realized her mouth was hanging open and shut it with a snap. He moved to the camera case to take out extra backs for the Hasselblad, while her eyes followed him like those of a hungry puppy. As he stepped close to show her how to load the several backs in advance, the scent of his aftershave set her quivering. "Each roll has only twelve shots, you know, so I thought I'd bring the extra backs. You can preload them," he said. But it was hard for her to concentrate on the words. She watched his long fingers showing her how to line up two double dots on the back of the camera if she wanted to double expose.

With an effort Allison forced her mind from Rick Lang to the business at hand. The renowned Finelli offered advice on back-lighting the hair with a colored filter to achieve a sunset effect. She produced the color print of the book cover, showing how she'd used the same technique with blue filters to create the effect of moon glow. He complimented her, watched as she proceeded, and offered kindly, "Young lady, it looks to me like you're wasting your time here. I'll move along to someone who needs my advice."

She looked up to see Rick stepping toward her. "Mind if I see that?"

She handed it to him silently, and they both studied Rick Lang leaning over Vivien Zuchinski with his hand near the side of her breast.

"It's damn good," he said quickly.

She looked at his temple as he studied the picture. "You're damn good." Before he could look into her eyes, she turned back to the camera.

By the end of the day's workshops it was four P.M. and both Allison and Rick were exhausted, yet curiously exhilarated. Heading back toward the van, he asked, "Is this going to be one of those nights when you're too high to sleep?"

She squeezed her eyes shut, opened them again, flung her arms wide, and bubbled joyously, "Yes! Yes! Yes!"

He watched the back of her hair swinging as she walked a step ahead of him, so energized she seemed ready to do cartwheels up the sidewalk.

"In that case I won't be keeping you from sleeping if I take you out to dinner."

"Oh, you don't have to do that." She turned to insist, but found her shoulder nearly colliding with his chest as he walked along, the sweater slung over his shoulder on two fingers.

"I know. I want to."

They studied each other for a silent moment. "Yeah?" she inquired cutely.

"Yeah," he repeated, grinning at her tilted chin and giving her a slow-motion mock punch on the jaw.

"Don't mind if I do," she decided. "I hardly touched my lunch, I was so off in another world. Sorry I get that way, but I can't help it. Lord, but I'm half starved, and I just realized it when you mentioned dinner."

"Half starved? Then how about a kiss to hold you over?"

She raised her eyes in surprise, feeling the thrill of anticipation already leaping up in the form of a blush. But he only pulled one of the paper-wrapped candy kisses from his pocket, and held it between index and middle fingers, offering it to Allison.

Their eyes met above it as they continued along the sidewalk. Her heart suddenly felt as if spring were burgeoning within it as well as in the apple, myrtle, and plum trees along the Madison streets.

"Oh, is that all?" she asked impishly. She plucked the candy from his fingers, opened it, and popped it into her mouth.

It seemed preordained that he drive again. "Where to?" he inquired, nosing the van into the busy end-of-the-day traffic near the Capitol.

"Back the way we came. There are plenty of cut-rate motels out that way." Without another word he headed out to Washington Avenue.

They entered the lobby of the Excel Motel together, each of them signing the register separately, ignoring the assessing glances cast their way by the clerk who asked, "Smoking or nonsmoking?"

Rick and Allison gaped at each other, then at the clerk.

"What?" they asked in unison.

"We got smoking rooms and nonsmoking rooms. Which one you want?"

"Nonsmoking," they answered, again in unison, and the clerk let his eyes drift from Allison to Rick as if to say, separate rooms, huh? He picked two keys from the wall, dropped them on the desk, and said, "Enjoy your stay."

On their way to the van—obviously the only vehicle parked out front, obviously the vehicle in which they had arrived together, obviously the vehicle which would take them to door C and rooms 239 and 240—Allison could feel the clerk's eyes following them.

"Do you think he believed us?" Rick asked, casting her a sidelong glance.

"Not after we both spouted out 'Nonsmoking.' Have you ever heard of such a thing before?"

"Never."

"Me neither."

They climbed into the van, and Allison couldn't resist wagging two fingers at the desk clerk as they pulled away from the sidewalk—shades of the night watchman in days past.

In the hall, standing between the two assigned doors that were exactly opposite each other, Rick asked, "Which one do you want?"

"Where's east?"

"That way." He pointed to 240.

"Then that one. I like the sun in the morning."

"Two-forty, milady," he said with a slight bow from the waist after he'd opened the door and dropped the key into her palm. She stepped uncertainly inside. It was vaguely creepy going into the motel room alone. She poked her nose around the corner to eye the double bed, the floor, the closed draperies, then glanced over her shoulder to find Rick standing in the open doorway to his room, watching her.

"How's yours?" he asked.

She shivered and shrugged. "Cold."

"There's probably a heater they leave turned off until guests are in. Just a minute." He hung up his clothing bag on the rack in his closet and crossed the hall, moving into her room without apparent self-consciousness, while she felt as if every eye in Madison, Wisconsin, was somehow watching them on closed-circuit TV. He bent to the heater on the wall and studied its dials. Abruptly he stood up. "Nope, that's just for air." He came toward her, and she stood as if rooted to the floor. "Excuse me," he said, taking her by the elbows to move her aside to adjust the thermostat behind her.

"There, it'll warm up in a minute. Everything else okay?"

"Sure, thanks." But suddenly she didn't want him to go back across the hall. The room seemed too impersonal and quiet, a queer, lonely place when she faced it alone.

Rick paused in the doorway. "Would it be all right if we didn't go to dinner right away? I thought I'd lie down awhile and catch a nap. It was a long drive. Maybe you should do the same."

"I don't mind."

"What time then?"

She shrugged again, feeling more lost and lonely than ever,

realizing he was, indeed, going to leave her and close himself away in his own room. She wondered despondently if nothing more personal would come of the two days than candy kisses.

After all, she had been the one to give the May basket; the next move was up to him.

"Sixish?" she suggested now, her spirits definitely flattened.

"Six it is." He tossed up his room key, caught it, winked at her, and said, "Pick you up at your place." Then he was gone, closing the door behind him.

CHAPTER

Eleven

ALLISON COULDN'T SLEEP. If the exhilaration of the day's workshops hadn't kept her awake, the butterflies in her stomach would have. She turned on the television and tried a cable station, but a horror movie was playing—hardly uplifting or relaxing. She flicked the TV off, flounced onto the bed, crossed her hands behind her head, and lay there like a ramrod.

Was he actually asleep over there while she lay here so keyed up over . . . over *everything* that it felt like she'd put a dime in the vibrator bed when she hadn't? How could he! The unsettled situation between them was as effective as any bottled stimulant on the druggist's shelves and getting more potent as the time for their "date" neared.

How should she act? As if she'd never shared a night of intimacy with Rick Lang that ended in near disaster? As if she had invited him to Madison, Wisconsin, solely to pose for her? As if she wasn't dying inside as each passing hour made her doubt she had the wherewithal to attract him as she once had?

By five o'clock her nerves were strung out like taut twine, and she ran a tub full of water—something she never did at home, it seemed sinful.

Sinking into bubbles up to her neck, she eased back, closing her eyes, willing herself to relax, be natural, just be her old full-of-piss-and-vinegar self. That was the girl he'd liked once. Crack a joke. Wear a smile. Banter. Tease.

But she felt like doing none of these. She felt like telling Rick Lang she loved him more than any man on the face of the earth, and if he didn't do something about it soon, she'd be a basket case.

She emerged from the bath wrinkled like a prune, having discovered that she had actually managed to fall asleep when she hadn't meant to. It was twenty minutes to six!

Forsaking shampoo, she settled for a quick recurling job with the hot iron, her usual light makeup, slightly heavier on the mascara for evening wear and a deeper shade of lipstick, almost umber, which shone like quicksilver when she checked her reflection in the mirror.

Cologne! She checked her watch—four minutes left. Rummaging through her bag, she came up with her favorite perfume and spared no immodesty, lavishing it on every intimate part of her body.

A knock on the door!

Oh Lord! He was two minutes early and she didn't have her dress on yet!

She flew to the coat rack, tore the yellow two-piece suit off the hanger, and clambered into the skirt, snatching a white eyelet blouse, trying to button up both at once.

He knocked again and called through the door, "Allison, are you awake?"

Her fingers seemed to be made of Silly Putty as she buttoned the minuscule pearl buttons of the blouse, which were round and insisted on slipping out of the holes nearly as fast as they went in.

"Allison?"

She yanked open the door, stopping his knuckles in midair as he raised them to rap again. For the second time that day his appearance brought her to a dead halt. This time he was dressed in an extremely formal vested suit of cocoa brown with an off-white shirt and Windsor-knotted tie in complementary stripes. The sight of Rick Lang in such clothing took Allison's breath away.

Her cheeks were as pink as crabapple blossoms, her hair lying in soft feathery ruff about her shoulders. His eyes traveled downward. Her hands were behind her back, closing the button on her skirt, and the strain at the front of the blouse made the top button pop open. His eyes moved lower to her feet, in nylons but no shoes. He cocked an eyebrow.

"Everything went wrong . . . I'm sorry," she wailed.

Dark, smiling eyes moved back to hers. "There's not a thing wrong with what I can see."

"I tried to sleep, but I couldn't. So I decided to take a bath, then fell asleep in the tub, of all things. And when I woke up it was nearly twenty to six already!" She turned away to rummage through her suitcase, coming up with high spike heels, all black patent-leather straps. He watched, fascinated, as she leaned to brace a hand on the bed, her back to him while she slipped the sling-back pumps on one shapely heel, then the other. It was the first time he'd ever seen her in a skirt. Her legs were thin but curved, and from behind, in the flattering shoes, they totally captivated Rick's eyes, which traveled up their shapely length to the enticing curve of her derrière as she leaned over, working on the second shoe.

He saw her check her bodice, then rebutton the top button of her blouse, her back still toward him. Leaning over her suitcase, she took out something from a tiny white box, raised her elbows, and fastened it about her neck. The scent she'd put on was everywhere in the room, and as she lifted her graceful elbows, it filled his nostrils, mesmerizing him, just as he was mesmerized by the sight of her adding these last feminine touches.

She turned. A tiny gold heart hung from a delicate chain in the hollow of her throat. The vanity mirror was just beside the door where Rick stood. She moved toward it while his eyes followed. Her bewildering, powdery scent became headier as she neared him, leaned over the vanity toward the mirror, and put tiny gold hoop earrings into her pierced ears. His eyes traveled down to where she bent at the hip. When he looked up he found Allison watching him while she put the back on the second earring. Once more the top button of her blouse had come undone. He followed her fingers in the mirror as they closed it yet again.

From the coat rack she took a yellow long-sleeved jacket that matched her skirt. He crossed the short expanse to her side, and when she turned, Allison found him at her shoulder.

"I'll trade you," he said, producing from behind his back a

single long-stemmed red rose that suddenly seemed to be reflected in her cheeks as her startled eyes caressed it.

It occurred to Allison that while she was deriding him for calmly napping, he'd been out buying the flower. Wordlessly she took it, relinquishing the jacket to his waiting hands, closing her eyes, and breathing deeply of the flower's fragrance while her back was turned, and he assisted her into the jacket.

When she faced him again, she held the stem of the rose in both hands, looking down at it, then up into his eyes. "Rick, I don't deserve this." Tears suddenly burned her eyes. "Oh God, Rick, I'm so sorry."

His face was somber. He did not touch her. "I'm sorry, too."

"You have nothing to apologize for. I . . . I hurt you so badly. I was so unfair . . . I know that now."

"Allison, you weren't ready. You tried to tell me that, but I wouldn't listen."

"No, Rick, I was such a damn fool. But I had some growing up to do, some sorting out. I was mixed up and angry and unsure."

"And how are you now?"

She didn't know what to say, was afraid to admit how totally committed she'd become to making up everything to him, to letting their relationship thrive. If only he'd touch her, give her some clue to his feelings.

"I'm . . . I'm sorted out, and no longer angry, and sure." Touch me, hold me, tell me I'm forgiven, her heart cried.

But his touch was only a brief pat on her elbow. "Let's talk about it after dinner." He took her elbow and guided her out the door, down the hall and into the brisk May evening.

He drove to a restaurant called the Speakeasy where the waiters wore striped shirts and arm bands and parted their hair down the middle. But neither Allison nor Rick really noticed.

The menus were the size of billboards. Still Rick managed to study her over his. She looked up. The candle put lights into his eyes, color in his cheeks, and shadows about his lips, which still did not smile. Studying his somber face, Allison wondered again what he would say if she simply told him the truth that ached to be spoken.

I love you, Rick Lang. I want you in my bed. I want you in my life.

The waiter approached, tugging her back to earth.

While they waited for swordfish and well-done filet mignon, the wine steward brought wine, flamboyantly exercising his skill in removing cork, testing the bouquet, pouring, and offering a sample for Rick's approval.

Rick tasted, nodded. The steward filled two glasses and faded away.

"How did I do? Was I convincing?" Rick asked.

"Very." She brightened falsely. "I'd have sworn you were a connoisseur of . . ." She checked the label on the bottle, but could not pronounce it.

"Moonshine '82," Rick filled in, and they laughed at their ignorance. But the gay mood was forced.

"And I've never known anyone who ate filet well-done. Did you see the scowl the waiter gave you?"

She shrugged. "I feel rare enough tonight without rare steak, too."

He leaned forward, bracing tailored sleeves on the edge of the table, blue eyes moving over hers. "Do you? Do you really?"

"Yes, I do . . . really."

He lifted his glass in a toast. "Then here's to a rare night."

They drank, less of the wine than of each other across the tops of their glasses. Resting his footed goblet upon the linen cloth, Rick made small circles with it, studying it momentarily before his hand fell still and he watched her face as flickering candlelight changed its dancing shadows. Silently he reached, laid his hand, palm up, on the tabletop.

Her eyes flickered to it, then back to his, cautiously.

"Allison, if I don't touch you soon, I'm going to go crazy," he said quietly, only the hand reaching, the rest of him leaning back with casual grace, ankle crossed over knee as if he'd only said, "Allison, the temperature outside is seventy-two degrees," while every atom in her body went into motion until she felt explosive.

"Oh God, me too." She slid her palm over his and he slowly closed his fingers until they were squeezing hers so tightly she thought her bones would break. He began moving his thumb, brushing it lightly across the backs of her knuckles as she sat stricken speechless, overwhelmed by the sensations that just his thumb could create within her body. She stared at their joined hands, wondering if he could feel the throbbing of her heart in her fingertips as she could.

"Do you dance?" he inquired quietly.

"Not very well."

"Me either, but I will if you will."

As they got to their feet the waiter brought Caesar salad. They turned toward the stamp-sized dance floor instead, where a man with an amiable smile played *Misty* on the piano.

Allison turned into Rick's arms, the two of them the only ones on the floor, neither even aware of it as his arm circled her waist and she moved near, resting her temple lightly against his jaw, her palm on his shoulder. Their movements were more of a gentle, unconscious sway than a dance, for they had not come here to dance, but to touch.

His after shave was faint, spicy, the shoulder of his suit coat firm and cool. The piano player began singing softly in a soulful voice, "Look at me, I'm as helpless as a kitten up a tree . . ." He smiled as he watched the handsome blond man wrap both arms around the tall, striking woman, and hers move up to circle his neck.

Rick rested his joined hands lightly on the hollow of Allison's spine, while his head dropped down and hers lifted. The words of the haunting old Erroll Garner song drifted about Allison, and she did feel helpless, clinging to a cloud, misty. Her hips rested lightly against Rick's, and the touch of his hands on the hollow of her spine sent shivers coursing upward. They moved in indolent swaying steps that took them nowhere but heaven as their thighs brushed and he leaned his forehead down to rest it on hers.

"I love you, Allison Scott, you know that, don't you?" he whispered.

She pulled back only far enough to see his face, while the beginning words of the song reverberated through her body, ringing now with triumph—*Look at me! Look at me! Look at me! Rick Lang just said he loves me!*

Her voice trembled and her eyes sparkled as she admitted,

"Yes . . . I know." She lay her fingertips on the back of his neck, above his collar—she suddenly had to touch his bare skin. "I love you, too, Rick Lang, you know that, don't you?"

"I've had my suspicions, but you put me through hell making me believe it."

"But you do?"

"I want to."

"Then do, because it's true."

He reached behind his neck to capture her right hand and reverted to the traditional waltz position. Her temple was again beside his ear. "Will you do something for me?" he asked.

"Anything."

"Maybe you shouldn't be so quick to answer 'anything.' This may be tough."

"Anything."

Again he stepped back and looked into her eyes. "Tell me about Jason."

Her steps faltered, a brief glint of uncertainty flickered in her eyes, but just then the music ended. He took her elbow and led her away from the floor. She watched the tips of her toes as they made their way back to the table. As Rick pulled her chair out, she felt a momentary sense of panic, then he was across from her, reaching for her hand again.

"Allison, you've just told me you love me. Will you trust me enough to tell me about Jason—everything, so his ghost will be exorcised? And this time without anger. If you can talk about him without anger, I'll know you're free of him at last, and ready for what you and I . . . well, just ready."

Wide brown eyes flickered to Rick's, then to the flame of the candle.

"Tell me . . . all of it."

She began softly. "He was my favorite, wonderful, sensational model. But first and foremost, he was a hedonist, only I never realized it until he'd left me." Tears glimmered in her eyes. She swallowed, pulling her hand from Rick's to hide her face. "Oh God," she said to the tabletop, "I don't know how to tell it. I was such a fool."

"Give me your hand," he ordered gently, "and don't look away from me."

She drew a deep, shuddering sigh as she began again, her hand in Rick's. She told him everything, how she'd begun by taking Jason's photo, then accepted the idea of his moving in; how she'd paid all the bills; how he'd used his body to get her to close her eyes to his shortcomings and character faults; how they'd collected the portfolio of photos; how he'd stolen them; even about his signature on the easel picture. She laughed sadly, softly, looking up into Rick's eyes. "And you know what?" Strangely, it hurt hardly at all to admit, "It was the only time he ever mentioned the word love."

Allison glanced at the wine bottle. "Could I have a little more of that?"

Rick released her hand. "No. You don't need it. Eat your salad while you finish. It'll take away the hollow feeling until I can."

Again she met his eyes, which did not smile or make light of his words. Neither did they denigrate her for the past she'd just revealed so blatantly. She sighed deeply and ate her salad.

The night was damp and cool, but scented with golden mock orange and lilac in full bloom. They walked with measured steps, Allison matching hers to Rick's as they crossed the parking lot to the door of the motel. She was tucked securely against his hip, wishing he'd walk faster. But he sauntered with torturous slowness, lugging the heavy glass door open without relinquishing his hold on her, laughing with Allison as they struggled inside, two abreast, bruising their hips.

They took the stairs in unison, eagerness growing with each step. Halfway up he stopped.

"I can't wait any longer." His arm swept around her and forced her back against the handrail as he gave her a taste of what lay in store. The sweet intoxication of his lips made her head spin.

"You keep that up and I'll be lying bruised and broken at the bottom of these steps, Mr. Lang. Don't you know better than to make a lady dizzy halfway up a flight of stairs?"

"I beg your pardon, Miss Scott. Common sense seems to have fled."

She pulled his head down to hers and mumbled against his mouth, "Oh, goody."

In the hallway between their two doors he asked simply, "My room or yours?"

"Tell me, Mr. Lang," she asked piquantly, arms looped about his neck, head tilted to one side, "do you like the sun in the morning?"

"I love the sun in the morning."

"Then mine."

She produced her key, handed it to him, and when the door swung wide open they stood for a moment studying each other, the smiles gone from their faces.

"I feel it only fair to warn you," he said, "that I've never before told a woman I love her before I made love to her."

"And how about after?"

"No, Allison, not even after."

"Supposing you don't after . . . well, after this one." Her eyes skittered down to her nervous fingers, than back up to his. "Just forget what I said one time about forsaking all others, okay? I'm . . . heck, I'm fifty years behind the times."

"Allison, I—"

"Shh." She covered his lips with her fingertips. "Just kiss me, Rick, hold me, and let's start starting over."

His palms molded her face, lifting it to receive his kiss, which spoke of an ardency that drove all memory of the past from her mind. With their lips still joined, they moved inside her room. He caught the door with his heel, and when it slammed they fell against it, lost in each other's arms.

"Allison, I'll never hurt you, never knowingly," he promised in a gruff voice. "That other time when I thought I had . . ." He swallowed, pinning her tightly against the length of his body, clasping her head against his chest. "Please, darling, just be honest with me, always."

"I promise," she vowed as she kissed the side of his neck, then pressed her forehead against it, feeling the thrum of his heart there momentarily before backing out of his embrace and looking into his eyes while she slowly, methodically began removing her clothes.

As her jacket came off, his hands were still. As she

reached for the button at the back of her skirt, he slowly, slowly began tugging the knot from his tie. They watched each other remove article by article until she stood before him in half-slip, panties and bra. Then he ordered, "Stop . . . let me."

Her hands fell still as he reached for the clasp of her bra. He was barefooted, only trousers and shirt still on, the latter pulled out of his waistband, hanging open to reveal the bare skin of his chest underneath.

Her suitcase lay open on the bed. In one motion he closed it and swept it to the floor, then flipped the covers down over the foot of the mattress.

He tugged her to the bed, urging her down until they lay facing each other, his hand on the bare band of skin above her slip. As his face moved over hers, blocking out the light from the bedside lamp, her eyes closed. Soft, seeking kisses urged her trembling lips to open. Warm, gentle palms encouraged her back to relax. Hard, golden arms prompted her hips to move closer. And when they had, the rapture began. He mastered her hesitation by again moving with a slow hand, at first only the heel of it slipping to the side of her breast, brushing against the silky fabric that covered it, pressing, caressing, yet at a lazy pace that lulled and suggested and made her want more. He explored her back with a widespread hand, sliding down over the shallows of her spine, making the silken fabric of the half-slip seduce her skin before easing his fingers inside its elastic to let his flesh take its place. And so he pressed her womanly core hard against his swollen body, moving rhythmically against her until her hands began moving up and down his shirt, then inside, against the warm skin of his back.

"Oh, how I missed you, missed you," Allison whispered greedily.

"I missed you, too, every day, every minute."

His tongue danced desirously upon hers, and she slipped her hands over his arms, until he shrugged out of the shirt, and it lay forgotten beneath him. He cupped her breast fully, pushing it upward to forcibly change its shape as he lowered his head and ran his tongue just above the transparent lily-shaped lace that edged her bra, revealing the dark, dusky nipple behind it. She dropped back, soft sounds coming from her throat, her eyes drifting closed as he leaned across her body and continued kissing only the tops of her breasts. There was a sweet yearning pain in her tightly gathered nipples that only his mouth could calm.

She arched off the mattress in invitation, and his hands slipped behind to release the clasp of the bra. She opened her eyes to watch his blond head dip once again to her naked skin and shuddered when his wet tongue touched, tempted.

Her hands blindly sought his body, skimming from chest to hard belly, then lower, caressing, cupping, inciting his breath to beat rapidly against her skin.

She pushed him up and away, the better to reach, and he fell back, tense, waiting, his eyes closed and nostrils flaring while she sat beside him, leaning back on one palm as she watched her hand play over him. His chest rose and fell with a driving beat while he lay, wrists up, drifting in pleasure. She released the hidden hook on the waistband of his trousers, then unzipped them, feeling his hand brushing softly against her back, though he lay as before, eyes closed, only that hand in motion.

There was nothing to equal the sense of celebration she knew as she undressed him fully, brushing his clothing away until he lay naked, golden brown, flat bellied, aroused, silent, waiting. She touched him, and he jerked once as if a jolt of electricity had sizzled through him, lifting his back momentarily off the bed. Then he lay as before, his fingertips lightly grazing her back while she stroked his bare leg, from inner thigh to sharp-boned knee that bent over the edge of the mattress.

"I love you so much," she uttered. And without compunction she captured his heat in her hand, leaned over, and kissed it briefly. "You're so beautiful."

"Allison, darling, come here." He tugged at her elbow, and she fell back beside him. "It's inside that I want to be beautiful for you. It's an accident if what you see is beautiful. But for you I want to have a beautiful soul . . . like yours is to me." His eyes were eloquent as he spoke into hers.

"Rick, I love you . . . I love you . . . body, soul, inside, outside. How could I ever have thought you were like him?" She clung to his neck, kissing his jaw, cheek, the corner of his mouth, then opened her lips beneath his to let him delve into the wet silk of her mouth.

His body was quivering as he pulled away. "Hey, where did you learn what you did a minute ago?"

"I told you, Jason was a hedonist. He had no compunctions about making his wishes known. He reveled in it."

"And that's why the song triggered your panic that night we were making love?"

"Yes."

He kissed the hollow just beneath her lower lip, speaking against her skin, his words rough-edged with passion. "I only take as good as I give, Allison, and with me it's ladies first, okay?"

Her answer was one of silent language, spoken with lithe limb and straining muscle, with wet tongue and willing skin. He shimmered the remaining garments down her legs, leaving her clothed in nothing but a tiny gold heart in the hollow of her throat. From there his lips began their downward journey. They traveled her body at will, tasting desire in its every quiver and shiver. He kissed her stomach, the soft valleys beside hip, behind knees, her ankles, thighs, lost in the fragrance he'd once watched her apply to secret, hidden places.

"I love you, Allison . . . beautiful Allison," he murmured and lifted himself above her, poised on the brink of a beauty surpassing the visual. And a moment later their bodies became one.

During the minutes that followed, stroking her to climax, he gave her the sense of self each being must have before giving that self to another, unfettered. It had been taken from her by another, in an eon far removed from now, but was returned in all its glory by this man Allison Scott had finally come to trust.

When they lay exhausted, damp and disheveled in a faultless disarray, limbs languid and lifeless, apart from each other yet knowing they would never truly be apart, he ran a bare sole along her calf. "Now who turns you on more, me or my Hasselblad?"

Her voice came lazily from two feet away. "Right now, my

darling Richard, ain't no way you could turn me on. I done been turned till I can't turn no more."

A replete chuckle came from his side of the bed, then a lethargic hand flopped down wherever it happened to flop. It landed on her ribs, felt around, discovered its whereabouts and rectified the mistake.

"Oh yeah? Want me to prove differently?"

She swatted the hand away, but it returned promptly, along with another to gather her against his long, naked body before he yanked the blankets up to cover them.

"I was shivering, that's why they were puckered up."

"Oh, and here all this time I thought it was the mention of my Hasselblad that did it."

"Oh, that too."

"Anything else?"

They were snuggled so close a bedbug couldn't have crawled between them.

"Nothing comes to mind."

"Nothing?"

She reached beneath the covers while she teased, "Not one eentsy-weentsy little thing."

He yanked her hand up and pinned both wrists over her head, laying across her chest. "That, you little snot, was a low blow. Just for that I may not suggest what I was just on the verge of suggesting when your sharp little tongue did you out of something you'd sell your soul for."

She struggled to lift her head to rain kisses of apology and giggling persuasion on his chin, nose, and mouth, but he backed far enough away that she couldn't reach.

"I take it back," she promised. "Especially since I know it's only temporary."

"Hey, lady, you want my Hasselblad for life, or don't you?"

"Do you come along with it?"

The pressure on her wrists disappeared. His lips swept down toward hers, a suggestive glint in his eyes as he answered, "You're damn right."

"For life?" she inquired. "For honest-to-goodness life?"

"For life."

"Forsaking all others?"

"Forsaking all others."

And ten minutes later she sold her soul for the second time that night.

A PROMISE
TO CHERISH

With
gratitude
to my friends in
Independence and Kansas City—
Bea, who gave me the map
Barbra, who showed me the old orchard
and
Vivien Lee, who took me to the "C C"

CHAPTER

One

As THE FIRST suitcase came clunking down the luggage return of Stapleton International Airport in Denver, Lee Walker checked her watch impatiently, drummed four coral fingernails against her shoulder bag, and studied the conveyor belt with a frown. It moved like a sedated snail! She glanced at her watch a second time—only one hour and ten minutes before the bid letting! If the damn suitcase didn't roll out soon, she'd end up at City Hall in these faded blue jeans!

Lee glowered at the flapping porthole until at last her suitcase came through. She sighed deeply and strained to reach it.

She plucked it off the conveyor belt and flew—a tall, dark-skinned flash of loose black hair and aqua feathers, the worn patches on the backside of her tight jeans attracting the eyes of several men she adroitly sidestepped. The feathers in her hair lifted with each long-legged slap of her moccasins on the terminal floor until she came at last, panting and winded by the thin Denver air, to the Economy Rent-A-Car booth.

Twenty minutes later the same suitcase hit the bed in Room 110 of the Cherry Creek Motel. Lee reached to yank the shirttails free of her jeans at the same time that she released the catch on the suitcase and flipped it open. Her hand halted. Her jaw dropped open.

"Oh my God," she whispered. Lifeless fingers forgot about buttons. Stricken eyes stared at the strange contents of the suitcase while one hand covered her lips, the other clasped her

suddenly queasy stomach. "Oh sh . . ." Her eyes took it in, but
her mind balked. "No . . . it can't be!" But she was staring not
at the mustard-colored envelope containing the bid for a sewage treatment plant she'd worked on for the last two weeks.
Instead, a half-naked blonde tootsie lifted a pair of enormous
breasts and smiled a come-hither message from the cover of
a . . . a *Thrust* magazine.

For a moment Lee was struck motionless with disbelief.
Thrust? She stood hunched over, horrified, her thoughts
whirling. Then frantically she scrambled through the suitcase,
throwing out item after item—a gray sweat suit, two pair of
dress trousers, a man's shaving kit, two neatly folded shirts,
royal blue jockey shorts—*royal blue?*—black socks, Rawhide deodorant, a pair of well-worn jogging shoes with filthy
laces, a hair blower, and a brush with very dark brown hair
caught in its white bristles.

She ran a thumb over them, then dropped it distastefully
and quit scrambling through the contents to grab the identification tag dangling from the suitcase handle.

> Sam Brown
> 8990 Ward Parkway
> Kansas City, Missouri 64110

With a groan Lee sank to the bed, leaned forward, and
clutched her forehead in both hands. *Oh, damn my hide, I've
really done it now. Old Thorpe will gloat over this for months!*
At the thought of Thorpe and his small, racist mind, panic
swept Lee, tightening the skin across her temples, making the
blood sing and swirl crazily as she burst to her feet. She
checked her watch. Frantic thoughts tumbled about in her
head, leaving her to stand in indecision, glancing from phone
to suitcase to the car keys on the bed.

Countless dire possibilities insinuated themselves into
Lee's thoughts while she wondered who to call first. Could
she possibly retrieve her own suitcase and make it to the bid
letting before two o'clock?

She wasted five minutes telephoning the airline's passenger
information, who told her to call lost and found, who
informed her they'd get back to her in half an hour. Frustrated

and angry at both herself and the airline, which hadn't had an attendant checking baggage-claim stubs, Lee finally returned to the airport. When a search of the baggage department proved futile, there seemed little to do except call the home office in Kansas City and admit her blunder.

Lee's stomach churned as she dialed. She pictured the fat belly and seedy little eyes of Floyd Thorpe, the company president and owner, who never lost an opportunity to remind Lee exactly why he'd hired her. Oh, he'd been waiting for this. Like the self-righteous bigot he was, how he'd been waiting. She knew full well Thorpe gritted his teeth every time they passed each other in the office. He probably visited his psychotherapist every payday after signing her check.

Well, you wanted to compete in a man's world and earn a man's salary, and you are!

But never in her three years in the construction industry had Lee earned it so dearly.

Floyd Thorpe's voice fairly shook with rage. He let out a blue streak of cuss words, ending with an order for Lee to "get your liberated female ass to that bid letting and find out who the hell was low bidder, and when you have, get on the next plane home because I'm not—by God—paying for any goddam *woman* to stay in a Colorado motel and eat on my company expense account when she doesn't know her ass from a catch basin, and any government bureaucrat who think it's easy to find *minority* employees who are worth diddly can shove his Minority Business Enterprise Goals—"

That's where Lee hung up.

Sexist, bigoted bastard! she raged silently, feeling again the ineffable futility of trying to change the jaundiced views of men like Floyd A. Thorpe.

Lee had no delusions about why she'd been hired. Not only was she a woman, she was also one-quarter American Indian, and either fact qualified her employer as a minority contractor in the eyes of the federal government as long as she was a corporation officer or owner. Furthermore, the federal government had proclaimed that ten percent of all federal monies allocated for public improvements were to be paid to minority contractors.

Considering the marked advantage of those contractors in

today's business world, Floyd A. Thorpe would have given the diamonds out of the opera windows of his Diamond Jubilee Lincoln Continental Mark V to be an Indian woman himself—if he could possibly manage it without being red and female! But Floyd Thorpe was not only male, he was also as Caucasian as the president himself, and he never let Lee forget it. Whenever she was around, he spit juice from the ever-present poke of tobacco that bulged his cheek. He hoisted up his pot belly with strutting tugs on his overstrained belt. He told dirty jokes and talked like the sewer rat he was. It got worse and worse as Lee continued to refuse his invitations to become a vice-president of Thorpe Construction. And if Lee Walker didn't like it, Thorpe's overbearing attitude clearly stated, she could go home and chew hides, plant maize, and raise a few papooses.

As Lee now spun from the telephone and crossed the airport terminal, she too gritted her teeth. Yes, she wanted equal pay, so once again she had to lick his boots and go out there and earn it!

She arrived at the bid letting five minutes late. As usual, she was the only woman in the room. Up front the city engineer was opening a sealed envelope as Lee slipped into a folding chair at the back of the room. From her purse she took a tablet and pen, then glanced surreptitiously at the lap of the man next to her as he entered the amount of the bid being read.

She wrote it quickly on her own paper, then leaned over to ask, "How many have been opened?"

He counted with the tip of a mechanical pencil. "Only six so far."

"Do you mind if I copy them?"

"Not at all."

He angled the pad her way, and Lee took down the six names and amounts. Glancing around the room, she found an unusually large number of contractors represented. The nation's slumping economy, coupled with relatively little new-home construction, had contractors traveling farther and bidding tougher in order to get work.

The Denver suburb of Aurora had attracted much attention, for it was one of the fastest growing mid-size cities in the nation. Aurora had solved its most serious problem—a shortage of water—by obtaining its own water supply and bringing it down from Leadville, a hundred miles away. But that water needed filtering and chemical treatment before use, adequate sewage treatment and removal after use. Every contractor in the room understood the value of getting in on the ground floor of the city's growth. To win this bid would be like plucking the first ripe plum in a highly productive orchard.

Suddenly Lee's back stiffened as the voice of the city engineer rang across the room, reading the name on the front of the next envelope.

"Thorpe Construction Company of Kansas City."

Lee stiffened and her heart did a double-whammy. There must be some mistake! She searched the room for anyone else from Thorpe, but she was the only one present. How could the envelope have gotten there? She scarcely had time to wonder before a brass letter opener sliced through the thick envelope with a raspy sound of authority, and while Lee still floundered in stunned surprise, her bid was read aloud:

"Four million two hundred forty-nine thousand."

Her heart thudded like a bass drum and she pressed a palm against it. *My God! I'm the low bidder so far!* Across the room faces fell as those who'd been beaten out sighed with disappointment.

Lee knew nothing to equal the exhilaration of moments like this. The sweet taste of revenge was already making her mouth water as she thought of returning to Kansas City and flinging the news in the beady little mustard seed eyes of one Floyd A. Thorpe, alias F.A.T., as Lee often thought of him.

Another bid was read: four million six. Hers was still low!

It took every effort to sit calmly in her chair and wait. How often she'd sat in sessions like this and known this giddy elation until someone else bested her at the last moment. There could be only one winner, and the larger the number of submissions, the greater the glory; the larger the job, the greater the possible profits. And this one was big . . .

Lee chewed her lower lip, trying to contain her growing

excitement as three more bids were opened and read, none of them lower than hers.

Finally the city engineer grinned and announced the last bid. "Brown and Brown, Inc., Kansas City, Missouri," he said as he lifted the bulky envelope and slit it. The room was as silent as outer space. Even before he read the amount aloud, the city engineer's smile broadened, and Lee experienced a premonition of doom.

"Four million two hundred forty-five thousand!"

The blood seemed to drop to Lee's feet. She wilted against the back of her chair and strove not to let her disappointment show. She swallowed, closed her eyes momentarily, and breathed deeply while the scuffle of shoes and the metallic clank of chairs filled the room. Her body felt like lead, but she forced herself to her feet. To lose was tough. To be second was harder. But to be second by only four thousand dollars on a job worth over four million was agony.

Four thousand dollars—Lee restrained an ironic grunt. It might as well have been four cents!

Could there by anything harder than congratulating the winner at a time like this? The man beside Lee moved toward the cluster of people who'd converged, Lee presumed, around the winning estimator. She caught a glimpse of a dark head, wide shoulders . . . and immediately squared her own.

Protocol, she thought dismally, wishing she could forgo congratulations.

The man was accepting them with obvious relish. His wide smile was turned upon a competitor who railed good-naturedly, "You did it again, Sam, damn ya! Why don't you leave some for the rest of us?"

The smile became a laugh as his darkly tanned hand pumped the much lighter colored one. "Next time, Marv, okay? My luck can't hold forever." Others shook his hand, and exchanged brief business comments while Lee waited her chance to approach him. His wide hand was enclosed around another when his eyes swung to find her in front of him. Those eyes were deep brown in a tan face. Pale crinkles at the corners of his eyes suggested he had squinted many hours into the sun. His nose was narrow, Nordic; the lips widely smiling, pleased at the moment. His neck was thick and his posture

more erect than any other man's in the room. Lee had a brief
glimpse of a silver and turquoise cross resting in the cleft of
his open collar as his shoulders swung her way. His palm slid
free of the man still addressing him, as if the brown-eyed
winner had forgotten him in the middle of a sentence.

"Congratulations . . . Sam, is it?" Lee extended her hand.
His grip was like that of a front-end loader.

"That's right. Sam Brown. And thank you. This one was
too close for comfort."

Lee's lips parted and her eyes widened. *Sam Brown?* The
coincidence was too great to be believed! *Sam Brown?* The
same Sam Brown who read girlie magazines? He certainly
didn't look like the type who'd need to.

Lee quelled the inane urge to ask him if he used Rawhide
deodorant and instead lifted her eyes to his hair for verifica-
tion—it was indeed dark brown, straight, and appeared to be
blow-combed into the stylish, unparted sweep that touched
both ear and forehead and the very tip of his collar. In a
crazy-clear recollection, royal blue jockey shorts flashed
across Lee's mind, and she felt a flush begin to creep up from
her navel.

"You don't have to tell me it was too close for comfort,"
Lee replied. "I'm the one who just came in second." Sam
Brown's palm was hard and warm and captured hers too long.
"I'm Lee Walker, Thorpe Construction."

His black brows lifted in surprise, and she freed her hand at
last.

"Lee Walker?"

"Yes."

"Of Kansas City?"

"Yes."

The beginning of a grin appeared on his wide lips, and his
dark eyes drifted down over her wrinkled plaid shirt, faded
jeans, and scuffed moccasins. On their way back up, they
took on a distinct glint of humor.

"I think I have something of yours," he said, leaning a little
closer, his voice low and confidential.

Across her mind's eye paraded a file of personal items
from her suitcase—bras, pants, tampons, her daily journal.
His insinuating perusal made her uncomfortably aware that

she was dressed like a teenage runaway while attending a business function requiring professionalism in both comportment and dress. At the same time he—though missing his suitcase, too—was dressed in shiny brown loafers, neat cocoa brown trousers, an open throated peach-colored shirt, and a summer-weight oatmeal-colored sport coat.

The difference made Lee feel at a distinct disadvantage. She felt the heat reach her face and with it a wave of suspicion and anger. Yes he certainly *did* have something of hers—a job worth over four million dollars! But this was no place to accuse him. Other people stood within earshot, thus she was forced to reply with only half the rancor she felt.

"Then it *was* you who turned in my bid."

"It was."

"And I suppose you think I should thank you for it?"

His smile only deepened the indentations on either side of his lips. "Didn't anyone ever tell you always to carry anything of immediate importance on the plane with you?"

Stung by the fact that he was undeniably right, she could only glare and splutter, "Perhaps you should consider teaching a workshop on the *dos* and *don'ts* of preparing bids for a public bid letting. I'm sure the class could learn innumerable new techniques from you."

He had the grace to back off and decrease the wattage of his grin.

"How dare you turn in someone else's bid!" she challenged.

"Under the circumstances, I felt it the only honorable thing to do."

"Honorable!" she nearly yelped, then forcibly lowered her voice. "You honorably looked it over first, though, didn't you!"

His half grin changed to a scowl. *"You're* the one who got the wrong suitcase. I picked—"

"I don't care to discuss it here, if you don't mind," she hissed in a stage whisper, glancing in a semicircle to find too many curious ears nearby. "But I *do* want to discuss it!" Her eyes blazed, but she forced restraint into her tones, though she wanted to let him have it with both barrels. "Where is it?"

Contrarily he slipped a lazy hand into his trouser pocket

and slung his weight on one hip. "Where is what?"

"My suitcase," she ground out with deliberate diction as if explaining to a dimwit.

"Oh, that." He looked away disinterestedly. "It's in my car."

She waited with long-suffering patience but he refrained from offering to get it for her.

"Shall we trade?" she suggested with saccharine sweetness.

"Trade?" Again his dark gaze turned to her.

"I believe I have something of yours, too."

Now she had his full attention. He leaned closer. "You have *my* suitcase?"

"Not exactly, but I know where it is."

"Where?"

"I returned it to the airport."

His brows curled, and he checked his watch hurriedly. But at that moment an enormous red-faced man clapped a big paw on Sam Brown's shoulder and turned him around. "Sam, if we're going to talk about that subcontract, we'd better get going. I have"—he, too, bared a wrist to check the time—"at the outside, an hour and a half."

Brown nodded. "I'll be right with you, John. Give me a minute." He turned hastily back to Lee. "I'm sorry I have to run. Where are you staying? I'll bring your suitcase no later than six o'clock." He was already easing toward the door.

"Hey, wait a minute, I—"

"Sorry, but I have a previous commitment. What motel?" John was in the doorway, waiting impatiently.

"I have to catch a plane! Don't you dare leave!"

Sam Brown had reached the door. "What motel?" he insisted.

"Damn!" she muttered as her hands gripped her hips, and she all but stamped a foot in frustration. "Cherry Creek Motel, but I can't wait—"

"Cherry Creek Motel," he repeated, and raised an index finger. "I'll deliver it." Then he was gone.

For the next three hours Lee sat like a caged rabbit in Room 110 of the Cherry Creek Motel while her irritation grew with each passing minute. By six o'clock she felt like a time bomb. She was hot and dirty. Denver in July was like an inferno, and Lee wanted nothing so much as a cool, refreshing bath. But she couldn't take one without her suitcase. Old Thorpe was going to be hotter than a cannibal's stewpot when he found out she hadn't returned to Kansas City as ordered. A check on late-leaving flights confirmed that Lee had already missed the suppertime flight, and the next one didn't leave till 10:10 P.M. She was damned if she'd stay up half the night just to get into the office bright and early for Thorpe's self-righteous tirade. After all, it wasn't her fault. And she'd had a harrowing day and still had a bone to pick with the "honorable" Sam Brown.

Every time she thought of him, her temperature rose a notch. To leave her high and dry and sashay off without returning her property was bad enough, but worse was the dirty, underhanded trick he'd pulled with her bid. She couldn't wait to tear into him and tell him exactly what a sneaky, low, lying dog he was!

At 6:15 she stormed to the TV and slammed a palm against the off button. She didn't give two hoots what tomorrow's weather would be like in Denver. All she wanted was to get out of this miserable city!

When a knock finally sounded, Lee's head snapped up and she stopped pacing momentarily, then stormed across and flung the door open.

Sam Brown stood on the sidewalk with two identical suitcases in his hands.

"You're late!" she snapped, glaring up at him with black, angry eyes.

"Sorry I had to run off like that. I got here as soon as I could."

"Well, it's not soon enough. I've already missed my flight, and my boss is going to be livid!"

"I said I was sorry, but you're the one who caused all this by grabbing the wrong luggage at the airport."

"Me! How about you! How dare you run off with my suitcase!"

"As I said before, you ran off with mine."

She gritted her teeth, knowing a frustration so overwhelming it turned her vision blazing red. "I'm not talking about at the airport. I'm talking about after the bid letting. You left me here to sit and stew and not even a brush to brush my hair with or clean clothes so I could take a bath or . . . or . . ." Disgusted, she yanked a suitcase from his hand and flung it onto the bed. Again she spun on him and ordered, "You've got some explaining to do. I'd suggest you begin."

He stepped inside obligingly, closed the door, set the other suitcase down, glanced around, and asked, "May I?" Then, as unruffled as you please, he carefully tugged at the crease in his impeccable pants before easing down in one of the two chairs beside the small round table.

With her hands on her hips, Lee spat out, "No . . . you . . . may . . . not!"

But instead of getting up, he spread his knees, leaned both elbows on them, and let his hands dangle limply between them. "Listen, Miss Walker, it's been a helluva—"

"*Ms*. Walker," she interrupted.

He raised one brow, paused a moment, then repeated patiently, "*Ms*. Walker." He flexed his shoulder muscles, kneaded the back of his neck, and continued, "It's been a long day and I'd like to get out of these clothes."

"You opened my suitcase," she stated unsympathetically, scarcely able to keep her temper under control.

"I what?"

She leaned forward and riveted him with snapping, black eyes. "You opened my suitcase!"

"Why, hell yes, I opened it. I thought it was mine."

"But you did more than just open it! You looked through it!"

"Oh did I, now?"

"Are you denying it?"

"Well, what about you? Are you saying you didn't open mine?"

"Don't change the subject!"

"The subject, I believe, is suitcases, and women who are sore losers."

"Sore losers . . . *sore losers!*" She stepped closer, towering over him. "Why, you lying, cheating . . . crook!" she shouted.

"What the hell are you driving at, *Ms*. Walker?"

"You opened my suitcase, found my unsealed bid, saw that it already had all the necessary signatures, looked it over, and undercut me by a stinking four thousand dollars, then played the benevolent Good Samaritan by turning in my envelope at the bid letting . . ."

In one swift motion Sam Brown came up out of his chair, swung her around, and stabbed two blunt fingers in the middle of her chest. The poke sent her reeling backward till she landed with an undignified bounce on the bed.

"That's a mighty serious allegation, lady!"

"That's a might narrow margin . . . *man!*" she sneered, leaning back on her hands as he stood above her, one of his knees pressing hard against hers. His face wore a thunderous look, made all the more formidable by the swarthiness of his skin and brows. Suddenly, though, he backed off, hands on hips as he cast a deprecating glance along her length.

"Oh, one of those," he intoned knowingly.

She rebounded off the bed, planted a palm on his chest, shoved him back two feet, stepped around him, then faced him squarely.

"Yes, one of those. I'm sick and tired of men who think a woman can't compete in this all-male sewer and water industry of theirs!"

"That's not what I meant when I called you lady, so don't put ulterior meanings on it."

"Oh, isn't it? Then why did you make the distinction? Isn't it because once you realized that suitcase belonged to a woman, you also realized the bid must have been prepared by a woman and you couldn't face getting stung at a public bid letting by losing to her?"

He pointed a long brown finger at her nose and leaned at a dangerous angle from the hip.

"Lady . . ." he began, but cut the word in half and tried again. "Ms. Walker, you're an opinionated, egotistical . . . suffragette! What makes you think nobody else in the world can bid a job better than you?" He began pacing in the small space before the table and chairs. "My God, take a look at the economy, at the number of contractors who are folding every month. Count the number who showed up at that bid letting today. That job will keep crews working for an entire season! Everybody wanted it. The margin was bound to be narrow!"

"Four thousand on four million is too narrow to be accidental, especially from a man who had possession of my suitcase during the earlier part of the day."

A look of pure disgust turned his features to granite. He stood before her, stalk still, jaw clamped tight. Momentarily his expression altered to a heavy-lidded perusal. His lips softened. His eyes traveled slowly down the madras shirt, not quite reaching her hips before starting back up again. His voice fell to a distasteful purr as he backed a step away and mused with strained male tolerance. "From what I saw in your suitcase, it's to be expected you'd be testy at this time of the month, so I'll chalk this up to female taboos and won't take further issue over your ch—"

Crack!!

She smacked him across the side of the mouth with an open palm. It knocked him momentarily off balance, and he teetered back in stunned surprise.

"Why . . . you . . . degenerate," she grated. "I might have expected something like that out of a . . . pervert who carried porno magazines in his suitcase on a business trip!"

Four red stripes in the shape of her fingers appeared to the left of his lips. His fists clenched. The cords along his neck stood at attention. His eyes glowered like chips of resin, and his lips were a thin, tight line.

Fear coursed through Lee at her own temerity. What had she done? She was alone in a motel room with a total stranger who was dishonest enough to cheat her in business, and she'd just knocked him clear into next week. He might very well decide to knock her clear into the one after that!

Her own trembling hand covered her lips, but he only straightened his shoulders, muscle by muscle, his anger held fiercely in check as he relaxed slowly, slowly. Without a word he retrieved his suitcase, opened the door, and paused, his eyes never leaving Lee's face.

"Just *who* looked through *whose* suitcase," he drawled, then added sarcastically, ". . . *lady?*"

He paused long enough to cause a warm flush to darken her cheeks before disappearing from the door, taking a smug grin with him.

In his wake Lee slammed the door so hard the mirror on the wall threatened to come crashing to the floor.

CHAPTER

Two

A MINUTE LATER Lee opened her suitcase only to stare, dismayed at its contents. *Oh no, not again,* she groaned. The distasteful magazine was still inside. It beckoned to Lee's seamier instincts. She began to close the suitcase, but a bit of royal blue peeked from beneath a folded dress shirt, making something forbidden and prurient tingle her insides. She crossed her arms nonchalantly over her waist, covertly glanced at the closed drapes, then slipped an innocent forefinger between the magazine pages, running it up and down thoughtfully several times before finally flipping the magazine open and crossing her arms tightly over her abdomen again.

She stared, mesmerized by the undeniably stunning body stretched backward over a wide boulder on a riverbank. The skin was oiled, shimmering beneath drops of river spray with limbs laid open, hiding nothing. The model's eyes were closed, the expression on her face a combination of lust and fulfillment. The sultry, open lips were parted, the tongue peeking out between perfect teeth. Her long, scarlet nails rested against the dark triangle of femininity.

Lee swallowed, blushed, but turned the page. There followed more of the same. Skin and sin, she thought—exactly what one might expect of a man like Sam Brown. Still, she turned one more page.

The blood surged to her face, to her toes, to the backs of her knees, as she stared at the pornographic film clip from a current movie. Her stomach went weightless. Her chest felt tight, and the short hairs of her arms and thighs stood at attention. The man and woman were intimately entwined, limbs and teeth bared . . .

Sam Brown, you are disgusting! Abruptly she slapped the magazine shut, slammed the suitcase closed, and drew her hand back as if it had been singed, just as a knock sounded at her door.

Her head snapped up. She swallowed and pressed cool palms against hot cheeks before crossing the room and opening the door with much more control than she felt.

It was Sam Brown again. But this time his sport coat was gone and only one button held his shirt together at the waist. The shirttails were matted into a network of wrinkles, and in the deep V collar she again caught sight of the small silver cross set in turquoise. She dropped her eyes quickly from that bare chest only to find his feet bare too.

"Seems we've done it again," he ventured.

"Seems," she said crisply, not smiling.

She found it impossible to confront his eyes right after having confronted his girlie magazine. *Don't be silly, Walker, he's not a mind reader.* But still she felt that if he got a closer look, he'd know what she'd been doing when he knocked.

"I was getting set to go for a run when . . ." He flipped a palm up. "Same song, second verse." He peered past her to his suitcase which she knew was lying on the bed with the top closed but unzipped. Still she stood like a palace guard, holding the edge of the door with one hand, blocking his entrance.

"Listen, what I said before was inexcusable. I'd like to apologize," Sam Brown offered.

"I should think you would," Lee returned tightly, the image from the magazine still vivid in her mind.

He handed her the correct suitcase. "Is that any way to reply when I'm trying to bury the hatchet? The least you can do is be civil."

"All right. I . . . I shouldn't have slapped you either. I'm sorry. There, will that do?" But her voice was hard and cynical.

"Not quite." He pointed to his belongings. "I'd like my stuff back, too. I want to take a run and work off all my recent anger and frustration, but my sweats are in there."

He tilted a peace-offering grin at her, and she stepped back stiffly and motioned for him to come in and take what was his. She watched the wrinkles on his shirttails as he lifted the cover of the suitcase to check cursorily inside. The magazine lay on top. He studied it a moment, then spun to face her, a dark glower lowering his eyebrows.

"Look, just because a man buys a skin magazine doesn't make him a pervert."

"To each his own," she granted, but her tone was undeniably judgmental.

"The rag's got damn good interviews and movie reviews and—" Suddenly he turned sour-faced, slammed the top down, and zipped it with three jerks of the wrist. "I don't know why the hell I should justify myself to you. And anyway, why do you think you have the right to convict a man according to what you find in his suitcase?"

She sighed with overstrained patience. "Listen, do you mind? I've been in these clothes all day, and I'd like a bath and some supper. It's been a rough day."

"Fine . . . fine." He yanked the suitcase off the bed. "I'm leaving!"

She was waiting to close the door on his heels, but before she could, he wheeled to face her. Almost angrily he stated, "I *am* sorry for what I said. It was totally out of line, but so are you for not gracefully accepting my apology and letting me off the hook. Those eyes of yours are gl—"

"I said, apology accepted."

"Then how about if I buy you dinner and we can talk about . . . whatever? Anything but suitcases."

"No thank you, Mr. Brown. Not interested. I work for one insufferable sexist and can't help being around him an unavoidable amount of time each week, but beyond him, I'm careful about who I spend my time with."

Deep wrinkles appeared in his forehead as he scowled down at her. He looked ominous and ready to blow his cork again, but Lee held her ground, facing him squarely, one hand on the edge of the door. She was conscious again of how erect his posture was—even more so as he held his anger tightly in check—shoulders squared back, the inverted triangle of bare skin on his chest as taut as the head of a drum. He wore a tight-lipped expression as his dark eyes seemed to penetrate her for a long, threatening moment. Then he turned on a bare heel and stalked away.

With a shaky sigh of relief, Lee closed the door, leaned her forehead against it for a moment, then slipped the dead bolt home.

The tension of the day had keyed her up until her neck and shoulders felt stiff with fatigue. She leaned far back from the waist, slipped a thin hand to the nape of her neck, and kneaded. Eyes closed, hair trailing free, she wondered what had prompted Sam Brown to invite her to dinner. Then, recalling his choice of reading material, she thought she knew the answer.

Lee flopped tiredly on the bed, crossed her arms behind her head, and tried to rid her thoughts of Sam Brown. But his face intruded, as she'd first seen it at the bid letting when he was accepting handshakes—smiling, laughing, pleased with himself. She remembered the tiny wrinkles at the corners of his eyes and wondered how old he was? Mid-thirties? When he scowled, he looked older—and he'd done plenty of scowling today! But his look of displeasure also made his undeniably handsome face even more good looking.

She tossed a limp forearm over her brow. Handsome is as handsome does, she thought tiredly. She'd chalk this day up to experience and forget she had ever laid eyes on the man.

The face of Floyd A. Fat Thorpe nudged Brown's aside, and Lee wondered which of the two was more disturbing. Thorpe was going to be more offensive than ever after this fiasco. Especially since she had deliberately disobeyed orders and stayed the night in Denver. There were times when competing in a man's world didn't seem worth it. But she had to prove to herself she could . . . hadn't she? Hadn't she had to prove it not only to herself but also to everyone else who had helped wreck her life?

She fell into a fitful sleep with the faces of Thorpe and Brown mingling in a collage of other disturbing faces from her past—Joel's, the judge's . . .

* * *

Awakening with a start, Lee jerked her wrist up—seven thirty!—slid off the bed, and began undressing all in one motion.

She ran a tubful of water, took a quick refreshing bath, and cursed the thin motel towels and cheap soap that scarcely lathered. Drying herself, she stepped to the vanity, then tossed the towel aside while she rummaged for her brush and began smoothing her hair. It reached just below her shoulder blades —a coarse, black mane thicker than wild prairie grass, so thick she leaned sideways at the waist as if its weight made her list. She leaned in the other direction, then stood straight, watching her breast rise and fall rhythmically with each brush stroke.

Her hand stopped in midair, the brush momentarily forgotten as she somberly assessed her naked reflection. Unbidden came the seductive pictures of the magazine and with them the vision of Sam Brown's face, his bare chest, his bare feet. She stared into her own dark eyes until her eyelids trembled, and she lowered her eyes. Her gaze moved down the long, lean neck to medium, pear-shaped breasts with dark nipples.

Hesitantly she brought the brush forward and ran the back of it around the outer edge of her right breast. The cool, yellow plastic was strangely smooth and welcome against her skin. She drifted it along the hollow beneath the breast, then up to the nipple. Tingles of remembrance came fluttering.

It had been a long time.

There were things a woman's body needed.

She closed her eyes as she turned the brush over, thinking of the whiskers on a firm jaw as she felt the light scrape of bristles along the side of her full breast, down her ribs, across her abdomen to the hollow of her hip.

A deep loneliness aroused memories of a past when her youthful dreams had consisted of rosy pictures of how life would turn out. Marriage, children, happy ever after. What had happened to all that? Why was she standing alone in a motel room in Denver, Colorado, remembering Joel Walker? He was married to someone else now, and, truth to tell, Lee no longer loved him. What she loved was the memory of those dreams she'd had when they'd first met, the wild want

of each other's bodies that they'd thought was enough upon
which to build a marriage. She ached for the time before all
the mistakes had been made, before Jed and Matthew had
been born.

Lee opened her eyes to find an empty, sad woman before
her. A woman with pale stretch marks snaking from hip to
abdomen as the only reminder of two pregnancies. She spread
her fingers upon them and slumped against the vanity. Then
she pushed herself erect and lifted her eyes. *Damn you, Lee,
you promised yourself not to get bogged down in recrimina-
tions over what can't be changed!*

She took a firmer grip on the brush and began styling her
hair, angrily brushing so hard her scalp hurt, dragging the
heavy black mass around the back of her head and securing it
just above and behind an ear in a heavy, smooth knot. Her
skin was naturally bronze and needed neither foundation nor
blush, but she accented her eyelids with silver shadow, curled
her lashes, and applied eyeliner and mascara. Her lipstick was
two-toned, a rich claret accented by white lipliner. She dashed
a touch of perfume behind each ear and turned to get dressed.

She donned a pair of baggy white pants that tapered at the
ankle above high-heeled wedgies of canvas and rope, then a
cavalry-style shirt of pale blue stripes that buttoned off center
and had short puffed sleeves ending in ruffles at the elbow. A
generous ruffled collar stood up around Lee's jaws, which she
knew emphasized her long, graceful neck. Stepping to the
mirror, again she added the ever-present feathers—this time
hanging them in her ears, light blue wisps that dangled when
she turned to retrieve her purse and head down to dinner.

The dining room was almost empty. Night had nearly fallen
and the lights of Denver were glimmering on one by one
beyond the windows. Lee paused in the doorway, peering into
the dimness where unobtrusive music played quietly. In a far
corner a gray-haired couple was sipping coffee. The only
other occupied table in the room was taken by Sam Brown.
He glanced up from a newspaper as Lee paused in the doorway. Their eyes met briefly before he turned expressionlessly
back to his reading, angling the paper to catch the last fading
light from the window beside him. Lee waited, feeling awkward and conspicuous as she studied the back of the cash

register. At last a waitress led her to a seat.

Unfortunately it was in the middle of the floor and faced Sam Brown. Again he lifted his eyes. Again they returned laconically to his newspaper, and Lee felt more than ever like the lead act in a one-ring circus.

The waitress handed Lee a menu. "Kind of slow tonight," the woman commented, her voice ringing like a clarion in the empty room.

"So I see."

"Can I get you anything from the bar?"

"Yes, a Smith and Kurn." Lee was conscious of Sam Brown's eyes directed her way again. "I know it's an after-dinner drink, but somehow I'm always too full then." She laughed nervously, damning herself for explaining, knowing she'd done it not for the waitress's benefit but for Sam Brown's. What did she care what he thought?

The waitress crossed to his table. She handed him a menu, and their voices also resounded clearly through the room.

"Something from the bar, sir?"

"An extra dry martini with pickled mushrooms, if you've got 'em."

My, aren't we fussy, Lee thought testily. Pickled mushrooms!

"We sure do," the waitress replied, and moved away to leave the room with nothing but that dim music which could scarcely fill the uncomfortable tension spinning between their two tables.

Lee searched her menu, immediately spotted what she wanted, but taking refuge behind the wide folder for a full five minutes until the waitress finally arrived with her drink, giving Lee someplace else to focus her attention.

The chocolate-flavored drink was refreshing. Lee sipped and followed the waitress with her eyes as the uniformed back hid Sam Brown momentarily from view.

"We gave you a couple extra mushrooms. How's that?" came the pleasant question.

"Great, thank you." His deep voice reverberated in Lee's ears.

When the woman stepped back, Sam's eyes caught Lee's.

Immediately she ducked to take a sip of her drink. The glass felt slippery in her hand. She dried her palm on her thigh, and applied herself to the menu again, ever so studiously, damning the waitress for walking off without asking if she was ready to order.

The woman returned at last with pencil and pad. So far Lee had managed to keep her eyes off the table by the window.

"Can I take your order now?"

Does a one-legged duck swim in a circle? Lee bit back the snippy retort and forcibly pasted a pleasant smile on her face. She attempted to speak softly, but the words came ringing off the walls like gunshots.

"I'll have ocean perch, no potato, and Thousand Island dressing on my salad."

"Would you like something in place of the potato?"

"Would I ever, but I'm being firm with myself tonight." There followed a false laugh which Lee hardly recognized as her own while Brown's eyes probed once again. She suddenly felt as if she'd told him something personal that he had no right to know and damned herself for making the innocent comment.

He ordered prime rib, medium rare, baked potato with both butter and sour cream, the house dressing—without being told what it was, which for some reason irritated Lee, who ate in restaurants seldom enough not to be adventurous—and a cup of coffee.

This time when the waitress moved away, the eyes of the two diners met and hesitated on each other for a longer moment, Sam Brown now leaned back in his chair with lazy nonchalance, one shoulder angling lower than the other as he rested a negligent elbow on the table and touched the rim of his glass with five fingertips.

Lee sipped her drink and looked pointedly away, but the distracting memory of his magazine pictures came niggling again. She felt his eyes on her and for a moment had the disquieting impression he was stacking her up against his naked tootsies, wondering how she'd compare. To Lee's dismay, the memory of her stretch marks emblazoned itself across her mind.

"Did you get your bath?"

At the sound of his lazy question her eyes flew up, and she colored as if he'd just spoken an obscenity, then glanced quickly at the old couple in the corner. They were sipping silently, paying no attention whatsoever.

"Yes. Did you have your run?"

He smiled crookedly. "I tried, but the damn air in this city is so thin I felt like I was having a heart attack."

"A pity you didn't." She quirked one eyebrow and made the ice cubes bob with a poke of her finger.

"Still don't believe me, huh?"

She lifted her glass, eyed him over its rim, took a long, sweet sip, then slowly shook her head from side to side. "Uh-uh."

He shrugged indifferently, took a pull on his cocktail, and studied the view outside the window. The way he had one shoulder back farther than the other made the yellow knit shirt hug his chest like a wet buckskin. The front zipper was lowered several inches and the silver cross winked at Lee while she tried to pretend he wasn't there. But it was impossible when, a moment later, the old couple arose, paid their bill, and went away, leaving Lee and Sam the only two in the room.

The waitress returned, deposited their first courses, and disappeared again.

Lee dove into her salad like a sinner into a confessional. But every clink of fork upon bowl seemed amplified and disturbing. The sound of her own chewing seemed explosive in the room. She scarcely kept from wriggling in her chair while feeling Sam Brown's steady gaze resting on her in an increasingly distracting manner.

His voice split the quiet again. "You know this is ridiculous, don't you?"

She looked up to find him with hands resting idly next to his salad bowl.

"What is?" she managed.

"Sitting here like a couple of little kids who just had a fight over who broke the mud pie."

She couldn't think of a single sane reply. With an engaging

grin he went on. "So, you're gonna stay in your yard and I'm gonna stay in mine, and we're going to glare at each other over the fence and be lonely and miserable while neither of us will make the first move."

She stared at him, gulped down what felt like an entire, unbroken head of lettuce, and said not a word.

"Can I bring my salad over there?" he asked finally, then added charmingly, "If I promise not to break your mud pie?"

The wisp of a smile threatened her lips and before she could control it she had chuckled, the sound bringing a wash of relief. "Yes, come ahead. It's awful sitting here trying not to look at you."

He and his salad and his pickled mushrooms were up and across the floor in three seconds. He settled himself at her table, gave her an audacious grin, and declared, "There, that's better," then dug into his lettuce with gusto.

She had called him a liar, a cheat, and a pervert. What possible course of conversation could successfully follow that? she wondered uneasily. To her relief, he came up with one.

"I have to admit, you're the first lady estimator I've ever seen."

"I'm the first lady estimator *I've* ever seen," she admitted.

The deep lines on either side of his mouth dented in. "How long have you been one?"

"I began in the business three years ago and have been an estimator for a little over a year."

"Why?"

Her eyebrows curled in puzzlement. "What do you mean, why?"

"Why choose a career in a tough business like this that's traditionally been dominated by men?"

"Because it pays well."

He accepted that with a nod of the head. "You work for old Floyd Thorpe, huh?"

"Yes, I'm sorry to say I do."

"He's a hell-raiser that one—a real shyster."

Startled, she looked into his dark eyes. "You know him?"

"He's been around Kansas City a long time. Everybody

there knows old Floyd. It's his kind that give construction companies a bad reputation. He's as crooked as a dog's hind leg."

"But he knows how to make money so he's excused, right?" she questioned sarcastically.

Refusing to rise to the bait, Sam asked, "If you dislike him so much, why work for him?"

"With the construction industry tied directly to new-home starts, need you ask?"

He wiped his mouth on a napkin. "No, I guess there aren't a lot of job openings right now, are there?"

She poked at the fleshy wedge of tomato in her bowl as if it were Thorpe's fat belly. "The only opening I've seen lately is the one between Floyd Thorpe's front teeth when he spits his slimy tobacco juice at my feet."

Brown laughed appreciatively, prompting Lee to look up with a devilish expression on her face. "Can I share a very private joke with you? One that's exceedingly irreverent?"

"I love irreverent jokes."

Lee sucked on her bottom lip, then confessed, "Privately, when I'm disgusted with my boss, which I usually am, I call him by his initials."

"Which are?"

"F.A.T." Brown rocked back in his chair and laughed while she continued, "He doesn't like it generally known what his middle initial is. Maybe that's why I take such pleasure in including it."

The fine white lines about Brown's eyes disappeared as he crinkled a smile and watched as she jabbed repeatedly at the tomato. His eyes passed over high, wide cheekbones, the proud, straight nose, the black straight hair caught behind her ear, in a plump, smooth bun, the copper skin and near-black eyes.

"You're Indian, right?"

Her eyes flashed up defiantly, and the feathers swung against her jaws. "One quarter Cherokee. He never lets me forget it."

Brown glanced at the feathers but withheld comment. "What you're saying is old Fat knows which side his bread is buttered on, huh?"

"Exactly. He's asked me no less than five times to accept the *honorary* title of vice-president."

"Let me guess." Brown leaned forward. "That would qualify him as a minority contractor, right?"

She grinned ruefully. "*And* make him eligible to bid any and all Minority Business Enterprise jobs the federal government lets, either as prime contractor or subcontractor. As you know, they seem to be the best bet going right now."

He studied her from beneath black brows shaped like boomerangs. "I take it you've declined the vice-presidency."

"With great relish."

Again Sam Brown leaned back in his chair and laughed richly. "There are a few contractors in the Kansas City area who'd grin from ear to ear to hear somebody put one over on F.A. after all the times he's pulled underhanded deals."

"I'd grin wider myself if it weren't for the increase in pay I'm turning down just to make Fat Thorpe eat crow."

"Or—more aptly—Cherokee?" Sam quipped, watching her closely.

She chuckled and her dark eyes sparkled momentarily before a pensive look overcame them. She nudged a few remaining pieces of lettuce around her salad bowl and folded her knuckles beneath her chin. She braced one elbow on the table, rested her other forearm against the edge of the table, and stroked the damp sides of her cold glass. "You know," she mused to the ice cubes in the empty tumbler, "there are some things my pride just won't let me do. Not even for money."

"But I thought you said money was why you took the job."

"It was. But I earn enough to support myself now. That's all I need."

She saw his eyes drop to the hand toying with the glass. It bore only a large oval turquoise in a sterling silver setting.

"You're not married?" he asked.

His eyes moved higher, met hers, and her fingers stopped stroking the damp glass.

"No," she answered tersely, realizing she should qualify the answer, then disregarded her conscience, thinking she owed this man nothing. They were simply sharing a table— two strangers in a lonely city away from home.

Their main course arrived, and Sam Brown changed the

subject. "I take it *the Fat* is going to hit the fan when he hears you lost the bid, huh?"

Lee looked up, chuckled appreciatively, and noted, "You *do* have an irreverent sense of humor, don't you? He's always hitting the fan over one thing or another. It's a way of life with him. If it's not over losing the bid, it'll be over me staying overnight on his precious company credit card, which he warned me not to do."

"But you're doing it anyway?" A frown tilted his brows.

"It was either that or get into Kansas City in the middle of the night after missing the six P.M. flight out of here. After the day I've put in, I wasn't about to spend half the night in a plane."

"All because I had your suitcase, right?"

She met his eyes, but only shrugged and returned to her dinner.

The waitress brought coffee, interrupting them momentarily. When they were alone again, Lee studied Sam thoughtfully and asked, "If you've been around the K.C. area long enough to know about the questionable business practices of my illustrious boss, why haven't we met before?"

"Probably because we've been primarily involved with plumbing contracting and only recently decided to expand into sewer and water work."

"We?" she asked curiously. "Who's the other Brown in Brown and Brown?"

"It was my dad. He was the one who knew every contractor's secrets around town. He was in the contracting business for years."

"Was?"

"He died four years ago," Sam stated unemotionally, cutting into his prime rib.

"I . . . I'm sorry."

He looked up brightly. "Oh, don't be. My father had a hell of a good life, did everything he ever wanted to do, died a happy man . . . on a golf course, no less, on the sixth tee." His brown eyes twinkled. "That sixth tee always did give him trouble."

Even though Sam Brown pronounced all this with no apparent sadness, Lee felt awkward sharing his private history this way when she scarcely knew him. But he went on. "He was a hard-drinking, hard-working Norwegian—"

"A Norwegian named *Brown?*"

"Comes from Brunvedt, somewhere back along the line."

"I'm sorry . . . I interrupted."

"Well as I said, he was a hard-headed Norwegian, and when I say he did everything he wanted, that included disobeying doctor's orders. He'd had a small stroke and was given orders to take it easy for a few months, but when a stubborn Norwegian takes it into his head he's going to go golfing, there's no stopping him."

Lee found she was enjoying Sam Brown's company immensely by now and surprised even herself by replying, "And when a stubborn Norwegian takes it into his head that he's going to go to dinner with a woman, there's no stopping him either, is there?"

Sam angled a smile at the knot of hair behind her ear, then at her eyes, and finally her lips. It occurred to Lee that he looked nothing whatever like any Norwegian she'd ever met. His hair was a rich chestnut color, his eyes and skin so dark they seemed to reflect her very face as he reached blindly for his coffee cup and—without taking his eyes from her— teased, "Well, it wasn't so painful after all, was it?"

She wished she could answer otherwise, but she found it impossible. "Admittedly, no it wasn't."

"Maybe we can do it again sometime in Kansas City."

For a moment she was tempted, but recalling the less estimable aspects of his personality, she warned, "Don't plan on it. Not unless *I've* won the bid."

"Mmm . . ." He lifted his coffee. Devilish eyes sparkled above the cup. "Might be worth fixing the bid in your favor next time."

"I have no doubt you'd do it." She studied him for some time, then admitted, "I have a habit of coining titles for people I meet. You know what I've dubbed you?"

"What?"

Their eyes tangled in a delightful duel of wits.

"The Honorable Sam Brown."

"Hey, I like that . . . that's clever."

"And pure, unvarnished sarcasm. Brown, you're a completely dishonorable scoundrel, and I don't know why I'm sitting at this table with you right now."

He tipped his chair back until it balanced on two legs. "Because you wanted to find out if I'm as perverted as my reading material led you to suspect. They say every woman is attracted to the wrong kind of man at least once in her life. Who knows? Maybe I'm it for you."

"Then again maybe you're not." She tipped her head and studied him closely. He was a highly delicious looking male specimen—she'd grant him that. And his nasty sense of humor didn't hurt a bit. But Lee reminded herself again that he wasn't the sort with whom she should be bantering about sexually provocative things. Conversations such as this provoked vibrations that said much more than the mere words, and she was by no means ready for such vibrations again. Her wounds hadn't healed from the last disastrous relationship. But even while she chided herself for indulging in such give-and-take, Sam's eyes were steady on her as his chair came down on all fours. He leaned crossed arms on the table edge, and pitched slightly toward her.

"Tell me," he said, his voice gone low and intimate. "What'd you think of the one stretched out on the rock beside the river?"

Damned if she was going to look like some nilly-witted teenager caught peeping at African breasts in *National Geographic!* Lee looked Brown smack in the eye and replied levelly, "The photographer must have missed oiling the inner side of her right calf. The water didn't bead up there."

Sam Brown rewarded her with a full-throated, appreciative peal of laughter while Lee scolded herself for her own precociousness. A moment later he had flung his soiled napkin on the table, picked up the check and was standing behind her chair, waiting to pull it back. But before he did, he leaned close and, just beside an aqua feather, said, "Chief Sitting Bull would have excommunicated you from the tribe if he'd ha . . . ha . . ." He turned away just in time. *"Aaa-chooo!"*

She glanced over her shoulder with a cheeky grin. "My goodness, Brown, it looks like you're allergic to me. Don't get so close next time."

He was rubbing his nose with a handkerchief. "It's that perfume you're wearing."

"My apologies." She grinned, not feeling the least bit of contrition.

It's just as well, she thought. She had no business being with him in the first place. But still she had to smile, for on the way back to their rooms he sneezed three more times, and by the time they reached her door he was giving her a good six-foot clearance.

CHAPTER
Three

FLOYD A. THORPE kept his office like he kept his teeth—brown around the edges. Rolls of plans, soil samples, drill bits, cast-iron pipe fittings, test plugs, incoming mail, hydrant wrenches, and used coffee cups created a random scattering of litter that was rarely cleared or dusted, for F.A. raised particular hell if anyone monkeyed with his "filing system." The room had an unpleasant smell, a mixture of rancid chewing tobacco, dust, stale alcohol, tar, and dried clay, topped off with the peculiar smell of cast iron. When Lee had taken the job at Thorpe Construction, F.A. had been in the middle of one of his sporadic drying-out periods, during which he became less abusive and more reasonable. The office had been cleaner, and so had he.

But he'd been off the wagon for months now. His nose shone like a beacon, and his cheeks wore the mottled red puffiness of the serious drinker. It was all Lee could do to face him the following morning across the junk on his desk.

"He what!" bellowed F.A.

Lee took a step backward. Thorpe's breakfast Manhattan was offensive the second time around.

"He got my suitcase by mistake, found the bid inside, and turned it in along with his own."

"And took the goddam job away from you like candy from a baby!" F.A. fumed and paced, then picked up a coffee can and spit into it. Lee studied a piece of P.V.C. pipe on a littered file cabinet behind him rather than observe the distasteful sight of his brown spume. "By a measly four thousand dollars!" F.A. whammed his fist into the center of the desk, lifting dust and making the telephone dance. He dropped into his desk chair and glowered at Lee, then turned suddenly pensive. "That's old Wayne Brown's kid, isn't it? Mmm . . . appears the kid's got more brains than his old man." Thorpe's eyes narrowed shrewdly, and he chuckled deep in his throat. Then he turned his beady eyes on Lee again. "I hope you learned your lesson from this. Everybody's out to screw everybody else in this world, and Sam Brown proved it!" With a quick shift of weight, he leaned back in his chair. "You thought any more about that vice-presidency I offered you?"

"Sorry, I prefer estimating."

Again he banged his fist on the desk. "Damn it, Walker, I put up with a lot from you, carrying your bids in a suitcase like some green recruit, then picking up the wrong damn one at the other end of the line and losing me a job worth over four million bucks! How long do you think I'm going to put up with screw-ups like this! I want your name on them corporation papers. It's the least you can do after the mess you made out of this Denver bid."

"I'm sorry about losing the suitcase, but the rest of it wasn't my fault. If Sam Brown checked my bid against his, he wouldn't admit it."

"Why, hell no, who would?" F.A.'s pot belly was so hard it scarcely depressed when he crossed his hands on it. "Tell you what, girlie. I'll give you till Friday to think it over. Either you help me out with this here minority business thing and agree to become vice-president, or you can find yourself someplace else to work. You're costin' me money, and unless you help me make a little of it back, I got no use for you."

Back in her own neat office, Lee strode angrily to her chair, deposited herself in it with great vexation, cursed under her breath, and considered marching back in there and telling F.A.T. where to put his vice-presidency *and* his tobacco cud! There'd be nothing so sweet as to walk out there and show that fat, smelly boar she didn't need his precious job or his calculating little mind one moment longer.

But the bitter truth was, she did.

She had no husband across town bringing in a paycheck from another job to support her. She was self-reliant now and needed a weekly salary to survive. Sam Brown had been right when he'd summed up the estimator's job market right now—there was none! Two years ago, before the recession had gripped the country, Kansas City and its surrounding suburbs had had perhaps twenty more general contractors than it did now. Now the industry grapevine buzzed constantly with news of this one or that one on the verge of folding, and they all held their breaths, hoping the next one to go under wouldn't be themselves.

The phone interrupted Lee's reverie. She punched line one and answered, "Lee Walker."

"You made it back."

The voice surprised Lee.

"Brown, is that you?"

"That's right, the Honorable Sam Brown. I looked for you on my flight. Thought we might sit together and share my magazine."

She didn't feel in the least like smiling but couldn't help it. Damn the man, making her laugh when he'd been the initial cause of the altercation she'd just had with Thorpe!

"Oh, you did, huh? I took an earlier flight. I've been back since ten o'clock."

A brief pause, then, "How did Thorpe take the news?"

She laughed, a single mirthless huff. "Need you ask?"

"Well, you win a few and you lose a few. He should know that by now."

"That isn't even remotely funny, Brown. Not after what you did to me! He came down on me like a tent when the circus is over, and what really irritates me is that Fat Thorpe actually seems to admire you for your duplicity. His exact words were, 'The kid's got more brains than his old man.' It appears you're two peas in a pod, you and my boss."

His unconcerned laughter came over the wire. "We're both a couple of degenerates, is that it?"

"That's it," she agreed.

"Well, how would you like a chance to try your hand at reforming me . . . say over dinner Friday night?"

Lee came close to sputtering, the dressing down she'd just

taken from F.A. still burning beneath her collar. "Dinner! What, again? And ruin my reputation around this town by being seen with a known pervert? I told you, Brown, I don't know why I ate with you the first time!"

"I'll take you to the American Restaurant," he bribed.

The American! Lee was suddenly crestfallen and undeniably tempted. The American Restaurant at the Crown Center was the *crème de la crème* of eateries in the Kansas City area.

"Brown, that's a dirty, rotten low blow, and you know it."

"I know," he agreed mirthfully, a smile in his voice.

"I told you, not until *I'm* the low bidder, and right now I'm not, as you well know." *The American Restaurant,* she thought woefully, kissing the chance good-bye.

"Okay, Cherokee, but I'll hold you to it . . . when you're low bidder."

"Ch . . ." Now Lee did sputter! "Ch . . . Cherokee! Brown, don't you ever call me that ag . . . Brown?" She clicked the disconnect button. "Brown!"

But he'd hung up. Then she did too, slamming the receiver down so hard it jumped back off the cradle. "Cherokee!" she spit out crossing her arms and glaring at the instrument guilty of carrying his damn sexy, teasing voice to her when she was in no mood to be manipulated by a smooth talker like him.

How dare he call her Cherokee when . . . when . . .

But a moment later her lips betrayed her and she found herself grinning at the phone. It was the last time she grinned that day.

Things went from bad to worse. Fat Thorpe pounded in and out, cussing like a marine and demanding test borings on jobs Lee knew were too wet to even consider bidding; ordering installation of inferior quality pipe they'd had trouble with before; demanding last minute changes in a bid she'd all but finished. He became more overbearing and demanding as the day passed. Lee required all her teeth-gritting strength to maintain her composure.

By the time she left the office, her nerves were at the breaking point. She arrived at her townhouse tired, angry, and depressed. In the front foyer she stripped off her shoes and pantyhose and left them lying in a heap. There was something about bare feet that seemed to take the stress off her head.

In the rear-facing kitchen she reached unseeingly into the refrigerator for a peach, and sank her teeth into it while roaming over to the sliding glass door and staring at her tiny private patio, fantasizing about calling the Human Rights Commission to complain that she was being discriminated against. But what could the complaint be? That Old Fat wanted to make her vice-president and give her a raise but she was declining the offer? There was nothing illegal about Thorpe's ploy to make his firm eligible as a minority contractor. It was only unethical! And Lee adamantly refused to be his patsy in the scheme.

She prowled the living room, heaping curses on Old Fat's fat head! Spying the newspaper, she checked the *Kansas City Star*, but as she'd suspected, no one wanted estimators. *The Construction Bulletin* turned up nothing more, and Lee's depression grew.

Sitting on the floor, her back to the sofa, she crossed her arms over upraised knees and rested her forehead there. The peach pit grew warm and slippery in her hand. She raised her head wearily and propped her chin on an arm, studying the precision pleats of the off-white custom-made draperies she was still paying off in monthly installments.

She'd worked so hard to get this place. She brushed a hand over the thick nap of the rich, rust carpet. She'd bought the townhouse only six months ago, and though she had a long way to go before it was completely decorated, she loved the furniture she'd managed to buy so far. She had modest dreams of adding decorator items piece by piece, of completing the finishing touches as she could afford them.

She sighed, slunk low onto her tailbone, and caught the nape of her neck on the cushion of the tuxedo sofa, which was covered with an arresting Mayan design of rich, deep earth tones, its soft depths strewn with plump matching cushions. Lee's eyes moved to the spots where she wanted side chairs.

But the room made her suddenly feel lonelier than ever. She studied the plants in the baskets, willing them to grow faster and fill up the extra space. Her eyes moved next to the only other item the room possessed—a loosely strung God's-eye on the wall behind the sofa, its rust, brown and ecru yarns so inexpertly stretched around the crossed dowels, that there could be no question it had been done by a child's hand.

Yes, the room was decidedly bare and lonely, but it was a beginning, and if she lost her job, she would lose this too.

Dejected, she wandered back to the kitchen, threw out the peach pit, rinsed off her hands and opened the refrigerator again only to find herself, some two minutes later, still staring into its almost empty space, remembering a day when she had shuffled and rearranged, trying to make room for family leftovers.

She closed the door on her memories, wishing the judge could see now what she'd made of herself since she'd faced him in court. Carrying a quart of milk onto the patio, she sank into a webbed lounge chair and drank the remainder of her supper right out of the red and white carton, too dispirited to care if it was in a glass or not.

It was much later when she finally plodded upstairs. The second floor of the townhouse had two bedrooms and a bath. As she neared the door of the smaller room, she slowed. Stopping, she reached inside and switched on the light. A pair of twin beds with heavy pine headboards took up the far wall. Between them stood a matching chest of drawers whose rich, dark wood looked richer against the bright scarlet carpet, but whose tops were bare—nothing there but a lamp and an unopened box of paper tissues. Still, the room was completely decorated. The bedspreads and draperies were crisp and new, with an all-over design of NFL insignias in a blaze of basic colors. On the wall beside one bed hung two Kansas City Chiefs pennants.

Lee studied the room sullenly, biting back tears that stung her eyes, feeling again the frustrating sense of unfairness that she could never shake at the thought of the boys.

She counted the days.

A brown and white cat padded silently into the room and preened his fur against Lee's ankle.

"Oh, P. Ewing, you've been on the bed again, haven't you?"

Lee looked down, watched the cat move sinuously against her, then crossed to one of the beds to plump its pillow and smooth the spread. On her way out she scooped up the cat, buried her face in his fur, and reached for the light switch. But she paused in the doorway and turned, assessing the silent room once more. "Oh, P. Ewing, what if I lose my job?" she lamented. "I'll have to give up this place."

On Friday morning Lee was working on a bid for a simple sewer and water installation in Overland Park, which would service an area where a shopping mall was to be built. The bid letting was scheduled for two that afternoon. These last few hours were always the worst. The phone constantly jangled with calls from salesmen giving last minute quotes on materials, from reinforced concrete pipe to catch basin castings. She'd just received a price quote on sod replacement which was several cents under the previous low bidder and was recomputing the labor subcontract cost when the phone rang. Preoccupied, fingers still flying over the calculator buttons, Lee reached unconsciously for the receiver, cradling it between shoulder and ear as her eyes continued scanning a column of numbers.

A moment later she realized she'd picked up a call meant for F.A. A smooth, masculine voice was saying, ". . . can come to terms on that twelve-inch reinforced concrete pipe we've had laying around the yard. The flaws are in the reinforcing, not in the concrete itself, so it'd be mighty tough to detect."

F.A. chuckled, then returned in a silky tone, "And we'll split the difference right up the middle?"

Horrified, Lee jerked the receiver away from her ear, clutching it in white knuckles, realizing she should have hung up the moment she'd identified the call as someone else's. But it had happened so fast! She rested the receiver on her job sheets and stared at the lighted button on the face of the phone, waiting, digesting what she'd heard. With each passing second her disgust grew. She'd heard it said many times that F.A. knew every dishonest trick in the book and wasn't afraid to use them. But she'd never had proof before. Using substandard materials, price fixing, collusion, buying off the competition before bids—there were countless deceits it was possible to practice. Some were illegal, some merely dishonest. But either way, until now it had been no more than hearsay.

The light blinked off, and Lee slipped the receiver silently back in place.

She was still sitting there in a turmoil when F.A. rounded the doorway into her office. This morning the gnawed stub of an unlit cigar was clenched in his teeth.

"Whoever you got to supply the twelve-inch reinforced concrete pipe on that Overland Park job, we won't be goin' with them. Gonna get that pipe from Jacobi."

"Oh?" Lee retorted coldly.

"Yeah, you can figure it at twelve-fifty a foot, materials only."

"And what margin of profit are you working on at twelve dollars and fifty cents a foot?"

His beady little eyes narrowed on her like laser beams. The cigar stub shifted to the opposite corner of his mouth. "Never mind, just figure it at twelve-fifty a foot."

Lee erupted from her chair. "No, *you* figure it at twelve-fifty a foot!"

"Me! That bid's due at two o'clock this afternoon and—"

"And it won't be turned in by me, not with flawed pipe from Jacobi figured into it!"

His sausagelike fingers slowly extracted the wet cigar from his lips. "So, Little Miss Big Ears has been listening in on somebody else's phone conversations, huh?"

"Yes, I heard you and Jacobi on the phone just now, but it was entirely unintentional. As a matter of fact, I only heard about ten seconds worth of the conversation."

"But it was enough to give you a sudden case of *morality,* is that it?" He managed to make the word sound quite dirty.

Lee's insides quivered. She pressed a thigh against the edge of her desk to steady the nerves that wanted to fly in six directions. "It's dishonest!"

Thorpe shifted till his shoulder leaned toward her like a baseball pitcher studying signals from a catcher. He jabbed the cigar butt before her nose. "It's profit. And don't you forget it!"

"Profit earned at the expense of the taxpayer . . . *and* the environment, I might add!"

"Well, bye-dee-ho!" F.A. ran his eyes around the walls of her office as if searching for something. "Too bad we ain't got a stake around here so you can tie yourself to it and strike a match," he sneered.

Lee was already jerking her desk drawers open, setting her briefcase on the chair, snapping it open, separating personal items from company items.

"I refuse to be a party to your . . . your flawed materials or your scheme to qualify as a minority contractor. Why, I wouldn't be an officer of this company if Geronimo himself were president!" She piled up address book, legal pads, and portfolios in the center of her desk, each sharp slap like an exclamation point in the room.

"Geronimo wouldn't have the smarts it takes to run a business like this and turn a profit during a year as tough as this's been! In one phone call I clear a smooth ten thousand. Now what the hell kind of fool would turn down money like that?"

Lee stopped packing, rested her knuckles on the desktop, and skewered him with a feral glare. "And nobody's the wiser when five years from now the pipe breaks and untreated sewage infiltrates somebody's water supply, or . . . or runs into the Missouri River or—"

"A regular Albert Schweitzer, ain't you? Well, supposing I was to cut you in on a share of my take on this little deal, and you make me a minority contractor after all. Would a few thousand ease your conscience any?"

His cocky, self-assured belief that anybody could be bought off only sickened Lee all the more. She was suddenly very, very sure she was doing what should have been done months ago. Suddenly her anger disappeared and a renewed sense of well-being swept over her. Her lips relaxed; her voice quieted.

"Suppose it would. And what would be the next unethical thing you'd ask me to do? And the next? And how long would it be before you asked me to make the transition from unethical to illegal? You know, F.A., it isn't just the money—it's something much deeper than that. It's something born in an Indian that can't be programmed out. Call it elemental respect for the earth . . . or whatever you like. It's part of the reason I do what I do. I can't stop development or urban sprawl. But I *can* do my part to see that it doesn't completely annihilate the environment. I agree with you, Geronimo probably wouldn't be a rich man if he ran this company or one like it, but he'd probably rather drink clean water than deposit ten thousand dollars in the bank." Lee scanned her cleared desktop, then chuckled and smiled at F.A. "Come to think of it, Indians never were famous for saving for a rainy day, were they?"

Lee's belongings were piled on the desk and the chair. She snapped the briefcase shut, picked up an armful of notebooks and folders, and turned toward the door.

"But what about that bid for this afternoon?" Thorpe squawked.

"Finish it yourself."

"Girlie, you walk out of here, you give up unemployment checks, cause I ain't claimin' I laid you off. And don't look for no recommendations from—"

The outside door cut off his spate. As if his recommendation was worth anything at all around this town, Lee thought, as she headed toward the parking lot.

Her red Ford Pinto was parked right beside Thorpe's long, sleek Diamond Jubilee Mark V. The navy blue sedan was covered with a fine layer of dust, as if he'd recently driven through a jobsite. Lee dumped her load on the back seat of the Pinto, then straightened and studied Floyd's dusty status symbol. Imbedded in the glass of the opera window—still intact —was the illustrious but now lusterless diamond.

With a sardonic smile Lee leaned over, breathed on it, lifted an elbow, and polished it carefully. She stepped back to survey it critically, nodded once, then clambered into her Pinto and drove away.

But her cocky attitude had totally disappeared when, three days later, she'd turned up absolutely nothing resembling a job opening. As she paced the floor, she told herself she'd done the only thing possible. She was reviewing the miles she'd put on both her car and her feet during the past three days when her phone rang. Picking it up from the kitchen counter, the Honorable Sam Brown's was the last voice on earth she expected at the other end of the line.

"Who the hell are you trying to hide from?" he said without preamble.

"What!"

"I've been trying to get your damn phone number for three days!"

"And just who might this be?" she queried with undisguised sugar in every syllable.

"This, my little Indian, is the Honorable Sam Brown speaking. Just why in hell aren't you listed in the phone book?"

"Because I'm divorced and I don't want any obscene phone calls. And why didn't you just call Thorpe Construction for my number?"

"I did, but it seems Fat Floyd developed a conscience—belatedly, I might add—and declined to give out confidential information."

"Why that fat rat!"

"My sentiments exactly."

"So how did you get it?"

"I spent sixty-five bucks taking out a dumb redhead and buying her dinner, then plying her with a German wine because she works for Ma Bell."

Lee was dumbfounded. "You *whaaaat!*"

"And all she was good for at the end of the evening was a chaste good night kiss." He chuckled wickedly.

"I told you, Brown, I don't accept obscene phone calls."

"Too bad, cause the redhead finally gave over—your phone number, of course."

"Brown, you scheming weasel, are you saying you bribed the girl to get my unlisted number?"

"Call it what you will . . . I got it, didn't I?"

"For what?"

"I heard Fat Floyd gave you the ax."

"Well, you heard wrong. I quit."

"Bully for you. Have you got another job yet?"

"Are you kidding? I've been beatin' feet from one end of this town to the other, but it's hopeless."

"Listen, I've got a proposition for you."

"I'll just bet you do, but I'm not that desperate yet. If it's the same one you offered the redhead on her doorstep, keep it."

"You're the most suspicious woman I ever paid sixty-five dollars for, you know that?"

"And I'll bet there've been plenty, right?"

"Quit your goading, Cherokee, this is legitimate business. I'd like to talk to you about coming to work for me."

"You wh—"

"But I won't discuss it on the phone. I never carry out an interview by phone, only face to face. Are you busy tomorrow night?"

"Brown, you're crazy!"

He went on as if she hadn't spoken. "I'm busy all day tomorrow, including lunch, or we could get together then. But I'll be free by—oh, say, four thirty. Why don't we meet someplace for cocktails and discuss it then?"

"Brown, I can't come to work for you. It'd be like jumping from the pot into the fire!"

"Listen, I'd like to stay and listen to all this sweet talk, but I'm on the run as it is. Meet me at fifty-three oh-one State Line Road and we'll discuss it sensibly. Fifty-three oh-one State Line . . . got that?"

"Sam Brown, I don't trust you. What makes you think—"

But he'd done it again.

"Brown? . . . Brown, come back here!"

He'd left her with a dead receiver, and before the address escaped Lee's head, she was scrambling for a pencil.

CHAPTER

Four

FIVE-THREE-OH-ONE State Line Road turned out to be a place so grandiose that Lee drove right past it two times without even considering it might be the right spot. It was magnificent. Perched imposingly at the crest of a hill, it dominated the view with a white facade that reminded Lee of an antebellum mansion. Staring up at it, she fully expected Scarlett O'Hara to come flouncing through the door. The horseshoe-shaped drive rose toward the building, encircling a curve of lush green grass and an imposing flower bed that provided the only clue to the building's identity—a stunning "C C" formed by vibrant red and white geraniums.

It appeared to be a country club, backing up to Ward Parkway, perhaps the most prestigious street in town with its countless fountains and mansions built by the oldest, moneyed forefathers. Lee had no doubt whatever that the place had a private membership of the highest echelon.

And Sam Brown was a member of *this?*

Leaving the car, Lee critically swished a hand over her skirt—thank God she hadn't worn slacks! Even the dress seemed less than adequate, for it was only a casual two-piece cotton outfit of brown and white stripes, the top an athletic looking slipover with ribbed waist, cap sleeves, and boatneck styling.

The shrubbery around the entrance looked artificial, it was so perfectly manicured. Tubs of potted flowers blossomed in colorful profusion on either side of the steps. Halting just short of them, Lee pulled a wand of lipgloss from her purse, checked her face in a tiny mirror, and applied a gleaming line of amber to her lips. Clamping her clutch bag beneath an elbow, she entered the "C C"—whatever it was!

She found herself in a vast room with high, wide windows off to the left through which the afternoon sun lit a tasteful grouping of antique furniture. A fireplace flanked the conversation area while enormous bouquets of silk flowers made the elegant old furniture appear even more valuable.

A discreet voice made her jump. "Ms. Walker?"

Lee turned to find a faultlessly dressed woman smiling at her from behind rimless glasses with a chain dangling from their bows. The woman looked like she might very well own the place.

"Yes?" a puzzled Lee returned.

"Ah, I thought so by Mr. Brown's description of you. You'll find him downstairs in the lounge. Just follow that stairway around and it'll take you right to him." With a graceful wave of her hand, the woman withdrew.

Lee followed the stairs as directed to find herself in a low-ceilinged bar with reduced lighting. She scarcely had time to note that Sam Brown wasn't there before a smiling black man in formal waiter's attire approached to ask, much as the woman upstairs had, "Ms. Walker?"

"Yes."

"Mr. Brown is waiting for you in the lounge, if you'll follow me."

He led the way to another elegant room much like the one upstairs, only smaller and more intimate, with soft lighting from tasteful table lamps. Again there was a fireplace on the far wall and a scattering of plush furniture placed in cozy groupings. Sam Brown stretched his tall frame up from one of the antique wing chairs flanking the fireplace.

"Here she is, Mr. Brown," the waiter announced.

"Thank you, Walter." To Lee, Sam said, "I see you found the place all right."

"Not without some trouble," she admitted, taking in his dark gaze as it swept her hair and face.

"Will the lady be wanting a cocktail?" Walter inquired.

"Yes, a Smith and Kurn," Brown answered before the waiter left them discreetly alone. Then he turned to Lee, gesturing. "Sit down, Ms. Walker."

In spite of herself she was pleased that he'd remembered her drink preference, and it tempered her voice as she chided, "Don't you Ms. Walker me, Sam Brown. Why didn't you warn me what kind of place this was?"

She perched on a Chippendale love seat while Brown chose the spot beside her rather than the chair he'd been occupying earlier. He turned sideways, lifting a knee partially onto the cushioned seat and resting his arm along its back. He scrutinized her with a half smile.

"Why? You look great, Cherokee."

"And don't call me Cherokee." She looked around furtively to see if anyone had heard, but they were alone in the lounge.

"If Ms. Walker and Cherokee are both out, what should I call you?"

She didn't know. "Try Lee," she finally suggested.

"All right, Lee, you had some trouble finding the place?"

"Trouble! I drove right past it two times and never even gave it a glance. What is it, anyway?"

"It's the Carriage Club."

"And you're a member, I take it."

"Aha." He reached for his cocktail from an oval table in front of the sofa. The entire grouping, including the pair of wing chairs, faced the fireplace, ensconcing them in a private circle of their own.

She turned her eyes to the coffee table. In addition to a bouquet of freshly cut spider mums and carnations, it held a silver bowl of macadamia nuts. Her gaze moved over richly papered walls to the polished andirons and screen in the fireplace. Slowly Lee's eyes traveled back to Sam Brown to find him studying her.

"Is this supposed to change my opinion of . . . the decadent rich?" she asked.

He shrugged, but his grin remained.

Just then Walter returned with her Smith and Kurn, set it on the table, and inquired, "And will there be anything else for you, Mr. Brown?"

"Another of the same."

As soon as Walter had faded away, Lee couldn't resist querying, "What? Aren't you going to ask for pickled mushrooms?"

"The decadent rich don't need to ask. Walter knows exactly how I prefer my drinks."

"So . . . you're a member of good standing?"

His only answer was the continued amiable expression on his face, and against her will, Lee Walker *was* thoroughly impressed.

"I came here to talk business, Mr. Brown," she said.

"Of course." He leaned forward slightly. "Unlike most of the contracting firms in this city, mine has had a good year. The plumbing half of the firm has sustained the sewer and water half until it can get on its feet. All I need is one good estimator."

"And what makes you think I'm good?"

"You damn near beat me out of that Denver job, and you did beat out an impressive lineup of competition. I want anybody who can do that working for me, not against me."

"I did beat you out, and you know it," she accused in a soft voice.

"Are we going to beat that old dead horse again?"

"I couldn't resist."

His brown eyes crinkled. Distracted, she reached for some nuts.

"Are you interested in the job offer?"

She didn't want to be, but—damn his dark eyes!—she was. Walter intruded momentarily to lean low with a silver tray, and even over his back Lee could feel Sam Brown's eyes following her hand as she lifted the nuts to her mouth, then licked away the salt that caught on her glossy lipstick.

She raised her eyes to confront him head on. "I want you to know right off the bat—I don't do anybody's dirty work. I bid 'em straight and fair."

"I'll pay you forty thousand a year, plus a company car and all the usual fringe benefits—profit sharing, insurance, use of a company credit card."

While shock waves catapulted through Lee, she watched Sam lazily stir his drink, then lift a red plastic saber upon which four pickled mushrooms were skewered. His sparkling teeth slipped the first mushroom into his mouth, and his jaws began moving while hers went slack.

"Forty thousand a year?" The words scarcely peeped from her throat.

"Mmm-hmm." His eyes lingered indolently on hers as he clamped those perfect teeth around the second mushroom. Mesmerized, still not quite able to absorb his offer, she watched as he ate all four mushrooms.

Forty thousand dollars!

"You must be joking."

"Not at all. You'll work damn hard for it. If I say travel, you'll travel. We're bidding jobs in about eight states right now. Sometimes there'll be late nights if we're up against a deadline. Other times there'll be night flights in order to get connections to the right city. I pay my estimators well, but they earn every cent of it."

She was still too stunned to take it all in. "I don't even know where your offices are."

"On the other side of the creek, near Rainbow and Johnson Drive. I'll take you over later to see them, if you like."

Again she was astonished. The area he'd named was well known as one of the most prestigious in the city. It was generally referred to as the Plaza Area, named after the lush Country Club Plaza Shopping Center nearby. She was still pondering this when Sam Brown pulled a tie from the pocket of his blue linen sport coat, though she was so lost in thought she scarcely realized what he was doing. Without the aid of a mirror, he raised his collar, lay the tie underneath, buttoned his collar button, and began applying a Windsor knot to the tie by feel. Though her eyes were fixed on his hands, she was thinking instead of the pair of widewale corduroy armchairs she wanted so badly, thinking of the drapes she could pay off in no time, thinking of not having to give up the townhouse.

The ever-attentive Walter appeared as if out of nowhere. "Will there be anything more, Mr. Brown?"

"Ms. Walker and I will go into dinner now, Walter. Thank you."

"Of course, sir. I'll bring your drinks for you."

Lee finally slipped out of her reverie to realize that Sam

Brown was slipping a hand under her elbow and urging her to her feet. They followed at Walter's heels. "House rules," Sam whispered conspiratorially. "Men have to wear ties in the dining room."

Lee made a feeble attempt to pull away from his commanding grasp. This is all too perfect. It's going too fast!

"I'm not dressed—"

"You're dressed just fine." His eyes swept her from hair to her waist, and up again.

She felt obligated to resist one more time. "But . . . but I haven't even said I'd work for you, much less won a bid yet. And you invited me for a drink, not dinner."

He only grinned down at her cheek, squeezed the soft, bare skin of her inner elbow, and teased, "Let a man try to impress a lady when he's trying his damndest, okay, Cherokee?"

That word, perhaps more than any other, brought her back down to earth. Cherokee. But it was too late now. They'd reached the dining room doorway, which opened off the lounge. She felt helpless as she was propelled along beside him. His thumb was rough on her bare skin as they paused just inside, and he was again greeted by name. "Evening, Mr. Brown . . . ma'am. Your table is all ready." The man escorted them to a linen-covered table in front of a wide window that curved in a semicircle around half of the dining room. Lee looked onto a view of the swimming pool, ice rink, and tennis courts below. In the distance a line of tall trees indicated the meandering route of Brush Creek as it flowed eastward. The sun was slanting across the green lawn, from which Lee had difficulty pulling her eyes.

A nudge on the back of her knees reminded her that Sam Brown was solicitously waiting to push in her chair.

"Oh . . . thank you." She settled herself, subjected to the tantalizing scent that wafted about him as he sat down across from her. He had no more than hit the chair when yet another solicitous employee of the Carriage Club was immediately at hand to state, "The evening special is shrimp marinated in wine sauce, seasoned with tarragon and served with herb butter. And how are you this evening, Mr. Brown?" Menus were opened crisply and placed first in Lee's hands, then Sam's.

He raised his dark brows, and a smile lifted his lips.

"Hungry as a bear, Edward, and how are you?"

Edward leaned back and laughed softly. "I'm fine, sir. Leaving on my vacation tomorrow morning for my son's house in Tucson. He's got a new baby, you know, and we've never seen her."

"I imagine it's a little hard to keep your mind on marinated shrimp then, isn't it?"

"For you, sir, not at all. Service is the same as always."

They laughed together in the way of men who go through this ritual often. Lee noted the same camaraderie between Brown and yet another man who brought them goblets of ice water.

When they were alone with their menus at last, Lee admitted, "I am impressed, Brown. How could I help but be?"

"Tell me that when you've seen me in action in the office and it'll mean something."

She looked for signs of teasing and saw none.

This man, this Sam Brown, what did she know of him? Was he honorable or a scoundrel? Was his poise in these elegant surroundings an intentional smoke screen to hide his seamier side? He could charm the gold out of a person's teeth—she had no doubt about that—but could he also be ruthless? He was handsome enough to turn any woman's head, and that fact made it more difficult to assess his hidden traits. After all, she was making a business decision, and what he looked like had absolutely no bearing upon his character or his motives. Studying him now, Lee entwined her fingers, pressed her arms along the table edge, and bent forward until her breasts touched her wrists.

"Level with me, Brown. Would you hire me with the ulterior motive of exploiting me, like Thorpe did?"

She watched his eyes carefully as they registered faint surprise at her direct question, then glinted with brief amusement before that too disappeared and he asked matter-of-factly, "Could it be, Ms. Walker, that you have a hang-up about being Indian?" Immediately she bristled, but before she could respond he went on. "I did a little checking on you. You're good, you're honest, you're young and ambitious. A man could do worse than hire a person like that as an estimator, especially when his corporation has all its officers intact.

Besides that, it wouldn't be far for you to drive. That's always to an employer's advantage."

His answer set her back in her chair. "How do you know where I live?"

Again a glint of amusement filled his eyes. "You forget. Your suitcase had a tag on its handle just like mine did."

Of course! How could she forget what had led her here in the first place? Yet it was disconcerting to think he'd been asking people about her.

"Tell me, Mr. Brown," she began, "is there anything you don't know about me?"

He looked up from his menu and she became uncomfortably aware that she was wearing a necklace shaped like an Indian arrowhead strung around her neck on a leather thong. But his eyes returned to his menu as he answered, "Yes, I don't know why you bother to order your meals without potatoes when you don't need to. The food here is tremendous. Don't stint yourself tonight."

His answer raised an instant prickle of female vanity, but she warned herself to accept the compliment with a grain of salt. Just then the waiter approached to take their order.

The meal was delicious, as promised. They ate it while discussing upcoming jobs Sam would want her to bid, projects she had worked on, nothing more personal until, over coffee, he sat back with one shoulder drooping lower than the other in a way with which she was already becoming familiar.

"Actually, there is a question about you that puzzles me," he said.

She looked up, waiting.

"Why don't you have records of employment before Thorpe Construction?"

"I do. They're in St. Louis."

"St. Louis?" Sam quirked an eyebrow.

"Yes, that's where I lived before."

"Before what?" Though his eyes rested lightly on her, she had the feeling he was drilling into her head.

"Before I moved here three years ago," she answered with deliberate evasion.

"Ah." He tilted his chin up, and for a moment she thought he might question her further, but just then the waiter arrived and laid a small tray at Sam Brown's elbow and handed him a silver pen.

"Excuse me, Mr. Brown, your tab." Sam scrawled a quick signature and rose to his feet.

"Come on, I'll show you the office."

Lee breathed a sigh of relief at the interruption, for the subject of St. Louis was not one she wanted to pursue.

As they moved past the tables toward the doorway, they were interrupted by an impeccably dressed man who leaned back in a chair, half turning to extend a hand. "How's it going, Sam?"

"Fine. Took a job in Denver last week." Brown released his hold on Lee's elbow to shake hands, then politely performed introductions.

"Cassie and Don Norris . . . Lee Walker, my newest estimator."

Lee considered spouting a denial aloud, but instead she politely shook hands with the Norrises.

"Well, congratulations, Lee. You've chosen a damn fine company there," Don Norris offered. She murmured some comment, surprised at his unsolicited praise and hoping it was true. A moment later Sam urged her toward the door again.

As they moved through the lounge, she couldn't resist glancing up at Sam. "Your new estimator? Aren't you being a little presumptuous?"

Sam smiled and shrugged. "It eliminated a lengthy explanation. I could have said you were the woman who stole my suitcase in the Denver airport. Would that have been better?"

Lee turned to hide her grin as they reached the main lobby, crossed to the door, and stepped outside.

"You can ride with me," he suggested. "It's not far, and I can bring you back to your car afterward."

He led her to a classy, off-white Toronado. Inside, the car smelled like him—the agreeably masculine and tangy scent of what she took to be Rawhide cosmetics. The front seat was luxurious, equipped with a stereo that filled the void while they drove in the waning summer evening.

It had been a long time since Lee had been in a car with an attractive man—and Sam Brown was certainly that! She watched the contour of his wrist draped over the steering wheel, the gleam of a gold watch peeking from beneath his sleeve, the relaxed fingers with dark skin and well-kept nails. She recalled the pleasant meal they'd just shared, his easygoing camaraderie with everyone at the club, the compliment Norris had dropped in passing, Brown's glib sense of humor. She ventured a brief study of his hair, an ear, the side of his neck, but then his face swung her way and she looked quickly out her side window.

No doubt about it—she was beginning to like Sam Brown.

The office complex was new, modern, and pleasing to the eye. The late sun, slanting across its cinnamon-colored brick walls and smoked-glass windows, created deep triangles of shadow, accentuating the beauty of the buildings' architectural design. In keeping with Kansas City's claim that it had more fountains than any other city in the world except Rome, the buildings had been designed around a charming esplanade whose main attraction was a fountain whose running water created a design reminiscent of a dandelion gone to seed.

Sam guided Lee along curved concrete walks past cherry trees, and yews and more, every shrub so well-kept it appeared they were tended by a beautician instead of a gardener. The sprinkler system had come on, and as they sauntered between the buildings Lee breathed in the pungent scent of wet cedar chips clustered at the base of the decorative plants. Redwood benches had been placed strategically along the walks, and even the trash depositories were built of redwood, blending pleasantly into the environment. Tall ash trees had been planted alongside each building.

Sam unlocked the lobby door and held it open while Lee entered a spacious foyer carpeted in burnt orange. The stairs were carpeted as well and seemed to drop out of nowhere into the center of the lobby. A rich walnut handrail was smooth beneath Lee's palm as she ran her hand along it appreciatively.

If she'd expected Brown to be a smalltime hood, his surroundings were suggesting otherwise.

At Suite 204 he fitted a key into the lock, pushed the walnut door inward, and held it also as she passed before him. Fluorescent lights came on, flooding the reception area.

Lee glanced around nervously. There was something so gloomy and deserted about the silent, empty office. The room was decorated in tones of blue, from royal to wedgwood, and the walls were hung with posters depicting various moments in the company's history. They were framed in aluminum, fronted with glass, and hung on rich vinyl wallcovering that matched upholstered chairs and smoked-glass tables, where various construction magazines and equipment brochures lay.

The chink of keys brought Lee's attention back to Sam.

"This is obviously the reception area," he said, motioning her ahead of him around a free-standing wall that formed the backdrop for the receptionist's desk.

The payroll office was the first cubicle behind the wall. Inside, a computer hummed softly and photographs of two toddlers stood on a desk.

"The computer runs day and night," Sam informed Lee. "All our payroll and parts inventory are stored in it."

There was a separate office for the bookkeeper and his assistant, followed by a large open area, also carpeted in deep blue, where slant-topped drafting tables were lined up. The arrangement preserved an overall feeling of space, for the smoky windows ran nearly ceiling to floor, and the sight of the ash trees outside helped bring the outdoors in. The suite was at the southeast corner of the building, thus the fading sun left this area dimly lit, for Sam hadn't turned on the overhead lights here.

"This is where our draftsmen work," he explained unnecessarily. Lee was ever conscious of him hovering a step behind her. Occasionally the soft clink of keys told her how near he was. She looked across the pleasant, orderly expanse. Wide racks of blueprints hung neatly, like sheets on a clothesline. There were no rolled, wrinkled, or torn plans in sight. There were no chunks of dried clay on the carpet, no coffee-can cuspidors. "That's the copy room." Sam pointed, and Lee turned her head in time to catch the vague movement of his arm before he moved through the drafting area into a separate corner office. In the doorway he turned again to her, his stance inviting her in.

"Yours?" she asked.

He nodded.

Just inside the door she stopped, tingles of appreciation

running along her arms. The room was neat and orderly, and Lee couldn't help comparing it to Floyd Thorpe's pigpen. A modest-sized executive desk stood to one side, a credenza under the window. There was a game table, surrounded by rich leather armchairs on ball castors, which was obviously used as a conference table. The floor was carpeted in rich chocolate, the windows treated with vertical blinds of a lighter shade. Here again, plans and blueprints hung on neat racks. A tall schefflera plant stood in the corner where east and south-facing windows met.

Lee crossed to the south window and looked out. A moment later her nostrils were again filled with Sam's scent as he stepped behind her and pointed past the treetops. "That's where we were." From here she could see only the tip of the Carriage Club's main building. "Most of the time I move in a rather confined area."

"But a very pleasant one," she noted, turning and laying her fingertips on the polished surface of his desk. Her eyes met his, but there was no hint of teasing in them this time. "I like it very much."

The expression on his face told Lee it was one thing he'd wanted to hear. His fingers relaxed and the keys clinked softly.

"Would you like to see the estimating area?"

"I thought you'd never ask."

A smile broke on his face like sun over the horizon, and he led the way to another wide expanse much like that where the drafting tables were. Here the tables were flat and of desk height. The southern exposure gave the estimating area the same view as that from Sam's office. Lee looked out, thinking again of the three years she'd worked in Floyd Thorpe's office, wondering if she could possibly be wrong about Sam Brown's character, knowing it was fast losing importance in light of his fantastic offer and this enticing office.

"You're the first full-time estimator I've hired for the new portion of the business, so there's no designated area for you," Sam explained. "You'll just work in here with the plumbing estimators, if that's all right with you."

"Oh . . ." She turned from the window. "That's more than

all right, as I'm sure you're well aware. I've never seen a contractor's office as plush as this. But I'm sure you're well aware of that, too."

"Just because you dig in dirt for a living doesn't mean you have to live in it."

"No, not at all. Somebody should tell that to Floyd Thorpe."

He turned and indicated a desk across the way. "That would be yours."

The desks were placed in herringbone relationship to one another, giving the room an even more spacious aspect. Beside the desk Sam was pointing to stood a potted orange tree, that seemed to be thriving.

Lee crossed to *her* desk, pulled out *her* chair, and touched *her* orange tree. The chair rolled silently on a large slab of clear vinyl that protected the blue carpet. She sat down, and placed her palms flat on the desk top as if to test its temperature. A feeling of imminent excitement tightened her chest. My God, it was like a dream come true. She looked up at Sam, standing some distance across the room, watching every move she made.

"I think it fits." Accepting his offer, she was filled with anticipation.

"Agreed." He raised a hand and beckoned her over to him. "Come on, I'll drive you back to your car. You'll be spending enough time in that chair without staying in it now."

She pushed the chair back beneath the desk and moved to him. This time he didn't touch her, but before they rounded the corner she turned back, taking one last look at her desk.

Back in his car she didn't hear the music, didn't feel the plush seat, didn't watch his wrist on the wheel. She was too excited.

"My God, Brown, did you do all that or did your father?"

"He made it possible for me to do it. We didn't have that office until after he died."

She paused. "I imagine he would have loved it as much as I do."

"He was content at the old location," Sam said. "My mother was the one who encouraged me to move into the new building and add a touch of class to the operation. It turned out we'd made too damn much profit one year. The overhead became a healthy tax write-off after we rented this new place. Meanwhile we enjoy the surroundings."

"You know what I want to do the first day of work?" Lee rested her head back against the luxurious seat and closed her eyes.

"What?"

She rolled her head toward Sam and opened her eyes to find him studying the curve of her arched throat. "I want to bring my sack lunch and sit by that fountain and eat at high noon."

He laughed pleasantly, and she watched his lips change with the sound. "Whatever turns you on. There are several good restaurants in the complex—"

"Restaurants! Where's your sense of . . . of nature!"

"I get all the nature I need during the day. I spend more than half my time at jobsites. My old man taught me that's the only way to run a business—by keeping your eye on what's happening instead of leaving it up to someone else. At noon I like to go where it's cool and not dusty and let somebody serve me a decent meal on a plate."

Lee couldn't help wondering if he went out on the job dressed like that. His brown shoes certainly didn't look like they'd scuffed any dust today.

Just then, the Toronado turned into the horseshoe driveway of the Carriage Club, and Lee straightened in her seat. Brown swung the car into a parking spot, and before she could protest he was out his side and heading around to open her door. She beat him to the punch and met him beside the car.

He turned and together they ambled across the lot. "When do you want to start?" he asked.

She stopped him with a hand on his sleeve. "Brown, there's just one thing I have to ask for even before I say I'll take the job."

"What's that?"

She swallowed, knowing that what she had to ask was presumptuous. "I . . . I have to have the last week of August off." This was the last week of July—she knew it was a lot to ask. Nobody in the construction industry took time off during the busy summer season. As she stood waiting for Sam's response, she feared, too, that he might demand the reason for her request and sought frantically for a white lie. But in the end she had no need to produce one.

"Shouldn't be any problem," Sam said, "but usually we take vacations during the cold months when there's not much going on." He began moving on, but Lee grabbed his arm.

"Oh, I didn't mean I expect it off with pay! It's just . . ." She grew self-conscious holding his arm and dropped her hand.

"It's okay. As far as I can remember, there won't be any important bids around that time, so you can plan on it as yours."

"Thank you. In that case, back to your original question." She braved a sheepish smile. "Would Monday be too soon to start?"

He chuckled, came back to where she trailed along behind him, and lightly pressed a palm against the small of her back. "Are you that eager to work for this . . . reprobate?" he teased.

Moving toward her car, she admitted artlessly, "I need to make the house payment next week, just like you do." She was far too aware of the warmth of his palm through the thin knit of her top, but then it disappeared.

"I don't make house payments. I live in the old family rattrap with my mother."

This was the second time he'd mentioned his mother, and Lee couldn't help but wonder. Another case of apron strings? Though she'd never have thought it of Sam Brown, she'd learned her lesson once with Joel. Furthermore, Sam wasn't the only one who'd done some calculating after reading an address on a suitcase. The family "rattrap" of which he spoke was on exclusive Ward Parkway. She didn't have to see the house to imagine what it must be like.

"Speaking of rattraps"—they'd reached her Pinto—"this one is mine."

He gave it a cursory glance, then returned his attention to her. "Is there anything else you need to know about the job?"

"Nothing I can think of. Oh, what are office hours?"

"On a normal day I usually come in around seven and knock off at five."

There seemed little more to say, and while she studied Sam Brown's expression, it ceased to say "business" and took on the distinctly alarming look of "pleasure."

A slow hand reached for the silver arrowhead necklace that rested against her chest, still warm from her skin, and his eyes followed. His fingers closed around it, and she thought she felt the thong tighten at the back of her neck.

Panic clawed its way up to her throat. She wanted to say "Brown, don't!" for she thought he was going to kiss her and, since he was about to become her boss, she couldn't let him set such a dangerous precedent. She wanted his job, but no other complications. Besides, he lived on Ward Parkway in the family "rattrap" with his mother . . . and . . . and . . . oh God, Brown, you smell so good . . . let go . . .

But she was never to know Sam Brown's intentions, for a moment later he dropped the arrowhead against her chest and turned away before an enormous sneeze erupted from him.

Lee was laughing before the second sneeze clutched him. He tugged a hanky from his hip pocket, rubbed his nose, and stepped back three feet.

"You and your damn Renaldo la Pizzio!"

Even though she jammed her hands on her hips, Lee was still amused as she scolded, "Oh, you had yourself a regular heyday with my private belongings, didn't you?"

"I could order you to get rid of it before you show up at the office."

"You could, but you won't. After all, they write exposés in Washington about orders like that."

But even as she chuckled, her body felt weak with relief, for if he *had* tried to kiss her, she wasn't sure how long she'd have resisted.

CHAPTER

Five

THE NIGHT BEFORE her first day of work, Lee slept in that tenuous half-conscious state she often experienced before a day promising something special—a thin, filmy kind of sleep during which the excitement somehow managed to keep her so nearly alert that the morning alarm was stifled before its bell gave out more than a ting. She lay staring at the ceiling, which was tinted pale pink by the rising sun, and said in amazement, "Forty thousand dollars a year, can you beat that?"

Then she was on her feet, eagerness in every step as she switched on the radio, showered, washed her hair, took a sinful amount of time styling it, then applied her makeup. Her head was tilted back, a mascara wand darkening her stubby lashes, when she suddenly straightened, stared at her reflection, smiled, and told the woman in the mirror, "An orange tree . . . You have an orange tree by your desk!" Then the woman in the mirror replied, "Damn fool, Walker, finish your primping or you'll be late on your first day."

Lee considered long and hard before deciding between a warm rose slack outfit and a white slim skirt with a matching peplumed jacket. She chose the skirt in deference to the classy office, the white in deference to her own deep coloring. It complemented her dark skin and black hair so strikingly that Lee felt thoroughly pleased with her appearance when she was all dressed. The straight skirt added to her height and the peplum added to her hips—an altogether flattering combo.

After adding a single white bangle bracelet that matched white hoops in her ears, she was satisfied.

But as she smoothed the skirt one last time over her hips, she confronted her reflection in the mirror again and a worried frown formed between her eyebrows. Had she dressed so carefully to please Sam Brown? The possibility was disturbing. She dropped her eyes to the photographs of Jed and Matthew in a hinged frame on her dresser top. The familiar stab of loss cut through her momentarily, then she was removing the black combs that held her hair behind each ear, replacing them defiantly with others that trailed small, bronze feathers to the backs of her jaws.

You are what you are, Lee Walker, and you'd be wise not to forget it!

In the office Sam Brown seemed to scarcely notice what she was wearing. The sleeves of his plaid shirt were already rolled up past the elbows, and he held a set of plans in his hand. Though he greeted Lee with a pleasant, "Good morning . . . all set to meet the gang?" it was all business with Sam Brown.

Three others were already there when Lee arrived. Sam immediately introduced her as "the first permanent employee of the sewer and water division." Rachael Robinson, the office's gal friday, was efficient and energetic. She wore a pale yellow dress that looked smashing against her black skin and conveyed a very *now* look.

Immediately Lee could tell Frank Schultz was Sam Brown's right-hand man. Schultz was the head estimator of plumbing and had been working with Sam on the few sewer and water jobs they'd bid so far. A bull-headed Irishman named Duke was head superintendent of the outside crews, and under him worked several foremen who remained voices on the radio much of the time. Ron Chen was head bookkeeper, a small Chinese man with thick glasses and an ingratiating smile. His second in command was his own twenty-year-old daughter, Terri, who worked part time and attended the University of Missouri at Kansas City the rest of the week. The computer was manned by an older, portly woman named Nelda Huffman, who looked more like a cleaning lady than a payroll clerk. The pictures on Nelda's desk proved to be of her grandchildren.

By the time all the employees of Brown & Brown had begun their work day, Lee Walker felt as if she were in the amphitheater of the United Nations Building! She realized that nobody here would notice a feather in her hair, although Rachael did comment on how stylish it was.

Brown & Brown was a pleasant change from Thorpe Construction. Though Lee didn't have her own office as she'd had previously, she didn't mind a bit. Among the entire office crew there was a noticeable camaraderie that made up for the lack of privacy. And the atmosphere was so harmonious, the decor so tasteful, that Lee felt almost childishly eager to do well, learn fast, and prove her abilities so she could feel justified in taking over the desk and the orange tree.

At coffee break the copy room became a gathering spot. It contained not only copying and duplicator machines, but also a refrigerator, microwave oven, and coffee percolator that was kept constantly replenished by Rachael, who seemed to be the office staff's cheerful "ladybug." Everyone seemed to like her.

The day began with a short session at which Sam Brown, Frank Schultz, and Rachael discussed helping Lee learn her way around the place. After Lee had filled out the usual new-employee forms, Frank explained the general bidding procedure, psychology, and ratio of profit on which they worked.

Sam was gone at noon, and Lee ate her sack lunch by the fountain, feeling totally refreshed when she returned. She saw Sam again late in the afternoon when he came in briefly, dusty leather workboots and khaki-colored jeans attesting to his having been out in the field. When Frank Schultz began cleaning off his desk top at the end of the afternoon, Lee couldn't believe it was going on five o'clock already. The day had raced by so fast it seemed as if she'd just walked in the door!

The following morning she, Sam, and Frank worked together on a small bid. Immediately Lee saw that changes here were discussed sensibly before being made. No last minute surprises were sprung unless it was by mutual agreement. They talked together about upcoming jobs listed in *The Construction Bulletin* and decided which ones Lee should order plans for. Sam asked if Frank would have time the following day to take Lee out and show her around the jobs in progress so she could get a handle on the equipment the company owned, and also give her a complete inventory of it so she knew exactly what work capacity they could handle.

The third day, she and Frank drove in a company pickup, from jobsite to jobsite. At each, Lee was introduced to crew members and foremen alike.

Walking into the skeleton of a two-story steel-frame building, Lee was surprised to see Sam Brown, in hardhat and workboots, waving hello. He picked his way across pipes and fittings, removing a pair of soiled leather workgloves as he came.

"Got troubles, boss?" Frank inquired.

"Naw, nothing Duke can't handle." Sam smiled over his shoulder as Lee heard Duke in the background, his voice like the roar of a bull elephant, telling some laborer to jack that son of a bitch up and see she didn't bust again or his ass'd be higher than the goddam water table! Lee was laughing as Sam turned back to her. The rough language of construction superintendents was nothing new to her.

"Everything going okay so far, Lee?" Sam's question was simple and inconsequential, nothing at all to make her heart jump. Maybe it was the ordinary way he'd called her Lee, or the way he lifted his hardhat off the back of his head and mopped his forehead with a sleeve that sent her pulse racing.

"Not a single complaint," she answered. "We've been to all the jobsites but one. I'm getting a good idea of how much equipment the company has, but I can see there's not much in the way of heavy stuff."

"We've leased most of the heavy stuff up till now and we'll continue to do that until we're sure we want to stay in the sewer and water work," Sam explained.

"A couple of the jobs we discussed yesterday would require a nine-eighty front-end loader and I haven't seen one yet."

"I know. We don't own one. The biggest we've got is a nine-fifty. That's why I wanted you to make the rounds with Frank. I've got some decisions to make about buying new equipment, and I want you in on them." There was something

elemental about him standing in the hot sun with a dusty boot
on a section of pipe, settling the hardhat back on his head,
then tugging back on the filthy leather gloves. His rolled-up
sleeves exposed arms tanned to a cinnamon hue with hair
bleached almost red by the sun. A bead of sweat trickled from
under the hardhat along his temple, and Lee looked away.

In the background a machine started up, and Sam shouted
to be heard above the noise. "Frank, could you run out to the
Independence City Hall and pick up a set of plans for that
Little Blue River job?"

"Sure, Sam. We'll be over that direction anyway."

"Good. Lee and I will run out and take a look at it Friday
morning." At the mention of her name, she turned back to the
trickle of sweat, but it had become no less irresistible, collect-
ing dust as it moved downward. It drew her eyes as if it were
whitewater on the Colorado River rather than a single droplet
flowing along a man's hairline.

She pulled her eyes away again, hoping Sam hadn't
noticed the direction of her gaze. At first she thought he
hadn't, but in the end she wasn't sure, for as Frank pulled the
pickup away from the bumpy construction site, Lee looked
back over her shoulder to discover Sam standing where they'd
left him, his feet planted firmly apart, his eyes following
them.

On Thursday, just before Lee left for the day, Sam stopped
by her desk. "It's been a helluva busy week. Sorry I haven't
been around much."

Lee's elbows were propped on the desk top as she leaned
over a long jobsheet. Turning, she almost bumped against
Sam's thigh, he'd been standing so close. She tipped her chair
back to look up at him.

"Frank has taken good care of me. The week's been great."

Sam crossed his arms, leaned against the edge of her desk,
and stretched his legs out in front of him. "Good, glad to hear
it. Listen, would you mind wearing something . . ." For a
moment his eyes fell to her bare knee where her skirt was
hitched up slightly. "Well, put on some slacks tomorrow,
okay? We'll probably be walking through some rough stuff
when we go out to look at that job."

"Sure, whatever you say."

"Have you got any boots?" Now his eyes drifted down her calves to the sling-back high heels on her feet.

"Aha. Got just the thing."

"Good. Bring 'em along. We'll be going out first thing in the morning, and the dew can be heavy."

"Anything else?"

"Yeah." For the first time he glanced up to give a quick survey of the room, but several desks were already empty, and nobody who remained paid them any attention. His gaze returned to Lee. "Have you been bringing those sack lunches like you said?"

"Every day. The fountain is delightful with cheese on rye."

"Could you make enough for two tomorrow?" His eyes softened as he smiled down at her.

"Of course. What's the occasion?"

"No occasion. We might end up someplace out in the boonies at lunchtime, so if you'll bring the food, I'll bring us some cola in a cooler."

"Friday is bologna and pickle day."

"Sweet or dill?"

"Dill."

"Sold." He stood up. "See you here at eight."

The following morning dawned murky and muggy after a night of intermittent thundershowers. Low, gray clouds hid the sunrise, and the thick, sultry air seemed cloyingly sticky.

She dressed in blue jeans, tennis shoes, and a casual cotton knit pullover of navy and white stripes with a sailor collar and a ribbed waist, and took along a pair of rubber, lace-up duck hunting boots, a can of mosquito spray, and a brown paper bag containing three bologna sandwiches, potato chips, pickles, and some chocolate chip cookies.

She and Sam set out right after he returned from his morning rounds of all the jobs. He stopped at Rachael's desk to advise her where they'd be. "If you need us, give a call on the radio."

"Right, boss."

"We'll take my truck," Sam informed Lee as they crossed the parking lot toward a sleek pickup identifiable by its stan-

dard company color—a rich, metallic brown with the logo
B & B in white on its doors. Sam looked down at Lee's feet.

"Didn't you bring any boots?"

"They're in my car. Be right back." She was only too
happy to move away from Sam Brown, for her eyes, too, had
meandered down the length of his strong legs, and the sight of
them was altogether too compelling. What was it about him?
Whenever she was close to him her thoughts strayed to his
masculinity, ever since that first night in Denver when she'd
found his magazine.

He'd backed the pickup around and was waiting when she
turned from the Pinto with full hands. This time her eyes were
arrested by the sight of his long, bronzed arm in its white
rolled-up sleeve as he stretched across the truck seat to push
the door open for her. *Shape up, Lee Walker, and think business!* Dragging her thoughts back to safer footing, she clambered up onto the high seat beside him and dumped her
collection on the floor.

A roll of plans, his workgloves and hardhat lay between
them, and with a murmured apology, Sam scooped them
closer to his hip to make more room for her.

"It's okay," Lee assured him, flashing him a quick smile.

But it wasn't okay. There was something too close about
the relatively confining space of the single seat. And—dammit!—did Sam Brown's vehicles always have to smell like
him? It was his world, this masculine domain of hardhats,
laced-up leather boots, and pickups with column shifts.

"I'll drive, you navigate," Sam ordered as they started out.
Almost gratefully, Lee opened the wide set of plans and studied the map. But even so, she found herself too aware of the
tan arm with its relaxed wrist that shifted gears, the hand
vibrating on the stick. Covertly she watched the tightening of
muscles beneath the left leg of his blue jeans as he raised it to
press in the clutch. He was a runner, she remembered, and
supposed those muscles were hard and well toned. The denim
fit his leg like a rind fits an orange.

Suddenly she realized they were sitting still and raised her
eyes from Sam's leg to find he'd been watching her. For how
long? She felt herself turning as red as the light that had
stopped them as he smiled lazily.

"I see you brought the bologna sandwiches." His face was stunningly dark against the open collar of his white shirt, and it did foolish things to the pit of her stomach.

"As ordered. Where's the Coke?" she managed to ask in a surprisingly normal voice.

He gestured with a shoulder and a lift of his chin. "In the back." His lazy eyes made her feel light-headed, but just then the light changed and they rolled forward. Sam's gaze moved away from her, and she returned to navigating.

"Exit on Two ninety-one south," she ordered.

"Two ninety-one south," he repeated. Then there was only the high whine of the wheels on the blacktop and the shuddering jiggle rising up through the seat beneath Lee as they rode silently. She watched the riffling of his shirtsleeves in the wind from the opened window, then studied the view beyond her own, striving to feel at ease in his presence.

Suddenly Rachael's voice crackled across the radio. "Base to unit one. Come in, Sam."

From the corner of her eye, Lee watched him pluck the mike from the dash. His index finger curled around the call button and the mike almost touched his lips. "Unit one, Sam here. Go ahead, Rachael."

"I've got a long-distance call from Denver. It's Tom Weatherall returning your call, so I thought you'd want to know."

"It's nothing important, just an inquiry I made about an equipment auction that's coming up. Tell him I'll get back to him on Monday."

"Right, boss . . . base clear."

"Thanks, Rachael. Unit one clear."

The white shirtsleeve strained diagonally across Sam's upper arm as he replaced the mike, and Lee turned her eyes resolutely away, again resisting the urge to study him. But to her chagrin, she found she need not look to remember. He was dressed in blue jeans, white shirt, and leather boots—no different from what a thousand laboring men wore every day. Yet he looked better than a thousand men, the basic no-nonsense work clothes lending him a magnetic sex appeal totally different from the dress slacks and sport coat he'd worn the first few times she'd seen him.

*Keep your mind on your map, Walker, he didn't even kiss
you.*

They turned off 291 at her directions and took increasingly
smaller roads until they came to a gravel road that led out into
the country. "I think this is it." Lee pointed to an abandoned
farm off to their right.

The pickup swerved to the side of the road to idle again
while Sam hooked his left elbow over the steering wheel,
rested his right hand along the back of the seat, and peered out
her window. She was served up a tantalizing whiff of his
aftershave as his knuckles passed before her face and he
pointed.

"Looks like it'll start just this side of those trees and move
off across the edge of that field. We might as well get out and
walk it."

Lee was only too glad to escape the close proximity to Sam
Brown, and she jumped from the cab with a shaky, indrawn
breath of relief. She sat down on the running board to untie
her tennis shoes and replace them with the olive drab water-
proof boots, conscious now that Sam was standing with his
hands on his hips watching her. She tucked her pantlegs
into the boot tops, but left the yellow strings dangling. Still
he stood, his weight balanced evenly on both feet, making
her skin prickle with awareness. It had been a long time
since a man had watched her change her clothes, even any
as impersonal as shoes, and this man seemed to be studying
the process all too closely. She straightened, got to her feet,
and gave her ribbed waistband a businesslike tug to pull it
back into place. His face wore a disturbingly appre- ciative
half grin, his gaze centered on the thin band of skin at her
waist, which quickly disappeared as she adjusted her shirt.

"What are you staring at, Brown?" she demanded.

He seemed to shake himself back to the present. "Estimators look different than they used to," he teased.

Keep it light, her saner self warned as his comment aroused
a small thrill. She displayed one foot, lifting it before her.
"Same as you, jeans and boots."

But as his eyes traveled down to her boots, she realized
that instead of minimizing her femininity, they accented it. To
her relief, at that moment Sam's hand slapped at his neck,

then he made a grab at the air, missing the mosquito that had just bitten him.

"Come here, I'll give you a spray." Lee picked up the can from the floor of the truck.

With a grin, he noted, "You come prepared, don't you?"

"In Missouri, in August, the morning after a healthy rain?" she asked pointedly. He came to stand before her while she shook the can and sprayed the front of him in long sweeps from neck to boots, noting even in that quick journey certain spots where his jeans were more worn. *Damn you, Walker, what's the matter with you?* "Turn around, I'll do your back." But his back presented as enticing a set of muscles as his front. His shoulders were wide and firm as she sprayed them, heading down toward where his shirt scarcely crinkled as it disappeared into the narrow waist of his jeans. His buns were so flat that they scarcely curved beneath the denim. Again she remembered that he was a runner. It seemed a long, long way down to his wide-spread boots.

He craned to look at her over his shoulder. "Hurry up. This stuff stinks."

As she stood up, she couldn't resist teasing. "Don't be such a baby, Brown. I don't think it smells so bad." And as if to prove the point, she gave him a shot inside the back of his collar, then pulled the can farther back and emitted a cloud at the back of his head. He doubled forward and let out an immense sneeze.

She burst out laughing as he moved out of range and whirled.

"Damn it all, if it isn't one thing it's another."

She puckered her face and feigned an apology. "Oh, I'm so-o-o sorry."

A wicked grin lifted his mouth as he returned wryly, "Yes, I can see just how sorry you are."

He took a menacing step toward her, and she backed away. "Now, Brown, it was an accident!" she warned, holding out a hand to fend him off. But he advanced a step farther.

"So will this be." He wrenched the can from her hand and shook it, a gleam of menace in his eye.

"Brown, I'm warning you!"

"You started it, now stand and take your medicine."

There was nothing she could do but turn her back on him, squeeze her eyes shut, and wait. He took his sweet time about it, while she grew increasingly uncomfortable. Finally she felt the spray at the back of her neck. Then it moved downward and stopped at her hips. "Put your arms up," he ordered. She gritted her teeth, did as ordered, but immediately realized her mistake, for when her arms went up, so did the shirt. A long moment passed in silence, and she felt herself beginning to blush. Then the hiss of the spray finished its trip down her backside, and he nudged her with the can, ordering, "Turn around." She spun about, chancing a quick peek at the top of his hair as he hunkered down before her, but quickly shutting her eyes as the cloud of spray moved upward. It stopped again, at her hips, and she suffered an agonizing moment, wondering what he was doing before a direct shot hit her in her bare navel.

She yelped and jumped backward. "Damn you, Brown!"

He chuckled devilishly. "I couldn't resist."

She glared at him as he knelt on one knee, his eyes nearly on a level with the ribbed waistband that she now hugged protectively in place. She was fighting a losing battle of trying to forget that Sam Brown was a man—and he wasn't helping one bit! The only resource she could draw upon was feigned indignation. She yanked the can from his hand, then stalked to the truck and flung it through the open window.

"We've got work to do, Brown. Enough of this fooling around!" And, thankfully, he followed her lead and got back down to business.

They set off through knee-high grass laden with dew and embroidered with spider webs to which droplets of moisture clung. They moved slowly, the only sounds those of their footsteps swishing through the grass, which occasionally squeaked as it brushed wetly against Lee's rubber boots. They stopped and stood shoulder to shoulder, each holding one side of the wide blueprints as they studied them.

There were a hundred considerations to be made when deciding whether or not to bid a job such as this one. The first and most obvious was the amount of dirt to be moved, where to, and with what. As they walked, they scanned the ups and downs, considering, discussing, doing mental calculations.

They left the fairly level edge of the cornfield and came to a section of uneven roughland—pasture for the most part—with gullies and swales, many filled with muddy potholes after last night's rains. The dampness of the soil was a second important consideration, so Sam and Lee often knelt, side by side, lifting handfuls of soil, noting where they wanted to do test borings.

Lee was conscious of the smell of mosquito spray and wet earth, and of Sam Brown's inviting masculine scent, as they squatted with their shoulders almost touching. They moved on again, following the route the pipe would take, crossing a thick stand of prairie thistle in full purple bloom, until they came to a marsh where red-winged blackbirds perched atop bobbing cattails. The birds' voices raised a cacophony while Sam and Lee stood unmoving for several minutes—just listening and enjoying. It was peaceful and private. Lee became aware that Sam's eyes were seeking her out as he stood behind her, his thumbs hooked on his hipbones. It took great effort to keep from looking back, but she resolutely refrained. Assuming a businesslike air, she noted, "Lots of birds out here."

Sam gave a cursory glance at the swamp and grunted in agreement, but immediately his eyes swung back to her.

"The Department of Natural Resources will require a permit before we mess around with their nesting area. I'll make a note of it." But when she jotted down the note, she braved a glance at him and caught him studying her in a disturbing way. Immediately she looked at the set of plans, but his next question made her forget the figures before her eyes.

"How long have you been divorced?"

The air was utterly still, everything washed clean by the night rains which still lingered on leaf and stem, turning into diamond beads when the sun occasionally broke through the patchy clouds overhead. Lee met Sam's eyes, realizing that if she answered it would be harder than ever to get back to business.

"Three years," she replied.

He seemed to consider before finally asking, "Does he live here?"

"No."

"In St. Louis?"

Though posed in a casual tone, his question brought her to her senses. "We're supposed to be looking for a corner lathe with a red flag on it," she reminded him.

"Oh." He shrugged, as if her deliberate evasion were of little importance. "Oh yeah . . . well, forget I asked."

She tried to do just that, but for the remainder of their walk the unanswered question hung between them.

CHAPTER

Six

BY THE TIME they finished their survey the sun was high and hot. They had made nearly a complete circle, which brought them at last to the foot of a hill below what had once been a thriving orchard and busy farmhouse. Lee could see the peak of the roof above the apple trees, and a large, rustic barn loomed up at her right. As they walked beneath the laden trees toward the crest of the hill, the shade felt soothing after the heat of the sun. The orchard had a scent of its own, a fecund mixture of loam and ripening fruit. Lee felt the lingering loneliness of old places whose thriving days have passed.

The house came into view. Like the barn, it had a fieldstone foundation. To Lee it seemed at once beautiful and sad, for the dreams that might have nurtured the building of this place were long dead with their dreamers. The voices of its past were long gone. Its windows, vacant now, had once reflected a yard filled with seasonal activity—cattle coming home at the end of deep afternoon, children at play . . .

At the thought, a sharp pain of regret knifed through Lee, and she clutched her stomach.

"Is something wrong?"

"No . . . no!" She turned back to Sam with assumed brightness and made a pretense of rubbing her stomach. "I . . . I'm just hungry, that's all."

He glanced in the direction of the truck. "I can probably make it up that old driveway yet. Why don't you wait here while I get the truck?"

He strode off, and she watched until he disappeared, swallowed up by the trees. The abandoned house drew her irresistibly, and her feet moved almost against her will. She wandered around the foundation, peeking in windows at old linoleum, remnants of wallpaper, a sagging pantry door, a rusted iron pump, a hole in the wall where a chimney had once been. She kicked at a fruit jar that had been left lying in the deep weeds and fought an intense ache brought on by the old place, whose memorabilia brought back memories of her own past.

A gay profusion of tiger lilies nodded on long stems beside the back stoop, and Lee sat down in the sun, dropping her forehead on her crossed arms and raised knees. The truck started, way off in the distance, but she scarcely heard it. Memories came flooding back, memories she wanted to blot out but couldn't—wallpaper on other walls...another kitchen sink with a child's dirty feet being washed at bedtime ...a table with two people, then two plus a baby in a high chair...the view from another kitchen window...a swing set where a child fell and called for Mommy...another back door with a mother swooping through on her way to soothe the child's cries...another backyard with day lilies blossoming in lemon brightness...

The truck came gunning up the steep, rutted incline, sending rocks rolling behind it, then coming to a stop under the apple trees.

"Lee?" Sam called as he stepped out of the cab. She raised her head slowly, pulling herself back to the present. "Come on down here. It's cooler in the shade." When she didn't move, his hand slipped from the door and his shoulders tensed. "Hey, are you okay?"

He started toward her, and immediately she pulled herself together and jumped off the step, brushing off her backside with a jauntiness she didn't feel.

"Yeah...yeah, sure." She would have strode right past him, but he reached out a hand, and before she could prevent it, he swung her around and tipped up her unsteady chin. He studied her closely and, after a long, uncomfortable scrutiny, stated, "You've been crying."

She squelched the sudden, overwhelming urge to throw herself into his arms.

"I have not," she declared stubbornly.

He dropped his eyes to her nostrils, and she made an effort to keep them from quivering. His gaze continued down to her lips, which felt puffy, then back up to her glistening eyes and damp lashes.

"Do you want to talk about it?" he invited very quietly.

No . . . yes . . . oh, please, let me go before I do . . . His eyes invited her confidence, and the corners of his lips turned down as she hovered on the brink of telling him everything, which would prove utterly disastrous, she was sure.

"No," she finally answered.

He seemed to consider for a moment, then his hand fell, and his voice came gay and bright. "All right. Then we'll just eat our lunch." He swung blithely toward the cab, reached inside, and came up with the sack lunch, then left the truck door open and the radio tuned to a country station as he turned to assess the area under the apple trees. "The ground's probably wet. Why don't we sit on the tailgate?"

"Fine," Lee answered, still thrown off guard by Sam's sudden levity when she had expected him to press her for answers. He lowered the tailgate, set the bag down, and turned to her with the same carefree air.

"Need a boost?" Before she could answer, Lee found herself deposited on the cool, brown metal. The truck bounced a little as Sam joined her then twisted to retrieve the cooler and pull out two icy cans of cola before popping their tops and handing her one. He tipped up his own and swilled nearly half its contents before licking his lips, running a hand across his mouth, and sighing with satisfaction.

He looked down pointedly at the sandwich bag between their hips, and Lee realized she'd been watching him with undivided interest, trying to figure him out.

"Oh! Help yourself," she offered.

"Thanks."

He took a sandwich, sank his teeth into it, and swung his feet in rhythm to the soft country songs coming from the cab behind them.

"Aren't you going to eat?" he asked.

Lee was brought back from her wool-gathering and, dutifully taking a bite of the sandwich, discovered she was hungrier than she'd thought. Soon they were sitting in companionable silence, munching and sipping, listening to the birds and the radio.

When Sam finished eating, he leaned back on one palm, hooked a boot heel over the edge of the tailgate, and draped his elbow indolently over an updrawn knee, swinging the cola can idly between his fingers. Lee grew increasingly aware of his scrutiny and of the privacy of the old orchard and abandoned farmyard.

"Are you still hung up on your husband?" Startled, Lee turned to find Sam's brown eyes steady on her face. They were undeniably stunning, their lashes longer than her own. His unsmiling lips had a symmetry and fullness that must have broken a heart or two in their time, she thought.

Unsettled by her observation, she looked at some distant point and answered, "No."

"That's not why you were crying, then?"

She gave up the senseless argument that she hadn't been crying. "I . . . no."

"Over somebody else, then?"

"No, there's nobody else."

A long silence followed, and she sensed him looking at her hair, then at her profile. "Well, then . . ." The ensuing pause was electric. She still felt his eyes on her face but was afraid to look at him. The hand with the can left his knee, then a single, cold index finger lifted her chin until she was forced to meet his eyes. She stared mutely into them—stunning, steady brown eyes—telling herself to turn away sensibly. Instead, she sat as if transfixed as his lips moved closer . . . and closer . . .

"Brown, don't," she said at the last moment, turning aside. Her voice was reedy and strained.

"Well, if it's not your ex-husband and it's not somebody else, there's no reason why I shouldn't kiss you, is there?"

There were a hundred reasons why not, but they all escaped Lee at that moment as he tipped her face up once more. The noon sun sent splinters of light through minute openings in the branches overhead into their private domain, like miniature green-gold starbursts. Somewhere in the distance a meadowlark warbled.

"Brown, you're my boss and I don't think—"

His kiss cut off her argument as he leaned over, pressing a palm against the floor behind her, and meeting her lips above the brown paper bag and the remains of their meal. His lips were cold from the drink, but soft and appealing as he tipped his head to the side and moved it in lazy, seductive motions back and forth. The coolness left the skin of his inner lips and was replaced by warmth from her own.

Oh, Brown, Brown, you're too damn good at this.

Lee found her common sense at last and pulled back, but Sam continued leaning toward her in that nonchalant pose. The wrist and can were on his knee again, but his eyes were on her mouth.

"I've been thinking about that since long before our walk today," he said.

"Don't say things like that." She frowned at his chin to convince him she was serious, though she suspected she was the one who needed convincing for it had suddenly become very hard to breathe.

"Why not?" he asked with a half smile.

"Because it could cause innumerable problems, and I'm not up to handling them."

He leaned even closer. "No problems—I promise." While she was still trying to sort out rationality from response, he kissed her again, sending tiny shudders up her arms and fluid fire through her veins. His warm tongue circled her lips, and even as she told herself this was dangerous, this man was too appealing and far, far too expert, her lips parted and answered his tongue with a first hesitant response. The kiss grew warmer and wider and better until Sam Brown's softly sucking mouth melted Lee's resistance, and she leaned toward him, realizing how much—how very much—she had missed this.

Oh, Brown, we never should have started this.

But even as she thought it, his mouth left hers and she watched, mesmerized, as he slipped the can from her fingers and placed it to one side with his own. He confiscated her sandwich, which now wore two flat-pressed fingerprints.

Methodically, he cleared away the rest of their lunch and placed the bag beside the soft drink cans on his far side. When he turned back to her, his intention was clear.

The pulse jumped in Lee's throat, and a band seemed to cinch about her chest, bringing with it a sweet expectation that rivaled the sweet scent of the orchard. Sam's right hand slipped to her ribs, his left to cup her hip and slide her over until she bumped firmly up against him. Then her head was tipping back and his warm lips opened over hers again.

A thousand forgotten feelings swept over Lee as Sam's hand slipped beneath the ribbing at her waist and her fingers found his collarbone. It had been so long . . . so long. Then, in one deft motion, he pulled her across his chest and took her backward with him, falling onto the bed of the pickup, little caring that it was hard and dirty and cold.

Her shirt slid up as his hand moved over her bare back and warm fingers slipped underneath the narrow band of elastic that crossed beneath her shoulder blades. His other hand slid down over her backside and expertly adjusted her length atop his own until she felt exactly how tough and hard all that running had made his thighs. And while he kissed and tempted her with a strong molding of tongue upon tongue, something more grew tough and hard beneath Lee's body. Her own body leaped to life.

And—oh, God—it felt so wonderful to be held again, caressed again. Sam's compelling lips shut out all thought of stopping the warm hand that curved around the side of her breast while his other arm pressed against her spine. He slipped his fingers inside the front of her bra, between lace and skin, the tips not quite reaching her nipple. A moment later he'd reached around her to release the clasp between her shoulder blades. His warm palms moved between their bodies, finding her freed breasts and caressing them slowly before rolling their tips between his fingers as if they were flowers he'd plucked on their stroll through the meadow.

He was ardent and persuasive and so undeniably tempting as she lay on him. She knew all the dangers of succumbing to his tantalizing sorcery, but she told herself not to think of them as her body responded fully.

But then Sam suddenly rolled her to her hip and reached

for the snap on her jeans, and she plummeted to earth again.

"Brown . . . this is crazy, stop it!" She caught his straying hand and dragged it to safer territory. Everything inside her had gone zinging-singing, turned-on crazy with incredible desire for him. His eyes glinted down into hers like dark, metallic sparks, and his fingers curled into the back of her hand until she whispered fiercely, "Don't!"

To Lee's immense surprise and relief, he rolled away and fell flat on his back, his hands coming to rest, knuckles down on the corrugated metal beneath him.

"Sorry, Cherokee."

That name again! It did the strangest things to her stomach. She sat up and drew a steadying breath, wondering what had ever possessed her to let things get so far out of hand. She was thoroughly embarrassed now, for even with her back to him she could feel his eyes on her. But she had little choice except to reach behind her for her bra.

Once again Sam Brown did the unpredictable. He sat up immediately and slipped his hands under her shirt. "Here, let me. I'm the one who messed it up." With a total lack of compunction he pushed her shirt up and found the trailing ends of the bra and hooked them together again. His putting it back on had an even greater sexual impact than when he'd released it. Goose bumps erupted over her skin and left her more tinglingly aware of him than ever. But he unselfconsciously pulled the shirt down to her waist, smoothed it into place, and dropped his hands from her. He seemed to dismiss the entire episode with an almost cheery note. "You're probably right. We should stop."

She was astonished by his mercurial change of mood. Somehow she'd expected him to be demanding or angry at her rebuff. But he sat beside her now as if they'd shared nothing more than a bag lunch. At least that was the impression he gave until his lopsided grin returned and he drawled devilishly, "But it *was* fun."

She bit back a smile and scolded, "Brown, have you no scruples whatsoever?"

"Well, I didn't see you exactly high-tailing it in the other direction."

"Oh no?" She boosted herself up and dropped off the tailgate, then turned to inform him from that safe distance, "I think it's time we headed back to town."

He only grinned, curled his hands over the edge of the tailgate, and swung his legs loosely from the knees.

"Whatcha doing this weekend, Cherokee?"

"Cut that out, Brown. I said I don't want problems."

"I've got another name besides Brown, you know."

"That's all we need—a little more familiarity between us, and everyone in the office will have their jaws wagging."

"What time do you get up on Saturdays?"

How was a woman supposed to fight an irresistible tease like him? It was all she could do to keep a straight face.

"None of your business. Are you coming or not?"

He leaped nimbly from the truck, revealing three dirty stripes down the back of his white shirt. As he slammed the tailgate shut he suggested, "How about we rent some roller skates and try the skate trails?"

"I said no!" She added in exasperation, "Oh, Lord, you're as striped as a polecat, Brown. Hold still while I get rid of the evidence."

She stepped quickly up behind him to whisk the dirt away, but as her hands brushed over his hard back, he grinned over his shoulder—a devastatingly charming grin. "You scared I might make a pass at you again and catch you in a weaker moment?" She felt a telltale blush creep across her cheeks and immediately stepped back and jammed her hands into her pockets.

"You know what your problem is? You read too many girlie magazines!"

Sam laughed and plucked an apple off a tree, then draped his elbows on top of the tailgate behind him as he took a lazy bite.

"Well, I just thought, since you'd changed your brand of perfume—"

"That wasn't perfume, that was mosquito spray!"

Again his rich peal of appreciation lifted through the orchard before his teeth snapped through the skin of the apple. He considered her unhurriedly. "What about tomorrow?"

The man was undauntable. If he kept it up, he'd break her down yet! She stamped her foot and declared, "No, no, a thousand times no!" then spun from him, strode to the pickup, and got in.

He flung the apple core beneath the trees and climbed in beside her as she wondered frantically how to break the sexual tension spinning between them. But as Sam started the engine, he managed to break it himself by glancing at her from the corner of his eye and teasing, "You know, you're cuter 'n hell when you're on the warpath, Cherokee."

She could resist no longer and burst out laughing. He was an outlandish tease and a tempting creature. But he was her boss and the last man in the world she should encourage— assuming she wanted to encourage any man, which she didn't. Yet even as she promised herself sternly to avoid being alone with Sam Brown, a glow of well-being spread from her smiling lips all the way down to her tingling toes.

CHAPTER
Seven

LEE SPENT THE following morning at her usual Saturday drudgery—cleaning house. She had changed the sheets, cleaned the upstairs, vacuumed the steps, and was shoving the vacuum cleaner along the living room carpet when she thought she'd heard the doorchime. She heard it again more clearly and, mumbling a curse, turned the machine off with a bare toe.

She opened her front door and stopped dead still. There, his hips against the wrought-iron handrail, sat Sam Brown, practically naked!

"Hi," he greeted, puffing hard. "This is an obscene house call."

Without warning, Lee burst out laughing. She covered her mouth with both hands and bent forward, overcome with mirth. "Oh, Brown, I believe you!"

There he sat, wearing nothing but his beat-up running shoes, a pair of white jogging shorts with a green stripe, and a red headband. Sweat ran down his heaving chest, making it shine in the sun. There was little hair on it, but what there was burned like red-gold sparks as trickles of perspiration ran down the center hollow toward his navel. His legs were crossed at the ankle, but his shoulders slumped forward as he panted laboriously.

"Don't tell me you ran all the way over here," Lee said.

He nodded, still trying to catch his breath.

"But it must be eight miles!"

"Eight mi . . . hiles is nothing. I'm in goo . . . hood shape."

"I can see that." And she could, in spite of his breathlessness. He looked like poured copper, wet and smooth and sleek and sculptured, the muscles of his legs as hard as an Olympian's, his shoulders glossy and well developed.

"Must've lost six pounds of sw . . . sweat on the way ov . . . over here though."

"I can see that, too."

He drew in a large gulp of air, his breathing growing even while he continued to slump against the rail. "You wouldn't turn a man away thirsty, would you?"

"And risk a darn good job?" Lee returned impertinently. "Come on."

Sam boosted himself away from the railing and followed Lee inside, making her uncomfortably conscious of her bare feet and legs and the strip of exposed skin between her skimpy bandeau top of white stretch terry and the faded denim cutoffs with strings dangling down her legs. She resisted an urge to run a hand over the single coarse braid that fell down her back and was as frayed around the edges as her cutoffs. She led Sam along the short hall to the rear of the house, where the kitchen's sliding glass door stood open to her small, shady patio. He stood before it, hands on hips, letting the draft cool his sweating body, as she opened the refrigerator.

"Here." She moved behind him with two clinking glasses.

"Thanks."

"Let's go out on the patio where it's more comfortable." She slid the screen open, and he followed. There was only a single webbed lounge chair, and before he could protest, Lee plopped down on the concrete, facing the lounge chair with her legs crossed Indian fashion. "Have a seat," she said.

"No, here, you take—"

"Don't be silly. You're the one who just ran eight miles, not me. Anyway, the concrete is cool."

He shrugged, dropped into the lounge chair, took a sip of tea, and glanced around at her pots of bright red geraniums, asparagus fern, and vinca vine. It was cool and restful in the shade, but Lee felt warm and uncomfortable as Sam's eyes returned to her. What should she say to this man who refused to accept her brush-off and appeared at her door the next day with incorrigible brashness . . . then made her laugh!

"Do you run every day?"

"I try to."

"I don't think I'd care to on a day like today. It's supposed to get up to ninety-five degrees."

"That's why I run in the morning."

"Mmm." She sipped her drink, aware of his eyes, which made a periodic sweep of the geraniums but always returned to her bare knees.

"Did I interrupt something important?" He glanced toward the house, where the vacuum cleaner was sprawled across the living room floor.

"Just the weekly house cleaning." Lee grimaced, then added, "Ugh!"

Sam laughed, then the corners of his lips remained in a teasing grin. "Heap big disgusting job, cleaning the teepee?"

She couldn't stop her smile. "Show some respect, would you, Brown?"

"Well, you should see yourself"—he gestured with his glass—"sitting there barefooted with your legs crossed and that braid dangling down your back and your skin the color of a too ripe peach. The name Cherokee fits better than ever." He polished off the rest of his tea in one gulp and set the glass down, still grinning.

"You know"—she tipped her head to one side—"it puzzles me why I let you get away with it. If anybody else said things like that to me, I'd give 'em a black eye."

"You tried that once on me too, remember?"

"You deserved it."

He threw his head back, closed his eyes, and crossed his hands over his naked belly. "Yeah, I did."

How was a woman supposed to deal with a man like him? There he sat, as composed as a potentate, looking for all the world like he was going to take a nap on her patio.

"If you just stopped by to catch forty winks, do you mind if I finish my cleaning?"

He opened one eye. "Not at all." The eye closed again, and a moment later Lee slid the screen door open. The vacuum cleaner wheezed on, and for some reason she found herself smiling. She heard nothing more from Sam Brown until about fifteen minutes later, when she was watering the living room plants. He stepped inside and stopped in the hall behind her. "Would you mind if I used your bathroom before I head back?"

She turned to see him filling the living room doorway with his bare shoulders and chest. "It's upstairs, to your right."

He sprinted up the steps as she turned back to watering the plants. But a moment later she remembered the open door to the extra bedroom and turned, ready to bolt up and close it before he emerged from the bathroom. But as she reached the bottom step, the door above clicked open and the muffled thud of his footsteps sounded across the hall, pausing momentarily while she backed up, listening, a hand pressed to her heart. Again his footseps neared, and she scurried out to the kitchen, where she was busily scouring the sink when he found her again.

"Thanks for the iced tea. I've got an eight-mile run yet, so I guess I'd better go."

She ran her hands under the water, grabbed a towel, and followed him idly toward the front door, conscious of a great reluctance to see him leave. They stepped out onto the sunny front stoop, and he moved down two steps, then turned as she leaned against the railing with the towel slung over her shoulder. "I'll see you Monday, Cherokee," he finally said. The sun lit his hair to russet and his skin to copper as he gazed up at her without making a move. In another minute he would turn and jog off across the city. And all of a sudden she couldn't let him go. "It's eighty-five degrees already. There's no need for you to run all the way home. I can give you a ride if you want."

"What about your house cleaning?"

"It's all done."

"In that case, I accept."

Her heart went light and happy. "Give me a minute to put on some decent clothes, okay?"

She'd already stepped through the front door when his question stopped her. "Do you have to?"

Over her shoulder she threw him a scolding expression, but he only raised his palms, shrugged, and grinned.

She returned shortly, dressed in white pedal pushers and a

red spaghetti-strap top that bloused at the waist and just above her breasts. As her bare feet slapped down the steps, a pair of red canvas sandals swung jauntily from two fingers, and white feathers bounced in her ears. Sam was leaning against the back fender of her dusty Pinto. He nudged himself upright and opened her door, waiting while she got in.

When he was seated beside her, she put the car into reverse. "If I remember right," she said, "you live on Ward Parkway . . . in the family rattrap." She gave him a sidelong grin.

"Everybody's got to live somewhere."

He settled back for the ride, and fifteen minutes later Lee was following Sam's finger as it pointed toward the cobbled drive of a majestic, well-preserved mansion.

Cradling the wheel in her arms, she stared in undisguised awe. Realizing Sam hadn't moved, she turned to give him a sheepish grin, then gazed up the ivy-covered chimney of the enormous stucco tudor home. "Nice little rattrap you live in," she said wryly.

"Would you like to see it?"

"Are you kidding?"

"Mother's not home. She's out golfing." The mention of his mother made Lee quail momentarily, though she wanted very badly to go inside his home and see where he lived, how he lived.

He seemed to sense her hesitation and turned, resting a knee on the seat between them, an arm along its back. "I'd like very much to spend the day with you, Cherokee. What do you say we do the town? Anything at all—think of the craziest, most illogical things you've ever thought of doing, and we'll try every one of 'em. And no more of what happened in the orchard yesterday. That's a promise."

It was a promise she would not have extracted had the choice been left up to her. "I *work* for you! Doesn't it sound just a little . . . well . . ."

"Hell, is that all? You think that if we end up more than friends you'll lose your job if and when the romance is over?"

"Something like that. Or at least it'll be a lot more strained when we bump into each other in the office every day."

Engaging creases crinkled the corners of his eyes. "Maybe

I should fire you here and now so the problem doesn't arise."

"Brown, you're impossible." But she couldn't help smiling as she shook her head at his foolish reasoning. Yes, he was impossible. Impossible to resist, with his dark good looks and his engaging sense of humor. She thrust her worries aside and promised herself a day of carefree fun. She would laugh and return his bantering and teasing and accept the fact that she enjoyed his company immensely.

"Say yes," he coaxed.

She gave him a wry corner-of-the-eye smirk. "You gonna fire me if I don't?"

"No."

"Then, yes, damn you."

The house was all cool class with an open stairway that dropped from the biggest fanlight window Lee had ever seen. Sam ran upstairs, leaving her to look around while he took a quick shower and changed. She wandered from room to room, hands clasped behind her back as if afraid to touch what she wasn't supposed to. The living room had two enormous sets of fanlight doors opening onto a glass-walled sunroom that overlooked the side yard, where the Kansas City traditions had been sustained—lush flower beds curving around ancient magnolia trees; a small fountain spouting water from a cupid's ewer; and wrought-iron benches enclosed on three sides by precision-trimmed boxwood hedges.

"Ready?"

Lee turned to find that Sam had come up silently behind her on the thick, white carpeting. He looked as inviting as his house and yard. She forced her eyes back to the luscious view outside. "I had no idea," she murmured.

"It gets kind of lonely sometimes," he replied.

Again she turned. He was standing nearer, smelling of fresh soap and that everlasting Rawhide scent. His car keys were in his hand.

"Let's go get crazy," she said, giving him a devilish look meant to suggest just that.

They took the city by storm, skittering across it like crazy bedbugs. Sam knew Kansas City well, both its fun spots and its history, and he introduced Lee to both. They rented roller

skates and wheeled through Loose Park, where the famed artist Christo had once covered the sidewalks with shimmering
gold cloth and entitled his work "Wrapped Walkways." They
bought bandages at the drugstore and entitled their works
"Wrapped Knees." They bought a rhinestone ring at the Country Club Plaza and put it on the finger of a fountain nymph in
the Crown Center, declaring a bond forever between the two
magnificent landmarks whose creators, Lee learned, had both
had the initials J. C. They got separated in the midst of the
colorful *Festa Italiana* in Crown Center Square and recovered
each other from the arms of exuberant Italian dancers. They
ate ice cream at Swenson's and drank piña coladas at Kelly's
Saloon, then nearly lost both on the Zambezi Zinger at Worlds
of Fun, and settled their stomachs by lying flat on their backs
between rows of markers at Mount Washington Cemetery.
They spit into the "Mighty Mo" off the middle of the Hannibal
Bridge, with laughing apologies to Octave Chanute, who
hadn't taken two and a half years creating it just to have two
zanies use it for this! They slipped into the Truman Library
and left a note commemorating the date in the *Encyclopedia
Britannica*—in Volume 7, page 754—promising to come
back a year from then and see if it was still there.

All day they walked along Kansas City streets named after
the city's founders—Meyer, Swope, Armour. Sam showed
Lee Kessler Boulevard, named after the landscape architect
who'd mapped out the entire beautification system of boule-
vards, gardens, and fountains which made the city a splendid
kaleidoscope of beauty. He told her the history of William
Rockhill Nelson, the founder of the *Kansas City Star*, who
had fought for the city's approval of the unique boulevard
network for fourteen years, and of how Jesse Clyde Nichols's
visionary planning had brought sculpture, fountains and art
objects to the city's intersections. They scampered, carefree,
through the sun-splashed Kansas City day, and when night fell
and the lights of the fountains lit their lilting waters to ruby,
emerald, and sapphire, Lee and Sam sat on the edge of one
eating Moo Goo Gai Pan and fried rice from little white card-
board containers.

"How's your knee?" Sam asked.

Lee lifted it and checked the bandage and the dried blood

on her white pedal pushers. "Still intact. Next time I won't let you talk me into doing three hundred sixty degree turns when I haven't been on skates in years."

He chuckled, but his eyes rested on her with a warm, appreciative glow.

"You're a helluva good sport, you know that, Cherokee?"

"Thanks. You ain't so bad yourself, Your Honor."

"You ready to call it a day?"

"Am I ever." She patted her stomach, sighed, then stacked the white cartons one inside the other. They meandered away from the fountain toward Sam's car, dropping their trash on the way . . . and somehow when he returned to her side, his hand took hers . . . and somehow she didn't mind a bit. A few minutes later, as their wide-swinging steps moved more lazily, Sam Brown looped an arm around Lee's neck and drew her close to his side. It felt good to be there, so she lifted a hand and hung it from his wrist, watching their feet go slower and slower.

Sam drove leisurely through the Kansas City night, listening to the night sounds of crickets and frogs through the open windows. The fountains along Ward Parkway *shushed* past, and Lee rested her head against the seat, wishing the evening needn't end at all. Sam pulled up in his driveway and turned off the engine. Neither of them moved.

"Thanks for a really fun day," she said softly.

"The pleasure was mine."

Still neither of them moved.

"I see Mother's home. Would you like to meet her?"

"Not tonight. It's late . . . and I've got bloody knees and Moo Goo Gai Pan on my shirt." The very thought of meeting his mother threatened to flaw the perfect day.

Lee felt Sam studying her across the car seat, and a moment later his voice came quietly. "Cherokee?"

"Yes?"

He hesitated before saying, "There's no Moo Goo Gai Pan on your shirt." Immediately she reached for her door handle, but his hand came out to detain her. "I'd really like you to meet my mother. Why are you running away?"

She laughed nervously and said to her lap, "I'm really not very good with mothers." She turned an entreating glance up at him and added softly, "I'd rather not."

His thumb moved softly, brushing the crook of her elbow. "Do you mind telling me why?"

She considered doing just that, then answered without rancor, "Yes, I do mind."

Disregarding her answer, he went on, "Let me guess. It's got something to do with your being part Indian."

She was stunned that he'd figured out that much of the truth and felt as if, for a moment, he'd looked into her very soul.

"H . . . how did you know?"

His eyes moved to the feathers at her ears and with a single finger he set one in motion, then explained, "You're very defensive about it, you know."

"Everybody wears Indian jewelry these days. It's very in."

"Don't get mad, Cherokee. It's been a great day, and I want to keep it that way. But I wish you'd level with me. So far you haven't told me much of anything about your past." A long pause followed before he encouraged softly, "Why don't you tell me now?"

She considered for a moment and realized she wanted very badly to tell him. But it was hard to explain. It had been so long.

"I . . . I don't know where to begin."

"Begin with your husband. Was he white?"

"Yes." She dropped her eyes.

"And?"

"And . . ."

When she didn't go on, he urged softly, "Look at me, Cherokee. And what?"

His eyes were pools of shadow as he leaned across the dark confines of the car, and at the concern in his voice she suddenly found herself wanting to tell him things she'd promised herself never to reveal. But she needed to put some distance between herself and Sam Brown while she told him, so she opened her door and got out, leaving him to follow. As they ambled slowly toward her car, she began haltingly.

"Joel married me in one of those . . . those idiotic rebounds from the woman he should have married in the first place. A very white woman of whom his mother heartily approved.

He'd . . . he'd had a fight with her, so when he met me it was . . ." She sighed and looked up at the stars. "Oh, I don't know what it was. A chemical mix-up, maybe. A stupid impulse. But we didn't think it out at all. We just did it. Too fast, too . . ." She shrugged and hugged her arms as they moved across damp grass. "Nothing about it was right, not from the very first, except maybe the sex. But that's not enough to sustain a marriage. After a while his mother's disapproval of me began to wear on Joel, and he began blaming me for alienating him from his family. Within a year after our divorce, he married the girl his mother had been telling him all along he should have married." They stopped at her car. "So now you know why I'm not too good with mothers."

The lights from the house spilled in long white splashes across the dark lawn behind them. Sam stood with a hand in his trouser pocket. Lee waited for his response. When it came, she was pleasantly surprised. The hand came out of his pocket and captured her elbow and he spoke in a soft, cajoling voice.

"Now that that's out of the way, come here." His gentle grip swung her around to face him, then he looped his arms around her waist till their hips rested lightly against each other. And suddenly she forgot about mothers and personal histories, for Sam Brown's face was smiling down at her through the warm, flower-scented night. It seemed as if the beguiling fountains of Kansas City itself danced within Lee's heart as she waited for one thing she needed to make this day end in total perfection. Then he lowered soft, warm open lips over hers, and she lifted her own, slightly parted, readily accepting the brush of his tongue upon hers . . . but softly, gently.

Ah, Brown, the things you do inside me.

He held her lightly, only the tips of her breasts brushing his shirt while she rested her hands on his biceps. Sam's tongue stroked and coaxed, and Lee's answered, her fingertips slipped up beneath the ribbing of his short knit sleeves in an unconscious invasion of his firm, hidden skin. The kiss was unhurried, almost lazy, a sweet lingual blandishment while they leaned a little apart and began to rock indolently from side to side. It was an aperitif of a kiss, designed to whet the appetite for more. But when it ended—slowly, lingeringly—

they refrained from partaking further.

Sam lifted his head to tease softly, "That's better than Swenson's ice cream."

Lee smiled and leaned back against the circle of his hands. "Mmm . . . and it won't give you a stomachache, either."

He smiled impishly and settled his hips more firmly against hers. "Oh no?"

But she knew it wasn't his stomach that ached. She could feel what ached, pressed hard and inviting against her pedal pushers.

So she was surprised when a moment later she found herself pushed gently away and turned toward her car by the Honorable Sam Brown, who was proving increasingly honorable indeed.

CHAPTER
Eight

EARLY MONDAY MORNING, plans got under way for bidding the
Little Blue River job. Again Lee noted the difference between
the way things were done at Brown & Brown and at Thorpe
Construction. Not only was there an ongoing sense of cooper-
ation where she worked now, but there was also a thorough-
ness that surprised her.

Accurate records of soil workability were kept for all major
jobs. Lee met the drill truck on site Monday afternoon to take
soil samples directly from the steel auger. These were
weighed, dried, and run through a series of nested copper
sieves. The amounts of material retained on each of the var-
iously gauged screens were weighed carefully and recorded on
a gradation chart. Lee and Sam worked side by side sieving
and recording the data. They compared their findings with
those of former jobs under similar soil conditions and used the
results to estimate the cost of such variables as dewatering and
sheeting to prevent cave-ins.

They sat in the coffee room, Frank perched on the edge of
a counter, Sam seated with his legs crossed and heels propped
up on an empty chair. The sense of belonging Lee felt in her
new job encouraged her to take full part in the decision making. To her surprise her personal relationship with Sam hardly
entered into their business dealings.

"Do you mind using Tri-State Drilling for dewatering?"
Sam asked. His elbows were pointed at the ceiling and his

fingers were clasped behind his neck as he leaned back comfortably.

"I was thinking of asking Griffin Wellpoint for a quote," Lee replied. "I've had good luck in dealing with them in the past." She held her breath. It was the first time she'd directly opposed the wishes of either Sam or Frank.

Sam only shrugged. "Great. We've had good luck with Tri-State, too, so either one is fine."

Lee ordered quotes from Griffin for dewatering, along with those from another subcontractor for installing pilings through the swampy area, which had proved to be mostly peat. She asked landscape contractors for quotes on sodding, seeding, mulching, and fertilizing. As the days passed and she waited for these quotes, the calculator on her desk whirred constantly.

She computed labor costs for pipe installation per foot, according to depth and soil conditions. Material costs were broken down into unit prices—and in the case of pipe—per-foot prices—and these extended out into lump sums.

As the week wore on and the day of the bid letting drew nearer, suppliers sent quotes on pipes, valves, manhole castings and hydrants. Throughout the week the tension seemed to grow as bid day—Friday—approached. As usual, quotes from subcontractors came in late, holding up progress to some degree and lending a sense of uncertainty to the work on the bid.

Late Thursday, Sam stopped by Lee's desk and asked, "Have all those quotes come in from the subs yet?"

"Still waiting on one from Greenway. You know how it is."

He chuckled, but the sound seemed tense for Sam, who was usually relaxed and easygoing. "Yeah, I know how it is."

"You want this job badly, don't you?"

His eyes met Lee's and for the first time that week seemed to convey thoughts beyond soil evaluations and price per linear foot. "I've got a rather personal stake in this one. Don't you?"

Thoughts of the orchard in all its seductive glory came back. "Yes, I do."

He gazed down at her for a moment longer, then seemed to drag himself from his reverie to scratch the side of his neck and glance at the pale green job sheets draped across her desk.

"Anyway, we could use this job since the Denver one doesn't get rolling till spring. There'd be time enough to get this one finished before winter."

Friday morning brought the usual eleventh-hour craziness Lee had come to expect in estimating. Somehow the spirit of competition never seemed to surface in suppliers until just before bid time. Within two hours of the deadline Lee received a call from the pipe supplier who was lowering his quote by twelve thousand dollars. Immediately subtotals and totals had to be changed on the official proposal form. Since the call came at 11:30 with bid time set for 2:00, Lee skipped lunch to change the figures, then run another calculator check of the math.

Sam came in at 12:45 to find her at her desk, her fingers flying over the machine, her bare feet curled up on the caster guards of her desk chair. "How's it going?" he asked.

She scarcely looked up. "What time is it?"

"Quarter to one."

"Will you double-check the addition on these sheets?"

"Sure." She extended the sheets without even turning her eyes his way. "Didn't you have lunch?"

She did glance up then, for about a half second. "No. American Pipe called and lowered their bid by twelve thousand dollars."

Sam sat down hastily at a nearby desk and his fingers, too, started flying over a calculator. "Why didn't you say something?"

She paused, looked up, and smiled at his dark head. "I'm too tense to eat anyway."

He pushed the total button, the machine clicked into silence, and Sam smiled across at Lee. "Relax, Cherokee, it's just a damn job."

But it wasn't, and they both knew it. It was *their* job. Their first joint effort, and something inside of Lee said they just had to win it! Still, she appreciated Sam's effort to put her at ease, and her smile said as much before they both set to work again.

Fifteen minutes later the changes were all entered in ink on the official bid proposal, and Sam leaned over Lee's desk to initial each one and put his signature beside the company seal impressed on the final sheet. His shoulder was almost touching her jaw as he bent to scratch his name on the paper. During the week, she'd had little trouble controlling personal feelings that intruded during business hours, but now, as he stood close and she watched his dark hands moving on the white paper, she was drawn to him by their singularity of purpose. He dropped the pen, straightened, and smiled down at her feet.

"You can put your shoes back on now. It's done."

She grinned sheepishly. "Takes the pressure off the head."

"Maybe off yours, but not off mine." He gave her feet an appreciative grin just as a group of draftsmen returned from lunch. "Well, I'm holding you up, huh?" It was one o'clock, and she still had to drive clear across the city to the Independence City Hall.

She drew in a deep breath, raked a hand through her hair, and gave Sam a shaky smile. "Well, here goes."

Brown & Brown's new estimator gathered up her papers, slipped the bid into a large gold envelope, licked it, pressed it shut, and lifted her eyes to find that her boss had been watching her every move.

"Good luck, Cherokee," he said softly.

"Thanks, Your Honor," she returned. Then she slipped on her shoes, picked up her purse, and left the office.

Brown & Brown took the Little Blue River job for $750,000, only $7,900 below the next highest bidder. When the last bid was read and the announcement made, Lee felt adrenaline swoop into her bloodstream in a giddy swoosh. She rose to her feet to accept handshakes, and her knees felt wobbly and weak. Her palms had been sweating throughout the opening of the envelopes, but now they itched to get to a telephone and call the office.

She suffered through what seemed like hours of felicitations before finally escaping to the pay phone in the hall.

Rachael's perky voice answered, "Brown & Brown."

"Rachael, we got it!" Lee announced without prelude.

"Lee! That's wonderful!"

"Isn't it, though?" Lee bubbled. "I'm ecstatic . . . and a little shaky."

Rachael laughed. "That part never changes, honey."

A little chuckle released the last of her nervousness, then Lee requested, "Put Sam on, will you, Rachael?"

She listened to the silence on the line for a brief moment, basking in a deep sense of satisfaction as she waited for his voice. When it came, it sounded full of smiles.

"Nice going, Cherokee."

"Hallelujah, we did it, Brown!"

He laughed. "Feels good, huh?"

"Does it ever."

"Just how good?"

Understanding his cryptic question, she replied, "Only seventy-nine hundred dollars good . . . that's how good."

"You mean that's all you left!"

"Yes!"

At his laugh of satisfaction, Lee pictured the smile carving grooves into his cheeks, and the pale laugh lines disappearing about his eyes.

"Who came in second?"

"Just a minute, I'll read you the list."

She relayed the remainder of the bids, then Sam asked, "You're coming back to the office, aren't you? We've got to celebrate your first victory."

"I'll be there in an hour or so."

"Good, see you then."

In the business of estimating, the days of defeat far outnumbered those of victory. On winning days, a special elation seeped into everyone, creating a spirit of camaraderie and good humor. Coming back into the office to find that everyone in the house had already heard the good news, Lee stopped to accept congratulations and share lighthearted jokes with her coworkers. But one was foremost in her mind.

Sam was beaming as he strode across the blue carpet dressed in casual gray slacks and a pale blue dress shirt with the sleeves rolled up to the elbow. Lord, she'd never been as proud as she was then, facing Sam Brown. Her smile was infectious as he extended his wide hand and clasped hers, squeezing hard, shaking it just once and holding it only a fraction of a second longer than necessary.

"Congratulations, Lee."

"Thank you, Sam." She wished she could lay her other hand over his and tell him how much she'd appreciated his faith in her during the past week, and what a true pleasure it had been preparing the bid in the congenial atmosphere of his office, among his cooperative employees and—of course—with him. But his hand slipped away, and the group of men continued chattering. Rachael, Nelda, and Ron Chen joined the group, and to Lee it felt like Christmas Eve.

Some people were already clearing off their tables, others still standing around shooting the breeze, when Rachael pulled herself away from a drafting table and turned toward the front. "Well, hi, Mary, how are you?"

A darkly tanned woman of about sixty had entered the office and was moving familiarly toward the cluster of men and women. Most of them greeted her by name and exchanged anecdotal greetings. Obviously they all knew her. She was dressed in a classy looking summer suit with brown and white spectator pumps and a matching purse. She exuded an air of quiet confidence.

"I understand congratulations are in order around here," she commented as she approached.

To Lee's amazement, Sam broke away from the others and greeted the woman with a light kiss on the cheek.

"Hi, Mother. You out slumming?" he teased.

"I heard the news. Thought it was time I met your new estimator."

"She's right here." Sam looped an arm around his mother's shoulder and directed her toward Lee, who stood stock still with amazement.

"Mother, this is Lee Walker—Lee, my mother, Mary Brown." He had placed his hands on his mother's shoulders, and his dark, amused eyes twinkled down at Lee as color rose to her cheeks. Like a robot she extended her hand, which was clasped in very dark, coppery fingers with wide knuckles and several flashy diamonds.

"I'm happy to meet you, Mrs. Brown," Lee managed, unable to keep her eyes from fleeing back to Sam, who stood as before, with his hands on his mother's shoulders, an undisguised look of merriment crinkling the corners of his eyes.

"So you've won your first bid for Brown and Brown," the

woman noted in a friendly fashion as she studied Lee from a face with wide, high cheekbones and a blunt, broad nose. Her hair was graying now, but was unmistakably coal black underneath the lighter strands.

"I . . . uh . . . yes, but not alone. Frank and . . . and your son worked with me on it."

"Sam wanted it quite badly. He mentioned it several times this week. Well, congratulations." She smiled, then added "And welcome to the company."

As Sam's hands fell from her shoulders, he grinned disarmingly at Lee, then turned to watch his mother visit with others before joining her. Just then the phone rang. One of the draftsmen picked it up.

"It's for you, Lee."

It was a salesman asking if she'd go out for a drink or dinner—standard procedure after winning a bid. The salesmen were always eager to write up orders. Lee was standing with her back to the room when she suddenly became aware that Sam had slipped quietly up behind her. She turned, glancing at him over her shoulder as she spoke into the receiver. "This afternoon?" She paused for the salesman's reply, then asked, "What time?" With the phone pressed to her ear, Lee watched Sam Brown reach for a pad and pencil and followed his movements as he wrote, "You owe me dinner . . ." He turned it her way and pierced her with a meaningful look as she tried valiantly to concentrate on what the voice on the phone was saying. Sam's hand moved again, adding, " . . . tonight." He punctuated the message with an exclamation point.

Lee turned her back on both Sam Brown and his message, stammering, "Ah . . . I'm sorry, Paul, what were you saying?" A quick glance over her shoulder told her that Sam had moved away again. "I'm sorry, Paul. Maybe we can make it Monday for lunch. I'm busy tonight."

They made arrangements to meet then, and by the time Lee hung up, the office was starting to empty. She looked around for Sam's mother, but found she had gone. Sam himself was coming toward Lee. She crossed her arms loosely over her chest and leaned against the desk as she watched him approach.

"Well, you've surprised me again, Your Honor." Lee smiled.

"Have I now?" His grin was utterly charming.

"You know perfectly well that you have. Your mother is more Indian than I am."

"Ah, you're very perceptive," he teased.

"Where is she?" Lee scanned the office again.

Sam shrugged, then smirked. "Probably gone home to clean the teepee."

A picture of his "teepee" flashed before Lee's mind, and she couldn't help laughing. "Sam Brown, you're impossible. Why didn't you tell me before this?"

"And let you stop thinking I hired you so I could become a minority contractor? I've had too much fun laughing about it to myself."

"At my expense?"

"It didn't cost you anything, did it?"

"Except my unflappable cool. I think you could've driven a front-end loader in my mouth when I got a look at her and realized she was your mother."

He smiled, but changed the subject abruptly. "What about that dinner?"

She cocked an eyebrow at him. "I take it you're holding me to my promise that I go out with you when I became low bidder."

"Exactly."

"And I *am* low bidder?"

"Yes you are."

"And I *do* keep my promises?"

His smile broadened. "I'll pick you up at your place at seven. Wear something dressy." He turned away, changed his mind, and returned momentarily to add, "And sexy." Then he left for good.

Lee chose white again—this time a sleek, lithe crepe de chine dress that slipped over her hips like water—not tight, not loose, but willowy. It was a simple cylinder, cinched by elastic above her breasts and at the waist, leaving her shoulders and upper chest bare, the perfect foil for a heavy turquoise and silver pendant shaped like a peyote bird that dropped onto her chest from a silvery chain. She touched it and looked at her reflection in the mirror, remembering Sam Brown's mother. How like him not to tell her the truth, then let her find it out as she had. She smiled, then hurried to insert tiny droplets of dangling turquoise in her ears. On her feet went the briefest straps of white leather and high, high heels. She tricked her hair into a froth of sassy curls, their disheveled control confined only by a fine white headband that crossed her temples and disappeared amid the bouncy tangle on her head.

Just then the doorbell rang. Without thinking, Lee snatched the framed picture of her sons from the dresser top and stuffed it into a drawer. On her way out she took a moment to close the door to the second bedroom. Downstairs she paused and pressed a hand against her churning stomach, then took a deep breath and went to greet Sam Brown.

He was leaning against the railing again, but he seemed to unfold in slow motion, coming up off the wrought iron muscle by muscle. As his ankles uncrossed, as his hand came out of his trouser pocket, as he pulled himself to his feet, his eyes shimmered down the length of Lee, and a smile of undisguised appreciation lifted his sculptured lips. When his dark eyes met her even darker ones, he said flat out, "You look absolutely sensational, Cherokee."

His approval brought a sweet ripple of pride up her spine as she took in the crisp lapels of his navy blue suit.

"Thank you, Your Honor, so do you." Did he ever! His white shirt set off the rusty hue of his face like a well-chosen matting about a painting, and she wondered how she could have been so naive as to have missed the truth about his heritage all this time. Yet from the first, she'd realized he didn't look like any full-blooded Scandinavian she'd ever known. He'd had his fun with her . . . but now, studying him, she couldn't help rejoicing at the final outcome. Yes, he was stunning, his silk tie knotted so flawlessly that it stood away from his collar band as if aroused.

At the thought she dropped her eyes and turned to fetch a tiny beaded purse.

When he'd seen her solicitously to her side of the car and started the engine, he turned to study her again. She met his gaze levelly, unconcerned that he was undoubtedly reading the admiration in her perusal, just as she was in his.

"Tonight it's the American. I, too, keep my promises."

"But it was supposed to be my treat." She knew she couldn't afford the American Restaurant.

"Oh, you're wrong about that."

"But—"

"It's a company dinner, on the boss. I'll write it off as a business expense."

"Oh, in that case . . . the American it is." But Lee felt far removed from business concerns at the moment. And as the evening progressed, that distance widened.

They approached the Crown Center by way of its ten-acre square of terraced lawns and fountains, passing the massive tent pavilion and the thirty-foot-high umbrellas beneath whose yellow peaks they'd lost and found each other last Saturday. Alexander Calder's stabile "Shiva" loomed up before them, and minutes later they were entering the luxurious Westin Crown Center Hotel.

Its multilevel lobby was carved into a rocky hillside of natural limestone, creating a dramatic garden of tropical foliage and full grown trees through which tumbled a sixty-foot waterfall. The rushing water created a refreshing background music for hotel guests, shoppers from the adjacent Crown Center shops, and sightseers who sauntered along the elevated catwalks above the lobby.

Had Hans Christian Andersen been alive to dream up a fairy tale setting, he could not have invented any more compellingly romantic than that through which they passed, Lee thought. She found it difficult to keep her eyes from Sam, and when they found themselves the only two people on the elevator carrying them up to the restaurant, she gave in to the urge.

He was leaning against the left wall, she against the right. They studied each other wordlessly, caught up in a sense of impending intimacy. Horizons lay ahead for them—it seemed understood—which would change their relationship forever. The knowledge intensified the moment, though to all outward appearances they were as casual as before.

Lee's senses seemed honed to a fine edge. She was keenly

attuned to Sam's familiar scent, to his expression which grew more and more thoughtful and sexually aware as the night wore on. Seated in the restaurant's lofty expanse with chrome and mirrors at her elbow and Kansas City spread out before her, Lee watched cars follow the arteries leading northeast toward the heart of the city. Yet time and again her gaze was pulled back to Sam's. As if her consciousness had been fine tuned, she absorbed every detail around her with acute perception—the soft hiss of bubbles in her stemglass; the sleek texture of pickled mushrooms from the toothpick Sam teasingly held toward her; the brush of his pant leg against her bare ankle under the table; the bite of woven caning against her bare shoulders as she relaxed in her bentwood chair; the heat of the flame from their Steak Diane as the waiter performed his culinary act; the sharp, tangy taste of broccoli, suddenly delectable when she'd never liked it before; the scent of starch in linen as she wiped her lips, which grew impatient for what now seemed a certainty; the sluggardly passage of time as Sam drew out their anticipation by ordering Cherries Jubilee; the flash of fire as a match was struck to liqueur; Sam's lips, tipped up only slightly at the corner as he slipped a scarlet cherry from a spoon and gave her a glimpse of his tongue stroking the succulent sauce from it; the heat flooding her body at his wordless suggestion.

Lee lounged all willowy in her chair, but she noted how often Sam's glance fell to the ruched line where her dress met her chest, then lower to the discernible shadows hinting of dusky, bare nipples within her silken bodice. Each time it happened her stomach tingled. But she lounged on, playing his waiting game with a restraint that keyed their sensuality to a higher pitch.

From the restaurant, across the square, to the car, and all the way home . . . he never touched her. Not with his hands. But his eyes were as tactile as the brush of warm flesh as they lingered on her. The city was dark, alive, waiting . . . just like Lee.

At the curb in front of her house the engine stopped and his car door opened, then he opened her door and waited for her to step out. Again they moved up the sidewalk, up the steps to the door without a word, without a touch.

She had left the outside light off. The shrubbery and over-hanging roof created deep shadows. Yet she turned to him, knowing his face without seeing it.

"Would you like to come in for a drink?" She remembered his preference for dry martinis with pickled mushrooms and added nervously, "I . . . I don't have any pickled mushrooms, but I do have olives."

A long, blank pause followed before he replied succinctly, "No, I wouldn't care for a drink or pickled mushrooms or olives."

Her stomach trembled, and she drew in a deep breath before asking softly, "What, then?"

She sensed him leaning toward her, just short of touching her as he answered in a husky voice, "I want you, Cherokee . . . you know that."

His answer sent her pulse pounding, and suddenly she didn't know what to say. She stood there in the dark, her nostrils filled with his scent, knowing the searching look in his eyes, though she could not see them. Then his voice came again, soft but intense. "Don't invite me in unless it's for that."

Still he didn't touch her, and though she wanted him to, she knew that once he did there'd be no turning back.

"You must know I still have reservations about it," she admitted shakily.

"Then why did you wear that dress tonight with nothing under it?"

He knew her better than she knew herself; it seemed foolish to deny it. She dropped her chin and admitted artlessly, "It was shameless of me, wasn't it?" She sensed him smiling in the dark doorway.

"Are you testing me, Cherokee, to see how far you can go before I make a move?"

"No . . . I . . . ." Her hands fluttered and her voice grew unsteady. "I'm just nervous."

After a thoughtful silence, he mused, "You're an enigma, you know that? I've seen you in action at a bid letting where there's a good reason to be nervous, yet there you're as unruf-fled as can be. Out in the tough business world you scrap and fight with the best of 'em. But what happens to that confident woman when a man finds her attractive?" His voice went softer. "What do you have to be nervous about?"

Suddenly there were tens of answers Lee could have given, any one of which would have been enough to stop her. But she withheld them all, realizing it had been half her doing that they were here together on the brink of something that would be splendid, she was certain. She did want him, and complications always went along with that, thus she suppressed her doubts and asked in a wistful way he could not mistake, "Would you like to come in for nothing so simple as . . . as pickled mushrooms or olives?"

In answer he reached out and gave her bare shoulder a brief squeeze that sent goosebumps down her arm.

"Give me your key," he ordered quietly.

Her hand trembled as she forfeited it. It chinked into his hand and a moment later the door swung inward, then closed behind them, securing them in a blanket of blackness.

She came to a halt in the middle of the hall, her back to Sam as she clutched her tiny purse in both hands. Oh, it had been so different with that other man, the one whose name she could barely remember, who had come oh so briefly after Joel. But she hadn't forgotten the sudden chill that had overcome her body and turned it unwilling at the last minute. What if that happened now? And what if . . . what if . . .

She ran a frenzied mental assessment of her body and found only its shortcomings—not only the stretchmarks but also the loss of firmness, the unmistakable contour of hips that were wider now, the few extra pounds she perhaps should have lost . . . and there was a single vein on . . .

Sam's hands sought her waist in the dark, and his fingers spread wide on her ribs, pulling her against him as he pressed his mouth into the curve of her neck, riding it back along the warm silver chain, pushing her hair aside to kiss the nape of her neck.

"Cherokee," he murmured, "you're so tense. There's no need to be."

In the dark he found the purse she still clutched and pulled it from her fingers. She heard the soft thud as it landed on a carpeted step before he returned his attentions to her neck.

She released the breath she'd held captive for too long and

forced the muscles of her neck to relax one by one as he nuzzled the warm hollow behind her ear until her head dropped forward, then to the side.

"How long has it been?" he asked with gruff tenderness.

She knew a moment of trepidation before answering honestly, "Three years." Three long, empty years.

At her answer he circled her with both arms, just below her breasts, and she covered the sleeves of his suit jacket with her own arms and the backs of his hands with hers.

"You mean I'm the first since your husband?" he asked softly near her temple.

She swallowed thickly, then admitted, "Yes . . . no . . . well, almost."

She felt him move as if to look down at her questioningly, but his arms remained as before, warm and secure about her midriff.

"Almost?"

"There was one other man. I was lonely and . . ." Again she swallowed, thinking he'd pull away if she admitted what had happened. "Well, I thought I could, but . . . when I changed my mind things got ugly."

His arms tightened more firmly around her, and he rocked her soothingly a time or two. "Oh, Cherokee, can't you feel that's not going to happen to us?"

And suddenly she could. She relaxed against him as he wet the soft skin of her neck with the tip of his tongue and slipped a hand over her left breast, warm and resilient within the tissue-fine fabric of her dress. Shudders of pleasure made her skin prickle. Doubts fled magically. She no longer remembered that the skin he touched was not as firm as it had once been. She only reveled in how good it felt to be caressed again. She closed her eyes, and braved the question she, too, needed to have answered.

"How long has it been for you?"

His hand continued its gentle exploration even as he told her, "Three months."

"With who?"

The hand stilled on her breast. "Does it matter?"

"If she still means something to you, it does."

"She doesn't."

She relaxed even further, relieved more than she could say by his answer. The crepe dress seemed to have no more substance than a cobweb as he cupped his wide palms about the lower swell of both breasts and made the fabric slip seductively across her nipples, tempting them, making her insecurities retreat farther and farther, replacing them with the vast need to be touched again, fondled, loved.

"Oh, Cherokee, you feel so good," he murmured against her naked shoulder, dropping his head forward and crushing her back against him.

"So do you." She covered his hands and pressed them firmly against her breasts as if to absorb every nuance of tenderness. The wide palms moved beneath her hands, gentling and arousing at once, appeasing the need for quiet exploration. "Oh, Brown," she admitted breathily, "I've needed this for so long."

"I know," came his gruff voice beside her ear. "We all do." Then his fingertips familiarized themselves with the belled shapes of her nipples. He folded them between his thumbs and the edges of his hands, lifting her breasts at the same time, sending tiny tuggings of ache feathering along her nerves.

She hardly realized she'd sighed until his voice whispered in the hair above her ear, "That's better, Cherokee . . . relax."

And she was—oh, she was—for his hands seemed to stroke away her lingering misgivings, and the easy pace he'd set won her trust. His hands were very hard, both front and back, yet their touch was sensitive, and she made no effort to stop one from escaping her light hold. It slid over her stomach, where the fingers spread wide for a moment, then closed again before pressing into the hollow beside her hip. His touch became feather light as with a single fingertip he scribed a twining grapevine upon the mound of femininity within her silken skirt. He sent a perceptible shiver through her, for his movement over the crepe made it slip across equally silky undergarments until the sleek touch of her clothing sent ripples of sensuality up her spine. It made her powerfully aware of her own sexuality, this touch that was half caress, half tickle, and all arousal. She sensed him gauging her reaction, listening to the accelerated beat of her heart, feeling it beneath the palm that still pleasured her breast. At last he slipped his hand fully over the curve of her femininity, bringing her to know a wild rapture, a lush awakening.

He murmured her name—Lee, and sometimes Cherokee —kissing her ear, her jaw, her shoulder, as his hands rustled over her, learning her contours, then traveling once more up her stomach and sides until his thumbs hooked the elastic at the top of her dress, taking it down to her waist and freeing her breasts to his palms, which lingered only momentarily before one slipped low within her garments to touch her intimately for the first time. His voice was ragged as he uttered, "Oh, Cherokee, I've wanted this since the first night I saw you in that motel room."

She smiled in the dark thinking back to that night, realizing she'd been fighting a losing battle ever since. "I . . . I tried not to think of you, but it . . . it was impossible after that."

His touch drove the breath from her lungs and set her pulse thrumming, while behind her his body invited with its pressure, then with a faint side to side movement. But it was far easier to accept the first touch than bestow it. As if sensing her hesitancy, he rested his jaw against her temple and encouraged, "You know, you don't have to ask permission if there's anything you feel like doing."

Was he teasing? Only a little, and in an engaging way that sent a new awareness through her body. Yet girlish uncertainty mingled with womanly yearning. His midsection pressed firmly against her backside, verifying the message in his words while she hesitated yet a moment longer.

Then he begged softly, "Please, Cherokee . . ."

At last she drew her arm back, circling behind him to rest upon the tail of his suit jacket. His hand fell still upon her body, and his breath beat harshly against her ear as he waited . . . waited.

It had been so long . . . so long. But during these moments of sweet expectation she realized this intimacy had almost been predestined, for she and Sam had felt that spark from the first, and since then they had revealed bits and pieces of each other in the hope that each would find something more substantial to bring to his act. And now it was here, and her turn had come.

Her hand moved tentatively between them, and Sam

backed away, giving her space and the right to know him. Her heart was like a wild thing in her breast as she touched him for the first time, a tentative caress that brought a strange, thick sound from his throat. She explored him through tailored gabardine until he lost the power to remain still beneath her fingers and ordered gruffly, "Turn around, Cherokee." Suddenly she was spun about by her shoulders, and her arms were lifting while their open mouths met like a crashing of worlds. She pressed her willing body against his, circling his neck, losing her fingers in thick hair at the back of his head, and exploring the contour of his skull before she felt herself being lifted off her feet.

"Your shoes . . ." he ordered against her lips.

Her toes worked the straps off her heels, as first one clunk sounded behind her, then another. A moment later her bare feet rested again on the cool tile floor, and his palms slid within the elastic at her waist, passing along her lower back. Down went the skirt, and with it pantyhose and silky briefs, to form a pool of fabric at her feet. He encircled her with powerful arms, lifted her off the floor for a second time, and kicked the garments aside. Another drugging kiss stretched into an abandoned celebration of discovery while hands, mouths, and hips paid homage. When he lifted his head a long time later, he asked hoarsely, "How do you feel about undressing a man?"

Perhaps it was then that she realized she could easily fall in love with Sam Brown, with this sensitive man who made it all so easy and kissed away the last remaining doubt.

She smiled and replied throatily, "Turn me loose and I'll show you."

The pressure fell away, and she slipped her hands under his jacket. Before it hit the floor she was working the knot of his tie from side to side. It joined the jacket. As he unbuttoned his cuffs, his forearms softly brushed her breasts, and his voice came low and husky and certain. "We're going to be good together, Cherokee. I just know it."

At that moment she knew it too, and she reached for his shirttails and pulled them free of his trousers.

She did it all, all that he wanted of her, removing each article of clothing with a newfound sense of freedom. And when he too was naked and reaching, her hips were taken firmly against his once more. Her fingertips found his bare chest, and she raised up on tiptoe to settle her bare breasts securely against it, and he ran his palms over her back.

He asked only a single word. "Where?"

"In the living room," she murmured against his mouth before she was turned around and pulled back against his naked thighs while his legs nudged hers and they made their way onto soft, plush carpeting. She felt the pressure of his lips against her shoulder and answered their tacit command by bending with him. As they knelt, with one of his knees between hers, he aroused her with a magical touch until she lost all sense of time and drifted into a sensual paradise where a three-year void was eradicated by his knowing hands. The heat came slowly, starting in her toes, up her legs, along her flanks until her head pressed back against his shoulder and waves of pleasure broke across her skin.

She groaned, a strangled sound of abandon, and he clamped a steadying arm just below her breasts, holding her tightly against him while bringing her again the sense of self she'd lost somewhere along the years.

Behind her he was tense and rigid as his fingers curled into her shoulders, and a moment later she was turned and lowered quickly to her back and spread-eagled against the soft living room carpet.

It was a wild, primitive act they shared this first time, as if neither could control the tempo or the pressure. Celibacy had given Lee a need to match Sam's, so neither was concerned about the way they displayed their wantonness. It happened, as it was meant to happen, in an elemental and satisfying way neither had planned or anticipated. And when it was over and he fell heavily across her, they knew they'd shared something exceptional, even rare.

"Cherokee . . ." was all he could find the breath to say, but the single word was an accolade.

"Your Honor . . ." In other times, other contexts, the title had taken on a note of teasing, but now it was a sigh.

"You're wonderful," he praised.

"So are you . . . and . . . different than I expected."

He braced up, though his weight still pinned her lower

half. "And what did you expect?"

"I . . . I don't know." With both hands she soothed the damp hair from his temples. Though it was still dark, her eyes had adjusted to the dimness, and she could discern the outlines of his features. "All I know is I was very unsure, and . . . and feeling rather inadequate, and you made me forget all that."

He ran an index finger along the rim of her nose. "Inadequate? Why?"

How foolish it seemed now, yet minutes ago she had felt uncertain. "The second time a woman loses the confidence that comes so easily with the first time."

He kissed the tip of her nose with exquisite tenderness. "You're anything but inadequate, Cherokee. But in case you still have doubts, I'm volunteering to do my best to soothe them—indefinitely."

She tried to chuckle, but it was hard with his weight pressing the air from her lungs. She settled comfortably at his side and lay with her head on his arm while his hand rested on her hip.

She had forgotten the deep lethargy and satisfying afterglow of love. She basked in it now, resting in the curve of his arm, cherishing this lazy time which was the antithesis of what had just passed, but equally as necessary.

She curled up even more securely against his side, listening to the thud of his heart against her ear and running a finger from the corner of his lips to the soft center. His kissed her finger, which slipped into the moist, lush interior of his mouth before he bit it very gently, then continued holding it between his teeth.

Ruminating on the minutes just past, she murmured, "That was terrible, wasn't it?"

"What was so terrible about it?"

"Uninhibited," she mumbled, slightly chagrined at the memory.

"Are you saying you want to take it a little slower next time?"

"Next time?" She reached up and playfully yanked a handful of his hair. "You certainly take a lot for granted."

"Oh, do I now?" He rolled her on top of him and settled her along his length, then ran his hands down her spine until his fingertips touched a part of her that disproved her words. And when they'd shared another ripple of mirth, he wrapped his arms around her securely and kissed her cheek.

"Cherokee, you're all woman, and you're more than enough to suit me. Mind if I hang around for a while?"

"Mmm . . . how long did you have in mind?"

"Oh . . . till morning, anyway." She heard the grin in his words, which brought a corresponding smile to her own lips.

But though she smiled and teased, "That long, huh?" the thought of morning was something to be reckoned with. Morning, with its bright revealing sun. She nudged the thought away, nestling against him, wanting him beside her throughout the night.

Morning would take care of itself.

CHAPTER

Nine

LEE WATCHED DAWN creep into the bedroom, all coral and cozy, illuminating their two bodies beneath strewn sheets, she on her belly, Sam on his back. Her eyes followed the brown and white cat that padded into the room, stopped beside the window where it lifted its nose to sniff the cool morning air, puffing the draperies gently from the sill, tapping the plastic bell on the end of the pull. Nose to the air, the cat stood for long minutes, then bounded onto the bed, landing in a most unfortunate spot.

Sam came up like a jack-in-the-box, uttering a sharp cry of surprise followed by an expletive. The cat went flying through the air like a missile as Lee braced up on both palms to observe Sam tenderly massaging his abused parts through the sheets.

She fell onto her belly again, chuckling into the pillow. "What's the matter? Was I too hard on you last night?"

"What the hell was that!"

"That was my cat, P. Ewing."

"Ohhh," he groaned. "I thought the bed was booby-trapped."

She laughed silently, hugged the pillow beneath one cheek, and peered up at him. "Can I help?"

He turned his head, all tousled and dark, and amusement curved his lips. "Your damn cat just . . . just pickled my mushrooms, woman, and you lie there making jokes?" It appeared he'd forgotten his discomforts now. He folded his arms behind his head and closed his eyes. "Don't talk to me, I'm pouting." But the corners of his lips twitched.

Lee studied him at leisure, noting that his beard had grown overnight, that his chest was wide and dark, that his nipples were the color of rosebuds. Pleasure came wafting over her at waking to the sight of such a man in her bed. He was as handsome as he was entertaining, and she let her eyes linger on his lips, brows, and eyelashes. She reached out and ran the tip of a fingernail just inside the rim of his nostril.

"Oh, Bro-o-w-wn?" she sing-songed seductively, going up and down the scale.

His nose twitched, but his eyes remained closed.

"Oh, Brow-w-wn . . ." she crooned again, tickling the edge of his other nostril. He wriggled his nose, then rubbed it distractedly before crossing his arms behind his head as before, with eyes still closed. She shimmied over beside him, propped her bare breasts coquettishly on his chest, and rested her chin on crossed wrists.

"Hey, Brown, you were right, this bed is booby-trapped. Wanna see?"

His chest shook silently, but he lay as before.

"Hmm?" she teased.

"Naw."

She snickered, unable to keep a straight face any longer. He opened one eye and looked down his nose at her.

"But I've got something here you might be interested in witnessing," he said.

"What's that?"

"A genuine Indian uprising."

They were dissolved by paroxysms of laughter then, even as his powerful arms closed around her and flipped her over. They shared a first good morning kiss, but before it ended the laughter had faded away. Lee held his face in both hands and said in a husky tone, "Oh, Brown, you're so good for me."

His ebony eyes ran over her face, touching her lips, nose, and tousled hair before meeting her own eyes.

"Lee," he requested in a strangely quiet way, "I'd like to hear you call me by my first name . . . just once."

She placed her palms in a light caress along his cheeks, then studied his face, feature by feature. It was a strong, compelling face, holding the color of the sun and his heritage in its copper tone. Her fingertips rested just beside his black-lashed eyes, which were as splendid in this new seriousness as ever they were when laughing. His cheekbones were high, his nose straight. She rested her thumbs on his full lips and brushed the soft skin lightly.

In the gentlest of voices she said his name. "Sam . . . Sam . . . Sam . . . I want you inside me again, Sam. You feel so good there." She drew his face down to hers, her mouth opening to receive his kiss as he moved over her, fitting his hips to hers, his firmness to her pliancy. Her eyes closed as his flesh stroked within hers—long, ardent strokes that took her back to that plane of rapture they'd shared more than once the night before.

"Open your eyes, Lee."

She opened them, losing herself in his brown, probing gaze that hovered just above her as their bodies blended rhythmically together. They watched each other's faces mirror what was happening inside as they moved closer to glory, reveling in not only what they took but also in what they gave.

As Lee witnessed a parade of feelings cross Sam's face, she found new meaning in the act, and realized with utter certainty that it was not one into which he had entered lightly.

When it was over and her hands had brushed away the sheen of moisture from Sam's back, she gathered him close, wondering if he would understand that what she'd just experienced seemed a blending of spirits as well as of bodies. Holding him tightly, she whispered against his neck, "Oh, we are good together, aren't we, Sam?"

"Yes we are, Cherokee. I told you that last night." He braced his elbows on either side of her, and his thumbs smoothed her hairline, and once again they assessed each other, but looking deeper now.

"I'm glad it wasn't just me," she began. "I mean . . . I needed this very badly and I thought maybe that's why it was . . . exceptional."

He smiled and kissed the side of her nose. "No, it wasn't

just you. It was exceptional for me too."

Her heart seemed to soar. "Was it really? You're not just saying that to be gallant?"

"Shall I stick around and convince you of that too?"

"Oh yes, Your Honor, please do."

And he did. They spent the weekend together, laughing and loving and learning about each other. And she came to know Sam Brown as a man of many facets.

That morning he insisted that she join him on an early run and produced from the trunk of his car a tote bag containing the same jogging clothes she'd seen once before. When she argued that it was Saturday, she had to clean the house, he said he'd help her when they got back. When she argued that she was out of shape, he said running would get her in shape —though he wasn't complaining. When she argued that it was hot, he said he'd cool her off.

They put on their sweatbands and headed out.

After a quarter of a mile Lee was lagging and panting. After half a mile her muscles burned. After that she tried to put her misery out of her mind, realizing what self-discipline it took to exercise like this every day. Her head hung. Her legs felt like deflated inner tubes. She followed Sam blindly, trailing doggedly at his heels and watching the slap of her feet . . .

He led her smack through the lawn sprinklers of Turner Golf Course!

She shrieked and threw her arms up over her head as the icy water brought her to a halt. "Brown, you're crazy!"

Still jogging, he turned to look at her over his shoulder. "I told you I'd cool you off," he called, then continued unceremoniously through the line of sprinklers. What could she do but laugh and follow?

When they returned home, he was the essence of solicitousness, laying her out on her stomach on the living room floor, then massaging her weary muscles with expert hands and soothing care. With her eyes closed and her cheek pressed against her crossed hands, she moaned, "Oh, Brown, how could you put me through that?"

"It'll keep you from getting fat and decadent," he replied cheerily, then completed her rubdown but refused to let her bask on the floor any longer. With a sharp slap on the rump, he ordered, "You have to keep moving or those muscles will tighten up."

With a groan she dragged herself up off the floor only to be hauled toward the shower. Without a flicker of embarrassment he joined her, and though it started out with Lee insisting she couldn't stand up for another minute, it ended with her soap-slicked body pressed flat against the cold ceramic tile and one knee hooked over Sam Brown's arm.

Afterward he made her breakfast, an ungodly concoction he called a Chinese omelette, declaring he had a passion for bean sprouts and water chestnuts. It was delicious after all, and the first meal a man had ever prepared for Lee. While they lounged at the table over cups of tea, Sam tipped his chair back on two legs, stretched a long arm toward the telephone on the counter behind him, called his mother, keeping his eyes on Lee all the time.

"Thought you might be worried," was the gist of his message.

When he'd hung up, he explained without compunction, "We don't interfere in each other's lives, but we share the same house. She'd do the same for me if she planned to be gone for an entire weekend."

And again, Lee looked at Sam in a new light.

There followed yet another surprise, for he was as good as his word and helped her with the house cleaning, showing an amazing lack of macho ego as he pushed the vacuum cleaner and emptied garbage cans. Joel had considered it "woman's work" and had never helped her with domestic tasks. Yet watching Sam Brown performing them now seemed to add to his masculinity rather than detract from it. She promised him a reward for his help and fulfilled that promise on the long sofa in the newly cleaned living room.

In the afternoon she remembered she'd made an appointment at the garage to have the oil changed in the Pinto. "Why not do it in the company shop and save yourself some money?" Sam suggested.

"Who, me?" she asked, surprised.

"Why not? The shop's got a hoist and any tools you need. Most of the guys who work for me take advantage of it. I don't mind."

"But . . ."

He leaned against the counter, crossed his arms, and cocked a dark eyebrow. "Don't tell me you're going to say, 'But I'm a woman.' Not after I just finished your vacuuming."

He had her there. She bit her tongue.

"I'll show you how, if you want me to. It's not hard," he offered.

And so Lee found herself doing the last thing in the world she'd ever have thought she'd do with Sam Brown—learning to buy the right size oil filter, the right weight oil; removing a drain plug, applying an oil-filter wrench, replacing the filter, then the plug, and finally the oil, and saving herself a considerable amount of money. And all at the suggestion of a man she'd once called rich and decadent.

But best of all, she'd earned Sam's respect, for as they headed back to her house, she knew he was pleased at the pluckiness she'd shown in her first attempt at auto maintenance.

They were scrubbing their hands at the bathroom sink when she looked up to find his approving eyes on her in the mirror. This time it was *he* who promised *her* a reward for her bravery, though he added with a charming grin that it would be the first time he'd ever made love to a mechanic.

While he went out to pick up a pizza, the "mechanic" prepared a homecoming.

Sam returned to a sight that stopped him dead in his tracks just inside the door. Lee posed at the far end of the hall haloed by the golden sunset coming through the patio door behind her. Her feet were bare. Her hair was loose. There were feathers in her ears and a white band around her forehead. Her palms rested on the walls above and beside her head while she slung her weight on one hip and the opposite thigh jutted forward. She wore nothing but a supple suede vest made up chiefly of swinging fringe. Several strands rode between her legs at the dark triangle of hair.

"Cherokee . . ." Sam breathed.

"Just so you don't get too used to me in a grease pit with a wrench in my hand."

"Come here, Cherokee," he said huskily.

They ate cold pizza.

* * *

At three o'clock in the morning Lee awakened with a charley horse in her leg and sprang up in pain. Sam was immediately at the foot of the bed, taking her calf in his hands and working the heel to ease the cramping muscles until the spasms passed.

"Better now, sweetheart?"

She sighed and relaxed. "Mmm-humm." His hands were like magic, soothing away the hurt. He'd called her sweetheart. She lay back, relaxed, letting him massage and manipulate the cramp away, thinking of what a study in contrasts Sam Brown had turned out to be. As if to bear out the point, a few minutes later he eased himself beside her again and pulled her into the curve of his body until they rested like two spoons in a drawer. As if to himself he mused, "Well, well . . . what's this now? I think I've discovered an Indian mound."

Lee burst out laughing and swatted him. "Sam Brown, you're awful!"

"Mmm . . . maybe I'll explore it."

"This one's been explored several times today."

"What? No more treasures left in it?"

Already he was searching for anything he might have missed. She knew that when he found it delight would surely follow, so she teased in return. "Well, there might be an old arrowhead left lying around."

Within minutes she had completely forgotten the lingering discomfort in her leg.

They ran again the next morning, then Lee cooked Sam breakfast while he did the Sunday crossword puzzle. Afterward she was sitting on the patio brushing her hair when he surprised her yet again by kneeling behind her, taking the brush from her hand, and pulling it gently through the tangled locks. As he braided the dark strands, they talked about their families and their pasts.

But there was one topic Lee never discussed—her children. She kept the door closed on the extra bedroom, hoping Sam wouldn't ask questions. And he didn't . . . until late Sunday afternoon, when they were once again lying naked on the living room floor.

She had fallen asleep and awoke to find Sam stretched out on his side, watching her, his jaw braced on a palm.

"Hi," he greeted softly.

"Hi." She smiled. "What are you doing?"

"Waiting."

"Have you been waiting long?"

"Not long. It's been an enjoyable wait."

She wondered how long he'd been studying her and resisted the urge to hide her stomach behind an arm. Even before he moved, she sensed what he was wondering.

Still lounging on his side, he dropped his eyes and slowly lifted his dark hand from his hip. It moved toward her stomach, then a single fingertip traced the faded line there, following it downward from her navel.

"What's this?" he asked in the quietest of voices, lifting his eyes to hers.

She swallowed and felt a flash of dread, wanting to be honest with him yet searching for an adequate lie. Finding none, she could only answer, "It's a stretch mark."

"And what's it from?" His unsmiling eyes remained locked with hers.

The words stuck in her throat, though she realized he deserved an answer—an honest answer. He had seen the marks many times during the past two days but had refrained from asking questions until it became apparent she was not going to offer an explanation without being prompted. She swallowed dryly, her throat tight with apprehension.

"It's . . . it's from a baby I once had."

A long moment passed, rife with unspoken questions. Then, without another word, he bent to her, resting his lips against the telltale line. Lee's heart threatened to burst beyond the bonds of her body as his warm mouth lingered. Tears suddenly filled her eyes at the sight of him twisted from the hip, his shoulder blade outlined sharply while he breathed softly against her skin.

When he raised his head at last, it was to study her eyes deeply as he asked, "When?"

"A long time ago."

He touched his thumb to the wet track from a tear. "Tears again, Cherokee, just like that day in the orchard?"

His compassion never failed to throw her off guard, for it was so unlike what she'd first expected from him. She turned her head sharply aside and stared out the window, unable to meet the concern in his gaze any longer. But he stretched out beside her again, wrapped her in his strong arms, and forced her to face him.

"Did it die, Cherokee?"

The natural assumption. She knew she should disabuse him of it here and now, but it was so hard . . . so hard. She closed her eyes, trapping more tears that wanted to escape, cutting off the sight of a tender, concerned Sam Brown, whom she knew she was deceiving by letting the misinterpretation go uncorrected.

"I can't talk about it. I . . . I just can't, Sam."

To Lee's surprise, he acquiesced. "Okay, we won't talk about it now." He brushed the hair back from her temple with his wide palm, then kissed the top of her head. "Anyway, I think it's time I was going."

They were silent as they went upstairs and found his clothes—the same he'd worn there Friday night—and a robe for her. She walked him to the door, but the gaiety they'd shared all weekend was gone. They stood without speaking for a long moment, Lee staring at his feet, and Sam at the keys in his palm. Finally he sighed and took her into his arms.

"Listen, I have to fly to Chicago tomorrow. I'll be gone for a few days."

She was taken by surprise at how abandoned his announcement made her feel. They had spent two days together—nothing more. How could she feel this bereft after only two days?

Her arms circled his shoulders, suddenly strong and clinging as she raised up on tiptoe, but after a brief return of the pressure, he backed away and grinned down at her.

"Promise me you'll run every day without me?"

She dredged up a bright smile. "Promise."

He kissed her lightly. "I'll be back on Thursday or so." Again they fell silent. He drew in a deep breath and looked as if he were coming to a decision he didn't like. "It'll probably be good for us to be apart for a while, huh?"

"Sure," she agreed with that same false brightness, while

her heart seemed to crack around the edges.

He gave her a last smile. "Get some sleep. You look exhausted."

Then he turned toward the door, and she found herself gripping its edge with both hands while calling after him, "Call me when you get back?"

"Of course."

But during the days that followed she wondered if he really would call. Why had that last conversation come up? *Why?* Each time she thought of it she felt like a fist was gripping her heart. He had guessed the truth, she was sure. He had guessed and wanted her to admit it, but when she'd backed away he'd decided it was time to take a second look at things. That's what he was doing on this trip to Chicago—evaluating her from a distance.

She lived with the fear that he would return having decided he didn't want to invest any more time in a woman who couldn't be totally honest with him, and she promised herself that if he called when he got back, she'd tell him the truth immediately.

In that brief time he had made himself an integral part of her life. He lingered in almost every corner of it—in the office, where she often glanced toward his open door, wondering how his business was going in Chicago, who he was with, if he missed her too; in her townhouse, where they had laughed and slept and made love and left memories in nearly every room; in her car, which reminded her of what fun it had been learning from him. Even running through the warm August evenings reminded her that he had already encouraged this change in her lifestyle, for she kept her promise and jogged after work each day, improving her wind control by breathing in long draughts as he'd taught her instead of in rhythm with her footsteps.

Sometimes she asked herself if this sudden obsession with Sam Brown was only sexual. Was she nothing more than a desperate divorcee who'd tumbled for the first man who gave her a second look? The idea frightened her, for ever since her divorce she'd feared doing that. Was she that kind of woman? Admittedly, it had been a long dry spell for her, which she'd certainly made up for with Sam Brown. Yet, what they had experienced that weekend had taken her feelings for him far beyond the sexual.

He had revealed himself to be a caring person, self-disciplined, amusing, devoted, compassionate, honest. What a surprise to discover such a myriad of admirable qualities hidden beneath the surface person she'd so mistrusted at first.

Recalling his attributes, she grew to miss him in a sometimes terrifying way and wished he'd call. But he didn't, though he checked in with Rachael every day. In a way Lee was hurt that he didn't ask to speak to her, but he'd said it would be good for them to be apart, and apparently he was giving the test a full chance.

Lee found him on her mind far, far too often and realized things had happened very fast between them. Too fast—like the first time with Joel when neither of them had stopped to think past the here and now. Hadn't she learned her lesson then? Yet here she was, plunged into loneliness over Sam after only a two-day relationship.

Relationship. She considered the word. Yes, she admitted, she and Sam Brown had related to one another in many ways. That was why their last conversation had come to bear such great significance and why his parting mood had left her utterly despondent. Once again she promised herself that the minute he called she'd tell him the truth.

Every time the phone rang in the office on Thursday, Lee's eyes went to the lighted button, wondering if it was him. Every time somebody's shadow crossed the doorway, she looked up with her heart in her throat. But he hadn't returned by five o'clock, and she drove home trying to decide whether or not she should run. What if he called while she was gone? In the end she kept her promise and went for the longest run she'd taken yet, pushing herself until her hip sockets ached and her thigh muscles quivered. Back home, she showered and put on faded blue jeans and a T-shirt with an advertisement for Water Products Company on its front. If he didn't call, if he didn't come, at least she wouldn't find herself at the end of the evening removing clothing that indicated she'd fussed and waited for him. But she polished her nails and braided her hair and put on a new brand of perfume she'd chosen for its light, uncloying scent. She opened the refrigerator perhaps a dozen times, but nothing appealed to her. She rehearsed exactly how she'd tell him, but each time she said the words her palms grew damp.

When the phone rang at 7:45, her heart seemed to skitter to her throat and her stomach went fluttery. It rang again. She lurched and grabbed it.

"Hello?"

Sam's baritone voice held an unexpected teasing note as he announced, "This is a collect obscene phone call from the Honorable Sam Brown to Cherokee Walker. Will she accept the charges?"

Joy sluiced through Lee, bringing a faint weakness to her knees. She beamed at the ceiling and answered, "Yes, she will."

"And is this Cherokee Walker?"

"It is."

"The one with the Indian braid on cleaning day and the mole way low on the left side of her rump?"

"Yes." A gurgle of laughter escaped her lips.

"And the one with the neat, sexy breasts just about the size of the palm of my hand?"

"The same." This was obviously no time for serious matters.

"The one who makes love on the living room floor and against the bathroom wall?"

"Sam, where are you?"

"I'm home, but I'll be at your house in exactly"—A pause followed as if he were checking his watch—"thirteen and a half minutes."

Her heart was hammering against her ribs, and she was smiling fit to kill. She was so relieved she forgot to say anything.

"Cherokee, are you still there?"

"Yes . . . yes, I'm still here."

Silence hummed for a moment before his voice came low and husky. "I missed you to beat hell, babe."

A great outthrusting pressure formed across her chest as she held the receiver in both hands and returned in a half whisper, "I missed you too. Hurry, Sam."

When had she last felt this giddy, this impatient? She was fifteen years old again, waiting for that special boy to walk into English class. She was sixteen, planning an appealing pose that a certain boy couldn't help but notice. She was seventeen and trying to appear casual while every nerve and muscle in her body was taut with anticipation. She conjured up the image of Sam Brown, and it was flawless and godlike, and she told herself it was only her breathless eagerness that made him perfect in her memory. Yet when reality stepped through her door, the memory paled in comparison.

He came in without knocking. She was standing at the kitchen end of the hall, where she waited for his knock after hearing the car door shut. At his unannounced entry, she drew in a quick breath, then stood unmoving, staring at Sam as he hesitated with his hand on the door—copper skin, chestnut hair, trousers of cinnamon brown, an open-throated ivory dress shirt, and a look in his dark eyes that said the past four days had been as long for him as they'd been for her.

"Cherokee . . ."

"Sam . . ."

She felt a moment of intense elation, took a hesitant step, and then they were flying toward each other and his arms were around her and hers were about his neck as he lifted her from the floor and turned in a joyous circle, holding her crushed high against his chest with her nose pressed against his crisp collar, where the scent of him was just as she remembered. She closed her eyes, the better to absorb the almost dizzying satisfaction at having him back again. Sam . . . Sam. . . . He let her slip down, and even before her toes touched the floor, they were kissing, with pounding hearts pressed together so tightly they seemed to beat within a single body. Their tongues conveyed not only impatience, not only eagerness, but also that far more poignant message—you're as good as I remembered . . . even better. She held the back of his head in two greedy palms, felt it move as his mouth worked compellingly upon hers and his strong arms circled so far around her ribs that his fingertips touched the soft swells at the sides of her breasts. Then his palms ran the length of her back, caressing it through the T-shirt from neck to waist in a touch that was curiously unsexual, but a comfirmation of her presence in his arms once again, a celebration at having her back where she belonged.

In much the same way she slipped her fingers inside the back of his collar, seeking warm skin, kneading the hard knots of his neck as if to reaffirm his presence.

When the first wild rush of greeting had finally passed, he lifted his head and his voice shook. "God, I missed you."

His words sent shudders of relief down her spine. His hands slipped under her shirt, and he folded his elbows along the center of her back till his wide palms came up through the neck of her T-shirt to cradle her head. She lay back against them, looking up at him, taking her fill of him.

"I missed you too... incredibly." Words seemed inadequate to describe how all-consuming her thoughts of him had been. She touched him in an effort to tell him in another way what her days had been like without him. She caressed his cheeks, his eyebrows, his lips... and as she did, his fingers massaged her head on either side of the thick braid. He closed his eyes and turned his parted lips against her fingertips as they brushed past.

"Chicago was almost a lost cause. I couldn't keep my mind on business," he confessed, still with his eyes closed, still with his lips turned against her fingers.

"The office wasn't the same without you."

He opened his eyes again. They held the look of a man who had truly come home.

"Wasn't it?"

She shook her head no. "I almost hated being there."

He smiled. "I'm glad. Misery loves company."

"Every time I knew Rachael had talked to you, I *was* miserable."

"Good, because I was too." His eyes wandered up to her hairline then, and his hands slipped from under her shirt to bracket her hips and settle them comfortably against his own.

"Did you run, like you promised?"

She laced her fingers around the back of his neck, leaning at the waist. "I ran like a dervish, trying to get you off my mind."

"Did it work?" The well-remembered grin was back.

"No." She squeezed his neck briefly. "It only made matters

worse. But you'd be proud of me. I must have gone three miles today."

"Three miles! Hey, that's good." At his approval she was suddenly very, very glad she'd persevered with the running and felt a great rush of pride.

"Oh, and I went shopping, too, and got some decent running shoes."

He backed away and looked down at her feet. "Let's see— oh, very nice. No more charley horses?" He settled her back where she'd been and ran his hands idly over the curve of her spine.

"Nope. I'm getting tougher all the time." Again she thrilled at his grin of approval. Then he observed, "You shopped for something else while I was gone too, didn't you?"

"What?"

His head dipped briefly to her neck while his hands moved unhurriedly over her buttocks. "Some new perfume, I think."

"Do you like it?"

"Aha." His lips confirmed the answer with a soft nip at the skin beneath one ear.

"And it doesn't make you sneeze?"

"Un-uh."

She rocked lazily against him, smiling to herself while her fingers remained locked at the back of his neck.

"Good, because after the shoes I can't afford to try another kind."

He laughed, lifting his head, white teeth flashing, then asked, "Have you eaten yet?"

"No, and I'm ravenous now that you're back."

"So am I. Let's go get something, and you can fill me in on everything that went on around the office while I was gone."

"I'm not exactly dressed . . ." She backed away, tugging at the hem of the baggy sweatshirt and looking down at it critically.

"You look sensational to me." Sam turned her toward the door, looped an arm over her shoulders, and gave her a nudge. "Now, let's get this damn eating over with so I can bring you back home and tell you again how much I missed you."

It wasn't until later that Lee realized the subtle change that had come over their relationship with Sam's homecoming. When it struck her, the significance was overwhelming. They had taken the time to catch up on each other's lives, talk business, eat supper together—all before they'd made love. And each moment had been equally satisfying.

CHAPTER

Ten

As August lengthened, Lee and Sam grew used to seeing each other every day at the office and every evening, in private, but in spite of Lee's silent promises, she never brought up the subject of her children. Somehow the proper moment didn't present itself that first night, and as the days slipped by it became easier and easier to put it off.

Yet she saw more and more of Sam. She learned his favorite foods, favorite colors, favorite movie stars. They attended an outdoor concert at the Starlight Theater, and he helped her pick out chairs for her living room. They went to a preseason game of the Kansas City Chiefs at plush Arrowhead Stadium and ran together almost daily.

On the surface everything was calm, and their relationship thrived. But as the last week of August neared, an undeniable tension grew between them. Sam had never asked why she needed the week off, but she knew he wondered.

There were countless times when she could have told him, such as when he'd scooped up P. Ewing, looked the cat in the eye, and said, "Cat, I like your name. Where'd you get it?"

It was the perfect lead-in, so why didn't she take the opportunity to explain that it had come from Jed, who'd inadvertently stumbled upon it by exclaiming the kitten was "pew-ing" the first time it used the sandbox?

It would have been so much simpler had she listened to her conscience and told him in the beginning. But the longer she held the secret inside, the bigger it grew, until it lay like a malignancy she knew must be removed before it eventually killed her. But by now she'd put off telling him for so long that she'd become paranoid about it.

There were times when she looked up to find Sam's eyes studying her pensively, and she knew he was biting his tongue to keep from asking the question which by now he had every right to ask. Yet, honorably, he didn't. And the tension built . . . and built.

Until the night he took her to his home to have dinner with his mother. The evening was an unqualified success, and Lee realized it represented another step in their deepening relationship. But she knew too that Sam had not chosen this last evening before her week off without due consideration. He'd done it as if to say—there, another obstacle overcome; now it's your turn.

All the way home in the car tension grew between them. Outside, a storm raged with great slashes of lightning zagging over the plains followed by awesome thunderclaps. Rain pelted down. The windshield wipers beat out a rhythm and the tires hissed through the rainy streets while inside the car Sam refrained from taking Lee's hand, which he usually did when he drove.

At the townhouse he killed the engine and the lights, then laced his fingers on the steering wheel and stared straight ahead, as if waiting for an explanation.

"Lee—" he began at last.

But before he could get any farther, she interrupted, "There's no sense in two of us getting soaked. You stay here."

His silence seemed to say, "On our last night together?" Yet he continued brooding while the tension mounted still higher between them. Finally, unable to think of a graceful exit line, Lee leaned over and kissed his cheek. He sat as stiff as a ramrod, but as she reached for the door handle, his hand lashed out in the dark and grabbed her so roughly that she gasped. Immediately he loosened his grip, and his voice became contrite.

"Lee, I'm going to miss you."

"I . . . I'm going to miss you too." She waited breathlessly, but still he didn't ask the question, and still she didn't offer an explanation. She wanted so badly to be honest with him, but she was so afraid of looking inadequate in his eyes. The silence lengthened, and the tension in the car seemed ready to explode. Then, just when she thought she couldn't bear it another instant, Sam released her hand, sighed tiredly, and sank down against the seat. She searched his face in the shadows, and for a blinding second the car interior was lit by lightning. His eyes were closed, and he'd rolled his face away from her while he pinched the bridge of his nose.

"Lee, I'm not sure . . . no, let me start again." His hand fell away from his nose, but his voice was strained and held an undeniable note of weariness. "I think I love you, Lee."

It was the last thing she'd expected him to say. Tears sprang to her eyes, and her heart pounded. She reached for his hand on the seat between them, took it in both of hers, and lifted it to her mouth. It was more than a kiss she placed on the back of it. It was a taking in of the texture, warmth and security of it. And it was an apology.

She straightened the long, lax fingers and pressed her cheek and eyebrow against his knuckles.

"Oh, Sam," she breathed sadly against his hand, then carried it to the side of her neck and pressed it beneath her jaw where the pulse raced. "I think I love you too."

Everything inside Lee's body felt as temptestuous as the storm outside. She ran her fingertips down his inner wrist and felt his wild pulse, but he sat as before, wedged low in the seat.

"What should we do about it?" he asked, and she knew it was as close as he would come to forcing her to tell him why she was about to drop mysteriously out of his life for a week.

"Wait and see. We both said we 'think.'"

But even to Lee, her answer sounded inadequate, and she sensed his frustration mounting. "Wait?" he snapped, anger boiling to the surface again as he demanded in a hard tone, "How long?" His fingers closed tightly around hers.

"Sam, let me go in."

He seemed to consider a moment, as if calculating the effect of his question before asking, "Can I come in with you?"

Immediately she let go of his hand. "No, Sam, not tonight."

"Why?" He sat up straighter and seemed to strain toward her.

"I . . ." But she couldn't explain it. She only knew it had something to do with the boys coming tomorrow and a feeling of her own unworthiness. But before she could conjure up an answer, his voice cut coldly through the tense space between them.

"All right then, come here." And before she could guess his intentions, he reached for her in an insolent way he'd never before used with her and pulled her roughly across the seat until she fell against his chest. He began kissing her with a bruising lack of sensitivity.

"S . . . Sam, don't!" She struggled up, recoiling instinctively against him. But he grabbed her by both wrists, and he was frighteningly powerful in his anger as they poised, faced off in a half-prone position across the car seat. His fingers bit into the tender skin where her pulse raced. Tears trembled on her eyelids, and fear swelled up in her throat.

"Why do you pull away? I'm wishing the lady good-bye, that's all."

"Sam . . ." But before more words escaped her stiff lips, she was flung backward against his hard chest with her right hand wrenched between their bodies, rendering it useless. And all the while his voice grated near her ear. "I've just said I think I love you, and you told me the same thing. Considering that, I think you deserve a proper good-bye." She fought him with her single free hand, but he controlled it with amazingly little difficulty as he roughly opened the front fastening of her slacks and plunged his hand inside.

"Sam . . . why . . . why are you doing . . . this?" she sobbed.

But he was relentless. "Why?" His hand invaded the part of her body he had never touched with anything but utmost tenderness, but his voice made a mockery of the act. "This is what you keep me around for, isn't it? This is what you want me for, isn't it?"

He plundered her with consummate skill while an unspeakable sense of loss washed over Lee. She was sobbing quietly now, and somewhere in the back of her mind she knew she'd brought on this anger herself, for his confession of love had been an invitation for her to confide in him, yet she'd refused once again. Tears ran down her face as she finally gave up struggling and lay passively on his hard, aroused body, letting him do with her what he would.

But just as swiftly as it had come, the fight went out of him. His hand fell still while his chest still heaved with emotion. His heartbeat reverberated through the thin fabric of Lee's blouse, and he swallowed convulsively. At the sound, she too choked back the thick tears that clotted her throat. Slowly his fingertips withdrew to rest on the soft, warm skin of her stomach. Neither of them spoke.

In those moments, as she lay upon him, feeling him breathe torturously against the back of her neck, she saw the death of a love that might have been. She held back the sobs she wanted to release for the annihilation of something they'd built slowly and carefully, something that had shown such bright promise only a short time ago.

And—oh God, oh God—it hurt.

He had seized upon one of her greatest vulnerabilities and used it against her, knowing full well that his accusation would debase her. She wished she could go back ten minutes and live them again. But she could only fling the back of a wrist over her eyes while her throat muscles worked spasmodically. All the while she lay on top of him like a plucked flower, wilted by the very sun that had once given it life.

She opened her eyes and stared unseeingly at the rivulets of rain oozing down the windshield, turning an unearthly green in the intermittent flashes of lightning. For a minute she felt disoriented and removed from herself.

Then she summoned up the will to move and pulled herself up, slowly, slowly, sitting on his sprawled thighs and running shaky fingers through her tousled hair, unable yet to find the strength to remove herself from him completely.

"Cherokee—"

"Don't!" His rasping utterance was cut in half by the stiffening of her shoulders and the harsh word. She had thrown up a hand in warning but still sat on him, still with her back to him. There followed a deadly silence, broken only by the ongoing thrum of rain on the roof and low growls of thunder.

Then, muscle by muscle, she dragged her weary body to the far side of the seat and untangled legs from his. In the same deliberate fashion he righted himself behind the wheel, then hung his hands on it, staring straight ahead for several seconds before slowly lowering his forehead onto his knuckles.

She tucked in her blouse, zipped and buttoned her slacks, and reached to slip her shoes from her feet, all with the stilted motions of an automaton. But when she reached for her purse and then for the door handle, Sam lifted his head and placed a detaining hand on her arm.

"Cherokee, I'm sorry. Let's talk about this."

"Don't touch me," she said lifelessly. "And don't call me Cherokee."

His hand fell away, but his voice held a note of entreaty. "This happened because you won't confide in me. If you go in now and stubbornly refuse to—"

The car door cut off his appeal as she stepped out into the torrents of rain and slammed it shut. A river of water rushed along the curb, but she scarcely felt it as her nylon-clad foot splashed through it. Then she was fleeing blindly toward the door. Behind her the engine started up, and the car tore away at breakneck speed, the tail lights fishtailing down the street on the slick pavement. At the stop sign up the block he only slowed, then tore off again with a second screech of tires and swerving of tail lights that bled off into the distance.

The night that followed was one of the worst in Lee's life. She was left utterly decimated by the rift between her and Sam while at the same time she realized she must buck up her spirits to face her sons. She damned Sam Brown for bringing this emotional turmoil into her life at a time that was already rife with it. Facing the boys brought again that sick-sweet lifting of the heart that was half joy, half pain, and as she knelt to greet them, it was with a foreknowledge that this visit was somehow doomed from the start.

Jed and Matthew had grown so much since she'd seen them. At six and eight, they now resisted her hello hugs. Telling herself not to feel slighted, she backed off, realizing she seemed strange to them and that it would take them a while to warm up. They loved her new townhouse, though, and claimed their new beds with exuberance and a few surprised "wows." They fell upon P. Ewing, seeming to have missed him more than their mother, and she looked on with heartsick emptiness, remembering how she and Joel had decided to get the cat because they'd been fighting more and more and thought the pet would be good for the boys.

Daddy, they said, was fine, and they liked his new wife, Tisha, real good. Tisha made the best lasagna in the world. No, Lee answered her younger son when he asked, she wasn't too handy at lasagna. How about spaghetti? But it seemed Matthew had lost the fetish for spaghetti she remembered.

They squealed with glee at her suggestion that she take them to a pro football game the second day they were there. But they didn't know the Kansas City players' names and before long squirmed in their seats and became occasionally disruptive, teasing each other and punching playfully, their bouncing and boisterousness drawing unfavorable glances from people in nearby seats. They left the game after the third quarter. On the way home Lee learned that soccer was their favorite game now. Daddy was coaching their team, and Tisha came to every game.

On Monday Lee won their hearts by taking them on an all-day outing to Worlds of Fun amusement park. They rode the Zulu, Orient Express, and Screamroller until Lee's feet hurt from standing around waiting. But after each ride she shared their renewed delight and robbed her pitifully poor pocketbook again and again for the junkfood they wanted. She forgot to bring suntan lotion, so by the end of the day the boys were both burned, thus irritable and uncomfortable in bed that night.

In her own bed, she thought about Sam and the day they'd ridden the Zambezi Zinger, but the day that had been so happy then only brought a bittersweet pang now and made her cry miserably. She missed him terribly, even while she hated him for the hurt he'd caused her. She considered calling him, but her emotional equilibrium was already strained to its limits by being with the boys again.

The boys. They hardly seemed like her sons anymore, and she felt increasingly inadequate. Nothing she did seemed right for their needs while everything Tisha did must be perfect. Tomorrow, she vowed, she'd make no mistakes.

That day she took them to the sixty acre Swope Park Zoo with its six hundred animals. But they'd been to Florida's Busch Gardens last year and had ridden down the African Safari Ride, where elephants spray you while you go past. The Swope trip seemed a definite second best to her sons.

Each night when they were asleep in their twin beds, Lee stepped to the doorway of their room and studied the dark heads on the pale pillow cases, and tears clogged her throat. At those moments, the disastrous days paled and were forgotten. She was desperately happy to have them here. The two sleeping children were hers again, flesh of her flesh, beings of her making. She loved them in a terrifying way, yet knew with a keen, piercing certainty that their stepmother's love was far more influential than her own. Soon she would become a shadow figure to them. Perhaps she already was.

Matthew had a bad dream the next night and awakened in tears. She sat on the edge of the bed while the backs of his sunburned hands smeared tears across his cheeks and he cried, "Where's Mommy?"

"I'm here, darling," she answered soothingly.

But, disoriented and accustomed to the securities of his life in another home, he cried, "No-o-o, I want Mommy."

By Friday both Jed and Matthew were discussing their friends at home and making plans for what they were going to play when they got back.

On Saturday they produced money "Mommy" had given them to buy a gift for Daddy. Lee took them to the store of stores—Halls, in the Crown Center—where there were items like nowhere else in the world. They bought Daddy a bar of soap shaped like a microphone so that he could sing in the shower.

On Sunday Lee dressed them each in a brand new outfit she'd bought and waited anxiously for their father to come and pick them up. She wondered what her reaction to Joel would be and felt a quailing in her stomach as the doorbell rang. The boys catapulted to answer it. But with him they babbled mostly about all the exciting things they'd done during the week. It was to Tisha, waiting in the car, to whom they ran with arms extended.

Joel looked healthy and happy, watching the boys gallop

across the lawn before he turned to her. She surveyed him with immense relief and realized he no longer posed a threat to her emotions. At some point she had stopped loving him, and she could face him now, comfortable with the fact.

"How are you, Lee?"

"Oh, I'm fine. Things are going well with my new job, and I've got the house now, and . . ." Her eyes wandered down the sidewalk to the boys, then back to Joel's face. "You and Tisha are doing a wonderful job with them, Joel."

"Thanks." He stood relaxed before her. "We're expecting another one in February."

"Well, congratulations!" She smiled. "I . . . well, please tell Tisha the same."

"I will." He made a move to leave and for the first time seemed slightly uncomfortable. "Well, I guess the guys will see you again at Christmas."

"Yes." The word sounded forlorn.

"Boys," Joel called, "come and kiss your mother goodbye."

They returned on the run, gave Lee the required kiss, then forgot everything except getting back into the car as fast as they could.

When they were gone, Lee wandered about the house like a lost soul, hugging her arms. The kitchen smelled like cherry popsicles and she found one melting down the sink, dropped there hastily when she'd said their daddy had arrived. She picked up the stick and threw it away, then rinsed the red liquid down the drain. But the pink stain remained. She stared at it for a long, long time until it grew wavery. A tear dripped down and landed beside it on the almond-colored porcelain, and a moment later she leaned an elbow on the sink edge and sobbed wretchedly. The sound of her crying made her weep all the harder, echoing as it did into the empty room. *My babies.* She clutched her stomach and let misery overwhelm her, leaning her face against her forearm until it grew slick. Her sobbing became so choppy and prolonged that it robbed Lee of breath, and she felt her knees buckle. She moved to the kitchen table and fell into a chair, dropping her head forward on her arms, crying until she thought there could be no more moisture in her body. *Where's Mommy?* P. Ewing came and rubbed up against her leg and purred, bringing a renewed freshet of misery. She needed a tissue, but had none in the kitchen, so she stumbled upstairs and blew her nose and dried her eyes. Clutching a handful of soggy tissues against her nose and mouth, she leaned against the bedroom doorway and felt her grief renewed at the sight of the twin beds and the pennants on the wall above them. Her head fell tiredly against the doorframe, and she cried until her throat and chest ached. *I love you, Jed. I love you, Matthew.* Her misery seemed to have eternal life. The convulsive sobs continued until her head was bursting, and she dragged herself to the bathroom for two aspirins. But at the sight of her ravaged face in the mirror, more tears burned her swollen eyelids and she thought that if she didn't hear the sound of another human voice soon, she would most certainly die.

She stumbled down to the kitchen and dialed, seeking help from the only person who could solace her. When she heard his voice, she tried to calm her own, but she lost control and sucked in unexpected gulps of air in the middle of words.

"Ss . . . S . . . ham?"

A moment of silence, then his concerned voice, "Lee, is that you?"

"S . . . Sam . . ." She couldn't get anything else out.

"Lee, what's the matter?" He sounded panicked.

"Oh, S . . . Sam, I n . . . need you so b . . . bad." A huge sob broke from her as she clutched the receiver with both hands.

"Lee, are you hurt?"

"No . . . No, n . . . not hurt . . . j . . . just hurting. Please . . . c . . . come . . ."

"Where are you?"

"At h . . . home," she choked.

"I'm coming."

When the line clicked, her arm wilted toward the floor with the phone dangling from her lifeless fingers and she begged him, "Pl . . . please hurry."

She was sitting slumped over the kitchen table ten minutes later when Sam Brown ran up the walk and burst through the front door. He skidded to a halt in the middle of the hall, chest heaving. "Lee?" He caught sight of her as she flew out of her chair. They met in the middle of the hall. She flung herself against him, sobbing abjectly and clinging to his comforting body as she burrowed into him.

"S . . . Sam, oh, Sam . . . h . . . hold me."

He crushed her to him protectively. "Lee, what is it? Are you all right?"

Her body was heaving so much no answer was possible just then. He closed his eyes and pressed a cheek against her disheveled hair as hot tears melded his shirt and his collarbone. Her tormented body was wracked by shudders so he wound his arms around her tightly, waiting for her to calm down.

"Sam . . . Sam . . ." she sobbed wretchedly, over and over.

Never had a body felt so good. His hard chest and arms were a haven of familiarity. His scent and texture comforted immeasurably while he stood like a rock, his feet widespread, his long length shielding her. Forgotten were the hurts they'd caused each other. All forgotten was the pain of separation. Barriers fell as she sought his strength, and he gave it willingly.

"I'm here," he assured her, spanning the back of her head with a wide hand and pressing her securely to him. "Tell me."

"My b . . . boys, m . . . my babies," she choked, the simple words becoming an outpouring of her soul while he remained unflinching, the solid foundation of her life.

"They were here?"

She could only nod against his neck.

"And now they're gone?"

Again she nodded and felt him stroke her hair. She pulled back. "How l . . . long have you known?"

His hands spanned almost the entire circumference of her head while his thumbs stroked the tears that were her healing. "Almost since the beginning."

She looked up through a bleary haze while her heart swelled with love for him. "Oh, Sam, I was s . . . so afraid to t . . . tell you." She buried herself against him.

"Why?" His voice was thick, and she heard in it vestiges of the hurt she'd caused and promised herself she would make it up to him. "Couldn't you trust me?"

Fresh tears spouted again while she clung to him. "I was so af . . . afraid of what you'd th . . . think of me." Her shoulders shook even as relief overwhelmed her because he knew at last.

"Shh, don't cry. Come here." He pushed her back gently and slipped an arm around her shoulders, urging her toward the stairs. He sat down on the third step and tugged her down between his knees on the step below, then pulled her back against him. His broad forearm crossed her chest and hugged her tightly while he squeezed her upper arm and rested his chin against the top of her hair. "Now tell me everything."

"I wanted to tell you the l . . . last time we were together. I wanted to so badly, b . . . but I didn't know what you'd think about a . . . a mother who had her kids taken away from her in a divorce court."

His lips pressed the top of her head. "Darling, I saw their beds the first day I came here. I've been waiting since then for you to tell me about it."

"You've known all that time. Oh, Sam, why didn't you ask?"

"I did once, but you let me believe they had died, and I realized then that *you* had to tell me. And that last night we were together, I . . . oh God, Cherokee, I'm so sorry for what I did. But it damn near killed me that you couldn't trust me enough to tell me then. I've had a miserable week, thinking of how I've hurt you and wondering if my suspicions about your kids were right. At times I even found myself wondering if you were with your ex-husband, and I told myself if you were, it was no more than I deserved." His arm tightened perceptibly across her chest.

"No, not that. He's married again and they're expecting another baby."

"You saw him this week, too?"

"Yes, he came to pick up the boys just before I called you."

"They live with him, then?" His quiet questions encouraged her to talk about them, and she marveled at having a man who understood her needs so well. His warm palm caressed her bare arm, and his voice was very soft and compelling.

"What are their names?"

She brushed his forearm and felt his breath warm on the top of her head. "Jed and Matthew." Just pronouncing their names brought a sharp sense of renewed heartache. She sat quietly for a long moment, thinking of their empty beds upstairs. But she rested her head against Sam's chest and drew strength from him as she continued. "Oh, Sam, I don't know if I'll ever get over l . . . losing them. That day in the courtroom was like . . . like judgment day, and I've been in hell ever since. It was totally unexpected. My lawyer was just as dumbfounded as I was when the judge declared that he was giving custody of the boys to Joel. But Joel had a high-powered attorney, one he could afford, and I had a less experienced one that I couldn't afford. I just never dreamed I'd lose. My attorney kept telling me there was something called the 'tender years concept,' meaning basically that little kids need their mother. The boys were only three and five then. But the judge said the court found it would be in the best interest of the children to have a strong male role model." Lee pulled away from Sam's body, crossed her arms on her knees, and rested her head on them. "Male role model, for God's sake. I didn't even know what it meant."

Sam studied her back, reached to cup a hand over her shoulders, and pulled her securely between his legs again.

"Go on," he ordered quietly, slipping his arm across her collarbone.

She closed her eyes and swallowed, then continued in a strained voice. "His lawyer brought up the subject of economics, and mine argued, but it seems economics enter into the . . . the emotional well-being of children. I had no means of support, no career, no prospects. I'd been a wife raising babies, how could I have?" A shudder went through her. She swallowed and opened her eyes. Tears slipped down her cheeks, and a lump lodged in her throat.

"Oh, Sam . . . have you any idea wh . . . what it's like to have your children t . . . taken away? What a failure you f . . . feel like?"

A hot tear dropped on his arm. He squeezed her shoulders and chest in a bone-crushing gesture of comfort, resting his cheek against her hair. "You're not a failure," he whispered thickly. "Not to me . . . because I love you."

How many times this week had she longed for those words? Yet at the moment they tore at her soul, for it was because she loved him too that she wanted to be perfect in his eyes. But she wasn't—oh, she wasn't—so, she went on purging herself. "This week I realized I'm totally inadequate as a mother. The courts were probably right to take them away ⌐ om me. She's done a better job than I ever could. I d . . . did everything wrong. I l . . . let them get s . . . sunburned and I—"

"Lee, stop it."

"I didn't know how to c . . . comfort Matthew when he had a b . . . bad dream and—"

"Lee!"

"And I . . . I . . ." The tears broke free again, and she struggled on in self-recrimination. "I c . . . can't m . . . make—" He grabbed her roughly and swung her around until her face was pressed against his chest where the last word came out a muffled sob—"lasagna."

"Oh God, Cherokee, don't do this to yourself."

"I d . . . did everything wrong." She clung to the back of his shirt, wailing out her pitiful litany.

"Shh . . ." He patted her hair and held her head tightly with both hands.

"They ran to h . . . her and f . . . forgot all about m . . . me when she . . ."

His mouth stopped her words. He had jerked her roughly up to him and held her now in an awkward embrace, twisted as she was at the waist while they perched on their two different steps. He kissed her savagely, then lifted his head and held her jaw as he studied her face.

"They've been away from you for a long time, and they're used to her now. That doesn't mean you're a failure. Don't blame yourself. It breaks my heart to see you like this."

And from the depths of her misery she realized what she had in Sam Brown. Strength, understanding, compassion. Her hurt was his hurt for he absorbed it and his eyes became a reflection of the pain he saw in hers. She trembled on the brink of understanding the true depth of love. And, not wanting to put him through more agony, she finally made a shaky effort to control her tears. When they eventually lessened, he pushed her gently away from him, but only far enough to raise one hip and pull a handkerchief from his back pocket. When she'd dried her eyes and blown her nose, she felt better. Heaving a giant sigh, she sat down beside him on the same step. Bracing both elbows on her knees, Lee gingerly covered her burning eyelids with her fingertips and declared unsteadily, "My eyes hurt. I haven't cried this much since the divorce."

"Then you needed it."

She lowered her hands and looked at his understanding face.

"I'm sorry I unloaded on you. But thank you for . . . for being here. I needed you so much, Sam."

He studied her swollen eyes with their red rims, the fingers behind which she hid her cheeks. He reached and took one of her hands and interlaced his fingers with hers. "That's what love is all about, being there when you need each other, isn't it?"

She touched his cheek with her free hand. "Sam . . ." she said, quiet now, overwhelmed by love for him, certain that what he said was true.

Their eyes held, then he turned a kiss into her palm. "Have you decided yet whether you love me or not?"

"I think I decided on the day you came over here in your jogging shorts."

A brief smile lifted his lips, then they fell serious again. He said quietly, "I'd like to hear you say it once, Lee."

They were sitting side by side in a curiously childish position, holding hands with only the sides of their knees touching as she said into his eyes, "I love you, Sam Brown."

"Then let's get married."

Her startled eyes opened wide. She stared at him for a full ten seconds, then stammered, "G . . . get married!"

He gave her a lopsided grin. "Well, don't look so surprised, Cherokee. Not after the last wild and wonderful month we've spent together."

"B . . . but . . ."

"But what? I love you. You love me. We even *like* each other! We're both in the same line of work, have terrific senses of humor, and we're even the same breed. What could make more sense?"

"But I'm not ready to get married again. I . . ." She looked away. "I tried it once and look what it's put me through."

"Cherokee, you're not going to go through this again, not if you marry me."

"Sam, please . . ."

"Please?" His voice took on an edge. "Please what?"

"Please don't ask. Let's just keep things as they are."

"As they are? You mean sex every night at your house and nothing more than a polite hello at the office? I said I love you, Lee. I've never said it to another woman. I want to live with you and hang our clothes in the same closet and have a family to—"

"A family!" She jumped off the step and stood at his feet facing him. "Haven't you heard a thing I've said? I had that once, and it was the worst tragedy of my life! I lost my sons—the only ones I ever plan to have—in a divorce court. I'm not equipped to be a mother. I told you that!"

"That's all in your head, Lee. You'll be as good a mother as—"

"It's not in my head!" She swung away toward the living room. "I . . . I'm insecure and hurt, and I've failed once at being both a wife and a mother. I don't think I'd be very good at either one again."

He stood behind her in the middle of the living room.

"That's your answer, then? You won't marry me because you're afraid?"

She swallowed and felt the damnable tears spring to her eyes again. "Yes, Sam, that's my answer."

"Lee." He placed a hand on her shoulder, but she shrugged it away. "Lee, I won't accept it, not if you really love me. The only way to get over being afraid of something is to try it again. You're . . . we're not going to fail. We've got too damn much going for us. I just know it."

"It's out of the question, Sam. I just don't understand how you . . ." She turned to face him. "Sam, you can't know how a thing like losing your children can undermine your self-confidence. I swore when it happened that I'd never go through such a thing again. I'd prove to the world that the judge was wrong. I wasn't just a . . . a stupid *squaw* with . . . with no career and no visible earning power. I had things to prove, and I'm not done proving them yet."

"Squaw?" he retorted angrily. "Is that what this is all about?"

"It's part of it. Nobody will ever convince me that judge wasn't influenced against me because I was Indian and Joel wasn't. It has as much to do with the decision as the fact that I couldn't support the kids. Well, I couldn't do anything about my heritage, but I certainly could about my financial status. I set out to earn as much money as any man, in a job only men have traditionally done, but I have a long way to go before I reach my goals."

Sam's face was grim. "Lee, you've got a red chip on your shoulder about the size of the original Indian nations! You carry it there, daring anybody to knock it off—that's why most people try. When are you going to learn you're melted into the pot here, and stop flaunting your heritage?"

Fresh anger flared through Lee. "You don't understand a thing I've said here today! Not a thing!"

"I understand it all, Lee. I'm just not willing to buy some of it. I love you and I accept you exactly as you are, without any question that we could make a successful marriage— babies and all. You're the one who doesn't understand that if you really love somebody past histories should be forgotten and you should put your entire trust in the strength of that love."

She reached out to touch him, her face tight with pain. "I *do* love you, Sam, I do. But do I have to prove it by marrying you?" He removed her hand from his chest and held it in his own.

"That's the usual way, Lee." He looked up, and his dark eyes held a glint of hurt before he added softly, "The honorable way."

What could she say? After the way they'd parted last time, the hurts they both carried since then, how could she argue with him? She saw a grave weariness settle over his features as he stood holding her palm with the tips of his fingers, brushing his thumb across her knuckles.

She stared at him, already stricken with loss. "Sam, don't go."

Again she saw his weariness and the burden of sadness that her refusal had so suddenly brought upon him. He looked into her eyes, and his own were heavy with regret.

"I have to, Cherokee. This time I have to."

"Sam, I . . . I need you."

He stepped close again, drew up her face, and placed a

good-bye kiss on her lips, which were swollen yet from crying.

"Yes, I believe you do," came his tender reply.

He studied her black pupils, touched a thumb to the purple skin of one lower eyelid, then turned, and a moment later the door closed behind him.

CHAPTER
Eleven

IF SHE WERE asked to define exactly who brought about the changes between them, Lee could not truthfully have named either Sam or herself. She only knew they'd reached an impasse that hurt deeply during the weeks that followed. Facing him each day at the office was sheer hell. He no longer passed her desk in the late afternoon to ask what time she'd be leaving for home. She no longer asked if he was coming over. Lee knew either of them could have broken down the invisible barrier that had sprung up between them. It would have taken no more than a single word, yet neither spoke it.

On the surface everything was the same. They consulted each other on bid work, bumped into each other in the copy room, pored over plans together. But through it all Sam maintained an incredibly unfluctuating air of normalcy, while Lee gave him neither pointed indifference nor veiled languishments. Instead they treated each other with neutral geniality, which made her wince inwardly. He opened doors for her if they were heading out together, and they chatted about jobs with a heartiness that distressed Lee's lovelorn soul.

One day in mid-September Sam passed her as she sat near the fountain eating lunch. He waved a roll of plans in greeting, never breaking stride as he called, "Hi, Lee. Enjoying the beautiful weather?" An acute sense of loss pierced her as she watched him stride purposefully into the building.

In late September six members of the office staff treated

Rachael to a birthday lunch at Leona's Restaurant in the Fair-way Shops. They all piled into Sam's car for the short ride. Lee ended up in the back seat. Being there brought back mem-ories of the days of intimacy with distressing clarity as she studied the back of Sam's head.

At Leona's, Lee found herself seated at a right angle to him. As they pulled their chairs in, their knees collided under the table. "Oh, excuse me!" Sam apologized. "It's these damn long legs of mine." His alacrity was as impersonal as if he had bumped Frank's knee, and again Lee felt raw inside. Yet she heard herself laugh and copy his nonchalance.

But for Lee being with him became a refined form of tor-ture. At times she studied him across a room, wondering if he had intentionally plotted this insipid neutrality to punish her. Was he aware of it? Did he maintain this jovial air knowing that every day now put her over the rack? Or had he simply chalked up their affair to experience and moved on to greener pastures? If he loved her, as he claimed he did, how could he be so . . . so damn mundane! When he caught her looking at him, he smiled and turned back to whatever he was doing without the slightest sign of constraint and certainly without flashing any intimate messages with his eyes. But then, did she herself flash any?

September crept to a close, and the first hint of fall tinged the air. Sam called Lee into his office one day, but again he was his ineffable genial self, announcing that she'd been there two months and he was giving her a raise because he was very pleased with her work. Though it was a small boost in pay he said, he meant it as a vote of confidence and ushered her to the open door, where they stood for a minute in full view of the draftsmen. He smelled so familiar that saliva pooled beneath Lee's tongue. The sight of his shirtsleeves rolled up to the elbow, exposing summer-bronzed forearms, and the famil-iar way he slipped a hand into his trouser pocket as they talked, raised goosebumps of awareness across the low reaches of Lee's stomach.

Sam leaned against the door jamb and crossed his arms over his chest, discussing some aspect of the Little Blue River job, which was in full swing by this time. The apples in the orchard would be ripe now, the mosquitoes gone, the red-winged blackbirds and goldfinches flown south. *Oh, Sam, Sam, I haven't stopped loving you.* He continued to discuss business as if nothing had ever happened between them. *Sam . . . Your Honor . . . I want to reach for you, burrow against you, and be part of your life again.* It was time to make some major decisions about equipment, he was saying, while from Lee's body came both a physical and emotional outpouring of need for him. *How can you act as if it never happened when every nerve in my body feels touched by you?* ". . . so Rachael will make the plane reservations. Plan to be gone overnight," Sam was saying.

"I . . . what?" Lee stammered.

"Plan to be gone overnight," he repeated. "I just don't see how we can fly to Denver, attend the equipment auction, and get back here in one day, especially if we end up buying something. There'll be financial arrangements to make, and we'll have to find a yard to rent."

His words hit her like a blow in the stomach. He'd been standing there making plans for the two of them to attend the heavy-equipment auction in Denver with no more compunction than he'd announce the same to Frank or Ron or any of the other guys. Lord o' mercy, did he expect her to go off on an overnight jaunt with him and keep it totally platonic? What did he think she was made of . . . PVC, like the pipes they laid in the ground? His lack of sensitivity infuriated her . . . and the prospect of being alone with him left her weak and trembling.

They flew out of Kansas City on a golden mid-October day, and as the plane looped westward, leaving the cloverleaf design of K.C. International Airport behind them, Lee had a feeling of *déjà vu*, because they were going back to the same place where they'd met.

Before they crossed over mid-Kansas, Sam had slumped back and fallen asleep beside her. He woke up long enough to decline breakfast, leaving Lee to eat alone, ever aware of his slow, slumberous breathing at her shoulder, remembering mornings when she'd awakened to that sound on the other side of her bed. He was still sleeping peacefully when the seatbelt sign flashed on in preparation for landing. She studied his shuttered eyes, the long, dark lashes fanning his cheeks, his lips and limbs in repose, and a renewed sense of longing sprang up inside her. Hesitantly she touched his arm, which lay lax over the armrest between them.

"Sam?"

His eyes opened abruptly and looked directly into hers. There was a moment of disorientation, a sweet, compelling return to the days when they'd awakened together, a sensual smile of hello beginning to tip up his unwary mouth before he seemed to realize where he was and curbed the warm response.

"We'll be landing in a minute," Lee said, casting her eyes away when he clasped his hands, stiffened his elbows, and stretched, uncoiling and shivering in the old, familiar way.

"God, I slept like the dead," he said, reaching for his seat-belt.

You always did, she wanted to say. Their elbows bumped when they were latching their buckles, and Lee wondered how she would survive this torture for two days.

Inside Stapleton International Airport they stood side by side, watching the luggage bump toward them, both reaching for the first familiar suitcase when it arrived. Lee backed off, letting Sam retrieve it and check its I.D. tag. "This one's yours," he stated, setting it at her ankle with no further comment or clue to what he was thinking. His suitcase arrived, and they set off to rent a car.

Sam stowed their identical suitcases in the trunk, unlocked the passenger door, and waited while Lee got in. How many times had he done this for her when they were lovers? Yet now there was only the impersonal politeness he'd show to any woman as a matter of course. When he was behind the wheel Lee was assaulted by the familiarity of his movements, his scent, his hands on the steering wheel.

The auction was to be held at the Adams County Fairgrounds in Henderson. By the time they arrived, Lee was only too happy to escape the confines of the car with its taunting reminders and inescapable memories. But the day proved as distressing as the ride, for it was a remarkably mellow one, the kind in which lovers revel. The Colorado sky was a cloudless cerulean blue, none of Denver's usual brown haze blocking out its deep color. The state's famed aspens were at their peak of brightness too, shimmering like golden coins beneath a butterscotch sun. Accompanying Sam, inspecting machinery, discussing the needs of the company for the upcoming spring job here where their relationship had begun, Lee had difficulty concentrating on business. Time and again she drifted into thoughts of the man at her elbow—the texture of his skin beneath the golden mountain sun; the shadows of his shoulder blades under the knit shirt that delineated the well-remembered shape of his chest and arms; the sheen of his dark hair, which she had first touched in a brush in a motel room not far from where they now stood; the outline of his thigh muscles within his trousers, those muscles she'd first seen on her doorstep on a summer's morning that changed her life forever; his voice which had spoken countless intimacies into her ear and soothed her shattered soul with reassurances when she'd most needed them.

Being alone with him this way yet not alone at all only tightened the string of emotional tension to a higher pitch, until Lee felt as if one more inadvertent nudge of his arm against hers would snap that tensile thread.

He bid on several pieces of machinery, bought two, and made arrangements for payment and pickup with the auctioneering company's financier.

By the time they made their way back toward the rented car, it was late afternoon and the Denver freeways were packed. Lee had no idea where they were staying, but feared Rachael might have made reservations at the Cherry Creek again. To her relief, Sam drove to a different hotel—an airport high-rise. They checked in side by side, but took two separate rooms. Sam extended his company credit card without the slightest hint of uneasiness. He handed Lee one of the keys, and they rode up to the ninth floor together. The hall was carpeted and silent as they moved toward adjacent doors.

Lee thought Sam might suggest meeting for dinner, but instead he unlocked his door, glanced inside, and remarked casually, "Mmm . . . looks like a nice room." Then he picked up his suitcase, turned and answered the question that had been burning within her all day: "See you in the morning, Lee."

It would have been graceless and ill-advised to declare that she was lonely and missed his company and wanted terribly to spend the night with him. Instead she stepped into her own lonely cell and leaned weakly against the closed door to stare at the avocado green carpeting and matching bedspread without seeing either. What she saw was the face and hands and body of the man she loved, the man separated from her by a plaster wall and the equally as palpable barrier of their self-imposed strictures. To know he was there, so close, yet untouchable, was torture. While she stared at the lonely room, tears threatened. A tight constriction squeezed her chest. She crossed to the window and took in the view of the Denver skyline—the Great West Towers, Denver Square, and Anaconda Towers off in the distance. The sun was setting behind the Rockies, which appeared in the foreground like a triple-tiered Mexican skirt, fading from dark purple to light lavender in three distinct layers, from the earth skyward.

She turned away from the stunning view and fell across the bed, battling tears. *You know I love you, Sam. Why are you doing this to me?* When she cried, she felt better and got up to wash her face, refresh her makeup, and go down to dinner, since it was obvious Sam had no intention of asking her to join him for the meal.

As she ate in solitude, anger began to replace her hurt. Her ego smarted. *Damn you, Sam Brown, damn you! Damn you! Damn you!*

Back in her room, she flung her key down on the dresser and glared at the wall. A minute later she pressed her ear to it. She thought she could make out the sound of his T.V. but wasn't certain. She turned on her own, but it had no appeal whatsoever. She flounced onto her bed, plumping the pillows behind her back, but the short-lived anger had dissipated now, leaving her with despair and a crushing yearning that blotted out common sense.

At five minutes after nine o'clock she picked up the telephone and dialed Room 914.

"Yes?" he answered.

She closed her eyes and rested her hand against the headboard. Her heart beat like a tom-tom, and her tongue felt dry and swollen.

"Th . . . this is an obscene phone call from Room 912. W

. . . will you pl . . . please come and . . . and . . ." But her voice faltered as she clutched the phone and swallowed.

"And what?"

Oh God, he wasn't going to help her at all. He was going to keep up this sham. She swallowed her pride, closed her eyes, and admitted, "I was going to say and make love to me, but I need you for so many more reasons than that. I miss you so much that nothing is good in my life anymore."

She thought she heard him sigh tiredly and pictured him, perhaps leaning his back against the wall only inches behind her. The earth seemed to turn one complete revolution before he finally asked, "Are you sure now, Lee?"

Tears seeped from the corners of her eyes. "Oh, Sam, what have you been trying to do to me these past weeks?"

"Give you a chance to heal."

Through her misery she felt a first glimmer of hope. She let her eyes drift closed, realizing it was what she too had been doing.

"Sam, please . . . please come over here."

"Okay," he agreed softly, and hung up.

An instant later a soft tap sounded on her door.

When she'd opened it, she stepped far back, interlacing her fingers and pressing them against her stomach. They stared at each other for an interminable moment as he leaned a shoulder against the doorframe. He was dressed in black socks, gray trousers, and a pale blue dress shirt held together by a single button at the waist. The shirttails hung out of his pants and it looked disheveled, as did his hair.

"Were you asleep already?" Lee asked guiltily.

He shook his head tiredly, no. "I don't think I've slept for the last six weeks—except on that plane today." How had she failed to notice the pinched lines at the corners of his eyes and the tired droop of his mouth?

"Because of me?" she asked hopefully.

He pulled himself away from the doorframe and, with his head drooping forward, turned and slowly closed the door. His shoulders rose in a great sigh, and at last he faced her again. "What do you think?" he asked quietly.

She stared back at him, blinded by pain and tears that threatened to spill from her lashes "I haven't known what to

think since you walked out of my house that night. I . . . you
. . . it's been . . ." Her palms flew to cover her face and sharp
sobs jerked her shoulders. "I . . . I . . . love you so," she
choked out against her hands.

He moved to stand before her, and his warm hands encircled her wrists, forcing them away from her face. He placed a
gentle kiss on the heel of each, where salty tears had left them
wet.

"I love you too," he said, his voice softened by pain.

With a small, throaty cry she flung herself against him,
arms looping up to circle his neck and cling. His arms, too,
clasped her tenaciously while he pressed his face against her
warm neck. He rocked her back and forth, back and forth,
standing with feet spread while holding her body firmly
molded to his, neither of them speaking, drawing comfort
from their nearness.

Her breasts, belly, and thighs flattened to his rigid body,
Lee's mind seemed filled with his name—Sam, Sam, Sam—
and the sweet realization that he was what she needed to complete not only her body but also her life, her *self*.

At last he raised his head and she hers. Their eyes delved,
dark into darker, speaking of the ache each had borne during
their separation, speaking of anguish about to end in triumph.

Their mouths met wordlessly and drank and sought to
make up for the emptiness of six weeks alone. Silky, wet
tongues twisted together, speaking of a want grown one hun-
dredfold since last they'd touched. The kiss lasted for endless,
reckless minutes—glorious! greedy!—until their hearts cla-
mored and their blood pounded. Sam bit Lee lightly, and her
tongue slid back to feel the texture of his teeth scraping atop
and below it. Her fingers found the warm hollow behind his
ear, and she made a throaty sound that sought to tell him
everything she felt for him.

His palms slid to her hips, moving them securely against
his own complementary curves. He pressed his face into the
scented side of her neck and as she tipped her head aslant, he
whispered roughly, "What are you doing with all these clothes
on?"

Her heart seemed to trip over itself as she raised her lips to his ear and answered in a tremulous voice, "Waiting for you to ask me again to marry you."

His head lifted in surprise, and a smile tugged at the corners of his mouth. "Bring it up later, when we have nothing better to talk about."

Then he sobered again, running his eyes over her hair, face, and breasts in a sweeping glance that brought them back once more to the black, searching Cherokee eyes that were alight with love and longing.

He lifted her chin, and his face lowered, while with infinite tenderness he circled her lips with the tip of his tongue. Then they were kissing again, open-mouthed and seeking, while she felt the flutter of his fingers at the valley between her breasts.

He lifted his head, and their eyes met again, then dropped together to his bronze fingers that slipped buttons through holes, then tugged the blouse from the waistband of her slacks. Wordlessly he slid it from her shoulders. Wordlessly, too, he reached behind her and when he backed away again the white brassiere was draped over his dark hands. He tossed it behind her and looked down at her stomach. A moment later he had freed the button at her waist and lowered the zipper beneath it, revealing a wedge of skin above low-slung briefs. He dropped to one knee, pressing his face within the open garment, kissing her stomach where weeks ago he'd traced the line she was so afraid to explain. He traced it again, this time with the feather-light tip of his tongue.

"There's nothing I don't love about you . . . nothing," he vowed as his strong arms cinched her hips and his eyes slid closed. He turned the side of his face against her flesh while his voice grew gruff with emotion. "You never have to be afraid to tell me anything. Always remember that."

Tears trembled close to the surface as she twined her fingers in the hair at the back of his head and pressed him nearer. She closed her eyes against the sweet swelling sensations his words brought to her chest, welcoming the faintly abrasive scratch of his whiskers. The top of his hair brushed the undersides of her breasts, and she leaned low over his head, cradling it in both arms.

"Oh, Sam, I was so afraid to have you see those marks the

first time. Afraid of your disapproval, and . . . and wanting to be perfect when I couldn't be. But that's what love does to you, makes you want to be flawless for the one you love."

He pulled back to look up at her. "Cherokee . . ." His dark eyes were eloquent with approval even before he spoke the words. "I wouldn't change a single thing about you, don't you know that?" He reached one dark hand up to cup a breast, lifting it slightly as he brushed its crest with his thumb, yet looking beyond it to her eyes.

And suddenly she did know it, just as she knew she loved this warm, complex man. She threaded the fingers of both hands back through the hair of his temples, then held the sides of his head while savoring the moment and him.

"I know," she finally breathed softly. Then she leaned to kiss his lips, lightly at first, but with growing ardor, until she felt his hands moving over her skin to the loosened waistband that was soon being eased over the backs of her thighs. When it threatened to trip her, he stood, his hands sliding up her ribs to her armpits until she felt herself being lifted into space. He held her effortlessly, his mouth teasing her jaw while she pressed her hands to his hard shoulders and kicked herself free of impediments. But when the clothes dropped to the floor, he still held her aloft.

"Sam, Sam, let me go," she said, feeling helpless and impatient, wriggled provocatively against him.

"Never." He smiled back, then she was sliding down his body, freeing the single button that held his shirt together at the waist. While he shrugged it off hastily, she loosened his belt buckle.

Suddenly she realized he was standing motionless, and her fingers fell still. She looked up to find him watching her with the faint hint of a smile on his lips. How incredible that after all they'd been through she could feel this abrupt shyness, as if it were her first time. His hands hung loosely at his sides, and the expression on his face was a mixture of enjoyment and anticipation.

"Be my guest," he said softly.

Her lips fell open. A thrill spiraled through her while the breath seemed caught in her throat. Then she accepted his invitation, pulling the last garments from between them.

When they were naked, it took no more than a step and he was against her, forcing her back until her calves struck the bed and she toppled backward, pulling him with her. Their bodies were all grace and harmony while their mouths spoke wordless intimate messages and their hands roamed over each other, familiarizing themselves once again. "Oh, Sam, how I missed you." His shoulders were sleek and firm, his hair the texture of mink, the tendons of his neck resilient as she ran her hands over them. He leaned above her, kissing her temple, her eyelids, catching her lip between his teeth while her eyes drifted closed and she took pleasure in his adulation.

He moved down, turning them onto their sides while trailing kisses from the underside of her chin along her throat and down the hollow between her breasts, detouring to bestow a lingering kiss on each before moving on. His elbow hooked the curve of her waist, and his forearm pressed silkily against her back while he dipped a pleasurably wet tribute into her navel. He pressed her back, easing lower to trace once more those pale lines she no longer thought of hiding, learning their texture with the tip of his tongue.

"Cherokee . . ." His voice was rough, his lips soft while he nuzzled lower . . . and lower. "Cherokee . . ."

Then all was sensation—rough to smooth, ebb to flow, texture to sleekness, man to woman. She made some inarticulate sound deep in her throat, raising her body while drifting in an ethereal realm of sensuality.

He took her just short of fulfillment, then came to her, lifting himself over her once again to join the force of his love with hers in movements that were as much a part of love's expression as its innermost urge to give and to share.

Lee's head was thrown back, her eyes closed as she reached above her for something to hold on to, finding nothing but a pillow into which her fingers curled while he watched the pleasure in her trembling eyelids.

His name ripped from her throat as they shared again that shattering force of feeling they'd known before, followed by the dissolving sigh of satisfaction. A kiss on her forehead, the weight shifting away, taking her with it to her side, a heavy hand threaded through her hair, then a blissful lassitude as they lay in each other's arms.

"Cherokee?" he murmured after a long, long time.

"Hmm?"

His chest was warm and damp where her forehead rested against it.

"Can we talk now?"

"The answer is yes," she said, smiling at the ebullient feeling it gave her to say the word at last.

"The . . . what?" He jerked back in surprise.

"The answer is yes." She looked up innocently into his eyes. "Yes, I'll marry you. Yes, yes, yes!" She kissed his chest with a quick, light smack.

And naturally he had to tease, "I didn't ask you yet."

"You were gonna."

"Oh, was I now?"

She snuggled up against him, wrapping her arms around him and nestling comfortably with her head tucked under his chin.

He lifted a knee, rested it on her hip, and pressed the sole of his foot in the warm hollow at the back of her leg. "You know what I kept thinking the last six weeks?" His tone was reflective. "Of what a damn fool I was the night I asked you to marry me. My timing stank. I know that now. You were in an emotional mess that night, and I had no business bringing up the subject just then. I thought . . ." He sifted his fingers through her hair as if it were sand. "I thought I'd give you some time to gain your equilibrium after seeing your kids and your ex-husband again."

"You had me so scared, Sam." She squeezed her eyes shut, then hugged him close with fierce possessiveness. "I've never suffered as badly as I have during the last six weeks. You were so . . . so . . . unaffected by it all."

"Unaffected!" he exclaimed, pushing her back to see her face. "Woman, I was dying a little bit each day, waiting for you to come to me and say you'd changed your mind."

"You were?" She widened her eyes in surprise. "You didn't act like you were dying. You acted as if I was just one of the boys."

"Just one of the boys?" The grin was back as he ran his eyes then his hand over one naked breast. "Oh, Cherokee, hardly. It's not one of the boys I want to share my house with . . . and my life with . . . to say nothing of my bed."

She smiled and felt a ripple of feminine vanity at his approval.

Then she fell serious, gazing up at him with concern. "Sam, have you really no fears at all?"

He pressed a kiss to her forehead. "None. Not since that first incredible weekend with you when we found out how much we can share."

"But . . ." She searched his eyes deeply, hoping he wouldn't misconstrue what she was about to say. "I do have fears, Sam. Please understand."

"I know, Cherokee, I know now."

"At least give me some time before we start a family, okay?"

His head snapped back and he braced up on one palm, a dark hand grasping her shoulder and rolling her onto her back. "You mean it, Cherokee? You've been thinking about . . . about kids?"

"Yes, Your Honor, I have to confess I have." She affected a scolding pout. "Not right away, mind you. After I have a little time to get used to the idea."

His smile was radiant, then to her amazement he gave a regular Indian war whoop and fell on his back beside her, rubbing his chest with an air of great satisfaction and smiling up at the ceiling.

She lay beside him, grinning at how happy she'd made him, wondering what one of their half-Indian babies would look like. It would have hair darker than his, beautiful eyes, with his long lashes instead of her short, stubby ones, and the prettiest lips this side of the Great Divide . . .

Her reverie was interrupted by the growing awareness that Sam was no longer looking at the ceiling but at her naked breasts. The message in his eyes was clear even before a dark finger came teasing.

"Hey, Cherokee, what do you say we jump in the shower together and start all over and celebrate? I've got some time to make up for."

She burst out laughing and shoved his finger aside. "What have you been doing over there in your room all by yourself? Reading your porn magazines again?"

"How did you guess?"

She pretended to consider a minute. "On second thought, I'm not sure if I should hitch up for life with a man who reads porn magazines when he's got a perfectly capable wife." She sat up saucily and was heading for the edge of the bed when her progress was checked abruptly. A second later she squealed, "Brown! Let me go, Brown! I gotta go to the bathroom!"

"Not alone, Cherokee! You're going with me, straight to the shower!" In a flash she was slung ignominiously over his shoulder, her black hair dangling down past his posterior while one dark forearm clamped behind her knees and his other hand rested on her upturned derrière.

"Brown, put me down!"

"Like hell." He chuckled and stalked off toward the bathroom.

"Pervert!" she squawked.

"You damn betcha," he agreed, then turned to bite her enticing backside playfully as it bounced along on his shoulder.

She could hardly breathe by the time they reached the bathroom and he let her slip to her feet. She landed in the cold, hard bathtub, and a minute later the colder spray hit her full in the face. Before it warmed, they were kissing and slipping against each other and groping for the tiny bar of soap.

While Sam unwrapped it, she pushed her sodden hair out of her eyes.

"Hey, Brown, I've got just one more question, and I think I deserve an answer."

Disgruntled by the interruption, he curled his brows. "Okay, what—but hurry up and get it over with so we can get on with the important stuff."

"Did you read the amount of my bid that day we first met?"

A slow, sly grin climbed his cheek. He shut his eyes, leaned his head back till the shower spray hit him full in the face, then brought it forward, shook his head like a dog, and opened his spiky-lashed eyes again. "I'll tell you what." He pulled her up close, settled his hips against hers, and taunted with a grin, "You do ev-v-verything I say and I'll think about answering that."

"Brown—" she started to scold playfully, but the word was cut in half by his wet lips, and a moment later the answer ceased to matter.

From the *New York Times* bestselling author
LaVyrle Spencer